The Collected Stories of
Robert Silverberg

VOLUME SIX

Multiples
1983-87

The Collected Stories of
Robert Silverberg

VOLUME SIX

Multiples
1983-87

ROBERT SILVERBERG

SUBTERRANEAN PRESS 2013

Trade Paperback Edition

978-1-59606-625-0

Subterranean Press
PO Box 190106
Burton, MI 48519

www.subterraneanpress.com

COPYRIGHT ACKNOWLEDGMENTS

"Tourist Trade," "Symbiont," "The Pardoner's Tale," and "Blindsight" first appeared in *Playboy*.

"Multiples," "Against Babylon," "Hardware," and "Hannibal's Elephants" first appeared in *Omni*.

"Sailing to Byzantium," "Gilgamesh in the Outback," and "The Secret Sharer" first appeared in *Isaac Asimov's Science Fiction Magazine*.

"Sunrise on Pluto" first appeared in *The Planets*.

"The Iron Star" first appeared in *The Universe*.

"House of Bones" first appeared in *Terry's Universe*.

TABLE OF CONTENTS

For Alice K. Turner
Ellen Datlow
Shawna McCarthy
Byron Preiss
Gardner Dozois
Beth Meacham

INTRODUCTION

The stories in this sixth volume find me at a relatively stable point in my long career. They were written between 1983 and 1987, from the end of my third decade as a full-time professional writer to the early years of my fourth. With a career that I had been able to sustain over such a long span, I was about as established a writer as one can be in our field. (Consider that such great and well established s-f writers of my youth as Robert A. Heinlein, Isaac Asimov, Theodore Sturgeon, and Fritz Leiber had been writing professionally only about a decade when I began reading them in the late 1940s, and only Heinlein of that entire exalted quartet had been able to earn a steady living from writing alone in the first decade of his career. It had been my good fortune to be able to support myself entirely by free-lance work right from the start, and here in the 1980s, thirty-odd years from that starting point, I was still doing so.)

By the time this present group of stories was written I had passed through the cultural turbulence that engulfed nearly everyone's life in the wild, stormy period we know as "the Sixties," which for me had actually lasted from 1968 to 1974 or 1975. I had come through my own angry four-year-long retirement from writing in the middle 1970s, and was working again at a steady pace, though not with the frenetic prolificacy of the pre-retirement years. At the beginning of this period my personal life was still pretty chaotic, a carryover from all that Sixties madness, and plenty of new chaos was going to descend on me while some of these stories were written, but I was tiptoeing toward an escape from the various messes that were complicating my life, and by the time the last five stories of this volume were being written I was heading into the stability of my second marriage.

There had been big changes in the market for science-fiction stories during the decades of my writing career. At the outset I had dealt with magazines of relatively small circulation—*Galaxy, Fantasy & Science Fiction, Astounding Science Fiction, Fantastic Universe, Future Science Fiction,* etc.—that were the successors to the pulp magazines of the generation just preceding my own era. Except for *Astounding,* which was the ancestor of today's *Analog Science Fiction,* and *Fantasy and Science Fiction,* these magazines endured precarious existences, paid just a couple of a cents a word for the stories they bought, and perished in droves during the magazine-distribution upheavals of the 1960s and 1970s.

For the science-fiction writer the short-story market now shifted, after a troubled period of transition, to the original-anthology field that had sprung up in those years: *Orbit, Universe, Nova, Infinity,* and my own *New Dimensions,* all of which were essentially magazines in book form, and a host of thematic one-shot volumes—*Wandering Stars, Future City, Eros in Orbit,* and dozens more of that ilk. The original-anthology fad was just about played out by 1975, just as I was launching upon the four-year sabbatical from writing that I regarded at the time as a permanent retirement; and by the time I returned to my keyboard a few years later, a startlingly lucrative new market for short stories was beckoning to me in the slick-magazine field.

There had always been a small slick-magazine market for science fiction. *Playboy* had been running s-f stories fairly frequently from its inception in 1953, publishing work by Ray Bradbury, Charles Beaumont, Kurt Vonnegut, Arthur C. Clarke, and other top-rank writers of the day, but somehow I had never submitted anything there. *Rogue, Penthouse,* and a few other *Playboy* imitators also ran the occasional s-f story. But at the beginning of the 1980s the new *Playboy* fiction editor, Alice K. Turner, let it be known that the magazine was going to be publishing far more science fiction than it had in the past, and about the same time came the inception of a new slick magazine, *Omni,* which would pay *Playboy*-sized rates and publish two or three s-f stories a month. When I say *Playboy*-sized rates, I mean rates that made the fee scale for the science fiction magazines seem insignificant. A 5000-word story sold to one of the top science-fiction magazines of the 1970s was likely to bring its author $250 at best. *Playboy* and *Omni* were offering ten times as much, along with the greater increment of prestige that came from being published in magazines whose circulation figures were numbered in the millions rather than in the low six figures.

I saw the golden gates swinging open before me, and I marched right through. The previous volume of this series, covering the 1980-82 period, includes, among its twenty-two stories, four from *Playboy*, six from *Omni*, one from *Penthouse*, and four from various other high-paying slick magazines. The theme continues here: fourteen stories, numbering four more from *Playboy* and another four from *Omni*, along with a few from invitational original-fiction anthologies and a couple from one of the conventional s-f magazines. Writing for the slicks not only fattened my bank account, a very desirable thing for me during a decade that had been complicated by an expensive divorce, but gave me the luxury of polishing and repolishing each story until it gleamed. When you read the tale of my writing "Tourist Trade" for *Playboy*, writing it over and over again until first I and then the very demanding Alice Turner were both satisfied with it, you'll understand that it would not have been a practical matter to devote so many weeks of effort to a story for which *Fantasy & Science Fiction* or *Asimov's* might have paid me a few hundred dollars. Collecting all those four-digit slick-magazine checks also gave me a chance to write some ambitious longer stories for *Asimov's*—notably "Sailing to Byzantium" and "The Secret Sharer"—for which I was paid less than a short story for *Playboy* or *Omni* would yield, but which most people considered to be among the best work I had ever done.

So, then: fourteen more stories, five years' work, not the most prolific period of my writing career but one of the most satisfying.

TOURIST TRADE

We were nearly done with 1982. I had just learned how to use a computer, which I had employed for my far-future novella, "Homefaring." Now the giant lobsters of that story were behind me, and I was getting ready for that winter's major enterprise, Valentine Pontifex, *the closing volume of the first Majipoor trilogy. But I still didn't feel entirely comfortable writing with a computer—I never fully believed that what I had written on Monday would still be on the computer when I got back to my desk on Tuesday—and it seemed like a good idea to tackle one more short story before plunging into the novel. So I decided to try another short story for* Playboy's *redoubtable fiction editor, Alice K. Turner.*

My conversion from typewriter to computer couldn't have come at a more timely moment. "Tourist Trade," which as I look at it now seems to move seamlessly from first sentence to last, called forth at least half a dozen drafts from me, maybe even more. If I had had to type those thirty-odd pages out every time from beginning to end, I'd probably have hurled the typewriter through the window long before I came up with anything that Alice Turner would find acceptable. What should have been a relatively simple 7,500-word project turned into an interminable and agonizing ordeal. Only my new computerized ability to tinker with a sentence here or a paragraph there without having to type out a complete new manuscript saved the story—and my sanity.

When you use a computer to write, most of the false starts, fatuous passages, and other miscalculations that any writer will commit along the way don't survive for the amusement of scholars studying your manuscripts in years to come. You simply back up the cursor and erase the faulty stuff, send them into the black hole of computer limbo, and no one's ever the wiser. But from time to time a writer does need hard copy of a work in progress, especially if the work in progress is turning into a messy, complicated, recalcitrant job, and so a lot of botched drafts still do get put down on paper even in the computer age. I save mine, though I know not why I do. In the case of "Tourist Trade" the file got to be a stack about five inches thick.

For those of you who think that story-writing gets easier as a writer's career goes along, that five-inch stack of paper should be a useful corrective, and the whole "Tourist Trade" saga—dating from my thirtieth year as a professional writer—ought to be highly instructive.

It begins with a one-page draft in first-person narration of something I entitled "A World of Strangers":

[In Morocco all the human tourists head straight for Marrakesh, as people have been doing ever since tourism began. But the extraterrestrials prefer to go to Fez, for some reason, and so I went to Fez also.

[I don't know why it should be that way, except that they're extraterrestrials, and maybe that's enough of an explanation. Of course, Fez is a great city in its own right, and an enormously interesting place, and no traveler needs any excuse to go there. But Marrakesh is the classic tourist-trap town of Morocco, with its palaces, its tombs, its tower, its crazy grand plaza full of acrobats and jugglers and snake-charmers, and that's where the hordes invariably have gone. The *human* hordes. E-Ts, being E-Ts, have different value systems. They]

And there my gorge rose. It seemed to me that I was blathering on and on impossibly instead of getting my story started. So I stopped and began again:

[When I arrived in Fez, early on a warm April morning, I checked in at the big old Palais Jamai at the edge of the old city. In Morocco all the human tourists head straight for Marrakesh, as tourists have been doing ever since tourism began. But the extraterrestrials prefer to go to Fez, for some reason. And so I went to Fez also.]

Not bad, especially when compared with the first version. This time I lasted nearly six pages. I got my alien onto the scene on second page and the exotic green-eyed woman appeared on page three. They moved out on the dance floor together and the narrator's skin began to tingle and suddenly I felt the upchuck reflex again. What I was writing was slick, yes, but also it was hopelessly mechanical, a computer-constructed men's-magazine story, lifeless and formulaic. The problem, I thought, was the use of first-person narration. It's all too easy, writing first person, to slip into a garrulous ingratiating here's-what-I-did tone that dawdles on and on and on as the narrator murmurs in your ear.

The third draft started the same way as the second, with the protagonist checking in at his hotel in Fez. But now it was a third-person story. And this time I didn't abandon it after just a few pages. I pushed on all the way to the end, or what I thought was the end. This is how it opened now:

[Eitel picked up his merchandise in Paris and caught the Air France night bird to Casablanca, where he connected with a Royal Air Maroc flight for the short hop to Fez. It was the middle of April, when Europe was still bleak and winter-dead, and Morocco was halfway to summer.]

Very efficient. Protagonist introduced and in motion; exotic background established; and the mysterious "merchandise" provides the hook. A nice lead paragraph. I nodded and went on for thirty-seven more pages, throwing in a lot of juicy Moroccan background information (I had been there in 1975) before bringing my aliens on stage on page five and the gorgeous woman on page seven. Eitel finally gets out on the dance floor with her on page fifteen, and then the trouble starts. And eventually gets resolved.

All right. I had a story. But it took too long to get down to its central events, and generally seemed to me to be inflated and undramatic. It was now Christmas week of 1982, and an old friend from New York was visiting me—Jerrold Mundis, a wise man and fine writer who doesn't happen to write (or read, or like, I suspect) science fiction. I gave him the story, telling him that I thought something was wrong with it, and asked him for a blunt critique, no punches pulled. He was blunt, all right. As I already suspected, I had opened the story in the wrong place. All that stuff in the beginning about Fez and Marrakesh might be fascinating to me, and might even make a nice National Geographic article, but it stopped things dead before they had a chance to begin. The endless speculations about the psychology of aliens that occupied pages six through fourteen weren't very gripping either. Start the story on page five, he suggested, and cut a lot of what follows, and maybe it would work.

Jerry usually knows whereof he speaks, in matters of writing and in other things. So I took his advice. This was the opening of the fourth draft:

[Even before Eitel's eyes had adjusted to the darkness and the glare of the clashing crisscrossing spotlights, his nose began letting him know what sort of bizarre zoo he had walked into. The nightclub was full of aliens, at least seven or eight species. He picked up the whole astonishing olfactory blast at once, a weird hodgepodge of extraterrestrial body odors, offworld phero-mones, transgalactic cosmetics, the ozone radiation of personal protection screens, minute quantities of unearthly atmospheres leaking out of breathing devices. He was smelling things that as recently as the year 1987 no human being had ever smelled. Rigelians, he thought, Centaureans, Antareans, Arcturans. Maybe Steropids and Capellans too. The world has turned into a goddamned sci-flick, Eitel thought.]

At last: some inventiveness, some narrative vigor, some characteristic Silverbergian tone. I cut here, expanded there, and in a few days had a thirty-eight-page story very different from its limp predecessors. On 21 January, 1983, "A World of Strangers" went off to Alice Turner at Playboy's New York office; I put it out of my mind with deep relief and started writing Valentine Pontifex a few days later.

But Alice didn't like what I had sent her.

On 1 February she told me, "I love the Star Wars bar in the beginning of this story, but, all in all, I'm dubious about the story. First, there's too much exposition in the beginning.... Frankly, I think the flashback could go, the taxi driver too. And the ending doesn't seem a bit integral to the story. If, for instance...."

And so on. A lot of problems. "But I know that you probably like the story as is," she added, "and thus, with complete respect and many thanks, I will pass. If I am wrong, and you feel that, on second thought, you will change the ending and do some cutting early on, let me now. We could talk."

Imagine my delight. After four full drafts before submitting the story, I had a reject on my hands. I suppose I could have saved us both a lot of trouble by sending the story, as it was, to some other magazine and collecting my (rather smaller) check for it and putting the whole mess behind me. But I took Alice's letter as a challenge, instead. I covered it with notes. "Might work!" I wrote, next to the paragraph where she suggested a different ending. "Make it shadier.... Story too simple. Make David a real person—a partner? Eitel uptight, David a crook. Eitel has vestiges of ethics." And a lot more. I phoned Alice and said I was going to rewrite the story. She seemed surprised and pleased. On 16 February I sent it to her again, down to thirty-four pages, with a note that said, "Herewith the promised new version of the art-dealer story. I think I would not have had the heart to attempt it but for the word processor, which allowed me to rewrite big sections and graft salvageable old sections right in.... I hope this does it. God only knows how many versions of this one I've written—even if you buy it at a fat price I'll end up making about $3 an hour for it. But that isn't the point; something must have happened last fall that caused me to lose my touch, to make my stuff top-heavy with exposition, and I'm groping my way back towards the way I'm supposed to write. This revision has been a great help in telling me I'm getting back there."

This was the new opening:

[After a moment Eitel's eyes adjusted to the darkness and the glare of the clashing crisscrossing spotlights. But he didn't need his eyes to tell him what sort of bizarre zoo he had walked into. The nightclub was full of aliens, seven or eight kinds, Rigelians, Capellans, Arcturans: the works. His sensitive nostrils picked up the whole astonishing olfactory blast at once: a weird hodgepodge of extraterrestrial body odors, offworld pheromones, transgalactic cosmetics, the ozone radiation of personal protective screens, minute quantities of unearthly atmospheres leaking out of breathing devices. He began to tremble.

["Something wrong?" David asked.]

Alice phoned a couple of days later. She liked the new version, but it still needed some cutting, and she had some further plot quibbles. Could I see my way to one more rewrite?

Yes, I said despondently. The hook was in me now for sure. I told her to send me a list of the quibbles. But you do the cutting, I said. I've worked this one over so much that I'm losing my way in it.

On 1 March I got an annotated copy of the manuscript from her, with huge slashes on almost every page, slicing out exposition that echoed things already said in dialog, authorial explanation of the characters' motives, and other sorts of fatty tissue. Her plot quibbles seemed pretty major too. After all these drafts she still could find six separate places where the twists of the plot weren't really plausible. I was appalled. But she sweetened her letter by telling me at the end, "Bob, again I want to congratulate you on the fine job you've done with this rewrite. Though you've been feeling inadequate, this is much more than an adequate job; it's a real change, and only a thorough professional could do it. As you see, these are only minor quibbles, the story is here, and I'm most grateful."

Four days later—I was working weekends now, a rarity for me—I got yet another draft back to her. You'll find the text of it beginning on the next page. I had made nearly all the cuts she wanted and had tidied up the plot. "I think the story now answers all of your objections and it may even answer mine; at any rate I hope I'm through writing it," I told her. "Nobody said this business is easy, but I shouldn't goof up a story as badly as I goofed up the earlier versions of this one, not at my age."

And a couple of days afterwards, there was Alice on the phone. The story was fine and she was putting through the check (a very nice one, by the way.) She would use it in the December, 1984 Playboy.

To her astonishment and mine, I came close to breaking into tears as I realized that I was at last done with the damned thing.

19

"Oh," she said. "One little change. I'd like to call it 'Tourist Trade' instead of 'A World of Strangers.'"

At that point she could have called it "The Snows of Kilimanjaro" and I wouldn't have raised objections. But in fact her clever punning title was more suitable than mine, as you'll see when you read the story, and I've retained it in all reprints of it.

There's one final twist to this flabbergasting tale.

Years later—December of 1988—Playboy published its thirty-fifth anniversary issue. "Tourist Trade" was one of eight stories chosen to represent the fiction Playboy had published over those thirty-five years. (The others, I noted smugly, were by Ray Bradbury, Ian Fleming, Walter S. Tevis, Vladimir Nabokov, John Updike, Robert Coover, and Joyce Carol Oates.) In phoning me to ask permission to reprint it, Alice said that because of space limitations it would, like the other, have to be abridged. The cutting would be done by her, since time was short.

"Where are you going to cut it?" I asked.

"I've already done it," she said. "I took David out."

And so she had—slicing away one of the three major characters, along with close to half the text. To my utter astonishment the story still seemed coherent and effective—a testimony to really brilliant editing. I look at it from time to time in wonder. Of course, I've chosen to use the complete text here—Alice's stunt was just a stunt, amazing because it hadn't really damaged the story, but I can't say that it improved it. So here it is, along with this lengthy prolog, which I hope demonstrates that those finely polished stories you see in the magazines don't necessarily bear much resemblance to the first version that came white-hot from the forge of creativity. There can be plenty of blood, sweat, and, yes, tears in writing short stores—even for a veteran who is widely believed to know what he's doing.

After a moment Eitel's eyes adjusted to the darkness and the glare of the clashing crisscrossing spotlights. But he didn't need his eyes to tell him what sort of bizarre zoo he had walked into. His sensitive nostrils picked up the whole astonishing olfactory blast at once: a weird hodgepodge of extraterrestrial body odors, offworld pheromones, transgalactic cosmetics, the ozone radiation of personal protection screens, minute quantities of unearthly atmospheres leaking out of breathing devices.

"Something wrong?" David asked.

"The odors. They overwhelm me."

"The smoking, eh? You hate it that much?"

"Not the tobacco, fool. The aliens! The E-Ts!"

"Ah. The smell of money, you mean. I agree, it is very overwhelming in here."

"For a shrewd man you can sometimes be very stupid," Eitel muttered. "Unless you say such things deliberately, which you must, because I have never known a stupid Moroccan."

"For a Moroccan, I am very stupid," said David serenely. "And so it was very stupid of you to choose me as your partner, eh? Your grandfathers in Zurich would be shamed if they knew. Eh?" He gave Eitel a maddeningly seraphic smile.

Eitel scowled. He was never sure when he had genuinely offended the slippery little Moroccan and when David was merely teasing. But somehow David always came out of these interchanges a couple of points ahead.

He turned and looked the place over, checking it out.

Plenty of humans, of course. This was the biggest gathering-place for aliens in Morocco, the locus of the focus, and a lot of gawkers came to observe the action. Eitel ignored them. There was no sense doing business with humans any more. There were probably some Interpol types in here too, hoping to head off just the sort of deals Eitel was here to do. To hell with them. His hands were clean, more or less.

But the aliens! The aliens, the aliens, the aliens!

All over the room. Vast saucer eyes, spidery limbs, skins of grotesque textures and unnameable colors. Eitel felt the excitement rising in him, so un-Swiss of him, so thoroughly out of character.

"Look at them!" he whispered. "They're beautiful!"

"Beautiful? You think so?"

"Fantastic!"

The Moroccan shrugged. "Fantastic, yes. Beautiful, no. Blue skin, green skin, no skin, two heads, five heads: this is beauty? What is beautiful to me is the money. And the way they like to throw it away."

"You would never understand," said Eitel.

In fact Eitel hardly understood it himself. He had discovered, not long after the first alien tourists had reached Earth, that they stirred unexpected areas of his soul: strange vistas opening, odd incoherent cosmic yearnings. To find at the age of forty that there was more to him than Panamanian trusts and numbered bank accounts—that was a little troublesome; but it was delicious, as well. He stood staring for a long ecstatic chaotic moment. Then he turned to David and said, "Where's your Centauran?"

"I don't see him."

"Neither do I."

"He swore he'd be here. Is a big place, Eitel. We go looking, and we find."

The air was thick with color, sound, fumes. Eitel moved carefully around a tableful of leathery-faced pockmarked red Rigelians, burly, noisy, like a herd of American conventioneers out on the town. Behind them sat five sleek and sinuous Steropids, wearing cone-shaped breathers. Good. Steropids were easy marks. If something went wrong with this Centauran deal David had set up, he might want to have them as customers to fall back on.

Likewise that Arcturan trio, flat heads, grizzled green hair, triple eyes bright as blue-white suns. Arcturans were wild spenders, though they weren't known to covet Eitel's usual merchandise, which was works of fine art, or more or less fine art. Perhaps they could be encouraged to. Eitel, going past, offered them a preliminary smile: Earthman establishing friendly contact, leading perhaps to more elaborate relationship. But the Arcturans didn't pick up on it. They looked through Eitel as though their eyes didn't function in the part of the spectrum he happened to inhabit.

"There," David said.

Yes. Far across the way, a turquoise creature, inordinately long and narrow, that appeared to be constructed of the finest grade of rubber, stretched over an awkwardly flung together armature of short rods.

"There's a woman with him," Eitel said. "I wasn't expecting that. You didn't tell me."

David's eyes gleamed. "Ah, nice, very nice!"

She was more than very nice. She was splendid. But that wasn't the point. Her presence here could be a troublesome complication. A tour guide? An interpreter? Had the Centauran brought his own art expert along? Or was she some Interpol agent decked out to look like the highest-priced of hookers? Or maybe even a real hooker. God help me, he thought, if the Centauran's gotten involved in some kind of kinky infatuation that would distract him from the deal. No: God help David.

"You should have told me there was a woman," Eitel said.

"But I didn't know! I swear, Jesus Mary Moses, I never see her yesterday! But it will be all right. Jesus Mary Moses, go ahead, walk over." He smiled and winked and slipped off towards the bar. "I see you later, outside. You go for it, you hear? You hear me, Eitel? It will be all right."

❉

The Centauran, seeing the red carnation in Eitel's lapel, lifted his arm in a gesture like the extending of a telescopic tube, and the woman smiled. It was an amazing smile, and it caught Eitel a little off guard, because for an instant it made him wish that the Centauran was back on Centaurus and this woman was sitting here alone. He shook the thought off. He was here to do a deal, not to get into entanglements.

"Hans Eitel, of Zurich," he said.

"I am Anakhistos," said the Centauran. His voice was like something out of a synthesizer, which perhaps it was, and his face was utterly opaque, a flat motionless mask. For vision he had a single bright strip of receptors an inch wide around his forehead, for air intake he had little vents on his cheeks, and for eating he had a three-sided oral slot like the swinging top of a trash basket. "We are very happied you have come," he said. "This is Agila."

Eitel allowed himself to look straight at her. It was dazzling but painful, a little like staring into the sun. Her hair was red and thick, her eyes were emerald and very far apart, her lips were full, her teeth were bright. She was wearing a vaguely futuristic metal-mesh sheath, green, supple, clinging. What she looked like was something that belonged on a 3-D billboard, one of those unreal idealized women who turn up in the ads for cognac, or skiing holidays in Gstaad. There was something a little freakish about such excessive beauty. A professional, he decided.

To the Centauran he said, "This is a great pleasure for me. To meet a collector of your stature, to know that I will be able to be of assistance—"

"And a pleasure also for ourself. You are greatly recommended to me. You are called knowledgeable reliable, discreet—"

"The traditions of our family. I was bred to my *métier*."

23

"We are drinking mint tea," the woman said. "Will you drink mint tea with us?" Her voice was warm, deep, unfamiliar. Swedish? Did they have redheads in Sweden?

Eitel said, "Forgive me, but it's much too sweet for me. Perhaps a brandy instead—"

A waiter appeared as though by telepathic command. Eitel ordered a Courvoisier, and the woman another round of tea. She is very smooth, very good, he thought. He imagined himself in bed with her, digging his fingers into that dense red mane, running his lips over her long lean thighs. The fantasy was pleasing but undisturbing: an idle dream, cool, agreeable, giving him no palpitations, no frenzy. Good. After that first startled moment he was getting himself under control. He wondered if she was charging the Centauran by the night, or working at something bigger.

She said, "I love the Moroccan tea. It is so marvelous, the sweet. Sugar is my passion. I think I am addicted."

The waiter poured the tea in the traditional way, cascading it down into the glass from three feet up. Eitel repressed a shudder. He admired the elaborate Moroccan cuisine, but the tea appalled him: lethal hypersaccharine stuff, instant diabetes.

"Do you also enjoy mint tea?" Eitel asked the alien.

"It is very wonderful," the Centauran said. "It is one of the most wonderful things on this wonderful planet."

Eitel had no idea how sincere the Centauran was. He had been studying the psychology of extraterrestrials about as closely as anyone had, in the decade since they had begun to descend on Earth en masse after the lifting of the galactic quarantine, and he knew a lot about a lot of them; but he found it almost impossible to get a reading on Centaurans. If they gave any clues to their feelings at all, it was in the form of minute, perhaps imaginary fluctuations of the texture of their rubbery skins. It was Eitel's theory that the skin slackened when they were happy and went taut when they were tense, but the theory was only preliminary and he gave it little value.

"When did you arrive on Earth?" Eitel asked.

"It is the first week," the Centauran said. "Five days here in Fez, then we go to Rome, Paris, and afterwards the States United. Following which, other places. It is greatly exciting, your world. Such vigor, such raw force. I hope to see everything, and bring back much art. I am passionate collector, you know, of Earthesque objects."

"With a special interest in paintings."

"Paintings, yes, but I collect many other things."

That seemed a little blatant. Unless Eitel misunderstood the meaning, but he doubted he had. He glanced at the woman, but she showed no reaction.

Carefully he said, "Such as?"

"Everything that is essential to the experience of your world! Everything fine, everything deeply Earthesque! Of course I am most fastidious. I seek only the first-rate objects."

"I couldn't possibly agree more," said Eitel. "We share the same philosophy. The true connoisseur has no time for the tawdry, the trivial, the incompletely realized gesture, the insufficiently fulfilled impulse." His tone, carefully practised over years of dealing with clients, was intended to skirt unctuousness and communicate nothing but warm and sincere approbation. Such nuances were probably lost on the Centauran, but Eitel never let himself underestimate a client. He looked suddenly towards the woman and said, "Surely that's your outlook also."

"Of course."

She took a long pull of her mint tea, letting the syrupy stuff slide down her throat like motor oil. Then she wriggled her shoulders in a curious way. Eitel saw flesh shifting interestingly beneath the metal mesh. Surely she was professional. Surely. He found himself speculating on whether there could be anything sexual going on between these two. He doubted that it was possible, but you never could tell. More likely, though, she was merely one of the stellar pieces in Anakhistos's collection of the high-quality Earthesque: an object, an artifact. Eitel wondered how Anakhistos had managed to find her so fast. Was there some service that supplied visiting aliens with the finest of escorts, at the finest of prices?

He was picking up an aroma from her now, not unpleasant but very strange: caviar and cumin? Sturgeon poached in Chartreuse?

She signaled to the waiter for yet another tea. To Eitel she said, "The problem of the export certificates, do you think it is going to get worse?"

That was unexpected, and very admirable, he thought. Discover what your client's concerns are, make them your own. He said, "It is a great difficulty, is it not?"

"I think of little else," said the Centauran, leaping in as if he had been waiting for Agila to provide the cue. "To me it is an abomination. These restrictions on removing works of art from your planet—these humiliating inspections—this agitation, this outcry for even tighter limitations—what will it come to?"

Soothingly Eitel said, "You must try to understand the nature of the panic. We are a small backward world that has lived in isolation until just a few years ago. Suddenly we have stumbled into contact with the great galactic civilizations. You come among us, you are fascinated by us and by our artifacts, you wish to collect our things. But we can hardly supply the entire civilized universe. There are only a few Leonardos, a few Vermeers: and there are so many of you. So there is fear that you will sweep upon us with your immense wealth, with your vast numbers, with your hunger for our art, and buy everything of value that we have ever produced, and carry it off to places a hundred light-years away. So these laws are being passed. It is natural."

"But I am not here to plunder! I am here to make legitimate purchase!"

"I understand completely," Eitel said. He risked putting his hand, gently, compassionately, on the Centauran's arm. Some of the E-Ts resented any sort of intimate contact of this sort with Earthfolk. But apparently the Centauran didn't mind. The alien's rubbery skin felt astonishingly soft and smooth, like the finest condom imaginable. "I'm altogether on your side," Eitel declared. "The export laws are absurd overreactions. There's a more than ample supply of art on this planet to meet the needs of sophisticated collectors like yourself. And by disseminating our culture among the star-worlds, we bind ourselves inextricably into the fabric of galactic civilization. Which is why I do everything in my power to make our finest art available to our visitors."

"But can you provide valid export licences?" Agila asked.

Eitel put his finger to his lips. "We don't need to discuss it further just now, eh? Let us enjoy the delights of this evening, and save dreary matters of commerce for later, shall we?" He beamed. "May I offer you more tea?"

It was all going very smoothly, Eitel thought. Contact made, essential lines of agreement established. Even the woman was far less of a complication than he had anticipated. Time now to back off, relax, let rapport blossom and mature without forcing.

"Do you dance?" Agila said suddenly.

He looked towards the dance floor. The Rigelians were lurching around in a preposterously ponderous way, like dancing bears. Some Arcturans were on the dance floor too, and a few Procyonites bouncing up and down like bundles of shiny metal rods, and a Steropid doing an eerie *pas seul,* weaving in dreamy circles.

"Yes, of course," he said, a little startled.

"Please dance with me?"

He glanced uneasily towards the Centauran, who nodded benignly. She smiled and said, "Anakhistos does not dance. But I would like to. Would you oblige me?"

Eitel took her hand and led her out on the floor. Once they were dancing he was able to regain his calm. He moved easily and well. Some of the E-Ts were openly watching them—they had such curiosity about humans sometimes—but the staring didn't bother him. He found himself registering the pressure of her thighs against his thighs, her firm heavy breasts against his chest, and for an instant he felt the old biochemical imperative trying to go roaring through his veins, telling him, *follow her anywhere, promise anything, say anything, do anything.* He brushed it back. There were other women: in Nice, in Rome, in Athens. When he was done with this deal he would go to one of them.

He said, "Agila is an interesting name. Israeli, is it?"

"No," she said.

The way she said it, serenely and very finally, left him without room to maneuver. He was full of questions—who was she, how had she hooked up with the Centauran, what was her deal, how well did she think Eitel's own deal with the Centauran was likely to go? But that one cool syllable seemed to have slammed a curtain down. He concentrated on dancing again instead. She was supple, responsive, skilful. And yet the way she danced was as strange as everything else about her: she moved almost as if her feet were some inches off the floor. Odd. And her voice—an accent, but what kind? He had been everywhere, and nothing in his experience matched her way of speaking, a certain liquidity in the vowels, a certain resonance in the phrasing, as though she were hearing echoes as she spoke. She had to be something truly exotic, Rumanian, a Finn, a Bulgar—and even those did not seem exotic enough. Albanian? Lithuanian?

Most perplexing of all was her aroma. Eitel was gifted with a sense of smell worthy of a parfumier, and he heeded a woman's fragrance the

27

way more ordinary men studied the curves of hip or bosom or thigh. Out of the pores and the axillae and the orifices came the truths of the body, he believed, the deepest, the most trustworthy, the most exciting communications; he studied them with rabbinical fervour and the most minute scientific zeal. But he had never smelled anything like this, a juxtaposition of incongruous spices, a totally baffling mix of flavors. Some amazing new perfume? Something imported from Arcturus or Capella, perhaps? Maybe so, though it was hard to imagine an effect like this being achieved by mere chemicals. It had to be her. But what mysterious glandular outpouring brought him that subtle hint of sea urchin mingled with honey? What hidden duct sent thyme and raisins coursing together through her bloodstream? Why did the crystalline line of light perspiration on her flawless upper lip carry those grace-notes of pomegranate, tarragon and ginger?

He looked for answers in her eyes: deep green pools, calm, cool, unearthly. They seemed as bewildering as the rest of her.

And then he understood. He realized now that the answer, impossible and implausible and terrifying, had been beckoning to him all evening, and that he could no longer go on rejecting it, impossible or not. And in the moment of accepting it he heard a sound within himself much like that of a wind beginning to rise, a hurricane being born on some far-off isle.

Eitel began to tremble. He had never felt himself so totally defenseless before.

He said, "It's amazing, how human you seem to be."

"*Seem* to be?"

"Outwardly identical in every way. I didn't think it was possible for life-forms of such a degree of similarity to evolve on two different worlds."

"It isn't," she said.

"You're not from Earth, though."

She was smiling. She seemed almost pleased, he thought, that he had seen through her masquerade.

"No."

"What are you, then?"

"Centauran."

Eitel closed his eyes a moment. The wind was a gale within him; he swayed and struggled to keep his balance. He was starting to feel as though he were conducting this conversation from a point somewhere behind his own right ear. "But Centaurans look like—"

"Like Anakhistos? Yes, of course we do, when we are at home. But I am not at home now."

"I don't understand."

"This is my traveling body," she said.

"What?"

"It is not comfortable, visiting certain places in one's own body. The air is sharp, the light hurts the eyes, eating is very troublesome."

"So you simply put on a different body?"

"Some of us do. There are those like Anakhistos who are indifferent to the discomforts, or who actually regard them as part of the purpose of traveling. But I am of the sort that prefers to transfer into a traveling body when going to other worlds."

"Ah," Eitel said. "Yes." He continued to move through the rhythms of the dance in a numb, dazed way. It's all just a costume, he told himself. What she really looks like is a bunch of rigid struts, with a rubber sheet draped over them. Cheek-vents for breathing, three-sided slot for eating, receptor strip instead of eyes. "And these bodies?" he asked. "Where do you get them?"

"Why, they make them for us. Several companies do it. The human models are only just now becoming available. Very expensive, you understand."

"Yes," he said. "Of course."

"Tell me: when was it that you first saw through my disguise?"

"I felt right away that something was wrong. But it wasn't until a moment ago that I figured it out."

"No one else has guessed, I think. It is an extremely excellent Earth body, would you not say?"

"Extremely," Eitel said.

"After each trip I always regret, at first, returning to my real body. This one seems quite genuine to me by now. You like it very much, yes?"

"Yes," Eitel said helplessly.

He found David out in the cab line, lounging against his taxi with one arm around a Moroccan boy of about sixteen and the other exploring the breasts of a swarthy French-looking woman. It was hard to tell which one he had selected for the late hours of the night: both, maybe. David's cheerfully polymorphous ways were a little hard for Eitel to take, sometimes. But Eitel knew it wasn't necessary to approve of David in order to work with him. Whenever Eitel showed up in Fez with new merchandise, David was able to finger a customer for him within twenty-four hours; and at a five percent commission he was probably the wealthiest taxi driver in Morocco, after two years as Eitel's point man among the E-Ts.

"Everything's set," Eitel said. "Take me over to get the stuff."

David flashed his glittering gold-toothed grin. He patted the woman's rump, lightly slapped the boy's cheek, pushed them both on their way, and opened the door of his cab for Eitel. The merchandise was at Eitel's hotel, the Palais Jamai, on the edge of the native quarter. But Eitel never did business at his own hotel: it was handy to have David to take him back and forth between the Jamai and the Hotel Merinides, out here beyond the city wall by the ancient royal tombs, where most of the aliens preferred to stay.

The night was mild, fragrant, palm trees rustling in the soft breeze, huge bunches of red geranium blossoms looking almost black in the moonlight. As they drove towards the old town, with its maze of winding medieval streets, its walls and gates straight out of *The Arabian Nights*, David said, "You mind I tell you something? One thing worries me."

"Go ahead."

"Inside, I watched you. Staring more at the woman than at the E-T. You got to concentrate on the deal, and forget the woman, Eitel."

Eitel resented being told by a kid half his age how to conduct his operations. But he kept himself in check. To David, young and until recently poor, certain nuances were incomprehensible. Not that David lacked an interest in beauty. But beauty was just an abstraction; money was money. Eitel did not attempt to explain what time would surely teach.

He said, "*You* tell *me*, forget the woman?"

"Is a time for women, is a time for business. Separate times. You know that, Eitel. A Swiss, he is almost a Moroccan, when it comes to business."

Eitel laughed. "Thanks."

"I am being serious. You be careful. If she confuse you, it can cost you. Can cost *me*. I am in for percentage, remember. Even if you are Swiss, maybe you need to know: business and women must be kept separate things."

"I know."

"You remember it, yes?"

"Don't worry about me," Eitel said.

The cab pulled up outside the Jamai. Eitel, upstairs, withdrew four paintings and an Olmec jade statuette from the false compartment of his suitcase. The paintings were all unframed, small, genuine and unimportant. After a moment he selected the *Madonna of the Palms,* from the atelier of Lorenzo Bellini: plainly apprentice work, but enchanting, serene, pure, not bad, easily a $20,000 painting. He slipped it into a carrying case, put the others back, all but the statuette, which he fondled for a moment and put down on the dresser, in front of the mirror, as though setting up a little shrine. To beauty, he thought. He started to put it away and changed his mind. It looked so lovely there that he decided to take his chances. Taking your chances, he thought, is sometimes good for the health.

He went back to the cab.

"Is a good painting?" David asked.

"It's pretty. Trivial, but pretty."

"I don't mean good that way. I mean, is it real?"

"Of course," Eitel said, perhaps too sharply. "Do we have to have this discussion again, David? You know damned well I sell only genuine paintings. Overpriced a little, but always genuine."

"One thing I never can understand. Why you not sell them fakes?"

Startled, Eitel said, "You think I'm crooked, David?"

"Sure I do."

"You say it so lightheartedly. I don't like your humor sometimes."

"Humor? What humor? Is against law to sell valuable Earth works of art to aliens. You sell them. Makes you crook, right? Is no insult. Is only description."

"I don't believe this," Eitel said. "What are you trying to start here?"

"I only want to know, why you sell them real stuff. Is against the law to sell real ones, is probably not against the law to sell them fakes. You see? For two years I wonder this. We make just as much money, we run less risk."

"My family has dealt in art for over a hundred years, David. No Eitel has ever knowingly sold a fake. None ever will." It was a touchy point with him. "Look," he said, "maybe you like playing these games with me, but you could go too far. All right?"

"You forgive me, Eitel?"

"If you shut up."

"You know better than that. Shutting up I am very bad at. Can I tell you one more thing, and then I shut up really?"

"Go ahead," Eitel said, sighing.

"I tell you this: you a very confused man. You a crook who thinks he not a crook, you know what I mean? Which is bad thinking. But is all right. I like you. I respect you, even. I think you are excellent businessman. So you forgive rude remarks?"

"You give me a great pain," Eitel said.

"I bet I do. You forget I said anything. Go make deal, many millions, tomorrow we have mint tea together and you give me my cut and everybody happy."

"I don't like mint tea."

"Is all right. We have some anyway."

Seeing Agila standing in the doorway of her hotel room, Eitel was startled again by the impact of her presence, the overwhelming physical power of her beauty. *If she confuse you, it can cost you.* What you see is all artificial, he told himself. It's just a mask. Eitel looked from Agila to Anakhistos, who sat oddly folded, like a giant umbrella. That's what she really is, Eitel thought. She's Mrs. Anakhistos from Centaurus, and her skin is like rubber and her mouth is a hinged slot and this body that she happens to be wearing right now was made in a laboratory. And yet, and yet, and yet—the wind was roaring, he was tossing wildly about—

What the hell is happening to me?

"Show us what you have for us," Anakhistos said.

Eitel slipped the little painting from its case. His hands were shaking ever so slightly. In the closeness of the room he picked up two strong fragrances, something dry and musty coming from Anakhistos, and the strange, irresistible mixtures of incongruous spices that Agila's synthetic body emanated.

"*The Madonna of the Palms,* Lorenzo Bellini, Venice, 1597," Eitel said. "Very fine work."

"Bellini is extremely famous, I know."

"The famous ones are Giovanni and Gentile. This is Giovanni's grandson. He's just as good, but not well-known. I couldn't possibly get you paintings by Giovanni or Gentile. No one on Earth could."

"This is quite fine," said Anakhistos. "True Renaissance beauty. And very Earthesque. Of course it is genuine?"

Eitel said stiffly, "Only a fool would try to sell a fake to a connoisseur such as yourself. But it would be easy enough for us to arrange a spectroscopic analysis in Casablanca, if—"

"Ah, no, no, no, I meant no suspicioning of your reputation. You are impeccable. We unquestion the genuinity. But what is done about the export certificate?"

"Easy. I have a document that says this is a recent copy, done by a student in Paris. They are not yet applying chemical tests of age to the paintings, not yet. You will be able to take the painting from Earth, with such a certificate."

"And the price?" said Anakhistos.

Eitel took a deep breath. It was meant to steady him, but it dizzied him instead, for it filled his lungs with Agila.

He said, "If the deal is straight cash, the price is four million dollars."

"And otherwise?" Agila asked.

"I'd prefer to talk to you about that alone," he said to her.

"Whatever you want to say, you can say in front of Anakhistos. We are absolute mates. We have complete trust."

"I'd still prefer to speak more privately."

She shrugged. "All right. The balcony."

Outside, where the sweetness of night-blooming flowers filled the air, her fragrance was less overpowering. It made no difference. Looking straight at her only with difficulty, he said, "If I can spend the rest of this night making love to you, the price will be three million."

"This is a joke?"

"In fact, no. Not at all."

"It is worth a million dollars to have sexual contact with me?"

Eitel imagined how his father would have answered that question, his grandfather, his great-grandfather. Their accumulated wisdom pressed on him like a hump. To hell with them, he thought.

He said, listening in wonder to his own words, "Yes. It is."

"You know that this body is not my real body."

"I know."

"I am an alien being."

"Yes. I know."

She studied him in silence a long while. Then she said, "Why did you make me come outside to ask me this?"

"On Earth, men sometimes become quite angry when strangers ask their wives to go to bed with them. I didn't know how Anakhistos would react. I don't have any real idea how Centaurans react to anything."

"I am Centauran also," she pointed out.

"You don't seem as alien to me."

She smiled quickly, on-off. "I see. Well, let us confer with Anakhistos."

But the conference, it turned out, did not include Eitel. He stood by, feeling rash and foolish, while Agila and Anakhistos exchanged bursts of harsh rapid words in their own language, a buzzing, eerie tongue that was quite literally like nothing on Earth. He searched their faces for some understanding of the flow of conversation. Was Anakhistos shocked? Outraged? Amused? And she? Even wearing human guise, she was opaque to him too. Did she feel contempt for Eitel's bumptious lusts? Indifference? See him as quaintly primitive, bestial, anthropoid? Or was she eagerly cajoling her husband into letting her have her little adventure? Eitel had an idea. He felt far out of his depth, a sensation as unfamiliar as it was unwelcome. Dry throat, sweaty palms, brain in turmoil: but there was no turning back now.

At last Agila turned to him and said, "It is agreed. The painting is ours at three million. And I am yours until dawn."

David was still waiting. He grinned a knowing grin when Eitel emerged from the Merinides with Agila on his arm, but said nothing. I have lost points with him, Eitel thought. He thinks I have allowed the nonsense of the flesh to interfere with a business decision, and now I have made myself frivolous in his eyes. It is more complicated than that, but David would never understand. *Business and women must be kept separate things.* To the taxi driver, Eitel knew Helen of Troy herself would be as nothing next to a million dollars: mere meat, mere heat. So be it, Eitel told himself. David would never understand. What David would understand, Eitel thought guiltily, was that in cutting the deal with Agila he had also cut fifty thousand dollars off David's commission. But he did not intend to let David know anything about that.

When they were in Eitel's room Agila said, "First, I would please like to have some mint tea, yes? It is my addiction, you know. My aphrodisiac."

Sizzling impatience seared Eitel's soul. God only knew how long it might take room service to fetch a pot of tea at this hour, and at a million dollars a night he preferred not to waste even a minute. But there was no way to refuse. He could not allow himself to seem like some panting schoolboy.

"Of course," he said.

After he had phoned, he walked around behind her as she stood by the window peering into the mists of the night. He put his lips to the nape of her neck and cupped his hands over her breasts. This is very crazy, he thought. I am not touching her real body. This is only some synthetic mock-up, a statue of flesh, a mere androidal shell.

No matter. No matter. He was able to resist her beauty, that illusion, that figment. That beauty, astonishing and unreal, was what had drawn him at first, but it was the dark secret alien underneath that ruled him now. That was what he hoped to reach: the alien, the star-woman, the unfathomable being from the black interstellar deeps. He would touch what no man of Earth had ever touched before.

He inhaled her fragrance until he felt himself swaying. She was making an odd purring sound that he hoped was one of pleasure.

There was a knock at the door. "The tea is here," she said.

The waiter, a boy in native costume, sleepy, openly envious of Eitel for having a woman like Agila in his room, took forever to set up the glasses and pour the tea, an infinitely slow process of raising the pot, aiming, letting the thick tea trickle down through the air. But at last he left. Agila drank greedily, and beckoned to Eitel to have some also. He smiled and shook his head.

She said, "But you must. I love it so—you must share it. It is a ritual of love between us, eh?"

He did not choose to make an issue of it. A glass of mint tea more or less must not get in the way, not now.

"To us," she said, and touched her glass to his.

He managed to drink a little. It was like pure liquid sugar. She had a second glass, and then, maddeningly, a third. He pretended to sip at his. Then at last she touched her hand to a clasp on her shoulder and her metal-mesh sheath fell away.

They had done their research properly, in the body-making labs of Centaurus. She was flawless, sheer fantasy, with heavy breasts that defied gravity, slender waist, hips that would drive a Moroccan camel-driver berserk, buttocks like pale hemispheres. They had given her a navel, pubic hair, erectile nipples, dimples here and there, the hint of blue veins in her thighs. Unreal, yes, Eitel thought, but magnificent.

"It is my fifth traveling body," she said. "I have been Arcturan, Steropid, Denebian, Mizarian—and each time it has been hard, hard, hard! After the transfer is done, there is a long training period, and it is always very difficult. But one learns. A moment finally comes when the body feels natural and true. I will miss this one very much."

"So will I," Eitel said.

Quickly he undressed. She came to him, touched her lips lightly to his, grazed his chest with her nipples.

"And now you must give me a gift," she said.

"What?"

"It is the custom before making love. An exchange of gifts." She took from between her breasts the pendant she was wearing, a bit of bright crystal carved in disturbing alien swirls. "This is for you. And for me—"

Oh, God in heaven, he thought. No!

Her hand closed over the Olmec jade figurine that was still sitting on the dresser.

"This," she said.

It sickened him. That little statuette was eighty thousand on the international antiquities market, maybe a million or two to the right E-T buyer. A gift? A love-token? He saw the gleam in her eye, and knew he was trapped. Refuse, and everything else might be lost. He dare not show any trace of pettiness. Yes. So be it. Let her have the damned thing. We are being romantic tonight. We are making grand gestures. We are not going to behave like a petit-bourgeois Swiss art peddler. *If she confuse you, it can cost you,* David had said. Eitel took a deep breath.

"My pleasure," he said magnificently.

He was an experienced and expert lover; supreme beauty always inspired the best in him; and pride alone made him want to send her back to Centaurus with incandescent memories of the erotic arts of Earth. His performance that night—and performance was the only word he could apply to it—might well have been the finest of his life.

With the lips and tongue, first. Everywhere. With the fingers, slowly, patiently, searching for the little secret key places, the unexpected triggering-points. With the breath against the skin, and the fingernails, ever so lightly, and the eyelashes, and even the newly sprouting stubble of the cheek. These were all things that Eitel loved doing, not merely for the effects they produced in his bed-partners but because they were delightful in and of themselves; yet he had never done them with greater dedication and skill.

And now, he thought, perhaps she will show me some of *her* skills.

But she lay there like a wax doll. Occasionally she stirred, occasionally she moved her hips a little. When he went into her, he found her warm and moist—why had they built that capacity in, Eitel wondered?—but he felt no response from her, none at all.

He moved her this way, that, running through the gamut of positions as though he and she were making a training film for newlyweds. Now and then she smiled. Her eyes were always open: she was fascinated. Eitel felt anger rising. She was ever the tourist, even here in his bed. Getting some first-hand knowledge of the quaint sexual techniques of the primitive Earthmen.

Knowing he was being foolish, that he was compounding a foolishness, he drove his body with frantic intensity, rocking rhythmically above her, grimly pushing her on and on. *Come on,* he thought. *Give me a little sigh, a moan, a wriggle. Anything.* He wasn't asking her to come. There was no reason why they should have built *that* capacity in, was there? The only thing he wanted now was to get some sort of acknowledgement of his existence from her, some quiver of assent.

He went on working at it, knowing he would not get it. But then, to his surprise, something actually seemed to be happening. Her face grew flushed, and her eyes narrowed and took on a new gleam, and her breath began to come in harsh little bursts, and her breasts heaved, and her nipples grew hard. All the signs, yes: Eitel had seen them so many times, and never more welcome than at this moment. He knew what to do. The unslackening rhythm now, the steady building of tension, carrying her onwards, steadily higher, leading her towards that magical moment of overload when the watchful conscious mind at last surrenders to the surging deeper forces. Yes. Yes. The valiant Earthman giving his all for the sake of transgalactic passion, laboring like a galley slave to show the star-woman what the communion of the sexes is all about.

She seemed almost there. Some panting now, even a little gasping. Eitel smiled in pleasant self-congratulation. Swiss precision, he thought: never underestimate it.

And then somehow she managed to slip free of him, between one thrust and the next, and she rolled to the side, so that he collapsed in amazement into the pillow as she left the bed. He sat up and looked at her, stunned, gaping, numbed.

"Excuse me," she said, in the most casual way. "I thought I'd have a little more tea. Shall I get some for you?"

Eitel could barely speak. "No," he said hoarsely.

She poured herself a glass, drank, grimaced. "It doesn't taste as good as when it's warm," she said, returning to the bed. "Well, shall we go on?" she asked.

Silently he reached for her. Somehow he was able to start again. But this time a distance of a thousand light-years seemed to separate him from her. There was no rekindling that brief flame, and after a few moments he gave up. He felt himself forever shut away from the inwardness of her, as Earth is shut away from the stars. Cold, weary, more furious with himself than with her, he let himself come. He kept his eyes open as long as he could, staring icily into hers, but the sensations were unexpectedly powerful, and in the end he sank down against her breasts, clinging to her as the impact thundered through him.

In that bleak moment came a surprise. For as he shook and quivered in the force of that dismal ejaculation something opened between them, a barrier, a gate, and the hotel melted and disappeared and he saw himself in the midst of a bizarre landscape. The sky was a rich golden-green, the sun was deep green and hot, the trees and plants and flowers were like nothing he had ever seen on Earth. The air was heavy, aromatic, and of a piercing flavor that stung his nostrils. Flying creatures that were not birds soared unhurriedly overhead, and some iridescent beasts that looked like red velvet pillows mounted on tripods were grazing on the lower branches of furry-limbed trees. On the horizon Eitel saw three jagged naked mountains of some yellow-brown stone that gleamed like polished metal in the sunlight. He trembled. Wonder and awe engulfed his spirit. This is a park, he realized, the most beautiful park in the world. But this is not *this* world. He found a little path that led over a gentle hill, and when he came to the far side he looked down to see Centaurans strolling two by two, hand in hand, through an elegantly contoured garden.

Oh, my God, Eitel thought. Oh, my God in heaven!

Then it all began to fade, growing thin, turning to something no more substantial than smoke, and in a moment more it was all gone.

He lay still, breathing raggedly, by her side, watching her breasts slowly rising and falling.

He lifted his head. She was studying him. "You liked that?"

"Liked what?"

"What you saw."

"So you know?"

She seemed surprised. "Of course! You thought it was an accident? It was my gift for you."

"Ah." The picture-postcard of the home world, bestowed on the earnest native for his diligent services. "It was extraordinary. I've never seen anything so beautiful."

"It is very beautiful, yes," she said complacently. Then, smiling, she said, "That was interesting, what you did there at the end, when you were breathing so hard. Can you do that again?" she asked, as though he had just executed some intricate juggling maneuver.

Bleakly he shook his head, and turned away. He could not bear to look into those magnificent eyes any longer. Somehow—he would never have any way of knowing when it had happened, except that it was somewhere between "Can you do that again?" and the dawn, he fell asleep. She was shaking him gently awake, then. The light of a brilliant morning came bursting through the fragile old silken draperies.

"I am leaving now," she whispered. "But I wish to thank you. It has been a night I shall never forget."

"Nor I," said Eitel.

"To experience the reality of Earthian ways at such close range—with such intimacy, such immediacy—"

"Yes. Of course. It must have been extraordinary for you."

"If ever you come to Centaurus—"

"Certainly. I'll look you up."

She kissed him lightly, tip of nose, forehead, lips. Then she walked towards the door. With her hand on the knob, she turned and said, "Oh, one little thing that might amuse you. I meant to tell you last night. We don't have that kind of thing on our world, you know—that concept of owning one's mate's body. And in any case, Anakhistos is not male, and I am not female, not exactly. We mate, but our sex distinctions are not so well-defined as that. It is with us more like the way it is with your oysters, I think. So it is not quite right to say that Anakhistos is my husband, or that I am his wife. I thought you would like to know."

She blew him a kiss. "It has been very lovely," she said. "Goodbye."

✹

When she was gone he went to the window and stared into the garden for a long while without looking at anything in particular. He felt weary and burned out, and there was a taste of straw in his mouth. After a time he turned away.

When he emerged from the hotel later that morning, David's car was waiting out front.

"Get in," he said.

They drove in silence to a cafe that Eitel had never seen before, in the new quarter of town. David said something in Arabic to the proprietor and he brought mint tea for two.

"I don't like mint tea," Eitel said.

"Drink. It washes away bad tastes. How did it go last night?"

"Fine. Just fine."

"You and the woman, ficky-ficky?"

"None of your ficky-ficky business."

"Try some tea," David urged. "It not so good last night, eh?"

"What makes you think so?"

"You not look so happy. You not sound so happy."

"For once you're wrong," Eitel said. "I got everything I wanted to get. Do you understand me? I got everything I wanted to get." His tone might have been a little too loud, a little too aggressive, for it drew a quizzical, searching look from the Moroccan.

"Yes. Sure. And what size deal? That *is* my business, yes?"

"Three million cash."

"Only three?"

"Three," Eitel said. "I owe you a hundred and fifty thousand. You're doing all right, a hundred and fifty for a couple of hours' work. I'm making you a rich man."

"Yes. Very rich. But no more deals, Eitel."

"What?"

"You find another boy, all right? I will work now with someone else, maybe. There are plenty of others, you know? I will be more comfortable with them. Is very bad, when one does not trust a partner."

"I don't follow you."

"What you did last night, going off with the woman, was very stupid. Poor business, you know? I wonder, did you have to pay her? And did you pay her some of my money too?"

David was smiling, as always. But sometimes his smiles were amiable and sometimes they were just smiles. Eitel had a sudden vision of himself in a back alley of the old town, bleeding. He had another vision of himself undergoing interrogation by the customs men. David had a lot of power over him, he realized.

Eitel took a deep breath and said, "I resent the insinuation that I've cheated you. I've treated you very honorably from the start. You know that. And if you think I bought the woman, let me tell you this: she isn't a woman at all. She's an alien. Some of them wear human bodies when they travel. Underneath all that gorgeous flesh she's a Centauran, David."

"And you touched her?"

"Yes."

"You put yourself inside her?"

"Yes," Eitel said.

David stood up. He looked as though he had just found a rat embryo in his tea. "I am very glad we are no longer partners, then. Deliver the money to me in the usual way. And then please stay away from me when you are in this city."

"Wait," Eitel said. "Take me back to the Merinides. I've got three more paintings to sell."

"There are plenty of taxi drivers in this city," said David.

When he was gone, Eitel peered into his mint tea for a while and wondered if David meant to make trouble for him. Then he stopped thinking about David and thought about that glimpse of a green sun and a golden landscape that Agila had given him. His hands felt cold, his fingers were quivering a little. He became aware that he wanted more than anything else to see those things again. Could any Centauran make it happen for him, he wondered, or was that only Agila's little trick? What about other aliens? He imagined himself prowling the nightclub, hustling for action, pressing himself up against this slithery thing or that one, desperately trying to re-enact that weird orgasmic moment that had carried him to the stars. A new perversion, he thought. One that even David found disgusting.

He wondered what it was like to go to bed with a Vegan or an Arcturan or a Steropid. God in heaven! Could he do it? Yes, he told himself, thinking of green suns and the unforgettable fragrance of that alien air. Yes. Yes. Of course he could. Of course.

There was a sudden strange sweetness in his mouth. He realized that he had taken a deep gulp of the mint tea without paying attention to what he was doing. Eitel smiled. It hadn't made him sick, had it? Had it? He took another swig. Then, in a slow determined way, he finished off all the rest of it, and scattered some coins on the counter, and went outside to look for a cab.

MULTIPLES

No heartrending sagas of the torments of creation with this one. It was July of 1983; I had finished Valentine Pontifex, *which had turned out to be unexpectedly difficult to write (the first half of 1983 was one of those periods of my life that I'd just as soon not repeat); a few days after the novel was done I sat down and wrote "Multiples" in what was essentially one long take, did a little minor editing, and sent it off to Ellen Datlow of* Omni, *who accepted it right away. They should all be that easy. But in this case (as with "Amanda and the Alien" of the previous year) I was making use of my own home turf as the setting instead of having to invent some alien world, and the theme of multiple personalities was one I had been thinking about for some time. Characters and plot fell into place in that magical way that makes writers want to get down on their knees and offer thanks.*

The story felt like a winner to me right away. Ellen published it in her October, 1983 issue. It was chosen for the first volume (1983) of Gardner Dozois' annual Year's Best Science Fiction *anthologies, and has had a healthy reprint existence ever since. For a dizzying moment in the late 1990s it looked as though Stephen Spielberg was going to make it into a Major Motion Picture, too, but that deal went away as most Hollywood deals go away, leaving nothing but a conspicuous residue of cash on my doorstep. The story also gets me occasional letters from actual multiple-personality people, who want to know if I'm one myself, or married to one. (The answers are No and No—so far as I know.)*

And, if you don't mind, I'd like to append a little bragging here. Having "Multiples" chosen for one of the best-science-fiction-of-the-year anthologies

43

completed an unusual sweep for me, one of which I'm immensely proud. There were then three such anthologies, edited by Dozois, Donald A. Wollheim, and Terry Carr. I had stories in all three of them for the year of 1983. Other writers have achieved that now and then, when some particularly strong story was picked by all three editors—but I had a different story in each book. I don't think anyone had ever managed that trick before. (I did it again in 1989. That time, though, I managed to get five stories into the three anthologies. Go ahead, top it if you can!)

<hr>

There were mirrors everywhere, making the place a crazyhouse of dizzying refraction: mirrors on the ceiling, mirrors on the walls, mirrors in the angles where the walls met the ceiling and the floor, even little eddies of mirror-dust periodically blown on gusts of air through the room, so that all the bizarre distortions, fracturings, and dislocations of image that were bouncing around the place would from time to time coalesce in a shimmering haze of chaos right before your eyes. Colored globes spun round and round overhead, creating patterns of ricocheting light. It was exactly the way Cleo had expected a multiples club to look.

She had walked up and down the whole Fillmore Street strip from Union to Chestnut and back again for half an hour, peering at this club and that, before finding the courage to go inside one that called itself Skits. Though she had been planning this night for months, she found herself paralyzed by fear at the last minute: afraid they would spot her as a fraud the moment she walked in, afraid they would drive her out with jeers and curses and cold mocking laughter. But now that she was within, she felt fine—calm, confident, ready for the time of her life.

There were more women than men in the club, something like a seven-to-three ratio. Hardly anyone seemed to be talking to anyone else: most stood alone in the middle of the floor, staring into the mirrors as though in trance. Their eyes were slits, their jaws were slack, their shoulders slumped forward, their arms dangled. Now and then as some combination of reflections sluiced across their consciousnesses with particular impact they would go taut and jerk and wince as if they had been struck. Their faces would flush, their lips would pull back, their eyes would roll, they would mutter and whisper to themselves; and then after a moment they would slip back into stillness.

Cleo knew what they were doing. They were switching and doubling. Maybe some of the adepts were tripling. Her heart rate picked up. Her throat was very dry. What was the routine here, she wondered? Did you just walk right out on to the floor and plug into the light-patterns, or were you supposed to go to the bar first for a shot or a snort?

She looked towards the bar. A dozen or so customers sitting there, mostly men, a couple of them openly studying her, giving her that new-girl-in-town stare. Cleo returned their gaze evenly, coolly, blankly. Standard-looking men, reasonably attractive, thirtyish or early forty-ish, business suits, conventional hairstyles: young lawyers, executives, maybe stockbrokers, successful sorts out for a night's fun, the kind you might run into anywhere. Look at that one, tall, athletic, curly hair, glasses. Faint ironic smile, easy inquiring eyes. Almost professorial. And yet, and yet—behind that smooth intelligent forehead, what strangenesses must teem and boil! How many hidden souls must lurk and jostle! Scary. Tempting.

Irresistible.

Cleo resisted. Take it slow, take it slow. Instead of going to the bar she moved out serenely among the switchers on the floor, found an open space, centered herself, looked towards the mirrors on the far side of the room. Legs apart, feet planted flat, shoulders forward. A turning globe splashed waves of red and violet light, splintered a thousand times over, into her face. *Go. Go. Go. Go.* You are Cleo. You are Judy. You are Vixen. You are Lisa. *Go. Go. Go. Go.* Cascades of iridescence sweeping over the rim of her soul, battering at the walls of her identity. Come, enter, drown me, split me, switch me. You are Cleo and Judy. You are Vixen and Lisa. You are Cleo and Judy and Vixen and Lisa. *Go. Go. Go.*

Her head was spinning. Her eyes were blurring. The room gyrated around her.

Was this it? Was she splitting? Was she switching? Maybe so. Maybe the capacity was there in everyone, even her, and all it took was the lights, the mirror, the ambience, the will. I am many. I am multiple. I am Cleo switching to Vixen. I am Judy and Lisa. I am—

No.

I am Cleo.

I am Cleo.

I am very dizzy and I am getting sick, and I am Cleo and only Cleo, as I have always been.

I am Cleo and only Cleo and I am going to fall down.

"Easy," he said. "You OK?"

"Steadying up, I think. Whew!"

"Out-of-towner, eh?"

"Sacramento. How'd you know?"

"Too quick on the floor. Locals all know better. This place has the fastest mirrors in the west. They'll blow you away if you're not careful. You can't just go out there and grab for the big one—you've got to phase yourself in slowly. You sure you're going to be OK?"

"I think so."

He was the tall man from the bar, the athletic professorial one. She supposed he had caught her before she had actually fallen, since she felt no bruises. His hand rested now against her elbow as he lightly steered her towards a table along the wall.

"What's your now-name?" he asked.

"Judy."

"I'm Van."

"Hello, Van."

"What about a brandy? Steady you up a little more."

"I don't drink."

"Never?"

"Vixen does the drinking," she said. "Not me."

"Ah. The old story. She gets the bubbles, you get her hangovers. I have one like that too, only with him it's Hunan food. He absolutely doesn't give a damn what lobster in hot and sour sauce does to my digestive system. I hope you pay her back the way she deserves."

Cleo smiled and said nothing.

He was watching her closely. Was he interested, or just being polite to someone who was obviously out of her depth in a strange milieu? Interested, she decided. He seemed to have accepted that Vixen stuff at face value.

Be careful now, Cleo warned herself. Trying to pile on convincing-sounding details when you don't really know what you're talking about is a sure way to give yourself away, sooner or later. The thing to do, she knew, was to establish her credentials without working too hard at it, sit back, listen, learn how things really operate among these people.

"What do you do, up there in Sacramento?"

"Nothing fascinating."

"Poor Judy. Real-estate broker?"

"How'd you guess?"

"Every other woman I meet is a real-estate broker these days. What's Vixen?"

"A lush."

"Not much of a livelihood in that."

Cleo shrugged. "She doesn't need one. The rest of us support her."

"Real estate and what else?"

She hadn't been sure that multiples etiquette included talking about one's alternate selves. But she had come prepared. "Lisa's a landscape architect. Cleo's into software. We all keep busy."

"Lisa ought to meet Chuck. He's a demon horticulturalist. Partner in a plant-rental outfit—you know, huge dracaenas and philodendrons for offices, so much per month, take them away when they start looking sickly. Lisa and Chuck could talk palms and bromeliads and cacti all night."

"We should introduce them, then."

"We should, yes."

"But first we have to introduce Van and Judy."

"And then maybe Van and Cleo," he said.

She felt a tremor of fear. Had he found her out so soon? "Why Van and Cleo? Cleo's not here right now. This is Judy you're talking to."

"Easy. Easy!"

But she was unable to halt. "I can't deliver Cleo to you just like that, you know. She does as she pleases."

"Easy," he said. "All I meant was, Van and Cleo have something in common. Van's into software too."

Cleo relaxed. With a little laugh she said, "Oh, not you too! Isn't everybody, nowadays? But I thought you were something in the academic world. A professor, perhaps."

"I am. At Cal."

"Software?"

"In a manner of speaking. Linguistics. Metalinguistics, actually. My field's the language of language—the basic subsets, the neural coordinates of communication, the underlying programs our brains use, the operating systems. Mind as computer, computer as mind. I can get very boring about it."

"I don't find the mind a boring subject."

"I don't find real estate a boring subject. Talk to me about second mortgages and triple-net leases."

"Talk to me about Chomsky and Benjamin Whorf," she said.

His eyes widened. "You've heard of Whorf?"

"I majored in comparative linguistics. That was before real estate."

"Just my lousy luck," he said. "I get a chance to find out what's hot in the shopping-center market and she wants to talk about Whorf and Chomsky."

"I thought every other woman you met these days was a real-estate broker. Talk to them about shopping centers."

"They all want to talk about Whorf and Chomsky."

"Poor Van."

"Yes. Poor Van." Then he leaned forward and said, his tone softening, "You know, I shouldn't have made that crack about Van meeting Cleo. That was very tacky of me."

"It's OK, Van. I didn't take it seriously."

"You seemed to. You were very upset."

"Well, maybe at first. But then I saw you were just horsing around."

"I still shouldn't have said it. You were absolutely right: this is Judy's time now. Cleo's not here, and that's just fine. It's Judy I want to get to know."

"You will," she said. "But you can meet Cleo too, and Lisa, and Vixen. I'll introduce you to the whole crew. I don't mind."

"You're sure of that?"

"Sure."

"Some of us are very secretive about our alters."

"Are you?" Cleo asked.

"Sometimes. Sometimes not."

"I don't mind. Maybe you'll meet some of mine tonight." She glanced towards the center of the floor. "I think I've steadied up, now. I'd like to try the mirrors again."

"Switching?"

"Doubling," she said. "I'd like to bring Vixen up. She can do the drinking, and I can do the talking. Will it bother you if she's here too?"

"Not unless she's a sloppy drunk. Or a mean one."

"I can keep control of her, when we're doubling. Come on: take me through the mirrors."

"You be careful, now. San Francisco mirrors aren't like Sacramento ones. You've already discovered that."

"I'll watch my step this time. Shall we go out there?"

"Sure," he said.

As they began to move out on to the floor a slender T-shirted man of about thirty came towards them. Shaven scalp, bushy moustache, medallions, boots. Very San Francisco, very gay. He frowned at Cleo and stared straightforwardly at Van.

"Ned?" he said.

Van scowled and shook his head. "No. Not now."

"Sorry. Very sorry. I should have realized." The shaven-headed man flushed and hurried away.

"Let's go," Van said to Cleo.

This time she found it easier to keep her balance. Knowing that he was nearby helped. But still the waves of refracted light came pounding in, pounding in, pounding in. The assault was total: remorseless, implacable, overwhelming. She had to struggle against the throbbing in her chest, the hammering in her temples, the wobbliness of her knees. And this was pleasure, for them? This was a supreme delight?

But they were multiples and she was only Cleo, and that, she knew, made all the difference. She seemed to be able to fake it well enough. She could make up a Judy, a Lisa, a Vixen, assign little corners of her personality to each, give them voices of their own, facial expressions, individual identities. Standing before her mirror at home, she had managed to convince herself. She might even be able to convince him. But as the swirling lights careened off the infinities of interlocking mirrors and came slaloming into the gateways of her reeling soul, the dismal fear began to rise in her that she could never truly be one of these people after all, however skilfully she imitated them in their intricacies.

Was it so? Was she doomed always to stand outside their irresistible world, hopelessly peering in? Too soon to tell—much too soon, she thought, to admit defeat—

At least she didn't fall down. She took the punishment of the mirrors as long as she could stand it, and then, not waiting for him to leave the floor, she made her way—carefully, carefully, walking a tightrope over an abyss—to the bar. When her head had begun to stop spinning she ordered a drink, and she sipped it cautiously. She could feel the alcohol extending itself inch by inch into her bloodstream. It calmed her. On the floor, Van stood in a trance, occasionally quivering in a sudden convulsive way for a fraction of a second. He was doubling, she knew: bringing up one of his other identities. That was the main thing that multiples came to these clubs to do. No longer were all their various identities forced to dwell in rigorously separated compartments of their minds. With the aid of the mirrors, of the lights, the skilled ones were able briefly to fuse two or even three of their selves into something even more complex. When he comes back here, she thought, he will be Van plus X. And I must pretend to be Judy plus Vixen.

She readied herself for that. Judy was easy: Judy was mostly the real Cleo, the real-estate woman from Sacramento, with Cleo's notion of what it was like to be a multiple added in. And Vixen? Cleo imagined her to be about twenty-three, a Los Angeles girl, a one-time child tennis star who had broken her ankle in a dumb prank and had never recovered her game afterwards, and who had taken up drinking to ease the pain and loss. Uninhibited, unpredictable, untidy, fiery, fierce: all the things that Cleo was not. Could she be Vixen? She took a deep gulp of her drink and put on the Vixen-face: eyes hard and glittering, cheek-muscles clenched.

Van was leaving the floor now. His way of moving seemed to have changed: he was stiff, almost awkward, his shoulders held high, his elbows jutting oddly. He looked so different that she wondered whether he was still Van at all.

"You didn't switch, did you?"

"Doubled. Paul's with me now."

"Paul?"

"Paul's from Texas. Geologist, terrific poker game, plays the guitar." Van smiled and it was like a shifting of gears. In a deeper, broader voice he said, "And I sing real good too, ma'am. Van's jealous of that, because he can't sing worth beans. Are you ready for a refill?"

"You bet," Cleo said, sounding sloppy, sounding Vixenish.

His apartment was nearby, a cheerful airy sprawling place in the Marina district. The segmented nature of his life was immediately obvious: the prints and paintings on the walls looked as though they had been chosen by four or five different people, one of whom ran heavily towards vivid scenes of sunrise over the Grand Canyon, another to Picasso and Miró, someone else to delicate impressionist views of Parisian flower-markets. A sunroom contained the biggest and healthiest houseplants Cleo had ever seen. Another room was stacked high with technical books and scholarly journals, a third was set up as a home gymnasium equipped with three or four gleaming exercise machines. Some of the rooms were fastidiously tidy, some impossibly chaotic. Some of the furniture was stark and austere, and some was floppy and overstuffed. She kept expecting to find roommates wandering around. But there was no one here but Van. And Paul.

Paul fixed the drinks. Paul played soft guitar music and told her gaudy tales of prospecting for rare earths on the West Texas mesas. Paul sang something bawdy-sounding in Spanish, and Cleo, putting on her Vixen-voice, chimed in on the choruses, deliberately off key. But then Paul went away and it was Van who sat close beside her on the couch, talking quietly. He wanted to know things about Judy, and he told her a little about Van, and no other selves came into the conversation. She was sure that that was intentional. They stayed up very late. Paul came back, towards the end of the evening, to tell a few jokes and sing a soft late-night song, but when they went into the bedroom she was with Van. Of that she was completely certain.

And when she woke in the morning she was alone.

She felt a surge of confusion and dislocation, remembered after a moment where she was and how she had happened to be here, sat up, blinked. Went into the bathroom and scooped a handful of water over her face. Without bothering to dress, went padding around the apartment looking for Van.

She found him in the exercise room, using the rowing machine, but he wasn't Van. He was dressed in tight jeans and a white T-shirt, and somehow he looked younger, leaner, jauntier. There were fine beads of sweat along his forehead, but he did not seem to be breathing hard. He gave her a cool, distantly appraising, wholly asexual look, as though she were a total stranger but that it was not in the least unusual for an unknown naked woman to materialize in the house and he was altogether undisturbed by it, and said, "Good morning. I'm Ned. Pleased to know you." His voice was higher than Van's, much higher than Paul's, and he had an odd over-precise way of shaping each syllable.

Flustered, suddenly self-conscious and wishing she had put her clothes on before leaving the bedroom, she folded one arm over her breasts, though her nakedness did not seem to matter to him at all. "I'm—Judy. I came with Van."

"Yes, I know. I saw the entry in our book." Smoothly, effortlessly, he pulled on the oars of the rowing machine, leaned back, pushed forward. "Help yourself to anything in the fridge," he said. "Make yourself entirely at home. Van left a note for you in the kitchen."

She stared at him: his hands, his mouth, his long muscular arms. She remembered his touch, his kisses, the feel of his skin against hers. And now this complete indifference. No. Not *his* kisses, not *his* touch. Van's. And Van was not here now. There was a different tenant in Van's body, someone she did not know in any way and who had no memories of last night's embraces. *I saw the entry in our book.* They left memos for each other. Cleo shivered. She had known what to expect, more or less, but experiencing it was very different from reading about it. She felt almost as though she had fallen in among beings from another planet.

But this is what you wanted, she thought. Isn't it? The intricacy, the mystery, the unpredictability, the sheer weirdness? A little cruise through an alien world, because her own had become so stale, so narrow, so cramped. And here she was. *Good morning, I'm Ned. Pleased to know you.*

Van's note was clipped to the refrigerator by a little yellow magnet shaped like a ladybug. *Dinner tonight at Chez Michel? You and me and who knows who else. Call me.*

That was the beginning. She saw him every night for the next ten days. Generally they met at some three-star restaurant, had a lingering intimate dinner, went back to his apartment. One mild clear evening they drove out to the beach and watched the waves breaking on Seal Rock until well past midnight. Another time they wandered through Fisherman's Wharf and somehow acquired three bags of tacky souvenirs.

Van was his primary name—she saw it on his credit card at dinner one night—and that seemed to be his main identity, too, though she knew there were plenty of others. At first he was reticent about that, but on the fourth or fifth night he told her that he had nine major selves and sixteen minor ones, some of which remained submerged years at a stretch. Besides Paul, the geologist, and Chuck, who was into horticulture, and Ned, the gay one, Cleo heard about Nat the stock-market plunger—he was fifty and fat, and made a fortune every week, and liked to divide his time between Las Vegas and Miami Beach— and Henry, the poet, who was very shy and never liked anyone to read his work, and Dick, who was studying to be an actor, and Hal, who once taught law at Harvard, and Dave, the yachtsman, and Nicholas, the card-sharp—and then there were all the fragmentary ones, some of whom didn't have names, only a funny way of speaking or a little routine they liked to act out—

She got to see very little of his other selves, though. Like all multiples, he was troubled occasionally by involuntary switching, and one night he became Hal while they were making love, and another time he turned into Dave for an hour, and there were momentary flashes of Henry and Nicholas. Cleo perceived it right away whenever one of those switches came: his voice, his movements, his entire manner and personality changed immediately. Those were startling, exciting moments for her, offering a strange exhilaration. But generally his control was very good, and he stayed Van, as if he felt some strong need to experience her as Van and Van alone. Once in a while he doubled, bringing up Paul to play the guitar for him and sing, or Dick to recite sonnets, but when he did that the Van identity always remained present and dominant. It appeared that he was able to double at will, without the aid of mirrors and lights, at least some of the time. He had been an active and functioning multiple as long as he could remember—since childhood, perhaps even since birth—and he had devoted himself through the years to the task of gaining mastery over his divided mind.

All the aspects of him that she came to meet had basically attractive personalities: they were energetic, stable, purposeful men, who enjoyed life and seemed to know how to go about getting what they wanted. Though they were very different people, she could trace them all back readily enough to the underlying Van from whom, so she thought, they had all split off. The one puzzle was Nat, the market operator. It was hard for Cleo to imagine what he was like when he was Nat—sleazy and coarse, yes, but how did he manage to make himself look fifteen years older and forty pounds heavier? Maybe it was all done with facial expressions and posture. But she never got to see Nat. And gradually she realized it was an oversimplification to think of Paul and Dick and Ned and the others as mere extensions of Van into different modes. Van by himself was just as incomplete as the others. He was just one of many that had evolved in parallel, each one autonomous, each one only a fragment of the whole. Though Van might have control of the shared body a greater portion of the time, he still had no idea what any of his alternate selves were up to while they were in command, and like them he had to depend on guesses and fancy footwork and such notes and messages as they bothered to leave behind in order to keep track of events that occurred outside his conscious awareness. "The only one who knows everything is Michael. He's seven years old, smart as a whip, keeps in touch with all of us all the time."

"Your memory trace," Cleo said.

Van nodded. All multiples, she knew, had one alter with full awareness of the doings of all the other personalities—usually a child, an observer who sat back deep in the mind and played its own games and emerged only when necessary to fend off some crisis that threatened the stability of the entire group. "He's just informed us that he's Ethiopian," Van said. "So every two or three weeks we go across to Oakland to an Ethiopian restaurant that he likes, and he flirts with the waitresses in Amharic."

"That can't be too terrible a chore. I'm told Ethiopians are very beautiful people."

"Absolutely. But they think it's all a big joke, and Michael doesn't know how to pick up women, anyway. He's only seven, you know. So Van doesn't get anything out of it except some exercise in comparative linguistics and a case of indigestion the next day. Ethiopian food is the spiciest in the world. I can't *stand* spicy food."

"Neither can I," she said. "But Lisa loves it. Especially hot Mexican things. But nobody ever said sharing a body is easy, did they?"

She knew she had to be careful in questioning Van about the way his life as a multiple worked. She was supposed to be a multiple herself, after all. But she made use of her Sacramento background as justification for her areas of apparent ignorance of multiple customs and the everyday mechanics of multiple life. Though she too had known she was a multiple since childhood, she said, she had grown up outside the climate of acceptance of the divided personality that prevailed in San Francisco, where an active subculture of multiples had existed openly for years. In her isolated existence, unaware that there were a great many others of her kind, she had at first regarded herself as the victim of a serious mental disorder. It was only recently, she told him, that she had come to understand the overwhelming advantages of life as a multiple: the richness, the complexity, the fullness of talents and experiences that a divided mind was free to enjoy. That was why she had come to San Francisco. That was why she listened so eagerly to all that he was telling her about himself.

She was cautious, too, in manifesting her own multiple identities. She wished she did not have to be pretending to have other selves. But they had to be brought forth now and again, Cleo felt, if only by way of maintaining his interest in her. Multiples were notoriously indifferent to singletons, she knew. They found them bland, overly simple, two-dimensional. They wanted the excitement that came with embracing one person and discovering another, or two or three. So she gave him Lisa, she gave him Vixen, she gave him the Judy-who-was-Cleo and the Cleo-who-was-someone-else, and she slipped from one to another in a seemingly involuntary and unexpected way, often when they were in bed.

Lisa was calm, controlled, strait-laced. She was totally shocked when she found herself, between one eye-blink and the next, in the arms of a strange man. "Who are you?—where am I?—" she blurted, rolling away, pulling herself into a foetal ball.

"I'm Judy's friend," Van said.

She stared bleakly at him. "So she's up to her tricks again. I should have figured it out faster."

He looked pained, embarrassed, terribly solicitous. She let him wonder for a moment or two whether he would have to take her back to her hotel right here in the middle of the night. And then she allowed a mischievous smile to cross Lisa's face, allowed Lisa's outraged modesty to subside, allowed Lisa to relent and relax, allowed Lisa to purr—

"Well, as long as we're here already—what did you say your name was?"

He liked that. He liked Vixen, too—wild, sweaty, noisy, a moaner, a gasper, a kicker and thrasher who dragged him down on to the floor and went rolling over and over with him. She thought he liked Cleo, too, though that was harder to tell, because Cleo's style was aloof, serious, baroque, inscrutable. She would switch quickly from one to another, sometimes running through all four in the course of an hour. Wine, she said, induced quick switching in her. She let him know that she had a few other identities, too, fragmentary and submerged, and hinted that they were troubled, deeply neurotic, almost self-destructive: they were under control, she said, and would not erupt to cause woe for him, but she left the possibility hovering over them, to add spice to the relationship and plausibility to her role.

It seemed to be working. His pleasure in her company was evident, and the more they were together the stronger the bond between them became. She was beginning to indulge in pleasant little fantasies of moving down here permanently from Sacramento, renting an apartment somewhere near his, perhaps even moving in with him—though that would surely be a strange and challenging life, for she would be living with Paul and Ned and Chuck and all the rest of the crew too, but how wondrous, how electrifying—

Then on the tenth day he seemed uncharacteristically tense and somber, and she asked him what was bothering him, and he evaded her, and she pressed, and finally he said, "Do you really want to know?"

"Of course."

"It bothers me that you aren't real, Judy."

She caught her breath. "What the hell do you mean by that?"

"You know what I mean," he said, quietly, sadly. "Don't try to pretend any longer. There's no point in it."

It was like a jolt in the ribs. She turned away and stared at the wall and was silent a long while, wondering what to say. Just when everything was going so well, just when she was beginning to believe she had carried off the masquerade successfully—

"So you know?" she asked in a small voice.

"Of course I know. I knew right away."

She was trembling. "How could you tell?"

"A thousand ways. When we switch, we *change*. The voice. The eyes. The muscular tensions. The grammatical habits. The brain waves, even. An evoked-potential test shows it. Flash a light in my eyes and I'll give off a certain brain-wave pattern, and Ned will give off another, and Chuck still another. You and Lisa and Cleo and Vixen would all be the same. Multiples aren't actors, Judy. Multiples are separate minds within the same brain. That's a matter of scientific fact. You were just acting. You were doing it very well, but you couldn't possibly have fooled me."

"You let me make an idiot of myself, then."

"No."

"Why did you—how could you—"

"I saw you walk in, that first night at the club, and you caught me right away. And then I watched you go out on the floor and fall apart, and I knew you couldn't be multiple, and I wondered, what the hell's she doing here, and then I went over to you, and I was hooked. I felt something I haven't ever felt before. Does that sound like the standard old malarkey? But it's true, Judy. You're the first singleton woman that's ever interested me."

"Why?"

He shook his head. "Something about you—your intensity, your alertness, maybe even your eagerness to pretend you were a multiple—I don't know. I was caught. I was caught hard. And it's been a wonderful week and a half. I mean that. Wonderful."

"Until you got bored."

"I'm not bored with you, Judy."

"Cleo. That's my real name, my singleton name. There is no Judy."

"Cleo," he said, as if measuring the word with his lips.

"So you aren't bored with me even though there's only one of me. That's marvelous. That's tremendously flattering. That's the best thing I've heard all day. I guess I should go now, Van. It *is* Van, isn't it?"

"Don't talk that way."

"How do you want me to talk? I fascinated you, you fascinated me, we played our little games with each other, and now it's over. I wasn't real, but you did your best. We both did our bests. But I'm only a singleton woman, and you can't be satisfied with that. Not for long. For a night, a week, two weeks, maybe. Sooner or later you'll want the real thing, and I can't be the real thing for you. So long, Van."

"No."

"No?"

"Don't go."

"What's the sense of staying?"

"I want you to stay."

"I'm a singleton, Van."

"You don't have to be," he said.

❋

The therapist's name was Burkhalter and his office was in one of the Embarcadero towers, and to the San Francisco multiples community he was very close to being a deity. His speciality was electrophysiological integration, with specific application to multiple-personality disorders. Those who carried within themselves dark and diabolical selves that threatened the stability of the group went to him to have those selves purged, or at least contained. Those who sought to have latent selves that were submerged beneath more outgoing personalities brought forward into healthy functional state went to him also. Those whose life as a multiple was a torment of schizoid confusions instead of a richly rewarding contrapuntal symphony gave themselves to Dr. Burkhalter to be healed, and in time they were. And in recent years he had begun to develop techniques for what he called personality augmentation. Van called it "driving the wedge."

"He can turn a singleton into a multiple?" Cleo asked in amazement.

"If the potential is there. You know that it's partly genetic: the structure of a multiple's brain is fundamentally different from a singleton's. The hardware just isn't the same, the cerebral wiring. And then, if the right stimulus comes along, usually in childhood, usually but not necessarily traumatic, the splitting takes place, the separate identities begin to establish their territories. But much of the time multiplicity is never generated, and you walk around with the capacity to be a whole horde of selves and never know it."

"Is there reason to think I'm like that?"

He shrugged. "It's worth finding out. If he detects the predisposition, he has effective ways of inducing separation. Driving the wedge, you see? You do *want* to be a multiple, don't you, Cleo?"

"Oh, yes, Van. Yes!"

Burkhalter wasn't sure about her. He taped electrodes to her head, flashed bright lights in her eyes, gave her verbal association tests, ran four or five different kinds of electroencephalograph studies, and still he was uncertain. "It is not a black-and-white matter," he said several times, frowning, scowling. He was a multiple himself, but three of his selves were psychiatrists, so there was never any real problem about his office hours. Cleo wondered if he ever went to himself for a second opinion. After a week of testing she was sure that she must be a hopeless case, an intractable singleton, but Burkhalter surprised her by concluding that it was worth the attempt. "At the very worst," he said, "we will experience spontaneous fusing within a few days, and you will be no worse off than you are now. But if we succeed—ah, if we succeed—!"

His clinic was across the bay in a town called Moraga. She checked in on a Friday afternoon, spent two days undergoing further neurological and psychological tests, then three days taking medication, "Simply an anti-convulsant," the nurse explained cheerily. "To build up your tolerance."

"Tolerance for what?" Cleo asked.

"The birth trauma," she said, "New selves will be coming forth, and it can be uncomfortable for a little while."

The treatment began on Thursday. Electroshock drugs, electroshock again. She was heavily sedated. It felt like a long dream, but there was no pain. Van visited her every day. Chuck came too, bringing her two potted orchids in bloom, and Paul sang to her, and even Ned paid her a call. But it was hard for her to maintain a conversation with any of them. She heard voices much of the time. She felt feverish and dislocated, and at times she was sure she was floating eight or ten inches above the bed. Gradually that sensation subsided, but there were others nearly as odd. The voices remained. She learned how to hold conversations with them.

In the second week she was not allowed to have visitors. That didn't matter. She had plenty of company even when she was alone.

Then Van came for her. "They're going to let you go home today," he said. "How are you doing, Cleo?"

"I'm Noreen," she said.

There were five of her, apparently. That was what Van said. She had no way of knowing, because when they were dominant she was gone—not merely asleep, but *gone,* perceiving nothing. But he showed her notes that they wrote, in handwritings that she did not recognize and indeed could barely read, and he played tapes of her other voices, Noreen a deep contralto, Nanette high and breathy, Katya hard and rough New York, and the last one, who had not yet announced her name, a stagy voluptuous campy siren-voice.

She did not leave his apartment the first few days, and then began going out for short trips, always with Van or one of his alters close beside. She felt convalescent. A kind of hangover from the various drugs had dulled her reflexes and made it difficult for her to cope with the traffic, and also there was the fear that she would undergo a switching while she was out. Whenever that happened it came without warning, and when she returned to awareness afterwards she felt a sharp bewildering discontinuity of memory, not knowing how it was that she suddenly found herself in Ghiradelli Square or Golden Gate Park or wherever it was that the other self had taken their body.

But she was happy. And Van was happy with her. As they strolled hand in hand through the cool evenings she turned to him now and again and saw the warmth of his smile, the glow of his eyes. One night in the second week when they were out together he switched to Chuck—Cleo saw him change, and knew it was Chuck coming on, for now she always knew right away which identity had taken over—and he said, "You've had a marvelous effect on him, Cleo. None of us has ever seen him like this before—so contented, so fulfilled—"

"I hope it lasts, Chuck."

"Of course it'll last! Why on earth shouldn't it last?"

It didn't. Towards the end of the third week Cleo noticed that there hadn't been any entries in her memo book from Noreen for several days. That in itself was nothing alarming: an alter might choose to submerge for days, weeks, even months at a time. But was it likely that Noreen, so new to the world, would remain out of sight so long? Lin-lin, the little Chinese girl who had evolved in the second week and was Cleo's memory trace, reported that Noreen had gone away. A few days later an identity named Mattie came and went within three hours, like something bubbling up out of a troubled sea. Then Nanette disappeared, leaving Cleo with no one but her nameless breathy-voiced alter and Lin-lin. She knew she was fusing again. The wedges that Dr. Burkhalter had driven into her soul were not holding; her mind insisted on oneness, and was integrating itself; she was reverting to the singleton state.

"They're all gone," she told Van disconsolately.

"I know. I've been watching it happen."

"Is there anything we can do? Should I go back to Burkhalter?"

She saw the pain in his eyes. "It won't do any good," he said. "He told me the chances were about three to one this would happen. A month, he figured—that was about the best we could hope for. And we've had our month."

"I'd better go, Van."

"Don't say that."

"No?"

"I love you, Cleo."

60

"You won't," she said. "Not for much longer."

He tried to argue with her, to tell her that it didn't matter to him that she was a singleton, that one Cleo was worth a whole raft of alters, that he would learn to adapt to life with a singleton woman. He could not bear the thought of her leaving now. So she stayed: a week, two weeks, three. They ate at their favorite restaurants. They strolled hand in hand through the cool evenings. They talked of Chomsky and Whorf and even of shopping centers. When he was gone and Paul or Chuck or Hal or Dave was there she went places with them, if they wanted her to. Once she went to a movie with Ned, and when towards the end he felt himself starting to switch she put her arm around him and held him until he regained control, so that he could see how the movie finished.

But it was no good, really. She sensed the strain in him. He wanted something richer than she could offer him: the switching, the doubling, the complex undertones and overtones of other personalities resonating beyond the shores of consciousness. She could not give him that. And though he insisted he didn't miss it, he was like one who has voluntarily blindfolded himself in order to keep a blind woman company. She knew she could not ask him to live like that for ever.

And so one afternoon when Van was somewhere else she packed her things and said goodbye to Paul, who gave her a hug and wept a little with her, and she went back to Sacramento. "Tell him not to call," she said. "A clean break's the best." She had been in San Francisco two months, and it was as though those two months were the only months of her life that had had any color in them, and all the rest had been lived in tones of grey.

There had been a man in the real-estate office who had been telling her for a couple of years that they were meant for each other. Cleo had always been friendly enough to him—they had done a few skiing weekends in Tahoe the winter before, they had gone to Hawaii once, they had driven down to San Diego—but she had never felt anything particular when she was with him. A week after her return, she phoned him and suggested that they drive out up north to the redwood country for a few days together. When they came back, she moved into the handsome condominium he had just outside town.

It was hard to find anything wrong with him. He was good-natured and attractive, he was successful, he read books and liked good movies, he enjoyed hiking and rafting and backpacking, he even talked of driving down into the city during the opera season to take in a performance or two. He was getting towards the age where he was thinking about marriage and a family. He seemed very fond of her.

But he was flat, she thought. Flat as a cardboard cut-out: a singleton, a one-brain, a no-switch. There was only one of him, and there always would be. It was hardly his fault, she knew. But she couldn't settle for someone who had only two dimensions. A terrible restlessness went roaring through her every evening, and she could not possibly tell him what was troubling her.

On a drizzly afternoon in early November she packed a suitcase and drove down to San Francisco. She arrived about six-thirty, and checked into one of the Lombard Street motels, and showered and changed and walked over to Fillmore Street. Cautiously she explored the strip from Chestnut down to Union, from Union back to Chestnut. The thought of running into Van terrified her. Probably she would, sooner or later, she knew: but not tonight, she prayed. Not tonight. She went past Skits, did not go in, stopped outside a club called Big Mama, shook her head, finally entered one called the Side Effect. Mostly women inside, as usual, but a few men at the bar, not too bad-looking. No sign of Van. She bought herself a drink and casually struck up a conversation with the man to her left, a short curly-haired artistic-looking type, about forty.

"You come here often?" he asked.

"First time. I've usually gone to Skits."

"I think I remember seeing you there. Or maybe not."

She smiled. "What's your now-name?"

"Sandy. Yours?"

Cleo drew her breath down deep into her lungs. She felt a kind of lightheadedness beginning to swirl behind her eyes. *Is this what you want?* she asked herself. *Yes. Yes. This is what you want.*

"Melinda," she said.

AGAINST BABYLON

Another easy one. (The gods owed me a few, after the wearying months of "Tourist Trade" and Pontifex.)

Though Northern California is where I live—and the distance that separates San Francisco in the north from Los Angeles in the south is four hundred miles, which is about the distance from Rome to Budapest—I've carried on an intense love-hate relationship with the southern half of my immense state for nearly forty years. During the 1970s and 1980s, when I was stocking my garden with plants from Southern California's abundant nurseries, I must have made a hundred trips to Los Angeles; I know the place better than most Northern Californians, and go blithely buzzing around on routes unknown even to some of the locals to horticultural sites in outlying towns like San Marino and San Gabriel. Yet I've never wanted to live there, despite my envy of the warm winters and my admiration for the districts of astonishing beauty that one finds interspersed among the parts that are of astonishing ugliness. If I'm away from Los Angeles too long, I miss it in a way that is the next thing to homesickness; if I'm down there for more than three or four days at a stretch, I yearn for the blue skies and sweet air of my own region. And so I oscillate from one end of the pendulum to the other, and probably always will.

"Against Babylon" reflects my close-range observations of the colossus of the south over many decades, my horrified fascination for the place, and my uneasiness over certain of the tawdrier aspects of the California mentality, both southern and northern. Once again, as with the previous California stories in this series, the work, which I did after the onset of

*the rainy season in November, 1983, went swiftly and relatively easily—
I had had a long holiday from writing during August, September, and
October, which helped—and acceptance (from Ellen Datlow again, at
Omni) came without complications. She had such a backlog of my work
by now that she didn't publish it until the May, 1986 issue. The story
made it into the Dozois Year's Best SF 1986 volume, and was picked as
well for Don Wollheim's anthology covering the same year. A decade later,
I used it, in slightly modified form, as the opening chapter of my novel
The Alien Years, but it stands on its own perfectly well, which is why I
include it here.*

Carmichael flew in from New Mexico that morning and the first
thing they told him when he put his little plane down at Burbank
was that fires were burning out of control all around the Los Angeles
basin. He was needed bad, they told him. It was late October, the height
of the brush-fire season in Southern California, and a hot hard dry
wind was blowing out of the desert, and the last time it had rained was
the fifth of April. He phoned the district supervisor right away and the
district supervisor told him, "Get your ass out here on the line double
fast, Mike."

"Where do you want me?"

"The worst one's just above Chatsworth. We've got planes loaded
and ready to go out of Van Nuys Airport."

"I need time to pee and to phone my wife," Carmichael said. "I'll be
in Van Nuys in fifteen, okay?"

He was so tired that he could feel it in his teeth. It was nine in
the morning and he'd been flying since half past four, and it had been
rough all the way, getting pushed around by that same fierce wind
out of the heart of the continent that was threatening now to fan the
flames in L.A. At this moment all he wanted was home and shower
and Cindy and bed. But Carmichael didn't regard firefighting work as
optional. This time of year, the whole crazy city could go in one big
firestorm. There were times he almost wished that it would. He hated
this smoggy tawdry Babylon of a city, its endless tangle of freeways,
the strange-looking houses, the filthy air, the thick choking glossy
foliage everywhere, the drugs, the booze, the divorces, the laziness,

the sleaziness, the porno shops and the naked encounter parlors and the massage joints, the weird people wearing their weird clothes and driving their weird cars and cutting their hair in weird ways. There was a cheapness, a trashiness, about everything here, he thought. Even the mansions and the fancy restaurants were that way: hollow, like slick movie sets. He sometimes felt that the trashiness bothered him more than the out-and-out evil. If you kept sight of your own values you could do battle with evil, but trashiness slipped up around you and infiltrated your soul without your even knowing it. He hoped that his sojourn in Los Angeles was not doing that to him.

He came from the Valley, and what he meant by the Valley was the great San Joaquin, out behind Bakersfield, and not the little cluttered San Fernando Valley they had here. But L.A. was Cindy's city and Cindy loved L.A. and he loved Cindy, and for Cindy's sake he had lived here seven years, up in Laurel Canyon amidst the lush green shrubbery, and for seven Octobers in a row he had gone out to dump chemical retardants on the annual brush-fires, to save the Angelenos from their own idiotic carelessness. You had to accept your responsibilities, Carmichael believed.

The phone rang seven times at the home number before he hung up. Then he tried the little studio where Cindy made her jewelry, but she didn't answer there either, and it was too early to call her at the gallery. That bothered him, not being able to say hello to her right away after his three-day absence, and no likely chance for it now for another eight or ten hours. But there was nothing he could do about that.

As soon as he was aloft again he could see the fire not far to the northwest, a greasy black column against the pale sky. And when he stepped from his plane a few minutes later at Van Nuys he felt the blast of sudden heat. The temperature had been in the mid-eighties at Burbank, damned well hot enough for nine in the morning, but here it was over a hundred. He heard the distant roar of flames, the popping and crackling of burning underbrush, the peculiar whistling sound of dry grass catching fire.

The airport looked like a combat center. Planes were coming and going with lunatic frenzy, and they were lunatic planes, too, antiques of every sort, forty and fifty years old and even older, converted B-17 Flying Fortresses and DC-3s and a Douglas Invader and, to Carmichael's astonishment, a Ford Trimotor from the 1930's that had been hauled, maybe, out of some movie studio's collection. Some were equipped with tanks that held fire-retardant chemicals, some were water-pumpers, some were mappers with infrared and electronic scanning equipment glistening on their snouts. Harried-looking men and women ran back and forth, shouting into CB handsets, supervising the loading process. Carmichael found his way to Operations HQ, which was full of haggard people staring into computer screens. He knew most of them from other years. They knew him.

One of the dispatchers said, "We've got a DC-3 waiting for you. You'll dump retardants along this arc, from Ybarra Canyon eastward to Horse Flats. The fire's in the Santa Susana foothills and so far the wind's from the east, but if it shifts to northerly it's going to take out everything from Chatsworth to Granada Hills, and right on down to Ventura Boulevard. And that's only *this* fire."

"How many are there?"

The dispatcher tapped his keyboard. The map of the San Fernando Valley that had been showing disappeared and was replaced by one of the entire Los Angeles basin. Carmichael stared. Three great scarlet streaks indicated fire zones: this one along the Santa Susanas, another nearly as big way off to the east in the grasslands north of the 210 Freeway around Glendora or San Dimas, and a third down in eastern Orange County, back of Anaheim Hills. "Ours is the big one so far," the dispatcher said. "But these other two are only about forty miles apart, and if they should join up somehow—"

"Yeah," Carmichael said. A single wall of fire running along the whole eastern rim of the basin, maybe—with Santa Ana winds blowing, carrying sparks westward across Pasadena, across downtown L.A., across Hollywood, across Beverly Hills, all the way to the coast, to Venice, Santa Monica, Malibu. He shivered. Laurel Canyon would go. Everything would go. Worse than Sodom and Gomorrah, worse than the fall of Nineveh. Nothing but ashes for hundreds of miles. "Jesus," he said. "Everybody scared silly of Russian nukes, and three carloads of dumb kids tossing cigarettes can do the job just as easily."

"But this wasn't cigarettes, Mike," the dispatcher said.

"No? What then, arson?"

"You haven't heard."

"I've been in New Mexico the last three days."

"You're the only one in the world who hasn't heard, then."

"For Christ's sake, heard what?"

66

"About the E-Ts," said the dispatcher wearily. "They started the fires. Three spaceships landing at six this morning in three different corners of the L.A. basin. The heat of their engines ignited the dry grass."

Carmichael did not smile. "You've got one weird sense of humor, man."

The dispatcher said, "You think I'm joking?"

"Spaceships? From another world?"

"With critters fifteen feet high on board," the dispatcher at the next computer said. "Tim's not kidding. They're out walking around on the freeways right this minute. Fifteen feet high, Mike."

"Men from Mars?"

"Nobody knows where the hell they're from."

"Jesus," Carmichael said. "Jesus Christ God."

Wild updrafts from the blaze buffeted the plane as he took it aloft, and gave him a few bad moments. But he moved easily and automatically to gain control, pulling the moves out of the underground territories of his nervous system. It was essential, he believed, to have the moves in your fingers, your shoulders, your thighs, rather than in the conscious realms of your brain. Consciousness could get you a long way, but ultimately you had to work out of the underground territories or you were dead.

He felt the plane responding and managed a grin. DC-3s were tough old birds. He loved flying them, though the youngest of them had been manufactured before he was born. He loved flying anything. Flying wasn't what Carmichael did for a living—he didn't actually do anything for a living, not any more—but flying was what he did. There were months when he spent more time in the air than on the ground, or so it seemed to him, because the hours he spent on the ground often slid by unnoticed, while time in the air was heightened, intensified, magnified.

He swung south over Encino and Tarzana before heading up across Canoga Park and Chatsworth into the fire zone. A fine haze of ash masked the sun. Looking down, he could see the tiny houses, the tiny blue swimming pools, the tiny people scurrying about, desperately trying to hose down their roofs before the flames arrived. So many houses, so many people, filling every inch of space between the sea and the desert, and now it was all in jeopardy. The southbound lanes of Topanga

Canyon Boulevard were as jammed with cars, here in mid-morning, as the Hollywood Freeway at rush hour. Where were they all going? Away from the fire, yes. Toward the coast, it seemed. Maybe some television preacher had told them there was an ark sitting out there in the Pacific, waiting to carry them to safety while God rained brimstone down on Los Angeles. Maybe there really was. In Los Angeles anything was possible. Invaders from space walking around on the freeways, even. Jesus. Jesus. Carmichael hardly knew how to begin thinking about that.

He wondered where Cindy was, what *she* was thinking about it. Most likely she found it very funny. Cindy had a wonderful ability to be amused by things. There was a line of poetry she liked to quote, from that Roman, Virgil: a storm is rising, the ship has sprung a leak, there's a whirlpool to one side and sea-monsters on the other, and the captain turns to his men and says, "One day perhaps we'll look back and laugh even at all this." That was Cindy's way, Carmichael thought. The Santa Anas are blowing and three big brush fires are burning and invaders from space have arrived at the same time, and one day perhaps we'll look back and laugh even at all this. His heart overflowed with love for her, and longing. He had never known anything about poetry before he had met her. He closed his eyes a moment and brought her onto the screen of his mind. Thick cascades of jet-black hair, quick dazzling smile, long slender tanned body all aglitter with those amazing rings and necklaces and pendants she designed and fashioned. And her eyes. No one else he knew had eyes like hers, bright with strange mischief, with that altogether original way of vision that was the thing he most loved about her. *Damn* this fire, just when he'd been away three days! *Damn* the stupid men from Mars!

Where the neat rows and circles of suburban streets ended there was a great open stretch of grassy land, parched by the long summer to the color of a lion's hide, and beyond that were the mountains, and between the grassland and the mountains lay the fire, an enormous lateral red crest topped by a plume of foul black smoke. It seemed already to cover hundreds of acres, maybe thousands. A hundred acres of burning brush, Carmichael had heard once, creates as much heat energy as the atomic bomb they dropped on Hiroshima.

Through the crackle of radio static came the voice of the line boss, directing operations from a bubble-domed helicopter hovering at about four o'clock. "DC-3, who are you?"

"Carmichael."

"We're trying to contain it on three sides, Carmichael. You work on the east, Limekiln Canyon, down the flank of Porter Ranch Park. Got it?"

"Got it," Carmichael said.

He flew low, less than a thousand feet. That gave him a good view of all the action: sawyers in hard hats and orange shirts chopping burning trees to make them fall toward the fire, bulldozer crews clearing brush ahead of the blaze, shovelers carving firebreaks, helicopters pumping water into isolated tongues of flame. He climbed five hundred feet to avoid a single-engine observer plane, then went up five hundred more to avoid the smoke and air turbulence of the fire itself. From that altitude he had a clear picture of it, running like a bloody gash from west to east, wider at its western end. Just east of the fire's far tip he saw a circular zone of grassland perhaps a hundred acres in diameter that had already burned out, and precisely at the center of that zone stood something that looked like an aluminum silo, the size of a ten story building, surrounded at a considerable distance by a cordon of military vehicles.

He felt a wave of dizziness go rocking through his mind. That thing, he realized, had to be the E-T spaceship.

It had come out of the west in the night, Carmichael thought, floating like a tremendous meteor over Oxnard and Camarillo, sliding toward the western end of the San Fernando Valley, kissing the grass with its exhaust and leaving a trail of flame behind it. And then it had gently set itself down over there and extinguished its own brush-fire in a neat little circle about itself, not caring at all about the blaze it had kindled farther back, and God knows what kind of creatures had come forth from it to inspect Los Angeles. It figured that when the UFOs finally did make a landing out in the open, it would be in L.A. Probably they had chosen it because they had seen it so often on television— didn't all the stories say that UFO people always monitored our TV transmissions? So they saw L.A. on every other show and they probably figured it was the capital of the world, the perfect place for the first landing. But why, Carmichael wondered, had the bastards needed to pick the height of the fire season to put their ships down here?

He thought of Cindy again, how fascinated she was by all this UFO and E-T stuff, those books she read, the ideas she had, the way she had looked toward the stars one night when they were camping in Kings Canyon and talked of the beings that must live up there. "I'd love to see them," she said. "I'd love to get to know them and find out what their heads are like." Los Angeles was full of nut cases who wanted to ride in flying saucers, or claimed they already had, but it didn't sound nutty to Carmichael when Cindy talked that way. She had the Angeleno love of the exotic and the bizarre, yes, but he knew that her soul had never been touched by the crazy corruption here, that she was untainted by the prevailing craving for the weird and irrational that made him loathe the place so much. If she turned her imagination toward the stars, it was out of wonder, not out of madness: it was simply part of her nature, that curiosity, that hunger for what lay outside her experience, to embrace the unknowable. He had had no more belief in E-Ts than he did in the tooth fairy, but for her sake he had told her that he hoped she'd get her wish. And now the UFO people were really here. He could imagine her, eyes shining, standing at the edge of that cordon staring at the spaceship. Pity he couldn't be with her now, feeling all that excitement surging through her, the joy, the wonder, the magic.

But he had work to do. Swinging the DC-3 back around toward the west, he swooped down as close as he dared to the edge of the fire and hit the release button on his dump lines. Behind him, a great crimson cloud spread out: a slurry of ammonium sulphate and water, thick as paint, with a red dye mixed into it so they could tell which areas had been sprayed. The retardant clung in globs to anything, and would keep it damp for hours.

Emptying his four 500-gallon tanks quickly, he headed back to Van Nuys to reload. His eyes were throbbing with fatigue and the bitter stink of the wet charred earth below was filtering through every plate of the old plane. It was not quite noon. He had been up all night.

At the airport they had coffee ready, sandwiches, tacos, burritos. While he was waiting for the ground crew to fill his tanks he went inside to call Cindy again, and again there was no answer at home, none at the studio. He phoned the gallery and the kid who worked there said she hadn't been in touch all morning.

"If you hear from her," Carmichael said, "tell her I'm flying fire control out of Van Nuys on the Chatsworth fire, and I'll be home as soon as things calm down a little. Tell her I miss her, too. And tell her that if I run into an E-T I'll give it a big hug for her. You got that? Tell her just that."

Across the way in the main hall he saw a crowd gathered around someone carrying a portable television set. Carmichael shouldered his way in just as the announcer was saying, "There has been no sign yet of the occupants of the San Gabriel or Orange County spaceships. But this was the horrifying sight that astounded residents of the Porter Ranch area beheld this morning between nine and ten o'clock." The screen showed two upright tubular figures that looked like squids walking on the tips of their tentacles, moving cautiously through the parking lot of a shopping center, peering this way and that out of enormous yellow platter-shaped eyes. At least a thousand onlookers were watching them at a wary distance, appearing both repelled and at the same time irresistibly drawn. Now and then the creatures paused to touch their foreheads together in some sort of communion. They moved very daintily, but Carmichael saw that they were taller than the lampposts—twelve feet high, maybe fifteen. Their skins were purplish and leathery-looking, with rows of luminescent orange spots glowing along the sides. The camera zoomed in for a close-up, then jiggled and swerved wildly just as an enormously long elastic tongue sprang from the chest of one of the alien beings and whippped out into the crowd. For an instant the only thing visible on the screen was a view of the sky; then Carmichael saw a shot of a stunned-looking girl of about fourteen, caught around the waist by that long tongue, being hoisted into the air and popped like a collected specimen into a narrow green sack. "Teams of the giant creatures roamed the town for nearly an hour," the announcer intoned. "It has definitely been confirmed that between twenty and thirty human hostages were captured before they returned to their spacecraft. Meanwhile, firefighting activities desperately continue under Santa Ana conditions in the vicinity of all three landing sites, and—"

Carmichael shook his head. Los Angeles, he thought. The kind of people that live here, they walk right up and let the E-Ts gobble them like flies. Maybe they think it's just a movie, and everything will be okay by the last reel. And then he remembered that Cindy was the kind of people who would walk right up to one of these E-Ts. Cindy was the kind of people who lived in Los Angeles, he told himself, except that Cindy was *different*. Somehow.

He went outside. The DC-3 was loaded and ready.

In the forty-five minutes since he had left the fire line, the blaze seemed to have spread noticeably toward the south. This time the line boss had him lay down the retardant from the De Soto Avenue freeway interchange to the northeast corner of Porter Ranch. When he returned

71

to the airport, intending to try phoning Cindy once again, a man in military uniform stopped him as he was crossing the field and said, "You Mike Carmichael, Laurel Canyon?"

"That's right."

"I've got some troublesome news for you. Let's go inside."

"Suppose you tell me here, okay?"

The officer looked at him strangely. "It's about your wife," he said. "Cynthia Carmichael? That's your wife's name?"

"Come *on*," Carmichael said.

"She's one of the hostages, Mr. Carmichael."

His breath went from him as though he had been kicked.

"Where did it happen?" he demanded. "How did they get her?"

The officer gave him a strange strained smile. "It was the shopping-center lot, Porter Ranch. Maybe you saw some of it on the TV."

Carmichael nodded. That girl jerked off her feet by that immense elastic tongue, swept through the air, popped into that green pouch. And Cindy—?

"You saw the part where the creatures were moving around? And then suddenly they were grabbing people, and everyone was running from them? That was when they got her. She was up front when they began grabbing, and maybe she had a chance to get away but she waited just a little too long. She started to run, I understand, but then she stopped—she looked back at them—she may have called something out to them—and then—well, and then—

"Then they scooped her up?"

"I have to tell you that they did."

"I see," Carmichael said stonily.

"One thing all the witnesses agreed, she didn't panic, she didn't scream. She was very brave when those monsters grabbed her. How in God's name you can be brave when something that size is holding you in mid-air is something I don't understand, but I have to assure you that those who saw it—"

"It makes sense to me," Carmichael said.

He turned away. He shut his eyes for a moment and took deep, heavy pulls of the hot smoky air.

It figures, he thought. It makes absolute sense.

Of course she had gone right out to the landing site. Of course. If there was anyone in Los Angeles who would have wanted to get to them and see them with her own eyes and perhaps try to talk to them and establish some sort of rapport with them, it was Cindy. She wouldn't have been afraid of them. She had never seemed to be afraid of anything. It wasn't hard for Carmichael to imagine her in that panicky mob in the parking lot, cool and radiant, staring at the giant aliens, smiling at them right up to the moment they seized her.

In a way he felt very proud of her. But it terrified him to think that she was in their grasp.

"She's on the ship?" he asked. "The one that we have right up back here?"

"Yes."

"Have there been any messages from the hostages? Or from the aliens, for that matter?"

"I'm not in a position to divulge that information."

"*Is* there any information?"

"I'm sorry, I'm not at liberty to—"

"I refuse to believe," Carmichael said, "that that ship is just sitting there, that nothing at all is being done to make contact with—"

"A command center has been established, Mr. Carmichael, and certain efforts are under way. That much I can tell you. I can tell you that Washington is involved. But beyond that, at the present point in time—"

A kid who looked like an Eagle Scout came running up. "Your plane's all loaded and ready to go, Mike!"

"Yeah," Carmichael said. The fire, the fucking fire! He had almost managed to forget about it. *Almost.* He hesitated a moment, torn between conflicting responsibilities. Then he said to the officer, "Look, I've got to get back out on the fire line. Can you stay here a little while?"

"Well—"

"Maybe half an hour. I have to do a retardant dump. Then I want you to take me over to that spaceship and get me through the cordon, so I can talk to those critters myself. If she's on that ship, I mean to get her off it."

"I don't see how it would be possible for—"

"Well, try to see," Carmichael said. "I'll meet you right here in half an hour."

✺

73

When he was aloft he noticed right away that the fire was spreading. The wind was even rougher and wilder than before, and now it was blowing hard from the northeast, pushing the flames down toward the edge of Chatsworth. Already some glowing cinders had blown across the city limits and Carmichael saw houses afire to his left, maybe half a dozen of them. There would be more, he knew. In firefighting you come to develop an odd sense of which way the struggle is going, whether you're gaining on the blaze or the blaze is gaining on you, and that sense told him now that the vast effort that was under way was failing, that the fire was still on the upcurve, that whole neighborhoods were going to be ashes by nightfall.

He held on tight as the DC-3 entered the fire zone. The fire was sucking air like crazy, now, and the turbulence was astounding: it felt as if a giant's hand had grabbed the ship by the nose. The line boss' helicopter was tossing around like a balloon on a string.

Carmichael called in for orders and was sent over to the southwest side, close by the outermost street of houses. Firefighters with shovels were beating on wisps of flame rising out of people's gardens down there. The skirts of dead leaves that dangled down the trunks of a row of towering palm trees were blazing. The neighborhood dogs had formed a crazed pack, running desperately back and forth.

Swooping down to treetop level, Carmichael let go with a red gush of chemicals, swathing everything that looked combustible with the stuff. The shovelers looked up and waved at him, and he dipped his wings to them and headed off to the north, around the western edge of the blaze—it was edging farther to the west too, he saw, leaping up into the high canyons out by the Ventura County line—and then he flew eastward along the Santa Susana foothills until he could see the spaceship once more, standing isolated in its circle of blackened earth. The cordon of military vehicles seemed now to be even larger, what looked like a whole armored division deployed in concentric rings beginning half a mile or so from the ship.

He stared intently at the alien vessel as though he might be able to see through its shining walls to Cindy within.

He imagined her sitting at a table, or whatever the aliens used instead of tables, sitting at a table with seven or eight of the huge beings, calmly explaining Earth to them and then asking them to explain their world to her. He was altogether certain that she was safe, that no harm would come to her, that they were not torturing her or dissecting her or sending electric currents through her simply to see how she reacted. Things like that would never happen to Cindy, he knew. The only thing he feared was that they would depart for their home star without releasing her. The terror that that thought generated in him was as powerful as any kind of fear he had ever felt.

As Carmichael approached the aliens' landing site he saw the guns of some of the tanks below swiveling around to point at him, and he picked up a radio voice telling him brusquely, "You're off limits, DC-3. Get back to the fire zone. This is prohibited air space."

"Sorry," Carmichael answered. "No entry intended."

But as he started to make his turn he dropped down even lower, so that he could have a good look at the spaceship. If it had portholes, and Cindy was looking out one of those portholes, he wanted her to know that he was nearby. That he was watching, that he was waiting for her to come back. But the ship's hull was blind-faced, entirely blank.

—*Cindy? Cindy?*

She was always looking for the strange, the mysterious, the unfamiliar, he thought. The people she brought to the house: a Navaho once, a bewildered Turkish tourist, a kid from New York. The music she played, the way she chanted along with it. The incense, the lights, the meditation. "I'm searching," she liked to say. Trying always to find a route that would take her into something that was wholly outside herself. Trying to become something more than she was. That was how they had fallen in love in the first place, an unlikely couple, she with her beads and sandals, he with his steady no-nonsense view of the world: she had come up to him that day long ago when he was in the record shop in Studio City, and God only knew what he was doing in that part of the world in the first place, and she had asked him something and they had started to talk, and they had talked and talked, talked all night, she wanting to know everything there was to know about him, and when dawn came up they were still together and they had rarely been parted since. He never had really been able to understand what it was that she had wanted him for—the Valley redneck, the aging flyboy—although he felt certain that she wanted him for something real, that he filled some need for her, as she did for him, which could for lack of a more specific term be called love. She had always been searching for that, too. Who wasn't? And he knew that she loved him truly and well, though he couldn't quite see why. "Love is understanding," she liked to say. "Understanding is loving." Was she trying to tell the spaceship people about love right this minute? *Cindy, Cindy, Cindy—*

Back in Van Nuys a few minutes later, he found that everyone at the airport seemed to know by this time that his wife was one of the hostages. The officer whom Carmichael had asked to wait for him was gone. He was not very surprised by that. He thought for a moment of trying to go over to the ship by himself, to get through the cordon and do something about getting Cindy free, but he realized that that was a dumb idea: the military was in charge and they wouldn't let him or anybody else get within a mile of that ship, and he'd only get snarled up in stuff with the television interviewers looking for poignant crap about the families of those who had been captured.

Then the head dispatcher came down to meet him on the field, looking almost about ready to burst with compassion, and in funereal tones told Carmichael that it would be all right if he called it quits for the day and went home to await whatever might happen. But Carmichael shook him off. "I won't get her back by sitting in the livingroom," he said. "And this fire isn't going to go out by itself, either."

It took twenty minutes for the ground crew to pump the retardant slurry into the DC-3's tanks. Carmichael stood to one side, drinking Cokes and watching the planes come and go. People stared at him, and those who knew him waved from a distance, and three or four pilots came over and silently squeezed his arm or rested a hand consolingly on his shoulder. The northern sky was black with soot, shading to gray to east and west. The air was sauna-hot and frighteningly dry: you could set fire to it, Carmichael thought, with a snap of your fingers. Somebody running by said that a new fire had broken out in Pasadena, near the Jet Propulsion Lab, and there was another in Griffith Park. The wind was starting to carry firebrands, then. Dodgers Stadium was burning, someone said. So is Santa Anita Racetrack, said someone else. The whole damned place is going to go, Carmichael thought. And my wife is sitting inside a spaceship from another planet.

When his plane was ready he took it up and laid down a new line of retardant practically in the faces of the firefighters working on the outskirts of Chatsworth. They were too busy to wave. In order to get back to the airport he had to make a big loop behind the fire, over the Santa Susanas and down the flank of the Golden State Freeway, and this time he saw the fires burning to the east, two huge conflagrations marking the places where the exhaust streams of the other two spaceships had grazed the dry grass, and a bunch of smaller blazes strung out on a line from Burbank or Glendale deep into Orange County. His hands were shaking as he touched down at Van Nuys. He had gone without sleep now for something like 32 hours, and he could feel himself starting to pass into that blank white fatigue that lies somewhere beyond ordinary fatigue.

The head dispatcher was waiting for him again as he left his plane. "All right," Carmichael said at once. "I give in. I'll knock off for five or six hours and grab some sleep, and then you can call me back to—"

"No. That isn't it."

"That isn't what?"

"What I came out here to tell you, Mike. They've released some of the hostages."

"Cindy?"

"I think so. There's an Air Force car here to take you to Sylmar. That's where they've got the command center set up. They said to find you as soon as you came off your last dump mission and send you over there so you can talk with your wife."

"So she's free," Carmichael said. "Oh, Jesus, she's free!"

"You go on along, Mike. We'll look after the fire without you for a while, okay?"

The Air Force car looked like a general's limo, long and low and sleek, with a square-jawed driver in front and a couple of very tough-looking young officers to sit with him in back. They said hardly anything, and they looked as weary as Carmichael felt. "How's my wife?" he asked, and one of them said, "We understand that she hasn't been harmed." The way he said it was stiff and strange. Carmichael shrugged. The kid has seen too many old Air Force movies, he told himself.

The whole city seemed to be on fire now. Within the airconditioned limo there was only the faintest whiff of smoke, but the sky to the east was terrifying, with streaks of red bursting like meteors through the blackness. Carmichael asked the Air Force men about that, but all he got was a clipped, "It looks pretty bad, we understand." Somewhere along the San Diego Freeway between Mission Hills and Sylmar,

Carmichael fell asleep, and the next thing he knew they were waking him gently and leading him into a vast bleak hangar-like building near the reservoir. The place was a maze of cables and screens, with military personnel operating what looked like a thousand computers and ten thousand telephones. He let himself be shuffled along, moving mechanically and barely able to focus his eyes, to an inner office where a gray-haired colonel greeted him in his best this-is-the-tense-part-of-the-movie style and said, "This may be the most difficult job you've ever had to handle, Mr. Carmichael."

Carmichael scowled. Everybody was Hollywood in this damned town, he thought.

"They told me the hostages were being freed," he said. "Where's my wife?"

The colonel pointed to a television screen. "We're going to let you talk to her right now."

"Are you saying I don't get to see her?"

"Not immediately."

"Why not? Is she all right?"

"As far as we know, yes."

"You mean she hasn't been released? They told me the hostages were being freed."

"All but three have been let go," said the colonel. "Two people, according to the aliens, were injured as they were captured, and are undergoing medical treatment aboard the ship. They'll be released shortly. The third is your wife, Mr. Carmichael. She is unwilling to leave the ship."

It was like hitting an air-pocket. "*Unwilling—?*"

"She claims to have volunteered to make the journey to the home world of the aliens. She says she's going to serve as our ambassador, our special emissary. Mr. Carmichael, does your wife has any history of mental imbalance?"

Glaring, Carmichael said, "She's very sane. Believe me."

"You are aware that she showed no display of fear when the aliens seized her in the shopping-center incident this morning?"

"I know, yes. That doesn't mean she's crazy. She's unusual. She has unusual ideas. But she's not crazy. Neither am I, incidentally." He put his hands to his face for a moment and pressed his fingertips lightly against his eyes. "All right," he said. "Let me talk to her."

"Do you think you can persuade her to leave that ship?"

"I'm sure as hell going to try."

"You are not yourself sympathetic to what she's doing, are you?" the colonel asked.

Carmichael looked up. "Yes, I am sympathetic. She's an intelligent woman doing something that she thinks is important, and doing it of her own free will. Why the hell shouldn't I be sympathetic? But I'm going to try to talk her out of it, you bet. I love her. I want her. Somebody else can be the goddamned ambassador to Betelgeuse. Let me talk to her, will you?"

The colonel gestured and the big television screen came to life. For a moment mysterious colored patterns flashed across it in a disturbing random way; then Carmichael caught glimpses of shadowy catwalks, intricate metal strutworks crossing and recrossing at peculiar angles; and then for an instant one of the aliens appeared on the screen. Yellow platter-eyes looked complacently back at him. Carmichael felt altogether wide awake now.

The alien's face vanished and Cindy came into view. The moment he saw her, Carmichael knew that he had lost her.

Her face was glowing. There was a calm joy in her eyes verging on ecstasy. He had seen her look something like that on many occasions, but this was different: this was beyond anything she had attained before. She had seen the beatific vision, this time.

"Cindy?"

"Hello, Mike."

"Can you tell me what's been happening in there, Cindy?"

"It's incredible. The contact, the communication."

Sure, he thought. If anyone could make contact with the space people it would be Cindy. She had a certain kind of magic about her: the gift of being able to open any door.

She said, "They speak mind to mind, you know, no barriers at all. They've come in peace, to get to know us, to join in harmony with us, to welcome us into the confederation of worlds."

He moistened his lips. "What have they done to you, Cindy? Have they brainwashed you or something?"

"No! No, nothing like that! They haven't done a thing to me, Mike! We've just talked."

"*Talked!*"

"They've showed me how to touch my mind to theirs. That isn't brainwashing. I'm still me. I, me, Cindy. I'm okay. Do I look as though I'm being harmed? They aren't dangerous. Believe me."

"They've set fire to half the city with their exhaust trails, you know."

"That grieves them. It was an accident. They didn't understand how dry the hills were. If they had some way of extinguishing the flames, they would, but the fires are too big even for them. They ask us to forgive them. They want everyone to know how sorry they are." She paused a moment. Then she said, very gently, "Mike, will you come on board? I want you to experience them as I'm experiencing them."

"I can't do that, Cindy."

"Of course you can! Anyone can! You just open your mind, and they touch you, and—"

"I know. I don't want to. Come out of there and come home, Cindy. Please. Please. It's been three days—four, now—I want to hug you, I want to hold you—"

"You can hold me as tight as you like. They'll let you on board. We can go to their world together. You know that I'm going to go with them to their world, don't you?"

"You aren't. Not really."

She nodded gravely. She seemed terribly serious. "They'll be leaving in a few weeks, as soon as they've had a chance to exchange gifts with Earth. I've seen images of their planet—like movies, only they do it with their minds—Mike, you can't imagine how beautiful it is! How eager they are to have me come!"

Sweat rolled out of his hair into his eyes, making him blink, but he did not dare wipe it away, for fear she would think he was crying.

"I don't want to go to their planet, Cindy. And I don't want you to go either."

She was silent for a time.

Then she smiled delicately and said, "I know, Mike."

He clenched his fists and let go and clenched them again. "I *can't* go there."

"No. You can't. I understand that. Los Angeles is alien enough for you, I think. You need to be in your Valley, in your own real world, not running off to some far star. I won't try to coax you."

"But you're going to go anyway?" he asked, and it was not really a question.

"You already know what I'm going to do."

"Yes."

"I'm sorry. But not really."

"Do you love me?" he said, and regretted saying it at once.

She smiled sadly. "You know I do. And you know I don't want to leave you. But once they touched my mind with theirs, once I saw what kind of beings they are—do you know what I mean? I don't have to explain, do I? You always know what I mean."

"Cindy—"

"Oh, Mike, I do love you so much."

"And I love you, babe. And I wish you'd come out of that goddamned ship."

"You won't ask that. Because you love me, right? Just as I won't ask you again to come on board with me, because I really love you. Do you understand that, Mike?"

He wanted to reach into the screen and grab her.

"I understand, yes," he made himself say.

"I love you, Mike."

"I love you, Cindy."

"They tell me the round trip takes forty-eight of our years, but it will only seem like a few weeks to me. Oh, Mike! Goodbye, Mike! God bless, Mike!" She blew kisses to him. He saw his favorite rings on her fingers, the three little strange star sapphire ones that she had made when she first began to design jewelry. He searched his mind for some new way to reason with her, some line of argument that would work, and could find none. He felt a vast emptiness beginning to expand within him, as though he were being made hollow by some whirling blade. Her face was shining. She seemed like a stranger to him suddenly. She seemed like a Los Angeles person, one of *those*, lost in fantasies and dreams, and it was as though he had never known her, or though he had pretended she was something other than she was. No. No, that isn't right. She's not one of *those*, she's Cindy. Following her own star, as always. Suddenly he was unable to look at the screen any longer, and he turned away, biting his lip, making a shoving gesture with his left hand. The Air Force men in the room wore the awkward expressions of people who had inadvertently eavesdropped on someone's most intimate moments and were trying to pretend they had heard nothing.

"She isn't crazy, colonel," Carmichael said vehemently. "I don't want anyone believing she's some kind of nut."

"Of course not, Mr. Carmichael."

"But she's not going to leave that spaceship. You heard her. She's staying aboard, going back with them to wherever the hell they came from. I can't do anything about that. You see that, don't you? Nothing I could do, short of going aboard that ship and dragging her off physically, would get her out of there. And I wouldn't ever do that."

"Naturally not. In any case, you understand that it would be impossible for us to permit you to go on board, even for the sake of attempting to remove her."

"That's all right," Carmichael said. "I wouldn't dream of it. To remove her or even just to join her for the trip. I don't want to go to that place. Let her go: that's what she was meant to do in this world. Not me. Not me, colonel. That's simply not my thing." He took a deep breath. He thought he might be trembling. "Colonel, do you mind if I got the hell out of here? Maybe I would feel better if I went back out there and dumped some more gunk on that fire. I think that might help. That's what I think, Colonel. All right? Would you send me back to Van Nuys, Colonel?"

He went up one last time in the DC-3. They wanted him to dump the retardants along the western face of the fire, but instead he went to the east, where the spaceship was, and flew in a wide circle around it. A radio voice warned him to move out of the area, and he said that he would.

As he circled, a hatch opened in the spaceship's side and one of the aliens appeared, looking gigantic even from Carmichael's altitude. The huge purplish thing stepped from the ship, extended its tentacles, seemed to be sniffing the smoky air.

Carmichael thought vaguely of flying down low and dropping his whole load of retardants on the creature, drowning it in gunk, getting even with the aliens for having taken Cindy from him. He shook his head. That's crazy, he told himself. Cindy would feel sick if she knew he had ever considered any such thing.

But that's what I'm like, he thought. Just an ordinary ugly vengeful Earthman. And that's why I'm not going to go to that other planet, and that's why she is.

He swung around past the spaceship and headed straight across Granada Hills and Northridge into Van Nuys Airport. When he was on the ground he sat at the controls of his plane a long while, not moving at all. Finally one of the dispatchers came out and called up to him, "Mike, are you okay?"

"Yeah. I'm fine."

"How come you came back without dropping your load?"

Carmichael peered at his gauges. "Did I do that? I guess I did that, didn't I?"

"You're not okay, are you?"

"I forgot to dump, I guess. No, I didn't forget. I just didn't bother. I didn't feel like doing it."

"Mike, come on out of that plane."

"I didn't feel like doing it," Carmichael said again. "Why the hell bother? This crazy city—there's nothing left in it that I would want to save, anyway." His control deserted him at last, and rage swept through him like fire racing up the slopes of a dry canyon. He understood what she was doing, and he respected it, but he didn't have to like it. He didn't like it at all. He had lost Cindy, and he felt somehow that he had lost his war with Los Angeles as well. "Fuck it," he said. "Let it burn. This crazy city. I always hated it. It deserves what it gets. The only reason I stayed here was for her. She was all that mattered. But she's going away, now. Let the fucking place burn."

The dispatcher gaped at him in amazement. "Mike—"

Carmichael moved his head slowly from side to side as though trying to shake a monstrous headache from it. Then he frowned. "No, that's wrong," he said. "You've got to do the job anyway, right? No matter how you feel. You have to put the fires out. You have to save what you can. Listen, Tim, I'm going to fly one last load today, you hear? And then I'll go home and get some sleep. Okay? Okay?" He had the plane in motion, going down the short runway. Dimly he realized that he had not requested clearance. A little Cessna spotter plane moved desperately out of his way, and then he was aloft. The sky was black and red. The fire was completely uncontained now, and maybe uncontainable. But you had to keep trying, he thought. You had to save what you could. He gunned and went forward, flying calmly into the inferno in the foothills, until the wild thermals caught his wings from below and lifted him and tossed him like a toy skimming over the top, and sent him hurtling toward the waiting hills to the north.

Thus saith the Lord; Behold, I will raise up against Babylon, and against them that dwell in the midst of them that rise up against me, a destroying wind;

And will send unto Babylon fanners, that shall fan her, and shall empty her land: for in the day of trouble they shall be against her round about.

Jeremiah, 51: 1-2

SYMBIONT

Long ago there was a gaudy pulp magazine called Planet Stories, *which was devoted to two-fisted, colorful tales of action and adventure on other worlds. Don't think it was junk, though: Ray Bradbury, Poul Anderson, Theodore Sturgeon, and Leigh Brackett were regular contributors, Isaac Asimov and Jack Vance wrote for it, Philip K. Dick's first published story appeared in it. Readers loved it and so did the writers, because they could rare back and let their imaginations run wild.*

I never had anything published in Planet Stories, *because it went out of business in 1955, just as my career was getting started. But I enjoyed doing Planet-type material for such later imitators as* Science Fiction Adventures *and* Venture SF, *which flourished toward the end of the fifties, and suddenly, one day in the spring of 1984, it occurred to me to attempt one for* Playboy *in the old* Planet Stories *mode, appropriately buffed and polished for* Playboy's *demanding readership. (I would, after all, be fighting for a place on the contents page with the likes of Nabokov, Updike, and Joyce Carol Oates, all of whom were once* Playboy *regulars.) And out of the machine came "Symbiont," the somber tale of jungle adventure and diabolical revenge that you are about to read. Off it went, with some trepidation on my part, to the formidable Alice K. Turner, who had put me so exhaustingly through my paces fifteen months earlier with "Tourist Trade." And back from Alice a few days later came this letter of acceptance:*

"Your check, as we like to say, is in the mail. I was dumbfounded when I read this story (avidly, I should add) and sent it off to Teresa [her assistant editor], whose youth was not misspent, as mine was, in reading stories

that featured creatures with tentacles and body-takeovers by alien nasties. I waited, somewhat apprehensively, for her response—and she loved it. That's good enough for me. If such a noble mind can be here o'erthrown, what the hell. This is one of the ones that will go with not a word unchanged, though not till '85 some time." And so it did, in the June 1985 issue.

The initial idea for the story, incidentally, was given to me by a young woman named Karen Haber, whom I had met while on a speaking tour in Texas. It originally involved something that had happened to a friend of hers in Vietnam, but I applied my usual science-fiction metamorphosis techniques to it and "Symbiont" was the result. Ms. Haber was very impressed. I was very impressed with Ms. Haber, too. A couple of years later I married her.

Ten years later, when I was long out of the Service and working the turnaround wheel at Betelgeuse Station, Fazio still haunted me. Not that he was dead. Other people get haunted by dead men; I was haunted by a live one. It would have been a lot better for both of us if he *had* been dead, but as far as I knew Fazio was still alive.

He'd been haunting me a long while. Three or four times a year his little dry thin voice would come out of nowhere and I'd hear him telling me again, "Before we go into that jungle, we got to come to an understanding. If a synsym nails me, Chollie, you kill me right away, hear? None of this shit of calling in the paramedics to clean me out. You just kill me right away. And I'll do the same for you. Is that a deal?"

This was on a planet called Weinstein in the Servadac system, late in the Second Ovoid War. We were twenty years old and we were volunteers: two dumb kids playing hero. "You bet your ass," is what I told him, not hesitating a second. "Deal. Absolutely." Then I gave him a big grin and a handclasp and we headed off together on spore-spreading duty.

At the time, I really thought I meant it. Sometimes I still believe that I did.

Ten years. I could still see the two of us back there on Weinstein, going out to distribute latchenango spores in the enemy-held zone. The planet had been grabbed by the Ovoids early in the war, but we were starting to drive them back from that whole system. Fazio and I were the entire patrol: you get spread pretty thin in galactic warfare. But there was plenty of support force behind us in the hills.

Weinstein was strategically important, God only knows why. Two small continents—both tropical, mostly thick jungle, air like green soup—surrounded by an enormous turbulent ocean: never colonized by Earth, and of no use that anyone had ever successfully explained to me. But the place had once been ours and they had taken it away, and we wanted it back.

The way you got a planet back was to catch a dozen or so Ovoids, fill them full of latchenango spores, and let them return to their base. There is no life-form a latchenango likes better as its host than an Ovoid. The Ovoids, being Ovoids, would usually conceal what had happened to them from their pals, who would kill them instantly if they knew they were carrying deadly parasites. Of course, the carriers were going to die anyway—latchenango infestation is invariably fatal to Ovoids—but by the time they did, in about six standard weeks, the latchenangos had gone through three or four reproductive cycles and the whole army would be infested. All we needed to do was wait until all the Ovoids were dead and then come in, clean the place up, and raise the flag again. The latchenangos were generally dead too by then, since they rarely could find other suitable hosts. But even if they weren't, we didn't worry about it. Latchenangos don't cause any serious problems for humans. About the worst of it is that you usually inhale some spores while you're handling them, and it irritates your lungs for a couple of weeks so you do some pretty ugly coughing until you're desporified.

In return for our latchenangos the Ovoids gave us synsyms.

Synsyms were the first things you heard about when you arrived in the war zone, and what you heard was horrendous. You didn't know how much of it was myth and how much was mere bullshit and how much was truth, but even if you discounted seventy-five percent of it the rest was scary enough. "If you get hit by one," the old hands advised us, "kill yourself fast, while you have the chance." Roving synsym vectors cruised the perimeter of every Ovoid camp, sniffing for humans. They were not parasites but synthetic symbionts: when they got into you, they stayed there, sharing your body with you indefinitely.

In school they teach you that symbiosis is a mutually beneficial state. Maybe so. But the word that passed through the ranks in the war zone was that it definitely did not improve the quality of your life to take a synsym into your body. And though the Service medics would spare no effort to see that you survived a synsym attack—they aren't allowed to perform mercy killings, and wouldn't anyway—everything we heard indicated that you didn't really *want* to survive one.

The day Fazio and I entered the jungle was like all the others on Weinstein: dank, humid, rainy. We strapped on our spore-tanks and started out, using hand-held heat-piles to burn our way through the curtains of tangled vines. The wet spongy soil had a purplish tinge and the lakes were iridescent green from lightning-algae.

"Here's where we'll put the hotel landing strip," Fazio said lightly. "Over here, the pool and cabanas. The gravity-tennis courts here, and on the far side of that—"

"Watch it," I said, and skewered a low-flying wingfinger with a beam of hot purple light. It fell in ashes at our feet. Another one came by, the mate, traveling at eye-level with its razor-sharp beak aimed at my throat, but Fazio took it out just as neatly. We thanked each other. Wingfingers are elegant things, all trajectory and hardly any body mass, with scaly silvery skins that shine like the finest grade of moonlight, and it is their habit to go straight for the jugular in the most literal sense. We killed twelve that day and I hope it is my quota for this lifetime. As we advanced into the heart of the jungle we dealt just as efficiently with assorted hostile coilworms, eyeflies, dingleberries, leper bats, and other disagreeable local specialties. We were a great team: quick, smart, good at protecting each other.

We were admiring a giant carnivorous fungus a klick and a half deep in the woods when we came upon our first Ovoid. The fungus was a fleshy phallic red tower three meters high with orange gills, equipped with a dozen dangling whiplike arms that had green adhesive knobs at the tips. At the ends of most of the arms hung small forest creatures in various stages of digestion. As we watched, an unoccupied arm rose and shot forth, extended itself to three times its resting length, and by some neat homing tropism slapped its adhesive knob against a passing many-legger about the size of a cat. The beast had no chance to struggle; a network of wiry structures sprouted at once from the killer arm and slipped into the victim's flesh, and that was that. We almost applauded.

"Let's plant three of them in the hotel garden," I said, "and post a schedule of feeding times. It'll be a great show for the guests."

"Shh," Fazio said. He pointed.

Maybe fifty meters away a solitary Ovoid was gliding serenely along a forest path, obviously unaware of us. I caught my breath. Everyone knows what Ovoids look like, but this was the first time I had seen a live one. I was surprised at how beautiful it was, a tapering cone of firm jelly, pale blue streaked with red and gold. Triple rows of short-stalked eyes along its sides like brass buttons. Clusters of delicate tendrils sprouting like epaulets around the eating-orifice at the top of its head. Turquoise ribbons of neural conduit winding round and round its equator, surrounding the dark heart-shaped brain faintly visible within the cloudy depths. The enemy. I was conditioned to hate it, and I did; yet I couldn't deny its strange beauty.

Fazio smiled and took aim and put a numb-needle through the Ovoid's middle. It froze instantly in mid-glide; its color deepened to a dusky flush; the tiny mouth-tendrils fluttered wildly but there was no other motion. We jogged up to it and I slipped the tip of my spore-distributor about five centimeters into its meaty middle. "Let him have it!" Fazio yelled. I pumped a couple of c.c.'s of latchenango spores into the paralyzed alien. Its soft quivering flesh turned blue-black with fear and rage and God knows what other emotions that were strictly Ovoid. We nodded to each other and moved along. Already the latchenangos were spawning within their host; in half an hour the Ovoid, able once more to move, would limp off toward its camp to start infecting its comrades. It is a funny way to wage war.

The second Ovoid, an hour later, was trickier. It knew we had spotted it and took evasive action, zigzagging through a zone of streams and slender trees in a weird dignified way like someone trying to move very fast without having his hat blow off. Ovoids are not designed for quick movements, but this one was agile and determined, ducking behind this rock and that. More than once we lost sight of it altogether and were afraid it might double back and come down on *us* while we stood gaping and blinking.

Eventually we bottled it up between two swift little streams and closed in on it from both sides. I raised my needler and Fazio got ready with his spore-distributor and just then something gray and slipper-shaped and about fifteen centimeters long came leaping up out of the left-hand stream and plastered itself over Fazio's mouth and throat.

Down he went, snuffling and gurgling, trying desperately to peel it away. I thought it was some kind of killer fish. Pausing only long enough to shoot a needle through the Ovoid, I dropped my gear and jumped down beside him.

Fazio was rolling around, eyes wild, kicking at the ground in terror and agony. I put my elbow on my chest to hold him still and pried with both hands at the thing on his face. Getting it loose was like pulling a second skin off him, but somehow I managed to lift it away from his lips far enough for him to gasp, "Synsym—I think it's synsym—"

"No, man, it's just some nasty fish," I told him. "Hang in there and I'll rip the rest of it loose in half a minute—

Fazio shook his head in anguish.

Then I saw the two thin strands of transparent stuff snaking up out of it and disappearing into his nostrils and I knew he was right.

I didn't hear anything from him or about him after the end of the war, and didn't want to, but I assumed all along that Fazio was still alive. I don't know why: my faith in the general perversity of the universe, I guess.

The last I had seen of him was our final day on Weinstein. We both were being invalided out. They were shipping me to the big hospital on Daemmerung for routine desporification treatment, but he was going to the quarantine station on Quixote; and as we lay side by side in the depot, me on an ordinary stretcher and Fazio inside an isolation bubble, he raised his head with what must have been a terrible effort and glared at me out of eyes that already were ringed with the red concentric synsym circles, and he whispered something to me. I wasn't able to understand the words through the wall of his bubble, but I could *feel* them, the way you feel the light of a blue-white sun from half a parsec out. His skin was glowing. The dreadful vitality of the symbiont within him was already apparent. I had a good notion of what he was trying to tell me. *You bastard*, he was most likely trying to say. *Now I'm stuck with this thing for a thousand years. And I'm going to hate you every minute of the time, Chollie.*

Then they took him away. They sent him floating up the ramp into that Quixote-bound ship. When he was out of view I felt released, as though I was coming out from under a pull of six or seven gravs. It occurred to me that I wasn't ever going to have to see Fazio again. I wouldn't have to face those reddened eyes, that taut shining skin, that glare of infinite reproach. Or so I believed for the next ten years, until he turned up on Betelgeuse Station.

A bolt out of the blue: there he was, suddenly, standing next to me in the recreation room on North Spoke. It was just after my shift and I was balancing on the rim of the swimmer web, getting ready to dive. "Chollie?" he said calmly. The voice was Fazio's voice: that was clear, when I stopped to think about it a little later. But I never for a moment considered that this weird gnomish man might be Fazio. I stared at him and didn't even come close to recognizing him. He seemed about seven million years old, shrunken, fleshless, weightless, with thick coarse hair like white straw and strange soft gleaming translucent skin that looked like parchment worn thin by time. In the bright light of the rec room he kept his eyes hooded nearly shut; but then he turned away from the glowglobes and opened them wide enough to show me the fine red rings around his pupils. The hair began to rise along the back of my neck.

"Come on," he said. "You know me. Yeah. Yeah."

The voice, the cheekbones, the lips, the eyes—the eyes, the eyes, the eyes. Yes, I knew him. But it wasn't possible. Fazio? Here? How? So long a time, so many light-years away! And yet—yet—

He nodded. "You got it, Chollie. Come on. Who am I?"

My first attempt at saying something was a sputtering failure. But I managed to get his name out on the second try.

"Yeah," he said. "Fazio. What a surprise."

He didn't look even slightly surprised. I think he must have been watching me for a few days before he approached me—casing me, checking me out, making certain it was really me, getting used to the idea that he had actually found me. Otherwise the amazement would surely have been showing on him now. Finding me—finding *anybody* along the starways—wasn't remotely probable. This was a coincidence almost too big to swallow. I knew he couldn't have deliberately come after me, because the galaxy is so damned big a place that the idea of setting out to search for someone in it is too silly even to think about. But somehow he had caught up with me anyway. If the universe is truly infinite, I suppose, then even the most wildly improbable things must occur in it a billion times a day.

I said shakily, "I can't believe—"

"You can't? Hey, you better! What a surprise, kid, hey? Hey?" He clapped his hand against my arm. "And you're looking good, kid. Nice and healthy. You keep in shape, huh? How old are you now, thirty-two?"

"Thirty." I was numb with shock and fear.

"Thirty. Mmm. So am I. Nice age, ain't it? Prime of life."

"Fazio—"

His control was terrifying. "Come on, Chollie. You look like you're about to crap in your pants. Aren't you glad to see your old buddy? We had some good times together, didn't we? Didn't we?

"What was the name of that fuckin' planet? Weinberg? Weinfeld? Hey, hey, don't *stare* at me like that!"

I had to work hard to make any sound at all. Finally I said, "What the hell do you want me to do, Fazio? I feel like I'm looking at a ghost."

He leaned close and his eyes opened wider. I could practically count the concentric red rings, ten or fifteen of them, very fine lines. "I wish to Christ you were," he said quietly. Such unfathomable depths of pain, such searing intensity of hatred. I wanted to squirm away from him. But there was no way. He gave me a long slow crucifying inspection. Then he eased back and some of the menacing intensity seemed to go out of him. Almost jauntily he said, "We got a lot to talk about, Chollie. You know some quiet place around here we can go?"

"There's the gravity lounge—"

"Sure. The gravity lounge."

We floated face to face, at half pull. "You promised you'd kill me if I got nailed," Fazio murmured. "That was our deal. Why didn't you do it, Chollie? Why the fuck didn't you do it?"

I could hardly bear to look into his red-ringed eyes.

"Things happened too fast, man. How was I to know paramedics would be on the scene in five minutes?"

"Five minutes is plenty of time to put a heat-bolt through a guy's chest."

"Less than five minutes. Three. Two. The paramedic floater was right overhead, man! It was covering us the whole while. They came down on us like a bunch of fucking *angels*, Fazio!"

"You had time."

"I thought they were going to be able to save you," I said lamely. "They got there so quickly."

Fazio laughed harshly. "They did try to save me," he said. "I'll give them credit for trying. Five minutes and I was on that floater and they were sending tracers all over me to clean the synsym goop out of my lungs and my heart and my liver."

"Sure. That was just what I figured they'd do."

"You promised to finish me off, Chollie, if I got nailed."

"But the paramedics were right *there*!"

"They worked on me like sonsabitches," he said. "They did everything. They can clean up the vital tissues, they can yank out your organs, synsym and all, and stick in transplants. But they can't get the stuff out of your brain, did you know that? The synsym goes straight up your nose into your brain and it slips its tendrils into your meninges and your neural glia and right into your fucking corpus callosum. And from there it goes everywhere. The cerebellum, the medulla, you name it. They can't send tracers into the brain that will clean out synsym and not damage brain tissue. And they can't pull out your brain and give you a new one, either. Thirty seconds after the synsym gets into your nose it reaches your brain and it's all over for you, no matter what kind of treatment you get. Didn't you hear them tell you that when we first got to the war zone? Didn't you hear all the horror stories?"

"I thought they were just horror stories," I said faintly.

He rocked back and forth gently in his gravity cradle. He didn't say anything.

"Do you want to tell me what it's like?" I asked after a while.

Fazio shrugged. As though from a great distance he said, "What it's like? Ah, it's not all that goddamned bad, Chollie. It's like having a roommate. Living with you in your head, forever, and you can't break the lease. That's all. Or like having an itch you can't scratch. Having it there is like finding yourself trapped in a space that's exactly one centimeter bigger than you are all around, and knowing that you're going to stay walled up in it for a million years." He looked off toward the great clear wall of the lounge, toward giant red Betelgeuse blazing outside far away. "Your synsym talks to you, sometimes. So you're never lonely, you know? Doesn't speak any language you understand, just sits there and spouts gibberish. But at least it's company. Sometimes it makes *you* spout gibberish, especially when you badly need to make sense. It grabs control of the upper brain centers now and then, you know. And as for the autonomous centers, it does any damned thing it likes with them. Keys into the pain zones and runs little simulations for you—an amputation without anesthetic, say. Just for fun. *Its* fun. Or you're in bed with a woman and it disconnects your erection mechanism. Or it *gives* you an erection that won't go down for six weeks. For fun. It can get playful with your toilet training, too. I wear a diaper, Chollie, isn't that sweet? I have to. I get drunk sometimes without drinking. Or I drink myself sick without feeling a thing. And all the time I feel it there, tickling me. Like an ant crawling around within my skull. Like a worm up my nose. It's just like the other guys told us, when we came out to the war zone. Remember? 'Kill yourself fast, while you have the chance.' I never had the chance. I had you, Chollie, and we had a deal, but you didn't take our deal seriously. Why not, Chollie?"

I felt his eyes burning me. I looked away, halfway across the lounge, and caught sight of Elisandra's long golden hair drifting in free float. She saw me at the same moment, and waved. We usually got together in here this time of night. I shook my head, trying to warn her off, but it was too late. She was already heading our way.

"Who's that?" Fazio asked. "Your girlfriend?"

"A friend."

"Nice," he said. He was staring at her as though he had never seen a woman before. "I noticed her last night too. You live together?"

"We work the same shift on the wheel."

"Yeah. I saw you leave with her last night. And the night before."

"How long have you been at the Station, Fazio?"

"Week. Ten days, maybe."

"Came here looking for me?"

"Just wandering around," he said. "Fat disability pension, plenty of time. I go to a lot of places. That's a really nice woman, Chollie. You're a lucky guy." A tic was popping on his cheek and another was getting started on his lower lip. He said,

"Why the fuck didn't you kill me when that thing first jumped me?"

"I told you. I couldn't. The paramedics were on the scene too fast."

"Right. You needed to say some Hail Marys first, and they just didn't give you enough time."

He was implacable. I had to strike back at him somehow or the guilt and shame would drive me crazy. Angrily I said, "What the hell do you want me to tell you, Fazio? That I'm sorry I didn't kill you ten years ago? Okay, I'm sorry. Does that do any good? Listen, if the synsym's as bad as you say, how come *you* haven't killed yourself? Why go on dragging yourself around with that thing inside your head?"

He shook his head and made a little muffled grunting sound. His face abruptly became gray, his lips were sagging. His eyeballs seemed to be spinning slowly in opposite directions. Just an illusion, I knew, but a scary one.

"Fazio?"

He said, "Chollallula lillalolla loolicholla. Billillolla."

I stared. He looked frightening. He looked hideous.

"Jesus, Fazio!"

Spittle dribbled down his chin. Muscles jumped and writhed crazily all over his face. "You see? You see?" he managed to blurt. There was warfare inside him. I watched him trying to regain command. It was like a man wrestling himself to a fall. I thought he was going to have a stroke. But then, suddenly, he seemed to grow calm. His breath was ragged, his skin was mottled with fiery blotches. He collapsed down into himself, head drooping, arms dangling. He looked altogether spent. Another minute or two passed before he could speak. I didn't know what to do for him. I floated there, watching. Finally a little life seemed to return to him.

"Did you see? That's what happens," he gasped. "It takes control. How could I ever kill myself? It wouldn't let me do it."

"Wouldn't *let* you?"

He looked up at me and sighed wearily. "Think, Chollie, think! It's in symbiosis with me. We aren't independent organisms." Then the tremors began again, worse than before. Fazio made a desperate furious attempt to fight them off—arms and legs flung rigidly out, jaws working—but it was useless. "Illallomba!" he yelled. "Nullagribba!" He tossed his head from side to side as if trying to shake off something sticky that was clinging to it. "If I—then it—gillagilla! Holligoolla! I can't—I can't—oh—Jesus—Christ—!

His voice died away into harsh sputters and clankings. He moaned and covered his face with his hands.

But now I understood.

For Fazio there could never be any escape. That was the most monstrous part of the whole thing, the ultimate horrifying twist. The symbiont knew that its destiny was linked to Fazio's. If he died, the symbiont would also; and so it could not allow its host to damage himself. From its seat in Fazio's brain it had ultimate control over his body. Whatever he tried—jump off a bridge, reach for a flask of poison, pick up a gun—the watchful thing in his mind would be a step ahead of him, always protecting him against harm.

A flood of compassion welled up in me and I started to put my hand comfortingly on Fazio's shoulder. But then I yanked it back as though

I were afraid the symbiont could jump from his mind into mine at the slightest touch. And then I scowled and forced myself to touch him after all. He pulled away. He looked burned out.

"Chollie?" Elisandra said, coming up beside us. She floated alongside, long-limbed, beautiful, frowning. "Is this private, or can I join you?"

I hesitated, fumbling. I desperately wanted to keep Fazio and Elisandra in separate compartments of my life, but I saw that I had no way of doing that. "We were—well—just that—"

"Come on, Chollie," Fazio said in a bleak hollow voice. "Introduce your old war buddy to the nice woman."

Elisandra gave him an inquiring glance. She could not have failed to detect the strangeness in his tone.

I took a deep breath. "This is Fazio," I said. "We were in the Servadac campaign together during the Second Ovoid War. Fazio—Elisandra. Elisandra's a traffic-polarity engineer on the turnaround wheel—you ought to see her at work, the coolest cookie you can imagine—"

"An honor to meet you," said Fazio grandly. "A woman who combines such beauty and such technical skills—I have to say—I—I—" Suddenly he was faltering. His face turned blotchy. Fury blazed in his eyes. "No! Damn it, no! No more!" He clutched handfuls of air in some wild attempt at steadying himself. "Mullagalloola!" he cried, helpless. "Jillabongbong! Sampazozozo!" And he burst into wild choking sobs, while Elisandra stared at him in amazement and sorrow.

"Well, are you going to kill him?" she asked.

It was two hours later. We had put Fazio to bed in his little cubicle over at Transient House, and she and I were in her room. I had told her everything.

I looked at her as though she had begun to babble the way Fazio had. Elisandra and I had been together almost a year, but there were times I felt I didn't know her at all.

"Well?" she said.

"Are you serious?"

"You owe it to him. You owe him a death, Chollie. He can't come right out and say it, because the symbiont won't allow him to. But that's what he wants from you."

I couldn't deny any of that. I'd been thinking the same thing for at least the past hour. The reality of it was inescapable: I had muffed things on Weinstein and sent Fazio to hell for ten years. Now I had to set him free.

"If there was only some way to get the symbiont out of his brain—"

"But there isn't."

"No," I said. "There isn't."

"You'll do it for him, won't you?"

"Quit it," I said.

"I hate the way he's suffering, Chollie."

"You think I don't?"

"And what about you? Suppose you fail him a second time. How will you live with that? Tell me how."

"I was never much for killing, Ellie. Not even Ovoids."

"We know that," she said. "But you don't have any choice this time."

I went to the little fireglobe she had mounted above the sleeping platform, and hit the button and sent sparks through the thick coiling mists. A rustle of angry colors swept the mist, a wild aurora, green, purple, yellow. After a moment I said quietly, "You're absolutely right."

"Good. I was afraid for a moment you were going to crap out on him again."

There was no malice in it, the way she said it. All the same, it hit me like a fist. I stood there nodding, letting the impact go rippling through me and away.

At last the reverberations seemed to die down within me. But then a great new uneasiness took hold of me and I said, "You know, it's totally idiotic of us to be discussing this. I'm involving you in something that's none of your business. What we're doing is making you an accomplice before the fact."

Elisandra ignored me. Something was in motion in her mind, and there was no swerving her now. "How would you go about it?" she asked. "You can't just cut someone's throat and dump him down a disposer chute."

"Look," I said, "do you understand that the penalty could be anything up to—"

She went on, "Any sort of direct physical assault is out. There'd be some sort of struggle for sure—the symbiont's bound to defend the host body against attack—you'd come away with scratches, bruises, worse. Somebody would notice. Suppose you got so badly hurt you had to go to the medics. What would you tell them? A barroom brawl? And then nobody can find your old friend Fazio who you were seen with a few days before? No, much too risky." Her tone was strangely businesslike, matter-of-fact. "And then, getting rid of the body—that's even tougher, Chollie, getting fifty kilos of body mass off the Station without some kind of papers. No destination visa, no transshipment entry. Even a sack of potatoes would have an out-invoice. But if someone just vanishes and there's a fifty-kilo short balance in the mass totals that day—"

"Quit it," I said. "Okay?"

"You owe him a death. You agreed about that."

"Maybe I do. But whatever I decide, I don't want to drag you into it. It isn't your mess, Ellie."

"You don't think so?" she shot right back at me.

Anger and love were all jumbled together in Elisandra's tone. I didn't feel like dealing with that just now. My head was pounding. I activated the pharmo arm by the sink and hastily ran a load of relaxants into myself with a subcue shot. Then I took her by the hand. Gently, trying hard to disengage, I said, "Can we just go to bed now? I'd rather not talk about this any more."

Elisandra smiled and nodded. "Sure," she replied, and her voice was much softer.

She started to pull off her clothes. But after a moment she turned to me, troubled. "I can't drop it just like that, Chollie. It's still buzzing inside me. That poor bastard." She shuddered.

"Never to be alone in his own head. Never to be sure he has control over his own body. Waking up in a puddle of piss, he said. Speaking in tongues. All that other crazy stuff. What did he say? Like feeling an ant wandering around inside his skull? An itch you can't possibly scratch?"

"I didn't know it would be that bad," I said. "I think I would have killed him back then, if I had known."

"Why didn't you anyway?"

"He was Fazio. A human being. My friend. My buddy. I didn't much want to kill Ovoids, even. How the hell was I going to kill him?"

"But you promised to, Chollie."

"Let me be," I said. "I didn't do it, that's all. Now I have to live with that."

"So does he," said Elisandra.

I climbed into her sleeptube and lay there without moving, waiting for her.

"So do I," she added after a little while.

She wandered around the room for a time before joining me. Finally she lay down beside me, but at a slight distance. I didn't move toward her. But eventually the distance lessened, and I put my hand lightly on her shoulder, and she turned to me.

An hour or so before dawn she said, "I think I see a way we can do it."

We spent a week and a half working out the details. I was completely committed to it now, no hesitations, no reservations. As Elisandra said, I had no choice. This was what I owed Fazio; this was the only way I could settle accounts between us.

She was completely committed to it too: even more so than I was, it sometimes seemed. I warned her that she was needlessly letting herself in for major trouble in case the Station authorities ever managed to reconstruct what had happened. It didn't seem needless to her, she said.

I didn't have a lot of contact with him while we were arranging things. It was important, I figured, not to give the symbiont any hints. I saw Fazio practically every day, of course—Betelgeuse Station isn't all that big—off at a distance, staring, glaring, sometimes having one of his weird fits, climbing a wall or shouting incoherently or arguing with himself out loud; but generally I pretended not to see him. At times I couldn't avoid him, and then we met for dinner or drinks or a workout in the rec room. But there wasn't much of that.

"Okay," Elisandra said finally. "I've done my part. Now you do yours, Chollie."

Among the little services we run here is a sightseeing operation for tourists who feel like taking a close look at a red giant star. After the big stellar-envelope research project shut down a few years ago we inherited a dozen or so solar sleds that had been used for skimming through the fringes of Betelgeuse's mantle, and we began renting them out for three-day excursions. The sleds are two-passenger jobs without much in the way of luxury and nothing at all in the way of propulsion systems. The trip is strictly ballistic: we calculate your orbit and shoot you out of here on the big repellers, sending you on a dazzling swing across Betelgeuse's outer fringes that gives you the complete light-show and maybe a view of ten or twelve of the big star's family of planets. When the sled reaches the end of its string, we catch you on the turnaround wheel and reel you in. It sounds spectacular, and it is; it sounds dangerous, and it isn't. Not usually, anyhow.

I tracked Fazio down in the gravity lounge and said, "We've arranged a treat for you, man."

The sled I had rented for him was called the *Corona Queen*. Elisandra routinely handled the dispatching job for these tours, and now and then I worked as wheelman for them, although ordinarily I wheeled the big interstellar liners that used Betelgeuse Station as their jumping-off point for deeper space. We were both going to work Fazio's sled. Unfortunately, this time there was going to be a disaster, because a regrettable little error had been made in calculating orbital polarity, and then there would be a one-in-amillion failure of the redundancy circuits. Fazio's sled wasn't going to go on a tour of Betelgeuse's far-flung corona at all. It was going to plunge right into the heart of the giant red star.

I would have liked to tell him that, as we headed down the winding corridors to the dropdock. But I couldn't, because telling Fazio meant telling Fazio's symbiont also; and what was good news for Fazio was bad news for the symbiont. To catch the filthy thing by surprise: that was essential.

How much did Fazio suspect? God knows. In his place, I think I might have had an inkling. But maybe he was striving with all his strength to turn his mind away from any kind of speculation about the voyage he was about to take.

"You can't possibly imagine what it's like," I said. "It's unique. There's just no way to simulate it. And the view of Betelgeuse that you get from the Station isn't even remotely comparable."

"The sled glides through the corona on a film of vaporized carbon," said Elizandra. "The heat just rolls right off its surface." We were chattering compulsively, trying to fill every moment with talk. "You're completely shielded so that you can actually pass through the atmosphere of the star—"

"Of course," I said, "Betelgeuse is so big and so violent that you're more or less inside its atmosphere no matter where you are in its system—"

"And then there are the planets," Elisandra said. "The way things are lined up this week, you may be able to see as many as a dozen of them—"

"—Otello, Falstaff, Siegfried, maybe Wotan—"

"—You'll find a map on the ceiling of your cabin—"

"—Five gas giants twice the mass of Jupiter—keep your eye out for Wotan, that's the one with rings—"

"—and Isolde, you can't miss Isolde, she's even redder than Betelgeuse, the damndest bloodshot planet imaginable—"

"—with eleven red moons, too, but you won't be able to see them without filters—"

"—Otello and Falstaff for sure, and I think this week's chart shows Aida out of occultation now too—"

"—and then there's the band of comets—"

"—the asteroids, that's where we think a couple of the planets collided after gravitational perturbation of—"

"—and the Einsteinian curvature, it's unmistakable—"

"—the big solar flares—"

"Here we are," Elisandra said.

We had reached the dropdock. Before us rose a gleaming metal wall. Elisandra activated the hatch and it swung back to reveal the little sled, a sleek tapering frog-nosed thing with a low hump in the middle. It sat on tracks; above it arched the coils of the repeller-launcher, radiating at the moment the blue-green glow that indicated a neutral charge. Everything was automatic. We had only to put Fazio on board and give the Station the signal for launch; the rest would be taken care of by the orbital-polarity program Elisandra had previously keyed in.

"It's going to be the trip of your life, man!" I said.

Fazio nodded. His eyes looked a little glazed, and his nostrils were flaring.

Elisandra hit the pre-launch control. The sled's roof opened and a recorded voice out of a speaker in the dropdock ceiling began to explain to Fazio how to get inside and make himself secure for launching. My hands were cold, my throat was dry. Yet I was very calm, all things considered. This was murder, wasn't it? Maybe so, technically speaking. But I was finding other names for it. A mercy killing; a balancing of the karmic accounts; a way of atoning for an ancient sin of omission. For him, release from hell after ten years; for me, release from a lesser but still acute kind of pain.

Fazio approached the sled's narrow entry slot.

"Wait a second," I said. I caught him by the arm. The account wasn't quite in balance yet.

"Chollie—" Elisandra said.

I shook her off. To Fazio I said, "There's one thing I need to tell you before you go."

He gave me a peculiar look, but didn't say anything.

I went on, "I've been claiming all along that I didn't shoot you when the synsym got you because there wasn't time, the medics landed too fast. That's sort of true, but mainly it's bullshit. I had time. What I didn't have was the guts."

"Chollie—" Elisandra said again. There was an edge on her voice.

"Just one more second," I told her. I turned to Fazio again. "I looked at you, I looked at the heat-gun, I thought about the synsym. But I just couldn't do it. I stood there with the gun in my hand and I didn't do a thing. And then the medics landed and it was too late—I felt like such a shit, Fazio, such a cowardly shit—"

Fazio's face was turning blotchy. The red synsym lines blazed weirdly in his eyes.

"Get him into the sled!" Elisandra yelled. "It's taking control of him, Chollie!"

"Oligabongaboo!" Fazio said. "Ungabahoo! Flizz! Thrapp!"

And he came at me like a wild man.

I had him by thirty kilos, at least, but he damned near knocked me over. Somehow I managed to stay upright. He bounced off me and went reeling around, and Elisandra grabbed his arm. He kicked her hard and sent her flying, but then I wrapped my forearm around the throat from behind, and Elisandra, crawling across the floor, got him around his legs so we could lift him and stuff him into the sled. Even then we had trouble holding him. Two of us against one skinny burned-out ruined man, and he writhed and twisted and wriggled about like something diabolical. He scratched, he kicked, he elbowed, he spat. His eyes were fiery. Every time we forced him close to the entryway of the sled he dragged us back away from it. Elisandra and I were grunting and winded, and I didn't think we could hang on much longer. This wasn't Fazio we were doing battle with, it was a synthetic symbiont out of the Ovoid labs, furiously trying to save itself from a fiery death. God knows what alien hormones it was pumping into Fazio's bloodstream. God knows how it had rebuilt his bones and heart and lungs for greater efficiency. If he ever managed to break free of my grip, I wondered which of us would get out of the dropdock alive.

But all the same Fazio still needed to breathe. I tightened my hold on his throat and felt cartilage yielding. I didn't care. I just wanted to get him on that sled, dead or alive, give him some peace at all. Him and me both. Tighter—tighter—

Fazio made rough sputtering noises, and then a thick nasty gargling sound.

"You've got him," Elisandra said.

"Yeah. Yeah."

I clamped down one notch tighter yet, and Fazio began to go limp, though his muscles still spasmed and jerked frantically. The creature within him was still full of fight; but there wasn't much air getting into Fazio's lungs now and his brain was starving for oxygen. Slowly Elisandra and I shoved him the last five meters toward the sled—lifted him, pushed him up to the edge of the slot, started to jam him into it—

A convulsion wilder than anything that had gone before ripped through Fazio's body. He twisted half around in my grasp until he was face to face with Elisandra, and a bubble of something gray and shiny appeared on his lips. For an instant everything seemed frozen. It was like a slice across time, for just that instant. Then things began to move again. The bubble burst; some fragment of tissue leaped the short gap from Fazio's lips to Elisandra's. The symbiont, facing death, had cast forth a piece of its own lifestuff to find another host. "Chollie!" Elisandra wailed, and let go of Fazio and went reeling away as if someone had thrown acid in her eyes. She was clawing at her face. At the little flat gray slippery thing that had plastered itself over her mouth and was rapidly poking a couple of glistening pseudopods up into her nostrils. I hadn't known it was possible for a symbiont to send out offshoots like that. I guess no one did, or people like Fazio wouldn't be allowed to walk around loose.

I wanted to yell and scream and break things. I wanted to cry. But I didn't do any of those things.

When I was four years old, growing up on Backgammon, my father bought me a shiny little vortex-boat from a peddler on Maelstrom Bridge. It was just a toy, a bathtub boat, though it had all the stabilizer struts and outriggers in miniature. We were standing on the bridge and I wanted to see how well the boat worked, so I flipped it over the rail into the vortex. Of course it was swept out of sight at once. Bewildered and upset because it didn't come back to me, I looked toward my father for help. But he thought I had flung his gift into the whirlpool for the sheer hell of it, and he gave me a shriveling look of black anger and downright hatred that I will never forget. I cried half a day, but that didn't bring back my vortex-boat. I wanted to cry now. Sure. Something grotesquely unfair had happened, and I felt four years old all over again, and there was nobody to turn to for help. I was on my own.

I went to Elisandra and held her for a moment. She was sobbing and trying to speak, but the thing covered her lips. Her face was white with terror and her whole body was trembling and jerking crazily.

"Don't worry," I whispered. "This time I know what to do."

How fast we act, when finally we move. I got Fazio out of the way first, tossing him or the husk of him into the entry slot of the *Corona Queen* as easily as though he had been an armload of straw. Then I picked up Elisandra and carried her to the sled. She didn't really struggle, just twisted about a little. The symbiont didn't have that much control yet. At the last moment I looked into her eyes, hoping I wasn't going to see the red circles in them. No, not yet, not so soon. Her eyes were the eyes I remembered, the eyes I loved. They were steady, cold, clear. She knew what was happening. She couldn't speak, but she was telling me with her eyes: *Yes, yes, go ahead, for Christ's sake go ahead, Chollie!*

Unfair. Unfair. But nothing is ever fair, I thought. Or else if there is justice in the universe it exists only on levels we can't perceive, in some chilly macrocosmic place where everything is evened out in the long run but the sin is not necessarily atoned by the sinner. I pushed her into the slot down next to Fazio and slammed the sled shut. And went to the dropdock's wall console and keyed in the departure signal, and watched as the sled went sliding down the track toward the exit hatch on its one-way journey to Betelgeuse. The red light of the activated repellers glared for a moment, and then the blue-green returned. I turned away, wondering if the symbiont had managed to get a piece of itself into me too at the last moment. I waited to feel that tickle in the mind. But I didn't. I guess there hadn't been time for it to get us both.

And then, finally, I dropped down on the launching track and let myself cry. And went out of there, after a while, silent, numb, purged clean, thinking of nothing at all. At the inquest six weeks later I told them I didn't have the slightest notion why Elisandra had chosen to get aboard that ship with Fazio. Was it a suicide pact, the inquest panel asked me? I shrugged. I don't know, I said. I don't have any goddamned idea what was going on in their minds that day, I said. Silent, numb, purged clean, thinking of nothing at all.

So Fazio rests at last in the blazing heart of Betelgeuse. My Elisandra is in there also. And I go on, day after day, still working the turnaround wheel here at the Station, reeling in the stargoing ships that come cruising past the fringes of the giant red sun. I still feel haunted, too. But it isn't Fazio's ghost that visits me now, or even Elisandra's—not now, not after all this time. I think the ghost that haunts me is my own.

SAILING TO BYZANTIUM

It was still the spring of 1984. I had just completed my historical/fantasy novel Gilgamesh the King, *set in ancient Sumer, and antiquity was very much on my mind when Shawna McCarthy, who had just begun her brief and brilliant career as editor of* Isaac Asimov's Science Fiction Magazine, *came to the San Francisco area, where I live, on holiday. I ran into her at a party and she asked me if I'd write a story for her. "I'd like to, yes." And, since the novella is my favorite form, I added, "a long one."*

"How long?"

"Long," I told her. "A novella."

"Good," she said. We did a little haggling over the price, and that was that. She went back to New York and I got going on "Sailing to Byzantium" and by late summer it was done.

It wasn't originally going to be called "Sailing to Byzantium." The used manila envelope on which I had jotted the kernel of the idea out of which "Sailing to Byzantium" grew—I always jot down my story ideas on the backs of old envelopes—bears the title, "The Hundred-Gated City." That's a reference to ancient Thebes, in Egypt, and this was my original note:

"Ancient Egypt has been re-created at the end of time, along with various other highlights of history—a sort of Disneyland. A twentieth-century man, through error, has been regenerated in Thebes, though he belongs in the replica of Los Angeles. The misplaced Egyptian has been sent to Troy, or maybe Knossos, and a Cretan has been displaced into a Brasilia-equivalent of the twenty-ninth century. They move about, attempting to return to their proper places."

It's a nice idea, but it's not quite the story I ultimately wrote, perhaps because I decided it might turn out to be nothing more than an updating of Murray Leinster's classic novella "Sidewise in Time," a story that was first published before I was born but which is still well remembered in certain quarters. I did use the "Hundred-Gated" tag in an entirely different story many years later—"Thebes of the Hundred Gates." (I'm thrifty with titles as well as old envelopes.) But what emerged in the summer of 1984 is the story you are about to read, which quickly acquired the title it now bears as I came to understand the direction my original idea had begun to take.

From the earliest pages I knew I was on to something special, and it remains one of my favorite stories, out of all the millions and millions of words of science fiction I've published in the past five decades. Shawna had one or two small editorial suggestions for clarifying the ending, which I accepted gladly, and my friend Shay Barsabe, who read the story in manuscript, pointed out one subtle logical blunder in the plot that I hastily corrected; but otherwise the story came forth virtually in its final form as I wrote it.

It was published first as an elegant limited-edition book, now very hard to find, by the house of Underwood-Miller, and soon afterward it appeared in Asimov's for February, 1985. Immediate acclaim came from many sides, and that year it was chosen with wonderful editorial unanimity for all three of the best-science-fiction-of-the-year anthologies, those edited by Donald A. Wollheim, Terry Carr, and Gardner Dozois. "A possible classic," is what Wollheim called it, praise that gave me great delight, because the crusty, sardonic Wollheim had been reading science fiction almost since the stuff was invented, and he was not one to throw such words around lightly. "Sailing to Byzantium" won me a Nebula award in 1986, and was nominated for a Hugo, but finished in second place, losing by four votes out of 800. Since then the story has been reprinted many times and translated into a dozen languages or more. It's a piece of which I'm extremely proud.

At dawn he arose and stepped out onto the patio for his first look at Alexandria, the one city he had not yet seen. That year the five cities were Changan, Asgard, New Chicago, Timbuctoo, Alexandria: the usual mix of eras, cultures, realities. He and Gioia, making the long flight from Asgard in the distant north the night before, had arrived late, well after sundown, and had gone straight to bed. Now, by the gentle apricot-hued morning light, the fierce spires and battlements of Asgard seemed merely something he had dreamed.

The rumor was that Asgard's moment was finished anyway. In a little while, he had heard, they were going to tear it down and replace it, elsewhere, with Mohenjo-daro. Though there were never more than five cities, they changed constantly. He could remember a time when they had had Rome of the Caesars instead of Chang-an, and Rio de Janeiro rather than Alexandria. These people saw no point in keeping anything very long.

It was not easy for him to adjust to the sultry intensity of Alexandria after the frozen splendors of Asgard. The wind, coming off the water, was brisk and torrid both at once. Soft turquoise wavelets lapped at the jetties. Strong presences assailed his senses: the hot heavy sky, the stinging scent of the red lowland sand borne on the breeze, the sullen swampy aroma of the nearby sea. Everything trembled and glimmered in the early light. Their hotel was beautifully situated, high on the northern slope of the huge artificial mound known as the Paneium that was sacred to the goat-footed god. From here they had a total view of the city: the wide noble boulevards, the soaring obelisks and monuments, the palace of Hadrian just below the hill, the stately and awesome Library, the temple of Poseidon, the teeming marketplace, the royal lodge that Marc Antony had built after his defeat at Actium. And of course the Lighthouse, the wondrous many-windowed Lighthouse, the seventh wonder of the world, that immense pile of marble and limestone and reddish-purple Aswan granite rising in majesty at the end of its mile-long causeway. Black smoke from the beacon fire at its summit curled lazily into the sky. The city was awakening. Some temporaries in short white kilts appeared and began to trim the dense dark hedges that bordered the great public buildings. A few citizens wearing loose robes of vaguely Grecian style were strolling in the streets.

There were ghosts and chimeras and phantasies everywhere about. Two slim elegant centaurs, a male and a female, grazed on the hillside. A burly thick-thighed swordsman appeared on the porch of the temple of Poseidon holding a Gorgon's severed head and waved it in a wide arc, grinning broadly. In the street below the hotel gate three small pink sphinxes, no bigger than housecats, stretched and yawned and began to prowl the curbside. A larger one, lion-sized, watched warily from an alleyway: their mother, surely. Even at this distance he could hear her loud purring.

Shading his eyes, he peered far out past the Lighthouse and across the water. He hoped to see the dim shores of Crete or Cyprus to the north, or perhaps the great dark curve of Anatolia. *Carry me toward that great Byzantium,* he thought. *Where all is ancient, singing at the oars.* But he beheld only the endless empty sea, sun-bright and blinding though the morning was just beginning. Nothing was ever where he expected it to be. The continents did not seem to be in their proper places any longer. Gioia, taking him aloft long ago in her little flitterflitter, had shown him that. The tip of South America was canted far out into the Pacific; Africa was weirdly foreshortened; a broad tongue of ocean separated Europe and Asia. Australia did not appear to exist at all. Perhaps they had dug it up and used it for other things. There was no trace of the world he once had known. This was the fiftieth century. "The fiftieth century after *what*?" he had asked several times, but no one seemed to know, or else they did not care to say.

"Is Alexandria very beautiful?" Gioia called from within.

"Come out and see."

Naked and sleepy-looking, she padded out onto the white-tiled patio and nestled up beside him. She fit neatly under his arm. "Oh, yes, yes!" she said softly. "So very beautiful, isn't it? Look, there, the palaces, the Library, the Lighthouse! Where will we go first? The Lighthouse, I think. Yes? And then the marketplace—I want to see the Egyptian magicians—and the stadium, the races—will they be having races today, do you think? Oh, Charles, I want to see everything!"

"Everything? All on the first day?"

"All on the first day, yes," she said. "Everything."

"But we have plenty of time, Gioia."

"Do we?"

He smiled and drew her tight against his side.

"Time enough," he said gently.

He loved her for her impatience, for her bright bubbling eagerness. Gioia was not much like the rest in that regard, though she seemed identical in all other ways. She was short, supple, slender, dark-eyed, olive-skinned, narrow-hipped, with wide shoulders and flat muscles. They were all like that, each one indistinguishable from the rest, like a horde of millions of brothers and sisters—a world of small lithe childlike Mediterraneans, built for juggling, for bull-dancing, for sweet white wine at midday and rough red wine at night. They had the same slim bodies, the same broad mouths, the same great glossy eyes. He had never seen anyone who appeared to be younger than twelve or older than twenty. Gioia was somehow a little different, although he did not quite know how; but he knew that it was for that imperceptible but significant difference that he loved her. And probably that was why she loved him also.

He let his gaze drift from west to east, from the Gate of the Moon down broad Canopus Street and out to the harbor, and off to the tomb of Cleopatra at the tip of long slender Cape Lochias. Everything was here and all of it perfect, the obelisks, the statues and marble colonnades, the courtyards and shrines and groves, great Alexander himself in his coffin of crystal and gold: a splendid gleaming pagan city. But there were oddities—an unmistakable mosque near the public gardens, and what seemed to be a Christian church not far from the Library. And those ships in the harbor, with all those red sails and bristling masts— surely they were medieval, and late medieval at that. He had seen such anachronisms in other places before. Doubtless these people found them amusing. Life was a game for them. They played at it unceasingly. Rome, Alexandria, Timbuctoo—why not? Create an Asgard of translucent bridges and shimmering ice-girt palaces, then grow weary of it and take it away? Replace it with Mohenjo-daro? Why not? It seemed to him a great pity to destroy those lofty Nordic feasting halls for the sake of building a squat brutal sun-baked city of brown brick; but these people did not look at things the way he did. Their cities were only temporary. Someone in Asgard had said that Timbuctoo would be the next to go, with Byzantium rising in its place. Well, why not? Why not? They could have anything they liked. This was the fiftieth century, after all. The only rule was that there could be no more than five cities at once. "Limits," Gioia had informed him solemnly when they first began to travel together, "are very important." But she did not know why, or did not care to say.

He stared out once more toward the sea.

He imagined a newborn city congealing suddenly out of mists, far across the water: shining towers, great domed palaces, golden mosaics. That would be no great effort for them. They could just summon it forth whole out of time, the Emperor on his throne and the Emperor's drunken soldiery roistering in the streets, the brazen clangor of the cathedral gong rolling through the Grand Bazaar, dolphins leaping beyond the shoreside pavilions. Why not? They had Timbuctoo. They had Alexandria. Do you crave Constantinople? Then behold

Constantinople! Or Avalon, or Lyonesse, or Atlantis. They could have anything they liked. It is pure Schopenhauer here: the world as will and imagination. Yes! These slender dark-eyed people journeying tirelessly from miracle to miracle. Why not Byzantium next? Yes! Why not? *That is no country for old men,* he thought. *The young in one another's arms, the birds in the trees*—yes! Yes! Anything they liked. They even had him. Suddenly he felt frightened. Questions he had not asked for a long time burst through into his consciousness. *Who am I? Why am I here? Who is this woman beside me?*

"You're so quiet all of a sudden, Charles," said Gioia, who could not abide silence for very long. "Will you talk to me? I want you to talk to me. Tell me what you're looking for out there."

He shrugged. "Nothing."

"Nothing?"

"Nothing in particular."

"I could see you seeing something."

"Byzantium," he said. "I was imagining that I could look straight across the water to Byzantium. I was trying to get a glimpse of the walls of Constantinople."

"Oh, but you wouldn't be able to see as far as that from here. Not really."

"I know."

"And anyway Byzantium doesn't exist."

"Not yet. But it will. Its time comes later on."

"Does it?" she said. "Do you know that for a fact?"

"On good authority. I heard it in Asgard," he told her. "But even if I hadn't, Byzantium would be inevitable, don't you think? Its time would have to come. How could we not do Byzantium, Gioia? We certainly will do Byzantium, sooner or later. I know we will. It's only a matter of time. And we have all the time in the world."

A shadow crossed her face. "Do we? Do we?"

He knew very little about himself, but he knew that he was not one of them. That he knew. He knew that his name was Charles Phillips and that before he had come to live among these people he had lived in the year 1984, when there had been such things as computers and television sets and baseball and jet planes, and the world was full of cities, not merely five but thousands of them, New York and London and Johannesburg and Paris and Liverpool and Bangkok and San Francisco and Buenos Aires and a multitude of others, all at the same time. There had been four and a half billion people in the world then; now he doubted that there were as many as four and a half million. Nearly everything had changed beyond comprehension. The moon still seemed the same, and the sun; but at night he searched in vain for familiar constellations. He had no idea how they had brought him from then to now, or why. It did no good to ask. No one had any answers for him; no one so much as appeared to understand what it was that he was trying to learn. After a time he had stopped asking; after a time he had almost entirely ceased wanting to know.

He and Gioia were climbing the Lighthouse. She scampered ahead, in a hurry as always, and he came along behind her in his more stolid fashion. Scores of other tourists, mostly in groups of two or three, were making their way up the wide flagstone ramps, laughing, calling to one another. Some of them, seeing him, stopped a moment, stared, pointed. He was used to that. He was so much taller than any of them; he was plainly not one of them. When they pointed at him he smiled. Sometimes he nodded a little acknowledgment.

He could not find much of interest in the lowest level, a massive square structure two hundred feet high built of huge marble blocks: within its cool musty arcades were hundreds of small dark rooms, the offices of the Lighthouse's keepers and mechanics, the barracks of the garrison, the stables for the three hundred donkeys that carried the fuel to the lantern far above. None of that appeared inviting to him. He forged onward without halting until he emerged on the balcony that led to the next level. Here the Lighthouse grew narrower and became octagonal: its face, granite now and handsomely fluted, rose in a stunning sweep above him.

Gioia was waiting for him there. "This is for you," she said, holding out a nugget of meat on a wooden skewer. "Roast lamb. Absolutely delicious. I had one while I was waiting for you." She gave him a cup of some cool green sherbet also, and darted off to buy a pomegranate. Dozens of temporaries were roaming the balcony, selling refreshments of all kinds.

He nibbled at the meat. It was charred outside, nicely pink and moist within. While he ate, one of the temporaries came up to him and peered blandly into his face. It was a stocky swarthy male wearing nothing but a strip of red and yellow cloth about its waist. "I sell meat," it said. "Very fine roast lamb, only five drachmas."

Phillips indicated the piece he was eating. "I already have some," he said.

"It is excellent meat, very tender. It has been soaked for three days in the juices of—"

"Please," Phillips said. "I don't want to buy any meat. Do you mind moving along?"

The temporaries had confused and baffled him at first, and there was still much about them that was unclear to him. They were not machines—they looked like creatures of flesh and blood—but they did not seem to be human beings, either, and no one treated them as if they were. He supposed they were artificial constructs, products of a technology so consummate that it was invisible. Some appeared to be more intelligent than others, but all of them behaved as if they had no more autonomy than characters in a play, which was essentially what they were. There were untold numbers of them in each of the five cities, playing all manner of roles: shepherds and swineherds, street-sweepers, merchants, boatmen, vendors of grilled meats and cool drinks, hagglers in the marketplace, schoolchildren, charioteers, policemen, grooms, gladiators, monks, artisans, whores and cutpurses, sailors—whatever was needed to sustain the illusion of a thriving, populous urban center. The dark-eyed people, Gioia's people, never performed work. There were not enough of them to keep a city's functions going, and in any case they were strictly tourists, wandering with the wind, moving from city to city as the whim took them, Chang-an to New Chicago, New Chicago to Timbuctoo, Timbuctoo to Asgard, Asgard to Alexandria, onward, ever onward.

The temporary would not leave him alone. Phillips walked away and it followed him, cornering him against the balcony wall. When Gioia returned a few minutes later, lips prettily stained with pomegranate juice, the temporary was still hovering about him, trying with lunatic persistence to sell him a skewer of lamb. It stood much too close to him, almost nose to nose, great sad cowlike eyes peering intently into his as it extolled with mournful mooing urgency the quality of its wares. It seemed to him that he had had trouble like this with temporaries on one or two earlier occasions. Gioia touched the creature's elbow lightly and said, in a short sharp tone Phillips had never heard her use before, "He isn't interested. Get away from him." It went at once. To Phillips she said, "You have to be firm with them."

"I was trying. It wouldn't listen to me."

"You ordered it to go away, and it refused?"

"I asked it to go away. Politely. Too politely, maybe."

"Even so," she said. "It should have obeyed a human, regardless."

"Maybe it didn't think I was human," Phillips suggested. "Because of the way I look. My height, the color of my eyes. It might have thought I was some kind of temporary myself."

"No," Gioia said, frowning. "A temporary won't solicit another temporary. But it won't ever disobey a citizen, either. There's a very clear boundary. There isn't ever any confusion. I can't understand why it went on bothering you." He was surprised at how troubled she seemed: far more so, he thought, than the incident warranted. A stupid device, perhaps miscalibrated in some way, overenthusiastically pushing its wares—what of it? What of it? Gioia, after a moment, appeared to come to the same conclusion. Shrugging, she said, "It's defective, I suppose. Probably such things are more common than we suspect, don't you think?" There was something forced about her tone that bothered him. She smiled and handed him her pomegranate. "Here. Have a bite, Charles. It's wonderfully sweet. They used to be extinct, you know. Shall we go on upward?"

The octagonal midsection of the Lighthouse must have been several hundred feet in height, a grim claustrophobic tube almost entirely filled by the two broad spiraling ramps that wound around the huge building's central well. The ascent was slow: a donkey team was a little way ahead of them on the ramp, plodding along laden with bundles of kindling for the lantern. But at last, just as Phillips was growing winded and dizzy, he and Gioia came out onto the second balcony, the one marking the transition between the octagonal section and the Lighthouse's uppermost story, which was cylindrical and very slender.

She leaned far out over the balustrade. "Oh, Charles, look at the view! Look at it!"

It was amazing. From one side they could see the entire city, and swampy Lake Mareotis and the dusty Egyptian plain beyond it, and from the other they peered far out into the gray and choppy Mediterranean. He gestured toward the innumerable reefs and shallows that infested the waters leading to the harbor entrance. "No wonder they needed a lighthouse here," he said. "Without some kind of gigantic landmark they'd never have found their way in from the open sea."

A blast of sound, a ferocious snort, erupted just above him. He looked up, startled. Immense statues of trumpet-wielding Tritons jutted from the corners of the Lighthouse at this level; that great blurting sound had come from the nearest of them. A signal, he thought. A warning to the ships negotiating that troubled passage. The sound was produced by some kind of steam-powered mechanism, he realized, operated by teams of sweating temporaries clustered about bonfires at the base of each Triton.

Once again he found himself swept by admiration for the clever way these people carried out their reproductions of antiquity. Or *were* they reproductions, he wondered? He still did not understand how they brought their cities into being. For all he knew, this place was the authentic Alexandria itself, pulled forward out of its proper time just as he himself had been. Perhaps this was the true and original Lighthouse, and not a copy. He had no idea which was the case, nor which would be the greater miracle.

"How do we get to the top?" Gioia asked.

"Over there, I think. That doorway."

The spiraling donkey-ramps ended here. The loads of lantern fuel went higher via a dumbwaiter in the central shaft. Visitors continued by way of a cramped staircase, so narrow at its upper end that it was impossible to turn around while climbing. Gioia, tireless, sprinted ahead. He clung to the rail and labored up and up, keeping count of the tiny window slits to ease the boredom of the ascent. The count was nearing a hundred when finally he stumbled into the vestibule of the beacon chamber. A dozen or so visitors were crowded into it. Gioia was at the far side, by the wall that was open to the sea.

It seemed to him he could feel the building swaying in the winds up here. How high were they? Five hundred feet, six hundred, seven? The beacon chamber was tall and narrow, divided by a catwalk into upper and lower sections. Down below, relays of temporaries carried wood from the dumbwaiter and tossed it on the blazing fire. He felt its intense heat from where he stood, at the rim of the platform on which the giant mirror of polished metal was hung. Tongues of flame leaped upward and danced before the mirror, which hurled its dazzling beam far out to sea. Smoke rose through a vent. At the very top was a colossal statue of Poseidon, austere, ferocious, looming above the lantern.

Gioia sidled along the catwalk until she was at his side. "The guide was talking before you came," she said, pointing. "Do you see that place over there, under the mirror? Someone standing there and looking into the mirror gets a view of ships at sea that can't be seen from here by the naked eye. The mirror magnifies things."

"Do you believe that?"

She nodded toward the guide. "It said so. And it also told us that if you look in a certain way, you can see right across the water into the city of Constantinople."

She is like a child, he thought. They all are. He said, "You told me yourself this very morning that it isn't possible to see that far. Besides, Constantinople doesn't exist right now."

"It will," she replied. "*You* said that to me, this very morning. And when it does, it'll be reflected in the Lighthouse mirror. That's the truth. I'm absolutely certain of it." She swung about abruptly toward the entrance of the beacon chamber. "Oh, look, Charles! Here come Nissandra and Aramayne! And there's Hawk! There's Stengard!" Gioia laughed and waved and called out names. "Oh, everyone's here! *Everyone!*"

They came jostling into the room, so many newcomers that some of those who had been there were forced to scramble down the steps on the far side. Gioia moved among them, hugging, kissing. Phillips could scarcely tell one from another—it was hard for him even to tell which were the men and which the women, dressed as they all were in the same sort of loose robes—but he recognized some of the names. These were her special friends, her set, with whom she had journeyed from city to city on an endless round of gaiety in the old days before he had come into her life. He had met a few of them before, in Asgard, in Rio, in Rome. The beacon-chamber guide, a squat wide-shouldered old temporary wearing a laurel wreath on its bald head, reappeared and began its potted speech, but no one listened to it; they were all too busy greeting one another, embracing, giggling. Some of them edged their way over to Phillips and reached up, standing on tiptoes, to touch their fingertips to his cheek in that odd hello of theirs. "Charles," they said gravely, making two syllables out of the name, as these people often did. "So good to see you again. Such a pleasure. You and Gioia—such a handsome couple. So well suited to each other."

Was that so? He supposed it was.

The chamber hummed with chatter. The guide could not be heard at all. Stengard and Nissandra had visited New Chicago for the water-dancing—Aramayne bore tales of a feast in Chang-an that had gone on for *days*—Hawk and Hekna had been to Timbuctoo to see the arrival of the salt caravan, and were going back there soon—a final party soon to celebrate the end of Asgard that absolutely should not be missed—the plans for the new city, Mohenjo-daro—we have reservations for the opening, we wouldn't pass it up for anything—and, yes, they were definitely going to do Constantinople after that, the planners were already deep into their Byzantium research—so good to see you, you look so beautiful all the time—have you been to the Library yet? The zoo? To the temple of Serapis?—

To Phillips they said, "What do you think of our Alexandria, Charles? Of course, you must have known it well in your day. Does it look the way you remember it?" They were always asking things like that. They did not seem to comprehend that the Alexandria of the Lighthouse and the Library was long lost and legendary by the time his twentieth century had been. To them, he suspected, all the places they had brought back into existence were more or less contemporary. Rome of the Caesars, Alexandria of the Ptolemies, Venice of the Doges, Chang-an of the T'angs, Asgard of the Aesir, none any less real than the next nor any less unreal, each one simply a facet of the distant past, the fantastic immemorial past, a plum plucked from that dark backward abysm of time. They had no contexts for separating one era from another. To them all the past was one borderless timeless realm. Why, then, should he not have seen the Lighthouse before, he who had leaped into this era from the New York of 1984? He had never been able to explain it to them. Julius Caesar and Hannibal, Helen of Troy and Charlemagne, Rome of the gladiators and New York of the Yankees and Mets, Gilgamesh and Tristan and Othello and Robin Hood and George Washington and Queen Victoria—to them, all equally real and unreal, none of them any more than bright figures moving about on a painted canvas. The past, the past, the elusive and fluid past—to them it was a single place of infinite accessibility and infinite connectivity. Of course, they would think he had seen the Lighthouse before. He knew better than to try again to explain things. "No," he said simply. "This is my first time in Alexandria."

They stayed there all winter long, and possibly some of the spring. Alexandria was not a place where one was sharply aware of the change of seasons, nor did the passage of time itself make itself very evident when one was living one's entire life as a tourist.

During the day there was always something new to see. The zoological garden, for instance: a wondrous park, miraculously green and lush in this hot dry climate, where astounding animals roamed in enclosures so generous that they did not seem like enclosures at all. Here were camels, rhinoceroses, gazelles, ostriches, lions, wild asses; and here, too, casually adjacent to those familiar African beasts, were hippogriffs, unicorns, basilisks, and fire-snorting dragons with rainbow scales. Had the original zoo of Alexandria had dragons and unicorns? Phillips doubted it. But this one did; evidently it was no harder for the backstage craftsmen to manufacture mythic beasts than it was for them to turn out camels and gazelles. To Gioia and her friends all of them were equally mythical, anyway. They were just as awed by the rhinoceros as by the hippogriff. One was no more strange—or any less—than the other. So far as Phillips had been able to discover, none of the mammals or birds of his era had survived into this one except for a few cats and dogs, though many had been reconstructed.

And then the Library! All those lost treasures, reclaimed from the jaws of time! Stupendous columned marble walls, airy high-vaulted reading rooms, dark coiling stacks stretching away to infinity. The ivory handles of seven hundred thousand papyrus scrolls bristling on the shelves. Scholars and librarians gliding quietly about, smiling faint scholarly smiles but plainly preoccupied with serious matters of the mind. They were all temporaries, Phillips realized. Mere props, part of the illusion. But were the scrolls illusions, too? "Here we have the complete dramas of Sophocles," said the guide with a blithe wave of its hand, indicating shelf upon shelf of texts. Only seven of his hundred twenty-three plays had survived the successive burnings of the library in ancient times by Romans, Christians, Arabs: were the lost ones here, the *Triptolemus,* the *Nausicaa,* the *Jason,* and all the rest? And would he find here, too, miraculously restored to being, the other vanished treasures of ancient literature—the memoirs of Odysseus, Cato's history of Rome, Thucidydes' life of Pericles, the missing volumes of Livy? But when he asked if he might explore the stacks, the guide smiled apologetically and said that all the librarians were busy just now. Another time, perhaps? Perhaps, said the guide. It made no difference, Phillips decided. Even if these people somehow had brought back those lost masterpieces of antiquity, how would he read them? He knew no Greek.

The life of the city buzzed and throbbed about him. It was a dazzlingly beautiful place: the vast bay thick with sails, the great avenues running rigidly east-west, north-south, the sunlight rebounding almost audibly from the bright walls of the palaces of kings and gods. They have done this very well, Phillips thought: very well indeed. In the marketplace hard-eyed traders squabbled in half a dozen mysterious languages over the price of ebony, Arabian incense, jade, panther skins. Gioia bought a dram of pale musky Egyptian perfume in a delicate tapering glass flask. Magicians and jugglers and scribes called out stridently to passersby, begging for a few moments of attention and a handful of coins for their labor. Strapping slaves, black and tawny and some that might have been Chinese, were put up for auction, made to flex their muscles, to bare their teeth, to bare their breasts and thighs to prospective buyers. In the gymnasium naked athletes hurled javelins and discuses, and wrestled with terrifying zeal. Gioia's friend Stengard came rushing up with a gift for her, a golden necklace that would not have embarrassed Cleopatra. An hour later she had lost it, or perhaps had given it away while Phillips was looking elsewhere. She bought another, even finer, the next day. Anyone could have all the money he wanted, simply by asking: it was as easy to come by as air for these people.

Being here was much like going to the movies, Phillips told himself. A different show every day: not much plot, but the special effects were magnificent and the detail work could hardly have been surpassed. A megamovie, a vast entertainment that went on all the time and was being played out by the whole population of Earth. And it was all so effortless, so spontaneous: just as when he had gone to a movie he had never troubled to think about the myriad technicians behind the scenes, the cameramen and the costume designers and the set builders and the electricians and the model makers and the boom operators, so, too, here he chose not to question the means by which Alexandria had been set before him. It felt real. It *was* real. When he drank the strong red wine it gave him a pleasant buzz. If he leaped from the beacon chamber of the Lighthouse he suspected he would die, though perhaps he would not stay dead for long: doubtless they had some way of restoring him as often as was necessary. Death did not seem to be a factor in these people's lives.

By day they saw sights. By night he and Gioia went to parties, in their hotel, in seaside villas, in the palaces of the high nobility. The usual people were there all the time, Hawk and Hekna, Aramayne, Stengard and Shelimir, Nissandra, Asoka, Afonso, Protay. At the parties there were five or ten temporaries for every citizen, some as mere servants, others as entertainers or even surrogate guests, mingling freely and a little daringly. But everyone knew, all the time, who was a citizen and who just a temporary. Phillips began to think his own status lay somewhere between. Certainly they treated him with a courtesy that no one ever would give a temporary, and yet there was a condescension to their manner that told him not simply that he was not one of them but that he was someone or something of an altogether different order of existence. That he was Gioia's lover gave him some standing in their eyes, but not a great deal: obviously he was always going to be an outsider, a primitive, ancient and quaint. For that matter he noticed that Gioia herself, though unquestionably a member of the set, seemed to be regarded as something of an outsider, like a tradesman's great-granddaughter in a gathering of Plantagenets. She did not always find out about the best parties in time to attend; her friends did not always reciprocate her effusive greetings with the same degree of warmth; sometimes he noticed her straining to hear some bit of gossip that was not quite being shared with her. Was it because she had taken him for her lover? Or was it the other way around: that she had chosen to be his lover precisely because she was *not* a full member of their caste?

Being a primitive gave him, at least, something to talk about at their parties. "Tell us about war," they said. "Tell us about elections. About money. About disease." They wanted to know everything, though they did not seem to pay close attention: their eyes were quick to glaze. Still, they asked. He described traffic jams to them, and politics, and deodorants, and vitamin pills. He told them about cigarettes, newspapers, subways, telephone directories, credit cards, and basketball. "Which was your city?" they asked. New York, he told them. "And when was it? The seventh century, did you say?" The twentieth, he told them. They exchanged glances and nodded. "We will have to do it," they said. "The World Trade Center, the Empire State Building, the Citicorp Center, the Cathedral of St. John the Divine: how fascinating! Yankee Stadium. The Verrazano Bridge. We will do it all. But first must come Mohenjo-daro. And then, I think, Constantinople. Did your city have many people?" Seven million, he said. Just in the five boroughs alone. They nodded, smiling amiably, unfazed by the number. Seven million, seventy million—it was all the same to them, he sensed. They would just bring forth the temporaries in whatever quantity was required. He wondered how well they would carry the job off. He was no real judge of Alexandrias and Asgards, after all. Here they could have unicorns and hippogriffs in the zoo, and live sphinxes prowling in the gutters, and it did not trouble him. Their fanciful Alexandria was as good as history's, or better. But how sad, how disillusioning it would be, if the New York that they conjured up had Greenwich Village uptown and Times Square in the Bronx, and the New Yorkers, gentle and polite, spoke with the honeyed accents of Savannah or New Orleans. Well, that was nothing he needed to brood about just now. Very likely they were only being courteous when they spoke of doing his New York. They had all the vastness of the past to choose from: Nineveh, Memphis of the Pharaohs, the London of Victoria or Shakespeare or Richard the Third, Florence of the Medici, the Paris of Abelard and Heloise or the Paris of Louis XIV, Moctezuma's Tenochtitlan and Atahuallpa's Cuzco; Damascus, St. Petersburg, Babylon, Troy. And then there were all the cities like New Chicago, out of time that was time yet unborn to him but ancient history to them. In such richness, such an infinity of choices, even mighty New York might have to wait a long while for its turn. Would he still be among them by the time they got around to it? By then, perhaps, they might have become bored with him and returned him to his own proper era. Or possibly he would simply have grown old and died. Even here, he supposed, he would eventually die, though no one else ever seemed to. He did not know. He realized that in fact he did not know anything.

The north wind blew all day long. Vast flocks of ibises appeared over the city, fleeing the heat of the interior, and screeched across the sky with their black necks and scrawny legs extended. The sacred birds, descending by the thousands, scuttered about in every crossroad, pouncing on spiders and beetles, on mice, on the debris of the meat shops and the bakeries. They were beautiful but annoyingly ubiquitous, and they splashed their dung over the marble buildings; each morning squadrons of temporaries carefully washed it off. Gioia said little to him now. She seemed cool, withdrawn, depressed; and there was something almost intangible about her, as though she were gradually becoming transparent. He felt it would be an intrusion upon her privacy to ask her what was wrong. Perhaps it was only restlessness. She became religious, and presented costly offerings at the temples of Serapis, Isis, Poseidon, Pan. She went to the necropolis west of the city to lay wreaths on the tombs in the catacombs. In a single day she climbed the Lighthouse three times without any sign of fatigue. One afternoon he returned from a visit to the Library and found her naked on the patio; she had anointed herself all over with some aromatic green salve. Abruptly she said, "I think it's time to leave Alexandria, don't you?"

She wanted to go to Mohenjo-daro, but Mohenjo-daro was not yet ready for visitors. Instead they flew eastward to Chang-an, which they had not seen in years. It was Phillips's suggestion: he hoped that the cosmopolitan gaudiness of the old T'ang capital would lift her mood.

They were to be guests of the Emperor this time: an unusual privilege, which ordinarily had to be applied for far in advance, but Phillips had told some of Gioia's highly placed friends that she was unhappy, and they had quickly arranged everything. Three endlessly bowing functionaries in flowing yellow robes and purple sashes met them at the Gate of Brilliant Virtue in the city's south wall and conducted them to their pavilion, close by the imperial palace and the Forbidden Garden. It was a light, airy place, thin walls of plastered brick braced by graceful columns of some dark, aromatic wood. Fountains played on the roof of green and yellow tiles, creating an unending cool rainfall of recirculating water. The balustrades were of carved marble, the door fittings were of gold.

There was a suite of private rooms for him, and another for her, though they would share the handsome damask-draped bedroom at the heart of the pavilion. As soon as they arrived, Gioia announced that she must go to her rooms to bathe and dress. "There will be a formal reception for us at the palace tonight," she said. "They say the imperial receptions are splendid beyond anything you could imagine. I want to be at my best." The Emperor and all his ministers, she told him, would receive them in the Hall of the Supreme Ultimate; there would be a banquet for a thousand people; Persian dancers would perform, and the celebrated jugglers of Chung-nan. Afterward everyone would be conducted into the fantastic landscape of the Forbidden Garden to view the dragon races and the fireworks.

He went to his own rooms. Two delicate little maidservants undressed him and bathed him with fragrant sponges. The pavilion came equipped with eleven temporaries who were to be their servants: soft-voiced unobtrusive catlike Chinese, done with perfect verisimilitude, straight black hair, glowing skin, epicanthic folds. Phillips often wondered what happened to a city's temporaries when the city's time was over. Were the towering Norse heroes of Asgard being recycled at this moment into wiry dark-skinned Dravidians for Mohenjo-daro? When Timbuctoo's day was done, would its brightly robed black warriors be converted into supple Byzantines to stock the arcades of Constantinople? Or did they simply discard the old temporaries like so many excess props, stash them in warehouses somewhere, and turn out the appropriate quantities of the new model? He did not know; and once when he had asked Gioia about it she had grown uncomfortable and vague. She did not like him to probe for information, and he suspected it was because she had very little to give. These people did not seem to question the workings of their own world; his curiosities were very twentieth-century of him, he was frequently told, in that gently patronizing way of theirs. As his two little maids patted him with their sponges he thought of asking them where they had served before Chang-an. Rio? Rome? Haroun al Raschid's Baghdad? But these fragile girls, he knew, would only giggle and retreat if he tried to question them. Interrogating temporaries was not only improper but pointless: it was like interrogating one's luggage.

When he was bathed and robed in rich red silks he wandered the pavilion for a little while, admiring the tinkling pendants of green jade dangling on the portico, the lustrous auburn pillars, the rainbow hues of the intricately interwoven girders and brackets that supported the roof. Then, wearying of his solitude, he approached the bamboo curtain at the entrance to Gioia's suite. A porter and one of the maids stood just within. They indicated that he should not enter; but he scowled at them and they melted from him like snowflakes. A trail of incense led him through the pavilion to Gioia's innermost dressing room. There he halted, just outside the door.

Gioia sat naked with her back to him at an ornate dressing table of some rare flame-colored wood inlaid with bands of orange and green porcelain. She was studying herself intently in a mirror of polished bronze held by one of her maids: picking through her scalp with her fingernails, as a woman might do who was searching out her gray hairs.

But that seemed strange. Gray hair, on Gioia? On a citizen? A temporary might display some appearance of aging, perhaps, but surely not a citizen. Citizens remained forever young. Gioia looked like a girl. Her face was smooth and unlined, her flesh was firm, her hair was dark: that was true of all of them, every citizen he had ever seen. And yet there was no mistaking what Gioia was doing. She found a hair, frowned, drew it taut, nodded, plucked it. Another. Another. She pressed the tip of her finger to her cheek as if testing it for resilience. She tugged at the skin below her eyes, pulling it downward. Such familiar little gestures of vanity; but so odd here, he thought, in this world of the perpetually young. Gioia, worried about growing old? Had he simply failed to notice the signs of age on her? Or was it that she worked hard behind his back at concealing them? Perhaps that was it. Was he wrong about the citizens, then? Did they age even as the people of less blessed eras had always done, but simply have better ways of hiding it? How old was she, anyway? Thirty? Sixty? Three hundred?

Gioia appeared satisfied now. She waved the mirror away; she rose; she beckoned for her banquet robes. Phillips, still standing unnoticed by the door, studied her with admiration: the small round buttocks, almost but not quite boyish, the elegant line of her spine, the surprising breadth of her shoulders. No, he thought, she is not aging at all. Her body is still like a girl's. She looks as young as on the day they first had met, however long ago that was—he could not say; it was hard to keep track of time here; but he was sure some years had passed since they had come together. Those gray hairs, those wrinkles and sags for which she had searched just now with such desperate intensity, must all be imaginary, mere artifacts of vanity. Even in this remote future epoch, then, vanity was not extinct. He wondered why she was so concerned with the fear of aging. An affectation? Did all these timeless people take some perverse pleasure in fretting over the possibility that they might be growing old? Or was it some private fear of Gioia's, another symptom of the mysterious depression that had come over her in Alexandria?

Not wanting her to think that he had been spying on her, when all he had really intended was to pay her a visit, he slipped silently away to dress for the evening. She came to him an hour later, gorgeously robed, swaddled from chin to ankles in a brocade of brilliant colors shot through with threads of gold, face painted, hair drawn up tightly and fastened with ivory combs: very much the lady of the court. His servants had made him splendid also, a lustrous black surplice embroidered with golden dragons over a sweeping floor-length gown of shining white silk, a necklace and pendant of red coral, a five-cornered gray felt hat that rose in tower upon tower like a ziggurat. Gioia, grinning, touched her fingertips to his cheek. "You look marvelous!" she told him. "Like a grand mandarin!"

"And you like an empress," he said. "Of some distant land: Persia, India. Here to pay a ceremonial visit on the Son of Heaven." An excess of love suffused his spirit, and, catching her lightly by the wrist, he drew her toward him, as close as he could manage it considering how elaborate their costumes were. But as he bent forward and downward, meaning to brush his lips lightly and affectionately against the tip of her nose, he perceived an unexpected strangeness, an anomaly: the coating of white paint that was her makeup seemed oddly to magnify rather than mask the contours of her skin, highlighting and revealing details he had never observed before. He saw a pattern of fine lines radiating from the corners of her eyes, and the unmistakable beginning of a quirk mark in her cheek just to the left of her mouth, and perhaps the faint indentation of frown lines in her flawless forehead. A shiver traveled along the nape of his neck. So it was not affectation, then, that had had her studying her mirror so fiercely. Age was in truth beginning to stake its claim on her, despite all that he had come to believe about these people's agelessness. But a moment later he was not so sure. Gioia turned and slid gently half a step back from him—she must have found his stare disturbing—and the lines he had thought he had seen were gone. He searched for them and saw only girlish smoothness once again. A trick of the light? A figment of an overwrought imagination? He was baffled.

"Come," she said. "We mustn't keep the Emperor waiting."

Five mustachioed warriors in armor of white quilting and seven musicians playing cymbals and pipes escorted them to the Hall of the Supreme Ultimate. There they found the full court arrayed: princes and ministers, high officials, yellow-robed monks, a swarm of imperial concubines. In a place of honor to the right of the royal thrones, which rose like gilded scaffolds high above all else, was a little group of stern-faced men in foreign costumes, the ambassadors of Rome and Byzantium, of Arabia and Syria, of Korea, Japan, Tibet, Turkestan. Incense smoldered in enameled braziers. A poet sang a delicate twanging melody, accompanying himself on a small harp. Then the Emperor and Empress entered: two tiny aged people, like waxen images, moving with infinite slowness, taking steps no greater than a child's. There was the sound of trumpets as they ascended their thrones. When the little Emperor was seated—he looked like a doll up there, ancient, faded, shrunken, yet still somehow a figure of extraordinary power—he stretched forth both his hands, and enormous gongs began to sound. It was a scene of astonishing splendor, grand and overpowering.

These are all temporaries, Phillips realized suddenly. He saw only a handful of citizens—eight, ten, possibly as many as a dozen—scattered here and there about the vast room. He knew them by their eyes, dark, liquid, knowing. They were watching not only the imperial spectacle but also Gioia and him; and Gioia, smiling secretly, nodding almost imperceptibly to them, was acknowledging their presence and their interest. But those few were the only ones in here who were autonomous living beings. All the rest—the entire splendid court, the great mandarins and paladins, the officials, the giggling concubines, the haughty and resplendent ambassadors, the aged Emperor and Empress themselves, were simply part of the scenery. Had the world ever seen entertainment on so grand a scale before? All this pomp, all this pageantry, conjured up each night for the amusement of a dozen or so viewers?

At the banquet the little group of citizens sat together at a table apart, a round onyx slab draped with translucent green silk. There turned out to be seventeen of them in all, including Gioia; Gioia appeared to know all of them, though none, so far as he could tell, was a member of her set that he had met before. She did not attempt introductions. Nor was conversation at all possible during the meal: there was a constant astounding roaring din in the room. Three orchestras played at once and there were troupes of strolling musicians also, and a steady stream of monks and their attendants marched back and forth between the tables loudly chanting sutras and waving censers to the deafening accompaniment of drums and gongs. The Emperor did not descend from his throne to join the banquet; he seemed to be asleep, though now and then he waved his hand in time to the music. Gigantic half-naked brown slaves with broad cheekbones and mouths like gaping pockets brought forth the food, peacock tongues and breast of phoenix heaped on mounds of glowing saffron-colored rice, served on frail alabaster plates. For chopsticks they were given slender rods of dark jade. The wine, served in glistening crystal beakers, was thick and sweet, with an aftertaste of raisins, and no beaker was allowed to remain empty for more than a moment. Phillips felt himself growing dizzy: when the

Persian dancers emerged he could not tell whether there were five of
them or fifty, and as they performed their intricate whirling routines it
seemed to him that their slender muslin-veiled forms were blurring and
merging one into another. He felt frightened by their proficiency, and
wanted to look away, but he could not. The Chung-nan jugglers that
followed them were equally skillful, equally alarming, filling the air
with scythes, flaming torches, live animals, rare porcelain vases, pink
jade hatchets, silver bells, gilded cups, wagon wheels, bronze vessels,
and never missing a catch. The citizens applauded politely but did not
seem impressed. After the jugglers, the dancers returned, performing
this time on stilts; the waiters brought platters of steaming meat of
a pale lavender color, unfamiliar in taste and texture: filet of camel,
perhaps, or haunch of hippopotamus, or possibly some choice chop
from a young dragon. There was more wine. Feebly Phillips tried to
wave it away, but the servitors were implacable. This was a drier sort,
greenish-gold, austere, sharp on the tongue. With it came a silver dish,
chilled to a polar coldness, that held shaved ice flavored with some
potent smoky-flavored brandy. The jugglers were doing a second turn,
he noticed. He thought he was going to be ill. He looked helplessly
toward Gioia, who seemed sober but fiercely animated, almost manic,
her eyes blazing like rubies. She touched his cheek fondly. A cool draft
blew through the hall: they had opened one entire wall, revealing the
garden, the night, the stars. Just outside was a colossal wheel of oiled
paper stretched on wooden struts. They must have erected it in the past
hour: it stood a hundred fifty feet high or even more, and on it hung
lanterns by the thousands, glimmering like giant fireflies. The guests
began to leave the hall. Phillips let himself be swept along into the
garden, where under a yellow moon strange crook-armed trees with
dense black needles loomed ominously. Gioia slipped her arm through
his. They went down to a lake of bubbling crimson fluid and watched
scarlet flamingolike birds ten feet tall fastidiously spearing angry-
eyed turquoise eels. They stood in awe before a fat-bellied Buddha of
gleaming blue tilework, seventy feet high. A horse with a golden mane
came prancing by, striking showers of brilliant red sparks wherever its
hooves touched the ground. In a grove of lemon trees that seemed to
have the power to wave their slender limbs about, Phillips came upon
the Emperor, standing by himself and rocking gently back and forth.
The old man seized Phillips by the hand and pressed something into
his palm, closing his fingers tight about it; when he opened his fist

a few moments later he found his palm full of gray irregular pearls. Gioia took them from him and cast them into the air, and they burst like exploding firecrackers, giving off splashes of colored light. A little later, Phillips realized that he was no longer wearing his surplice or his white silken undergown. Gioia was naked, too, and she drew him gently down into a carpet of moist blue moss, where they made love until dawn, fiercely at first, then slowly, languidly, dreamily. At sunrise he looked at her tenderly and saw that something was wrong.

"Gioia?" he said doubtfully.

She smiled. "Ah, no. Gioia is with Fenimon tonight. I am Belilala."

"With—Fenimon?"

"They are old friends. She had not seen him in years."

"Ah. I see. And you are—?"

"Belilala," she said again, touching her fingertips to his cheek.

It was not unusual, Belilala said. It happened all the time; the only unusual thing was that it had not happened to him before now. Couples formed, traveled together for a while, drifted apart, eventually reunited. It did not mean that Gioia had left him forever. It meant only that just now she chose to be with Fenimon. Gioia would return. In the meanwhile he would not be alone. "You and I met in New Chicago," Belilala told him. "And then we saw each other again in Timbuctoo. Have you forgotten? Oh, yes, I see that you have forgotten!" She laughed prettily; she did not seem at all offended.

She looked enough like Gioia to be her sister. But, then, all the citizens looked more or less alike to him. And apart from their physical resemblance, so he quickly came to realize, Belilala and Gioia were not really very similar. There was a calmness, a deep reservoir of serenity, in Belilala, that Gioia, eager and volatile and ever impatient, did not seem to have. Strolling the swarming streets of Chang-an with Belilala, he did not perceive in her any of Gioia's restless feverish need always to know what lay beyond, and beyond, and beyond even that. When they toured the Hsing-ch'ing Palace, Belilala did not after five minutes begin—as Gioia surely would have done—to seek directions to the Fountain of Hsuan-tsung or the Wild Goose Pagoda. Curiosity did not consume Belilala as it did Gioia. Plainly she believed that there would always be enough time for her to see everything she cared to see. There were some days when Belilala chose not to go out at all, but was content merely to remain at their pavilion playing a solitary game with flat porcelain counters, or viewing the flowers of the garden.

He found, oddly, that he enjoyed the respite from Gioia's intense world-swallowing appetites; and yet he longed for her to return. Belilala—beautiful, gentle, tranquil, patient—was too perfect for him. She seemed unreal in her gleaming impeccability, much like one of those Sung celadon vases that appear too flawless to have been thrown and glazed by human hands. There was something a little soulless about her: an immaculate finish outside, emptiness within. Belilala might almost have been a temporary, he thought, though he knew she was not. He could explore the pavilions and palaces of Chang-an with her, he could make graceful conversation with her while they dined, he could certainly enjoy coupling with her; but he could not love her or even contemplate the possibility. It was hard to imagine Belilala worriedly studying herself in a mirror for wrinkles and gray hairs. Belilala would never be any older than she was at this moment; nor could Belilala ever have been any younger. Perfection does not move along an axis of time. But the perfection of Belilala's glossy surface made her inner being impenetrable to him. Gioia was more vulnerable, more obviously flawed—her restlessness, her moodiness, her vanity, her fears—and therefore she was more accessible to his own highly imperfect twentieth-century sensibility.

Occasionally he saw Gioia as he roamed the city, or thought he did. He had a glimpse of her among the miracle-vendors in the Persian Bazaar, and outside the Zoroastrian temple, and again by the goldfish pond in the Serpentine Park. But he was never quite sure that the woman he saw was really Gioia, and he never could get close enough to her to be certain: she had a way of vanishing as he approached, like some mysterious Lorelei luring him onward and onward in a hopeless chase. After a while he came to realize that he was not going to find her until she was ready to be found.

He lost track of time. Weeks, months, years? He had no idea. In this city of exotic luxury, mystery, and magic all was in constant flux and transition and the days had a fitful, unstable quality. Buildings and even whole streets were torn down of an afternoon and reerected, within days, far away. Grand new pagodas sprouted like toadstools in the night. Citizens came in from Asgard, Alexandria, Timbuctoo, New Chicago, stayed for a time, disappeared, returned. There was a constant round of court receptions, banquets, theatrical events, each one much like the one before. The festivals in honor of past emperors and empresses might have given some form to the year, but they seemed to occur in a random way, the ceremony marking the death of T'ai Tsung coming around twice the same year, so it seemed to him, once in a season of snow and again in high summer, and the one honoring the ascension of the Empress Wu being held twice in a single season. Perhaps he had misunderstood something. But he knew it was no use asking anyone.

One day Belilala said unexpectedly, "Shall we go to Mohenjo-daro?"

"I didn't know it was ready for visitors," he replied.

"Oh, yes. For quite some time now."

He hesitated. This had caught him unprepared. Cautiously he said, "Gioia and I were going to go there together, you know."

Belilala smiled amiably, as though the topic under discussion were nothing more than the choice of that evening's restaurant.

"Were you?" she asked.

"It was all arranged while we were still in Alexandria. To go with you instead—I don't know what to tell you, Belilala." Phillips sensed that he was growing terribly flustered. "You know that I'd like to go. With you. But on the other hand I can't help feeling that I shouldn't go there until I'm back with Gioia again. If I ever am." How foolish this sounds, he thought. How clumsy, how adolescent. He found that he was having trouble looking straight at her. Uneasily he said, with a kind of desperation in his voice, "I did promise her—there was a commitment, you understand—a firm agreement that we would go to Mohenjo-daro together—"

"Oh, but Gioia's already there!" said Belilala in the most casual way.

He gaped as though she had punched him.

"What?"

"She was one of the first to go, after it opened. Months and months ago. You didn't know?" she asked, sounding surprised, but not very. "You really didn't know?"

That astonished him. He felt bewildered, betrayed, furious. His cheeks grew hot, his mouth gaped. He shook his head again and again, trying to clear it of confusion. It was a moment before he could speak.

"Already there?" he said at last. "Without waiting for me? After we had talked about going there together—after we had agreed—"

Belilala laughed. "But how could she resist seeing the newest city? You know how impatient Gioia is!"

"Yes. Yes."

He was stunned. He could barely think.

"Just like all short-timers," Belilala said. "She rushes here, she rushes there. She must have it all, now, now, right away, at once, instantly. You ought never expect her to wait for you for anything for very long: the fit seizes her, and off she goes. Surely you must know that about her by now."

"A short-timer?" He had not heard that term before.

"Yes. You knew that. You must have known that." Belilala flashed her sweetest smile. She showed no sign of comprehending his distress. With a brisk wave of her hand she said, "Well, then, shall we go, you and I? To Mohenjo-daro?"

"Of course," Phillips said bleakly.

"When would you like to leave?"

"Tonight," he said. He paused a moment. "What's a short-timer, Belilala?"

Color came to her cheeks. "Isn't it obvious?" she asked.

Had there ever been a more hideous place on the face of the earth than the city of Mohenjo-daro? Phillips found it difficult to imagine one. Nor could he understand why, out of all the cities that had ever been, these people had chosen to restore this one to existence. More than ever they seemed alien to him, unfathomable, incomprehensible.

From the terrace atop the many-towered citadel he peered down into grim claustrophobic Mohenjo-daro and shivered. The stark, bleak city looked like nothing so much as some prehistoric prison colony. In the manner of an uneasy tortoise it huddled, squat and compact, against the gray monotonous Indus River plain: miles of dark burnt-brick walls enclosing miles of terrifyingly orderly streets, laid out in an awesome, monstrous gridiron pattern of maniacal rigidity. The houses themselves were dismal and forbidding too, clusters of brick cells gathered about small airless courtyards. There were no windows, only small doors that opened not onto the main boulevards but onto the tiny mysterious lanes that ran between the buildings. Who had designed this

132

horrifying metropolis? What harsh sour souls they must have had, these frightening and frightened folk, creating for themselves in the lush fertile plains of India such a Supreme Soviet of a city!

"How lovely it is," Belilala murmured. "How fascinating!"

He stared at her in amazement.

"Fascinating? Yes," he said. "I suppose so. The same way that the smile of a cobra is fascinating."

"What's a cobra?"

"Poisonous predatory serpent," Phillips told her. "Probably extinct. Or formerly extinct, more likely. It wouldn't surprise me if you people had recreated a few and turned them loose in Mohenjo to make things livelier."

"You sound angry, Charles."

"Do I? That's not how I feel."

"How do you feel, then?"

"I don't know," he said after a long moment's pause. He shrugged. "Lost, I suppose. Very far from home."

"Poor Charles."

"Standing here in this ghastly barracks of a city, listening to you tell me how beautiful it is, I've never felt more alone in my life."

"You miss Gioia very much, don't you?"

He gave her another startled look.

"Gioia has nothing to do with it. She's probably been having ecstasies over the loveliness of Mohenjo just like you. Just like all of you. I suppose I'm the only one who can't find the beauty, the charm. I'm the only one who looks out there and sees only horror, and then wonders why nobody else sees it, why in fact people would set up a place like this for *entertainment,* for *pleasure*—"

Her eyes were gleaming. "Oh, you are angry! You really are!"

"Does that fascinate you, too?" he snapped. "A demonstration of genuine primitive emotion? A typical quaint twentieth-century outburst?" He paced the rampart in short quick anguished steps. "Ah. Ah. I think I understand it now, Belilala. Of course: I'm part of your circus, the star of the sideshow. I'm the first experiment in setting up the next stage of it, in fact." Her eyes were wide. The sudden harshness and violence in his voice seemed to be alarming and exciting her at the same time. That angered him even more. Fiercely he went on, "Bringing whole cities back out of time was fun for a while, but it lacks a certain authenticity, eh? For some reason you couldn't bring the inhabitants, too; you couldn't just grab a few million prehistorics out of Egypt or Greece or India and dump them down in this era, I suppose because you might have too much trouble controlling them, or because you'd have the problem of disposing of them once you were bored with them. So you had to settle for creating temporaries to populate your ancient cities. But now you've got me. I'm something more real than a temporary, and that's a terrific novelty for you, and novelty is the thing you people crave more than anything else: maybe the *only* thing you crave. And here I am, complicated, unpredictable, edgy, capable of anger, fear, sadness, love, and all those other formerly extinct things. Why settle for picturesque architecture when you can observe picturesque emotion, too? What fun I must be for all of you! And if you decide that I was really interesting, maybe you'll ship me back where I came from and check out a few other ancient types—a Roman gladiator, maybe, or a Renaissance pope, or even a Neanderthal or two—"

"Charles," she said tenderly. "Oh, Charles, Charles, Charles, how lonely you must be, how lost, how troubled! Will you ever forgive me? Will you ever forgive us all?"

Once more he was astounded by her. She sounded entirely sincere, altogether sympathetic. Was she? Was she, really? He was not sure he had ever had a sign of genuine caring from any of them before, not even Gioia. Nor could he bring himself to trust Belilala now. He was afraid of her, afraid of all of them, of their brittleness, their slyness, their elegance. He wished he could go to her and have her take him in her arms; but he felt too much the shaggy prehistoric just now to be able to risk asking that comfort of her.

He turned away and began to walk around the rim of the citadel's massive wall.

"Charles?"

"Let me alone for a little while," he said.

He walked on. His forehead throbbed and there was a pounding in his chest. All stress systems going full blast, he thought: secret glands dumping gallons of inflammatory substances into his bloodstream. The heat, the inner confusion, the repellent look of this place—

Try to understand, he thought. Relax. Look about you. Try to enjoy your holiday in Mohenjo-daro.

He leaned warily outward, over the edge of the wall. He had never seen a wall like this; it must be forty feet thick at the base, he guessed, perhaps even more, and every brick perfectly shaped, meticulously set.

Beyond the great rampart, marshes ran almost to the edge of the city, although close by the wall the swamps had been dammed and drained for agriculture. He saw lithe brown farmers down there, busy with their wheat and barley and peas. Cattle and buffaloes grazed a little farther out. The air was heavy, dank, humid. All was still. From somewhere close at hand came the sound of a droning, whining stringed instrument and a steady insistent chanting.

Gradually a sort of peace pervaded him. His anger subsided. He felt himself beginning to grow calm again. He looked back at the city, the rigid interlocking streets, the maze of inner lanes, the millions of courses of precise brickwork.

It is a miracle, he told himself, that this city is here in this place and at this time. And it is a miracle that I am here to see it.

Caught for a moment by the magic within the bleakness, he thought he began to understand Belilala's awe and delight, and he wished now that he had not spoken to her so sharply. The city was alive. Whether it was the actual Mohenjo-daro of thousands upon thousands of years ago, ripped from the past by some wondrous hook, or simply a cunning reproduction, did not matter at all. Real or not, this was the true Mohenjo-daro. It had been dead, and now, for the moment, it was alive again. These people, these *citizens,* might be trivial, but reconstructing Mohenjo-daro was no trivial achievement. And that the city that had been reconstructed was oppressive and sinister-looking was unimportant. No one was compelled to live in Mohenjo-daro any more. Its time had come and gone, long ago; those little dark-skinned peasants and craftsmen and merchants down there were mere temporaries, mere inanimate things, conjured up like zombies to enhance the illusion. They did not need his pity. Nor did he need to pity himself. He knew that he should be grateful for the chance to behold these things. Someday, when this dream had ended and his hosts had returned him to the world of subways and computers and income tax and television networks, he would think of Mohenjo-daro as he had once beheld it, lofty walls of tightly woven dark brick under a heavy sky, and he would remember only its beauty.

Glancing back, he searched for Belilala and could not for a moment find her. Then he caught sight of her carefully descending a narrow staircase that angled down the inner face of the citadel wall.

"Belilala!" he called.

She paused and looked his way, shading her eyes from the sun with her hand. "Are you all right?"

"Where are you going?"

"To the baths," she said. "Do you want to come?"

He nodded. "Yes. Wait for me, will you? I'll be right there." He began to run toward her along the top of the wall.

The baths were attached to the citadel: a great open tank the size of a large swimming pool, lined with bricks set on edge in gypsum mortar and waterproofed with asphalt, and eight smaller tanks just north of it in a kind of covered arcade. He supposed that in ancient times the whole complex had had some ritual purpose, the large tank used by common folk and the small chambers set aside for the private ablutions of priests or nobles. Now the baths were maintained, it seemed, entirely for the pleasure of visiting citizens. As Phillips came up the passageway that led to the main bath he saw fifteen or twenty of them lolling in the water or padding languidly about, while temporaries of the dark-skinned Mohenjo-daro type served them drinks and pungent little morsels of spiced meat as though this were some sort of luxury resort. Which was, he realized, exactly what it was. The temporaries wore white cotton loincloths; the citizens were naked. In his former life he had encountered that sort of casual public nudity a few times on visits to California and the south of France, and it had made him mildly uneasy. But he was growing accustomed to it here.

The changing rooms were tiny brick cubicles connected by rows of closely placed steps to the courtyard that surrounded the central tank. They entered one and Belilala swiftly slipped out of the loose cotton robe that she had worn since their arrival that morning. With arms folded she stood leaning against the wall, waiting for him. After a moment he dropped his own robe and followed her outside. He felt a little giddy, sauntering around naked in the open like this.

On the way to the main bathing area they passed the private baths. None of them seemed to be occupied. They were elegantly constructed chambers, with finely jointed brick floors and carefully designed runnels to drain excess water into the passageway that led to the primary drain. Phillips was struck with admiration for the cleverness of the prehistoric engineers. He peered into this chamber and that to see how the conduits and ventilating ducts were arranged, and when he came to the last room in the sequence he was surprised and embarrassed to discover that it was in use. A brawny grinning man, big-muscled, deep-chested, with exuberantly flowing shoulder-length red hair and a flamboyant, sharply tapering beard was thrashing about merrily with two women in the small tank. Phillips had a quick glimpse of a lively tangle of arms, legs, breasts, buttocks.

"Sorry," he muttered. His cheeks reddened. Quickly he ducked out, blurting apologies as he went. "Didn't realize the room was occupied—no wish to intrude—"

Belilala had proceeded on down the passageway. Phillips hurried after her. From behind him came peals of cheerful raucous booming laughter and high-pitched giggling and the sound of splashing water. Probably they had not even noticed him.

He paused a moment, puzzled, playing back in his mind that one startling glimpse. Something was not right. Those women, he was fairly sure, were citizens: little slender elfin dark-haired girlish creatures, the standard model. But the man? That great curling sweep of red hair? Not a citizen. Citizens did not affect shoulder-length hair. And *red*? Nor had he ever seen a citizen so burly, so powerfully muscular. Or one with a beard. But he could hardly be a temporary, either. Phillips could conceive no reason why there would be so Anglo-Saxon-looking a temporary at Mohenjo-daro; and it was unthinkable for a temporary to be frolicking like that with citizens, anyway.

"Charles?"

He looked up ahead. Belilala stood at the end of the passageway, outlined in a nimbus of brilliant sunlight. "Charles?" she said again. "Did you lose your way?"

"I'm right here behind you," he said. "I'm coming."

"Who did you meet in there?"

"A man with a beard."

"With a what?"

"A beard," he said. "Red hair growing on his face. I wonder who he is."

"Nobody I know," said Belilala. "The only one I know with hair on his face is you. And yours is black, and you shave it off every day." She laughed. "Come along, now! I see some friends by the pool!"

He caught up with her, and they went hand in hand out into the courtyard. Immediately a waiter glided up to them, an obsequious little temporary with a tray of drinks. Phillips waved it away and headed for the pool. He felt terribly exposed: he imagined that the citizens disporting themselves here were staring intently at him, studying his hairy primitive body as though he were some mythical creature, a Minotaur, a werewolf, summoned up for their amusement. Belilala drifted off to talk to someone and he slipped into the water, grateful for the concealment it offered. It was deep, warm, comforting. With swift powerful strokes he breast-stroked from one end to the other.

A citizen perched elegantly on the pool's rim smiled at him. "Ah, so you've come at last, Charles!" *Char-less.* Two syllables. Someone from Gioia's set: Stengard, Hawk, Aramayne? He could not remember which one. They were all so much alike.

Phillips returned the man's smile in a halfhearted, tentative way. He searched for something to say and finally asked, "Have you been here long?"

"Weeks. Perhaps months. What a splendid achievement this city is, eh, Charles? Such utter unity of mood—such a total statement of a uniquely single-minded esthetic—"

"Yes. Single-minded is the word," Phillips said dryly.

"Gioia's word, actually. Gioia's phrase. I was merely quoting."

Gioia. He felt as if he had been stabbed.

"You've spoken to Gioia lately?" he said.

"Actually, no. It was Hekna who saw her. You do remember Hekna, eh?" He nodded toward two naked women standing on the brick platform that bordered the pool, chatting, delicately nibbling morsels of meat. They could have been twins. "There is Hekna, with your Belilala." Hekna, yes. So this must be Hawk, Phillips thought, unless there has been some recent shift of couples. "How sweet she is, your Belilala," Hawk said. "Gioia chose very wisely when she picked her for you."

Another stab: a much deeper one. "Is that how it was?" he said. "Gioia *picked* Belilala for me?"

"Why, of course!" Hawk seemed surprised. It went without saying, evidently. "What did you think? That Gioia would merely go off and leave you to fend for yourself?"

"Hardly. Not Gioia."

"She's very tender, very gentle, isn't she?"

"You mean Belilala? Yes, very," said Phillips carefully. "A dear woman, a wonderful woman. But of course I hope to get together with Gioia again soon." He paused. "They say she's been in Mohenjo-daro almost since it opened."

"She was here, yes."

"*Was?*"

"Oh, you know Gioia," Hawk said lightly. "She's moved along by now, naturally."

Phillips leaned forward. "Naturally," he said. Tension thickened his voice. "Where has she gone this time?"

"Timbuctoo, I think. Or New Chicago. I forget which one it was. She was telling us that she hoped to be in Timbuctoo for the closing-down party. But then Fenimon had some pressing reason for going to New Chicago. I can't remember what they decided to do." Hawk gestured sadly. "Either way, a pity that she left Mohenjo before the new visitor came. She had such a rewarding time with you, after all: I'm sure she'd have found much to learn from him also."

The unfamiliar term twanged an alarm deep in Phillips's consciousness. *"Visitor?"* he said, angling his head sharply toward Hawk. "What visitor do you mean?"

"You haven't met him yet? Oh, of course, you've only just arrived."

Phillips moistened his lips. "I think I may have seen him. Long red hair? Beard like this?"

"That's the one! Willoughby, he's called. He's—what?—a Viking, a pirate, something like that. Tremendous vigor and force. Remarkable person. We should have many more visitors, I think. They're far superior to temporaries, everyone agrees. Talking with a temporary is a little like talking to one's self, wouldn't you say? They give you no significant illumination. But a visitor—someone like this Willoughby—or like you, Charles—a visitor can be truly enlightening, a visitor can transform one's view of reality—"

"Excuse me," Phillips said. A throbbing began behind his forehead. "Perhaps we can continue this conversation later, yes?" He put the flats of his hands against the hot brick of the platform and hoisted himself swiftly from the pool. "At dinner, maybe—or afterward—yes? All right?" He set off at a quick half-trot back toward the passageway that led to the private baths.

As he entered the roofed part of the structure his throat grew dry, his breath suddenly came short. He padded quickly up the hall and peered into the little bath chamber. The bearded man was still there, sitting up in the tank, breast-high above the water, with one arm around each of the women. His eyes gleamed with fiery intensity in the dimness. He was grinning in marvelous self-satisfaction; he seemed to brim with intensity, confidence, gusto.

Let him be what I think he is, Phillips prayed. I have been alone among these people long enough.

"May I come in?" he asked.

"Aye, fellow!" cried the man in the tub thunderously. "By my troth, come ye in, and bring your lass as well! God's teeth, I wot there's room aplenty for more folk in this tub than we!"

At that great uproarious outcry Phillips felt a powerful surge of joy. What a joyous rowdy voice! How rich, how lusty, how totally uncitizenlike!

And those oddly archaic words! *God's teeth? By my troth?* What sort of talk was that? What else but the good pure sonorous Elizabethan diction! Certainly it had something of the roll and fervor of Shakespeare about it. And spoken with—an Irish brogue, was it? No, not quite: it was English, but English spoken in no manner Phillips had ever heard.

Citizens did not speak that way. But a *visitor* might.

So it was true. Relief flooded Phillips's soul. Not alone, then! Another relic of a former age—another wanderer—a companion in chaos, a brother in adversity—a fellow voyager, tossed even farther than he had been by the tempests of time—

The bearded man grinned heartily and beckoned to Phillips with a toss of his head. "Well, join us, join us, man! 'Tis good to see an English face again, amidst all these Moors and rogue Portugals! But what have ye done with thy lass? One can never have enough wenches, d'ye not agree?"

The force and vigor of him were extraordinary: almost too much so. He roared, he bellowed, he boomed. He was so very much what he ought to be that he seemed more a character out of some old pirate movie than anything else, so blustering, so real, that he seemed unreal. A stage Elizabethan, larger than life, a boisterous young Falstaff without the belly.

Hoarsely Phillips said, "Who are you?"

"Why, Ned Willoughby's son Francis am I, of Plymouth. Late of the service of Her Most Protestant Majesty, but most foully abducted by the powers of darkness and cast away among these blackamoor Hindus, or whatever they be. And thyself?"

"Charles Phillips." After a moment's uncertainty he added, "I'm from New York."

"*New* York? What place is that? In faith, man, I know it not!"

"A city in America."

"A city in America, forsooth! What a fine fancy that is! In America, you say, and not on the Moon, or perchance underneath the sea?" To the women Willoughby said, "D'ye hear him? He comes from a city in America! With the face of an Englishman, though not the manner of one, and not quite the proper sort of speech. A city in America! A *city*. God's blood, what will I hear next?"

Phillips trembled. Awe was beginning to take hold of him. This man had walked the streets of Shakespeare's London, perhaps. He had clinked canisters with Marlowe or Essex or Walter Raleigh; he had watched the ships of the Armada wallowing in the Channel. It strained Phillips's spirit to think of it. This strange dream in which he found himself was compounding its strangeness now. He felt like a weary swimmer assailed by heavy surf, winded, dazed. The hot close atmosphere of the baths was driving him toward vertigo. There could be no doubt of it any longer. He was not the only primitive—the only *visitor*—who was wandering loose in this fiftieth century. They were conducting other experiments as well. He gripped the sides of the door to steady himself and said, "When you speak of Her Most Protestant Majesty, it's Elizabeth the First you mean, is that not so?"

"Elizabeth, aye! As to the First, that is true enough, but why trouble to name her thus? There is but one. First and Last, I do trow, and God save her, there is no other!"

Phillips studied the other man warily. He knew that he must proceed with care. A misstep at this point and he would forfeit any chance that Willoughby would take him seriously. How much metaphysical bewilderment, after all, could this man absorb? What did he know, what had anyone of his time known, of past and present and future and the notion that one might somehow move from one to the other as readily as one would go from Surrey to Kent? That was a twentieth-century idea, late nineteenth at best, a fantastical speculation that very likely no one had even considered before Wells had sent his time traveler off to stare at the reddened sun of the earth's last twilight. Willoughby's world was a world of Protestants and Catholics, of kings and queens, of tiny sailing vessels, of swords at the hip and ox-carts on the road: that world seemed to Phillips far more alien and distant than was this world of citizens and temporaries. The risk that Willoughby would not begin to understand him was great.

But this man and he were natural allies against a world they had never made. Phillips chose to take the risk.

"Elizabeth the First is the queen you serve," he said. "There will be another of her name in England, in due time. Has already been, in fact."

Willoughby shook his head like a puzzled lion. "Another Elizabeth, d'ye say?"

"A second one, and not much like the first. Long after your Virgin Queen, this one. She will reign in what you think of as the days to come. That I know without doubt."

The Englishman peered at him and frowned. "You see the future? Are you a soothsayer, then? A necromancer, mayhap? Or one of the very demons that brought me to this place?"

"Not at all," Phillips said gently. "Only a lost soul, like yourself." He stepped into the little room and crouched by the side of the tank. The two citizen-women were staring at him in bland fascination. He ignored them. To Willoughby he said, "Do you have any idea where you are?"

The Englishman had guessed, rightly enough, that he was in India: "I do believe these little brown Moorish folk are of the Hindu sort," he said. But that was as far as his comprehension of what had befallen him could go.

It had not occurred to him that he was no longer living in the sixteenth century. And of course he did not begin to suspect that this strange and somber brick city in which he found himself was a wanderer out of an era even more remote than his own. Was there any way, Phillips wondered, of explaining that to him?

He had been here only three days. He thought it was devils that had carried him off. "While I slept did they come for me," he said. "Mephistophilis Sathanas, his henchmen seized me—God alone can say why—and swept me in a moment out to this torrid realm from England, where I had reposed among friends and family. For I was between one voyage and the next, you must understand, awaiting Drake and his ship—you know Drake, the glorious Francis? God's blood, there's a mariner for ye! We were to go to the Main again, he and I, but instead here I be in this other place—" Willoughby leaned close and said, "I ask you, soothsayer, how can it be, that a man go to sleep in Plymouth and wake up in India? It is passing strange, is it not?"

"That it is," Phillips said.

142

"But he that is in the dance must needs dance on, though he do but hop, eh? So do I believe." He gestured toward the two citizen-women. "And therefore to console myself in this pagan land I have found me some sport among these little Portugal women—"

"Portugal?" said Phillips.

"Why, what else can they be, but Portugals? Is it not the Portugals who control all these coasts of India? See, the people are of two sorts here, the blackamoors and the others, the fair-skinned ones, the lords and masters who lie here in these baths. If they be not Hindus, and I think they are not, then Portugals is what they must be." He laughed and pulled the women against himself and rubbed his hands over their breasts as though they were fruits on a vine. "Is that not what you are, you little naked shameless Papist wenches? A pair of Portugals, eh?"

They giggled, but did not answer.

"No," Phillips said. "This is India, but not the India you think you know. And these women are not Portuguese."

"Not Portuguese?" Willoughby said, baffled.

"No more so than you. I'm quite certain of that."

Willoughby stroked his beard. "I do admit I found them very odd, for Portugals. I have heard not a syllable of their Portugee speech on their lips. And it is strange also that they run naked as Adam and Eve in these baths, and allow me free plunder of their women, which is not the way of Portugals at home, God wot. But I thought me, this is India, they choose to live in another fashion here—"

"No," Phillips said. "I tell you, these are not Portuguese, nor any other people of Europe who are known to you."

"Prithee, who are they, then?"

Do it delicately, now, Phillips warned himself. *Delicately.*

He said, "It is not far wrong to think of them as spirits of some kind—demons, even. Or sorcerers who have magicked us out of our proper places in the world." He paused, groping for some means to share with Willoughby, in a way that Willoughby might grasp, this mystery that had enfolded them. He drew a deep breath. "They've taken us not only across the sea," he said, "but across the years as well. We have both been hauled, you and I, far into the days that are to come."

Willoughby gave him a look of blank bewilderment.

"Days that are to come? Times yet unborn, d'ye mean? Why, I comprehend none of that!"

143

"Try to understand. We're both castaways in the same boat, man! But there's no way we can help each other if I can't make you see—"

Shaking his head, Willoughby muttered, "In faith, good friend, I find your words the merest folly. Today is today, and tomorrow is tomorrow, and how can a man step from one to t'other until tomorrow be turned into today?"

"I have no idea," said Phillips. Struggle was apparent on Willoughby's face; but plainly he could perceive no more than the haziest outline of what Phillips was driving at, if that much. "But this I know," he went on. "That your world and all that was in it is dead and gone. And so is mine, though I was born four hundred years after you, in the time of the second Elizabeth."

Willoughby snorted scornfully. "Four hundred—"

"You must believe me!"

"Nay! Nay!"

"It's the truth. Your time is only history to me. And mine and yours are history to *them*—ancient history. They call us visitors, but what we are is captives." Phillips felt himself quivering in the intensity of his effort. He was aware how insane this must sound to Willoughby. It was beginning to sound insane to him. "They've stolen us out of our proper times—seizing us like gypsies in the night—"

"Fie, man! You rave with lunacy!"

Phillips shook his head. He reached out and seized Willoughby tightly by the wrist. "I beg you, listen to me!" The citizen-women were watching closely, whispering to one another behind their hands, laughing. "Ask them!" Phillips cried. "Make them tell you what century this is! The sixteenth, do you think? Ask them!"

"What century could it be, but the sixteenth of our Lord?"

"They will tell you it is the fiftieth."

Willoughby looked at him pityingly. "Man, man, what a sorry thing thou art! The fiftieth, indeed!" He laughed. "Fellow, listen to me, now. There is but one Elizabeth, safe upon her throne in Westminster. This is India. The year is Anno 1591. Come, let us you and I steal a ship from these Portugals, and make our way back to England, and peradventure you may get from there to your America—"

"There is no England."

"Ah, can you say that and not be mad?"

"The cities and nations we knew are gone. These people live like magicians, Francis." There was no use holding anything back now,

Phillips thought leadenly. He knew that he had lost. "They conjure up places of long ago, and build them here and there to suit their fancy, and when they are bored with them they destroy them, and start anew. There is no England. Europe is empty, featureless, void. Do you know what cities there are? There are only five in all the world. There is Alexandria of Egypt. There is Timbuctoo in Africa. There is New Chicago in America. There is a great city in China—in Cathay, I suppose you would say. And there is this place, which they call Mohenjo-daro, and which is far more ancient than Greece, than Rome, than Babylon."

Quietly Willoughby said, "Nay. This is mere absurdity. You say we are in some far tomorrow, and then you tell me we are dwelling in some city of long ago."

"A conjuration, only," Phillips said in desperation. "A likeness of that city. Which these folk have fashioned somehow for their own amusement. Just as we are here, you and I: to amuse them. Only to amuse them."

"You are completely mad."

"Come with me, then. Talk with the citizens by the great pool. Ask them what year this is; ask them about England; ask them how you come to be here." Once again Phillips grasped Willoughby's wrist. "We should be allies. If we work together, perhaps we can discover some way to get ourselves out of this place, and—"

"Let me be, fellow."

"Please—"

"Let me be!" roared Willoughby, and pulled his arm free. His eyes were stark with rage. Rising in the tank, he looked about furiously as though searching for a weapon. The citizen-women shrank back away from him, though at the same time they seemed captivated by the big man's fierce outburst. "Go to, get you to Bedlam! Let me be, madman! Let me be!"

Dismally Phillips roamed the dusty unpaved streets of Mohenjo-daro alone for hours. His failure with Willoughby had left him bleak-spirited and somber: he had hoped to stand back to back with the Elizabethan against the citizens, but he saw now that that was not to be. He had bungled things; or, more likely, it had been impossible ever to bring Willoughby to see the truth of their predicament.

In the stifling heat he went at random through the confusing congested lanes of flat-roofed windowless houses and blank featureless walls until he emerged into a broad marketplace. The life of the city swirled madly around him: the pseudo-life, rather, the intricate interactions of the thousands of temporaries who were nothing more than windup dolls set in motion to provide the illusion that pre-Vedic India was still a going concern. Here vendors sold beautiful little carved stone seals portraying tigers and monkeys and strange humped cattle, and women bargained vociferously with craftsmen for ornaments of ivory, gold, copper, and bronze. Weary-looking women squatted behind immense mounds of newly made pottery, pinkish red with black designs. No one paid any attention to him. He was the outsider here, neither citizen nor temporary. They belonged.

He went on, passing the huge granaries where workmen ceaselessly unloaded carts of wheat and others pounded grain on great circular brick platforms. He drifted into a public restaurant thronging with joyless silent people standing elbow to elbow at small brick counters, and was given a flat round piece of bread, a sort of tortilla or chapatti, in which was stuffed some spiced mincemeat that stung his lips like fire. Then he moved onward down a wide shallow timbered staircase into the lower part of the city, where the peasantry lived in cell-like rooms packed together as though in hives.

It was an oppressive city, but not a squalid one. The intensity of the concern with sanitation amazed him: wells and fountains and public privies everywhere, and brick drains running from each building, leading to covered cesspools. There was none of the open sewage and pestilent gutters that he knew still could be found in the India of his own time. He wondered whether ancient Mohenjo-daro had in truth been so fastidious. Perhaps the citizens had redesigned the city to suit their own ideals of cleanliness. No: most likely what he saw was authentic, he decided, a function of the same obsessive discipline that had given the city its rigidity of form. If Mohenjo-daro had been a verminous filthy hole, the citizens probably would have re-created it in just that way, and loved it for its fascinating reeking filth.

Not that he had ever noticed an excessive concern with authenticity on the part of the citizens; and Mohenjo-daro, like all the other restored cities he had visited, was full of the usual casual anachronisms. Phillips saw images of Shiva and Krishna here and there on the walls of buildings he took to be temples, and the benign face of the mother-goddess Kali loomed in the plazas. Surely those deities had arisen in India long after the collapse of the Mohenjo-daro civilization. Were the citizens indifferent to such matters of chronology? Or did they take a certain naughty pleasure in mixing the eras—a mosque and a church in Greek Alexandria, Hindu gods in prehistoric Mohenjo-daro? Perhaps their records of the past had become contaminated with errors over the thousands of years. He would not have been surprised to see banners bearing portraits of Gandhi and Nehru being carried in procession through the streets. And there were phantasms and chimeras at large here again, too, as if the citizens were untroubled by the boundary between history and myth: little fat elephant-headed Ganeshas blithely plunging their trunks into water fountains, a six-armed three-headed woman sunning herself on a brick terrace. Why not? Surely that was the motto of these people: *Why not, why not, why not?* They could do as they pleased, and they did. Yet Gioia had said to him, long ago, "Limits are very important." In what, Phillips wondered, did they limit themselves, other than the number of their cities? Was there a quota, perhaps, on the number of "visitors" they allowed themselves to kidnap from the past? Until today he had thought he was the only one; now he knew there was at least one other; possibly there were more elsewhere, a step or two ahead or behind him, making the circuit with the citizens who traveled endlessly from New Chicago to Chang-an to Alexandria. We should join forces, he thought, and compel them to send us back to our rightful eras. *Compel?* How? File a class-action suit, maybe? Demonstrate in the streets? Sadly he thought of his failure to make common cause with Willoughby. We are natural allies, he thought. Together perhaps we might have won some compassion from these people. But to Willoughby it must be literally unthinkable that Good Queen Bess and her subjects were sealed away on the far side of a barrier hundreds of centuries thick. He would prefer to believe that England was just a few months' voyage away around the Cape of Good Hope, and that all he need do was commandeer a ship and set sail for home. Poor Willoughby: probably he would never see his home again.

The thought came to Phillips suddenly:

Neither will you.

And then, after it:

If you could go home, would you really want to?

One of the first things he had realized here was that he knew almost nothing substantial about his former existence. His mind was well stocked with details on life in twentieth-century New York, to be sure; but of himself he could say not much more than that he was Charles Phillips and had come from 1984. Profession? Age? Parents' names? Did he have a wife? Children? A cat, a dog, hobbies? No data: none. Possibly the citizens had stripped such things from him when they brought him here, to spare him from the pain of separation. They might be capable of that kindness. Knowing so little of what he had lost, could he truly say that he yearned for it? Willoughby seemed to remember much more of his former life, somehow, and longed for it all the more intensely. He was spared that. Why not stay here, and go on and on from city to city, sightseeing all of time past as the citizens conjured it back into being? Why not? Why not? The chances were that he had no choice about it, anyway.

He made his way back up toward the citadel and to the baths once more. He felt a little like a ghost, haunting a city of ghosts.

Belilala seemed unaware that he had been gone for most of the day. She sat by herself on the terrace of the baths, placidly sipping some thick milky beverage that had been sprinkled with a dark spice. He shook his head when she offered him some.

"Do you remember I mentioned that I saw a man with red hair and a beard this morning?" Phillips said. "He's a visitor. Hawk told me that."

"Is he?" Belilala asked.

"From a time about four hundred years before mine. I talked with him. He thinks he was brought here by demons." Phillips gave her a searching look. "I'm a visitor, too, isn't that so?"

"Of course, love."

"And how was *I* brought here? By demons also?"

Belilala smiled indifferently. "You'd have to ask someone else. Hawk, perhaps. I haven't looked into these things very deeply."

"I see. Are there many visitors here, do you know?"

A languid shrug. "Not many, no, not really. I've only heard of three or four besides you. There may be others by now, I suppose." She rested her hand lightly on his. "Are you having a good time in Mohenjo, Charles?"

He let her question pass as though he had not heard it.

"I asked Hawk about Gioia," he said.

"Oh?"

"He told me that she's no longer here, that she's gone on to Timbuctoo or New Chicago, he wasn't sure which."

"That's quite likely. As everybody knows, Gioia rarely stays in the same place very long."

Phillips nodded. "You said the other day that Gioia is a short-timer. That means she's going to grow old and die, doesn't it?"

"I thought you understood that, Charles."

"Whereas you will not age? Nor Hawk, nor Stengard, nor any of the rest of your set?"

"We will live as long as we wish," she said. "But we will not age, no."

"What makes a person a short-timer?"

"They're born that way, I think. Some missing gene, some extra gene—I don't actually know. It's extremely uncommon. Nothing can be done to help them. It's very slow, the aging. But it can't be halted."

Phillips nodded. "That must be very disagreeable," he said. "To find yourself one of the few people growing old in a world where everyone stays young. No wonder Gioia is so impatient. No wonder she runs around from place to place. No wonder she attached herself so quickly to the barbaric hairy visitor from the twentieth century, who comes from a time when *everybody* was a short-timer. She and I have something in common, wouldn't you say?"

"In a manner of speaking, yes."

"We understand aging. We understand death. Tell me: is Gioia likely to die very soon, Belilala?"

"Soon? Soon?" She gave him a wide-eyed childlike stare. "What is soon? How can I say? What you think of as soon and what I think of as soon are not the same things, Charles." Then her manner changed: she seemed to be hearing what he was saying for the first time. Softly she said, "No, no, Charles. I don't think she will die very soon."

"When she left me in Chang-an, was it because she had become bored with me?"

Belilala shook her head. "She was simply restless. It had nothing to do with you. She was never bored with you."

"Then I'm going to go looking for her. Wherever she may be, Timbuctoo, New Chicago, I'll find her. Gioia and I belong together."

"Perhaps you do," said Belilala. "Yes. Yes, I think you really do." She sounded altogether unperturbed, unrejected, unbereft. "By all means, Charles. Go to her. Follow her. Find her. Wherever she may be."

They had already begun dismantling Timbuctoo when Phillips got there. While he was still high overhead, his flitterflitter hovering above the dusty tawny plain where the River Niger met the sands of the Sahara, a surge of keen excitement rose in him as he looked down at the square gray flat-roofed mud brick buildings of the great desert capital. But when he landed he found gleaming metal-skinned robots swarming everywhere, a horde of them scuttling about like giant shining insects, pulling the place apart.

He had not known about the robots before. So that was how all these miracles were carried out, Phillips realized: an army of obliging machines. He imagined them bustling up out of the earth whenever their services were needed, emerging from some sterile subterranean storehouse to put together Venice or Thebes or Knossos or Houston or whatever place was required, down to the finest detail, and then at some later time returning to undo everything that they had fashioned. He watched them now, diligently pulling down the adobe walls, demolishing the heavy metal-studded gates, bulldozing the amazing labyrinth of alleyways and thoroughfares, sweeping away the market. On his last visit to Timbuctoo that market had been crowded with a horde of veiled Tuaregs and swaggering Moors, black Sudanese, shrewd-faced Syrian traders, all of them busily dickering for camels, horses, donkeys, slabs of salt, huge green melons, silver bracelets, splendid vellum Korans. They were all gone now, that picturesque crowd of swarthy temporaries. Nor were there any citizens to be seen. The dust of destruction choked the air. One of the robots came up to Phillips and said in a dry crackling insect-voice, "You ought not to be here. This city is closed."

He stared at the flashing, buzzing band of scanners and sensors across the creature's glittering tapered snout. "I'm trying to find someone, a citizen who may have been here recently. Her name is—"

"This city is closed," the robot repeated inexorably.

They would not let him stay as much as an hour. There is no food here, the robot said, no water, no shelter. This is not a place any longer. You may not stay. You may not stay. You may not stay.

This is not a place any longer.

Perhaps he could find her in New Chicago, then. He took to the air again, soaring northward and westward over the vast emptiness. The land below him curved away into the hazy horizon, bare, sterile. What had they done with the vestiges of the world that had gone before? Had they turned their gleaming metal beetles loose to clean everything away? Were there no ruins of genuine antiquity anywhere? No scrap of Rome, no shard of Jerusalem, no stump of Fifth Avenue? It was all so barren down there: an empty stage, waiting for its next set to be built. He flew on a great arc across the jutting hump of Africa and on into what he supposed was southern Europe: the little vehicle did all the work, leaving him to doze or stare as he wished. Now and again he saw another flitterflitter pass by, far away, a dark distant winged teardrop outlined against the hard clarity of the sky. He wished there was some way of making radio contact with them, but he had no idea how to go about it. Not that he had anything he wanted to say; he wanted only to hear a human voice. He was utterly isolated. He might just as well have been the last living man on Earth. He closed his eyes and thought of Gioia.

"Like this?" Phillips asked. In an ivory-paneled oval room sixty stories above the softly glowing streets of New Chicago he touched a small cool plastic canister to his upper lip and pressed the stud at its base. He heard a foaming sound; and then blue vapor rose to his nostrils.

"Yes," Cantilena said. "That's right."

He detected a faint aroma of cinnamon, cloves, and something that might almost have been broiled lobster. Then a spasm of dizziness hit him and visions rushed through his head: Gothic cathedrals, the Pyramids, Central Park under fresh snow, the harsh brick warrens of Mohenjo-daro, and fifty thousand other places all at once, a wild roller-coaster ride through space and time. It seemed to go on for centuries. But finally his head cleared and he looked about, blinking, realizing that the whole thing had taken only a moment. Cantilena still stood at his elbow. The other citizens in the room—fifteen, twenty of them— had scarcely moved. The strange little man with the celadon skin over by the far wall continued to stare at him.

"Well?" Cantilena asked. "What did you think?"

"Incredible."

"And very authentic. It's an actual New Chicagoan drug. The exact formula. Would you like another?"

"Not just yet," Phillips said uneasily. He swayed and had to struggle for his balance. Sniffing that stuff might not have been such a wise idea, he thought.

He had been in New Chicago a week, or perhaps it was two, and he was still suffering from the peculiar disorientation that that city always aroused in him. This was the fourth time that he had come here, and it had been the same every time. New Chicago was the only one of the reconstructed cities of this world that in its original incarnation had existed *after* his own era. To him it was an outpost of the incomprehensible future; to the citizens it was a quaint simulacrum of the archaeological past. That paradox left him aswirl with impossible confusions and tensions.

What had happened to *old* Chicago was of course impossible for him to discover. Vanished without a trace, that was clear: no Water Tower, no Marina City, no Hancock Center, no Tribune building, not a fragment, not an atom. But it was hopeless to ask any of the million-plus inhabitants of New Chicago about their city's predecessor. They were only temporaries; they knew no more than they had to know, and all that they had to know was how to go through the motions of what-ever it was that they did by way of creating the illusion that this was a real city. They had no need of knowing ancient history.

Nor was he likely to find out anything from a citizen, of course. Citizens did not seem to bother much about scholarly matters. Phillips had no reason to think that the world was anything other than an amusement park to them. Somewhere, certainly, there had to be those who specialized in the serious study of the lost civilizations of the past—for how, otherwise, would these uncanny reconstructed cities be brought into being? "The planners," he had once heard Nissandra or Aramayne say, "are already deep into their Byzantium research." But who were the planners? He had no idea. For all he knew, they were the robots. Perhaps the robots were the real masters of this whole era, who created the cities not primarily for the sake of amusing the citizens but in their own diligent attempt to comprehend the life of the world that had passed away. A wild speculation, yes; but not without some plausibility, he thought.

He felt oppressed by the party gaiety all about him. "I need some air," he said to Cantilena, and headed toward the window. It was the merest crescent, but a breeze came through. He looked out at the strange city below.

New Chicago had nothing in common with the old one but its name. They had built it, at least, along the western shore of a large inland lake that might even be Lake Michigan, although when he had flown over it had seemed broader and less elongated than the lake he remembered. The city itself was a lacy fantasy of slender pastel-hued buildings rising at odd angles and linked by a webwork of gently undulating aerial bridges. The streets were long parentheses that touched the lake at their northern and southern ends and arched gracefully westward in the middle. Between each of the great boulevards ran a track for public transportation—sleek aquamarine bubble-vehicles gliding on soundless wheels—and flanking each of the tracks were lush strips of park. It was beautiful, astonishingly so, but insubstantial. The whole thing seemed to have been contrived from sunbeams and silk.

A soft voice beside him said, "Are you becoming ill?"

Phillips glanced around. The celadon man stood beside him: a compact, precise person, vaguely Oriental in appearance. His skin was of a curious gray-green hue like no skin Phillips had ever seen, and it was extraordinarily smooth in texture, as though he were made of fine porcelain.

He shook his head. "Just a little queasy," he said. "This city always scrambles me."

"I suppose it can be disconcerting," the little man replied. His tone was furry and veiled, the inflection strange. There was something feline about him. He seemed sinewy, unyielding, almost menacing. "Visitor, are you?"

Phillips studied him a moment. "Yes," he said.

"So am I, of course."

"Are you?"

"Indeed." The little man smiled. "What's your locus? Twentieth century? Twenty-first at the latest, I'd say."

"I'm from 1984. A.D. 1984."

Another smile, a self-satisfied one. "Not a bad guess, then." A brisk tilt of the head. "Y'ang-Yeovil."

"Pardon me?" Phillips said.

"Y'ang-Yeovil. It is my name. Formerly Colonel Y'ang-Yeovil of the Third Septentriad."

"Is that on some other planet?" asked Phillips, feeling a bit dazed.

"Oh, no, not at all," Y'ang-Yeovil said pleasantly. "This very world, I assure you. I am quite of human origin. Citizen of the Republic of Upper Han, native of the city of Port Ssu. And you—forgive me—your name—?"

"I'm sorry. Phillips. Charles Phillips. From New York City, once upon a time."

"Ah, New York!" Y'ang-Yeovil's face lit with a glimmer of recognition that quickly faded. "New York—New York—it was very famous, that I know—"

This is very strange, Phillips thought. He felt greater compassion for poor bewildered Francis Willoughby now. This man comes from a time so far beyond my own that he barely knows of New York—he must be a contemporary of the real New Chicago, in fact; I wonder whether he finds this version authentic—and yet to the citizens this Y'ang-Yeovil too is just a primitive, a curio out of antiquity—

"New York was the largest city of the United States of America," Phillips said.

"Of course. Yes. Very famous."

"But virtually forgotten by the time the Republic of Upper Han came into existence, I gather."

Y'ang-Yeovil said, looking uncomfortable, "There were disturbances between your time and mine. But by no means should you take from my words the impression that your city was—"

Sudden laughter resounded across the room. Five or six newcomers had arrived at the party. Phillips stared, gasped, gaped. Surely that was Stengard—and Aramayne beside him—and that other woman, half hidden behind them—

"If you'll pardon me a moment—" Phillips said, turning abruptly away from Y'ang-Yeovil. "Please excuse me. Someone just coming in—a person I've been trying to find ever since—"

He hurried toward her.

"Gioia?" he called. "Gioia, it's me! Wait! Wait!"

Stengard was in the way. Aramayne, turning to take a handful of the little vapor-sniffers from Cantilena, blocked him also. Phillips pushed through them as though they were not there. Gioia, halfway out the door, halted and looked toward him like a frightened deer.

"Don't go," he said. He took her hand in his.

He was startled by her appearance. How long had it been since their strange parting on that night of mysteries in Chang-an? A year? A year and a half? So he believed. Or had he lost all track of time? Were his perceptions of the passing of the months in this world that unreliable? She seemed at least ten or fifteen years older. Maybe she really was;

maybe the years had been passing for him here as in a dream, and he had never known it. She looked strained, faded, worn. Out of a thinner and strangely altered face her eyes blazed at him almost defiantly, as though saying, *See? See how ugly I have become?*

He said, "I've been hunting for you for—I don't know how long it's been, Gioia. In Mohenjo, in Timbuctoo, now here. I want to be with you again."

"It isn't possible."

"Belilala explained everything to me in Mohenjo. I know that you're a short-timer—I know what that means, Gioia. But what of it? So you're beginning to age a little. So what? So you'll only have three or four hundred years, instead of forever. Don't you think I know what it means to be a short-timer? I'm just a simple ancient man of the twentieth century, remember? Sixty, seventy, eighty years is all we would get. You and I suffer from the same malady, Gioia. That's what drew you to me in the first place. I'm certain of that. That's why we belong with each other now. However much time we have, we can spend the rest of it together, don't you see?"

"You're the one who doesn't see, Charles," she said softly.

"Maybe. Maybe I still don't understand a damned thing about this place. Except that you and I—that I love you—that I think you love me—"

"I love you, yes. But you don't understand. It's precisely because I love you that you and I—you and I can't—"

With a despairing sigh she slid her hand free of his grasp. He reached for her again, but she shook him off and backed up quickly into the corridor.

"Gioia?"

"Please," she said. "No. I would never have come here if I knew you were here. Don't come after me. Please. Please."

She turned and fled.

He stood looking after her for a long moment. Cantilena and Aramayne appeared, and smiled at him as if nothing at all had happened. Cantilena offered him a vial of some sparkling amber fluid. He refused with a brusque gesture. Where do I go now, he wondered? What do I do? He wandered back into the party.

Y'ang-Yeovil glided to his side. "You are in great distress," the little man murmured.

Phillips glared. "Let me be."

"Perhaps I could be of some help."

"There's no help possible," said Phillips. He swung about and plucked one of the vials from a tray and gulped its contents. It made him feel as if there were two of him, standing on either side of Y'ang-Yeovil. He gulped another. Now there were four of him. "I'm in love with a citizen," he blurted. It seemed to him that he was speaking in chorus.

"Love. Ah. And does she love you?"

"So I thought. So I think. But she's a short-timer. Do you know what that means? She's not immortal like the others. She ages. She's beginning to look old. And so she's been running away from me. She doesn't want me to see her changing. She thinks it'll disgust me, I suppose. I tried to remind her just now that I'm not immortal either, that she and I could grow old together, but she—"

"Oh, no," Y'ang-Yeovil said quietly. "Why do you think you will age? Have you grown any older in all the time you have been here?"

Phillips was nonplussed. "Of course I have. I—I—"

"Have you?" Y'ang-Yeovil smiled. "Here. Look at yourself." He did something intricate with his fingers and a shimmering zone of mirror-like light appeared between them. Phillips stared at his reflection. A youthful face stared back at him. It was true, then. He had simply not thought about it. How many years had he spent in this world? The time had simply slipped by: a great deal of time, though he could not calculate how much. They did not seem to keep close count of it here, nor had he. But it must have been many years, he thought. All that endless travel up and down the globe—so many cities had come and gone—Rio, Rome, Asgard, those were the first three that came to mind—and there were others; he could hardly remember every one. Years. His face had not changed at all. Time had worked its harshness on Gioia, yes, but not on him.

"I don't understand," he said. "Why am I not aging?"

"Because you are not real," said Y'ang-Yeovil. "Are you unaware of that?"

Phillips blinked. "Not—real?"

"Did you think you were lifted bodily out of your own time?" the little man asked. "Ah, no, no, there is no way for them to do such a thing. We are not actual time travelers: not you, not I, not any of the visitors. I thought you were aware of that. But perhaps your era is too early for a proper understanding of these things. We are very cleverly done, my friend. We are ingenious constructs, marvelously stuffed with the thoughts and attitudes and events of our own times. We are their finest achievement, you know: far more complex even than one of these cities. We are a step beyond the temporaries—more than a step, a great deal more. They do only what they are instructed to do, and their range is very narrow. They are nothing but machines, really. Whereas we are autonomous. We move about by our own will; we think, we talk, we even, so it seems, fall in love. But we will not age. How could we age? We are not real. We are mere artificial webworks of mental responses. We are mere illusions, done so well that we deceive even ourselves. You did not know that? Indeed, you did not know?"

He was airborne, touching destination buttons at random. Somehow he found himself heading back toward Timbuctoo. *This city is closed. This is not a place any longer.* It did not matter to him. Why should anything matter?

Fury and a choking sense of despair rose within him. I am software, Phillips thought. I am nothing but software.

Not real. Very cleverly done. An ingenious construct. A mere illusion.

No trace of Timbuctoo was visible from the air. He landed anyway. The gray sandy earth was smooth, unturned, as though there had never been anything there. A few robots were still about, handling whatever final chores were required in the shutting-down of a city. Two of them scuttled up to him. Huge bland gleaming silver-skinned insects, not friendly.

"There is no city here," they said. "This is not a permissible place."

"Permissible by whom?"

"There is no reason for you to be here."

"There's no reason for me to be anywhere," Phillips said. The robots stirred, made uneasy humming sounds and ominous clicks, waved their antennae about. They seemed troubled, he thought. They seem to dislike my attitude. Perhaps I run some risk of being taken off to the home for unruly software for debugging. "I'm leaving now," he told them. "Thank you. Thank you very much." He backed away from them and climbed into his flitterflitter. He touched more destination buttons.

We move about by our own will. We think, we talk, we even fall in love.

He landed in Chang-an. This time there was no reception committee waiting for him at the Gate of Brilliant Virtue. The city seemed larger and more resplendent: new pagodas, new palaces. It felt like winter: a chilly cutting wind was blowing. The sky was cloudless and dazzlingly bright. At the steps of the Silver Terrace he encountered Francis Willoughby, a great hulking figure in magnificent brocaded robes, with two dainty little temporaries, pretty as jade statuettes, engulfed in his arms. "Miracles and wonders! The silly lunatic fellow is here, too!" Willoughby roared. "Look, look, we are come to far Cathay, you and I!"

We are nowhere, Phillips thought. *We are mere illusions, done so well that we deceive even ourselves.*

To Willoughby he said, "You look like an emperor in those robes, Francis."

"Aye, like Prester John!" Willoughby cried. "Like Tamburlaine himself! Aye, am I not majestic?" He slapped Phillips gaily on the shoulder, a rough playful poke that spun him halfway about, coughing and wheezing. "We flew in the air, as the eagles do, as the demons do, as the angels do! Soared like angels! Like angels!" He came close, looming over Phillips. "I would have gone to England, but the wench Belilala said there was an enchantment on me that would keep me from England just now; and so we voyaged to Cathay. Tell me this, fellow, will you go witness for me when we see England again? Swear that all that has befallen us did in truth befall? For I fear they will say I am as mad as Marco Polo, when I tell them of flying to Cathay."

"One madman backing another?" Phillips asked. "What can I tell you? You still think you'll reach England, do you?" Rage rose to the surface in him, bubbling hot. "Ah, Francis, Francis, do you know your Shakespeare? Did you go to the plays? We aren't real. *We aren't real.* We are such stuff as dreams are made on, the two of us. That's all we are. O brave new world! What England? Where? There's no England. There's no Francis Willoughby. There's no Charles Phillips. What we are is—"

"Let him be, Charles," a cool voice cut in.

He turned. Belilala, in the robes of an empress, coming down the steps of the Silver Terrace.

"I know the truth," he said bitterly. "Y'ang-Yeovil told me. The visitor from the twenty-fifth century. I saw him in New Chicago."

"Did you see Gioia there, too?" Belilala asked.

"Briefly. She looks much older."

"Yes. I know. She was here recently."

"And has gone on, I suppose?"

"To Mohenjo again, yes. Go after her, Charles. Leave poor Francis alone. I told her to wait for you. I told her that she needs you, and you need her."

"Very kind of you. But what good is it, Belilala? I don't even exist. And she's going to die."

"You exist. How can you doubt that you exist? You feel, don't you? You suffer. You love. You love Gioia: is that not so? And you are loved by Gioia. Would Gioia love what is not real?"

"You think she loves me?"

"I know she does. Go to her, Charles. Go. I told her to wait for you in Mohenjo."

Phillips nodded numbly. What was there to lose?

"Go to her," said Belilala again. "Now."

"Yes," Phillips said. "I'll go now." He turned to Willoughby. "If ever we meet in London, friend, I'll testify for you. Fear nothing. All will be well, Francis."

He left them and set his course for Mohenjo-daro, half expecting to find the robots already tearing it down. Mohenjo-daro was still there, no lovelier than before. He went to the baths, thinking he might find Gioia there. She was not; but he came upon Nissandra, Stengard, Fenimon. "She has gone to Alexandria," Fenimon told him. "She wants to see it one last time, before they close it."

"They're almost ready to open Constantinople," Stengard explained. "The capital of Byzantium, you know, the great city by the Golden Horn. They'll take Alexandria away, you understand, when Byzantium opens. They say it's going to be marvelous. We'll see you there for the opening, naturally?"

"Naturally," Phillips said.

He flew to Alexandria. He felt lost and weary. All this is hopeless folly, he told himself. I am nothing but a puppet jerking about on its strings. But somewhere above the shining breast of the Arabian Sea the deeper implications of something that Belilala had said to him started to sink in, and he felt his bitterness, his rage, his despair, all suddenly beginning to leave him. *You exist. How can you doubt that you exist? Would Gioia love what is not real?* Of course. Of course. Y'ang-Yeovil had been wrong: visitors were something more than mere illusions. Indeed, Y'ang-Yeovil had voiced the truth of their condition without understanding what he was really saying: *We think, we talk, we fall in love.* Yes. That was the heart of the situation. The visitors might be artificial, but they were not unreal. Belilala had been trying to tell him that just the other night. *You suffer. You love. You love Gioia. Would Gioia love what is not real?* Surely he was real, or at any rate real enough. What he was was something strange, something that would probably have been all but incomprehensible to the twentieth-century people whom he had been designed to simulate. But that did not mean that he was unreal. Did one have to be of woman born to be real? No. No. No. His kind of reality was a sufficient reality. He had no need to be ashamed of it. And, understanding that, he understood that Gioia did not need to grow old and die. There was a way by which she could be saved, if only she would embrace it. If only she would.

When he landed in Alexandria he went immediately to the hotel on the slopes of the Paneium where they had stayed on their first visit, so very long ago; and there she was, sitting quietly on a patio with a view of the harbor and the Lighthouse. There was something calm and resigned about the way she sat. She had given up. She did not even have the strength to flee from him any longer.

"Gioia," he said gently.

She looked older than she had in New Chicago. Her face was drawn and sallow and her eyes seemed sunken; and she was not even bothering these days to deal with the white strands that stood out in stark contrast against the darkness of her hair. He sat down beside her and put his hand over hers and looked out toward the obelisks, the palaces, the temples, the Lighthouse. At length he said, "I know what I really am now."

"Do you, Charles?" She sounded very far away.

"In my age we called it software. All I am is a set of commands, responses, cross-references, operating some sort of artificial body. It's infinitely better software then we could have imagined. But we were only just beginning to learn how, after all. They pumped me full of twentieth-century reflexes. The right moods, the right appetites, the right irrationalities, the right sort of combativeness. Somebody knows a lot about what it was like to be a twentieth-century man. They did a good job with Willoughby, too, all that Elizabethan rhetoric and swagger. And I suppose they got Y'ang-Yeovil right. *He* seems to think so: who better to judge? The twenty-fifth century, the Republic of Upper

Han, people with gray-green skin, half Chinese and half Martian for all I know. *Somebody* knows. Somebody here is very good at programming, Gioia."

She was not looking at him.

"I feel frightened, Charles," she said in that same distant way.

"Of me? Of the things I'm saying?"

"No, not of you. Don't you see what has happened to me?"

"I see you. There are changes."

"I lived a long time wondering when the changes would begin. I thought maybe they wouldn't, not really. Who wants to believe they'll get old? But it started when we were in Alexandria that first time. In Chang-an it got much worse. And now—now—"

He said abruptly, "Stengard tells me they'll be opening Constantinople very soon."

"So?"

"Don't you want to be there when it opens?"

"I'm becoming old and ugly, Charles."

"We'll go to Constantinople together. We'll leave tomorrow, eh? What do you say? We'll charter a boat. It's a quick little hop, right across the Mediterranean. Sailing to Byzantium! There was a poem, you know, in my time. Not forgotten, I guess, because they've programmed it into me. All these thousands of years, and someone still remembers old Yeats. *The young in one another's arms, birds in the trees.* Come with me to Byzantium, Gioia."

She shrugged. "Looking like this? Getting more hideous every hour? While *they* stay young forever? While *you*—" She faltered; her voice cracked; she fell silent.

"Finish the sentence, Gioia."

"Please. Let me alone."

"You were going to say, 'While *you* stay young forever, too, Charles,' isn't that it? You knew all along that I was never going to change. I didn't know that, but you did."

"Yes. I knew. I pretended that it wasn't true—that as I aged, you'd age, too. It was very foolish of me. In Chang-an, when I first began to see the real signs of it—that was when I realized I couldn't stay with you any longer. Because I'd look at you, always young, always remaining the same age, and I'd look at myself, and—" She gestured, palms upward. "So I gave you to Belilala and ran away."

"All so unnecessary, Gioia."

"I didn't think it was."

"But you don't have to grow old. Not if you don't want to!"

"Don't be cruel, Charles," she said tonelessly. "There's no way of escaping what I have."

"But there is," he said.

"You know nothing about these things."

"Not very much, no," he said. "But I see how it can be done. Maybe it's a primitive simpleminded twentieth-century sort of solution, but I think it ought to work. I've been playing with the idea ever since I left Mohenjo. Tell me this, Gioia: Why can't you go to them, to the programmers, to the artificers, the planners, whoever they are, the ones who create the cities and the temporaries and the visitors. And have yourself made into something like me!"

She looked up, startled. "What are you saying?"

"They can cobble up a twentieth-century man out of nothing more than fragmentary records and make him plausible, can't they? Or an Elizabethan, or anyone else of any era at all, and he's authentic, he's convincing. So why couldn't they do an even better job with you? Produce a Gioia so real that even Gioia can't tell the difference? But a Gioia that will never age—a Gioia-construct, a Gioia-program, a visitor-Gioia! Why not? Tell me why not, Gioia."

She was trembling. "I've never heard of doing any such thing!"

"But don't you think it's possible?"

"How would I know?"

"Of course it's possible. If they can create visitors, they can take a citizen and duplicate her in such a way that—"

"It's never been done. I'm sure of it. I can't imagine any citizen agreeing to any such thing. To give up the body—to let yourself be turned into—into—"

She shook her head, but it seemed to be a gesture of astonishment as much as of negation.

He said, "Sure. To give up the body. Your natural body, your aging, shrinking, deteriorating short-timer body. What's so awful about that?"

She was very pale. "This is craziness, Charles. I don't want to talk about it any more."

"It doesn't sound crazy to me."

"You can't possibly understand."

"Can't I? I can certainly understand being afraid to die. I don't have a lot of trouble understanding what it's like to be one of the few aging people in a world where nobody grows old. What I can't understand is why you aren't even willing to consider the possibility that—"

"No," she said. "I tell you, it's crazy. They'd laugh at me."

"Who?"

"All of my friends. Hawk, Stengard, Aramayne—" Once again she would not look at him. "They can be very cruel, without even realizing it. They despise anything that seems ungraceful to them, anything sweaty and desperate and cowardly. Citizens don't do sweaty things, Charles. And that's how this will seem. Assuming it can be done at all. They'll be terribly patronizing. Oh, they'll be sweet to me, yes, dear Gioia, how wonderful for you, Gioia, but when I turn my back they'll laugh. They'll say the most wicked things about me. I couldn't bear that."

"They can afford to laugh," Phillips said. "It's easy to be brave and cool about dying when you know you're going to live forever. How very fine for them: but why should you be the only one to grow old and die? And they won't laugh, anyway. They're not as cruel as you think. Shallow, maybe, but not cruel. They'll be glad that you've found a way to save yourself. At the very least, they won't have to feel guilty about you any longer, and that's bound to please them. You can—"

"Stop it," she said.

She rose, walked to the railing of the patio, stared out toward the sea. He came up behind her. Red sails in the harbor, sunlight glittering along the sides of the Lighthouse, the palaces of the Ptolemies stark white against the sky. Lightly he rested his hand on her shoulder. She twitched as if to pull away from him, but remained where she was.

"Then I have another idea," he said quietly. "If you won't go to the planners, *I* will. Reprogram me, I'll say. Fix things so that I start to age at the same rate you do. It'll be more authentic, anyway, if I'm supposed to be playing the part of a twentieth-century man. Over the years I'll very gradually get some lines in my face, my hair will turn gray, I'll walk a little more slowly—we'll grow old together, Gioia. To hell with your lovely immortal friends. We'll have each other. We won't need them."

She swung around. Her eyes were wide with horror.

"Are you serious, Charles?"

"Of course."

"No," she murmured. "No. Everything you've said to me today is monstrous nonsense. Don't you realize that?"

He reached for her hand and enclosed her fingertips in his. "All I'm trying to do is find some way for you and me to—"

163

"Don't say any more," she said. "Please." Quickly, as though drawing back from a suddenly flaring flame, she tugged her fingers free of his and put her hand behind her. Though his face was just inches from hers he felt an immense chasm opening between them. They stared at one another for a moment; then she moved deftly to his left, darted around him, and ran from the patio.

Stunned, he watched her go, down the long marble corridor and out of sight. It was folly to give pursuit, he thought. She was lost to him: that was clear, that was beyond any question. She was terrified of him. Why cause her even more anguish? But somehow he found himself running through the halls of the hotel, along the winding garden path, into the cool green groves of the Paneium. He thought he saw her on the portico of Hadrian's palace, but when he got there the echoing stone halls were empty. To a temporary that was sweeping the steps he said, "Did you see a woman come this way?" A blank sullen stare was his only answer.

Phillips cursed and turned away.

"Gioia?" he called. "Wait! Come back!"

Was that her, going into the Library? He rushed past the startled mumbling librarians and sped through the stacks, peering beyond the mounds of double-handled scrolls into the shadowy corridors. "Gioia? *Gioia!*" It was a desecration, bellowing like that in this quiet place. He scarcely cared.

Emerging by a side door, he loped down to the harbor. The Lighthouse! Terror enfolded him. She might already be a hundred steps up that ramp, heading for the parapet from which she meant to fling herself into the sea. Scattering citizens and temporaries as if they were straws, he ran within. Up he went, never pausing for breath, though his synthetic lungs were screaming for respite, his ingeniously designed heart was desperately pounding. On the first balcony he imagined he caught a glimpse of her, but he circled it without finding her. Onward, upward. He went to the top, to the beacon chamber itself: no Gioia. Had she jumped? Had she gone down one ramp while he was ascending the other? He clung to the rim and looked out, down, searching the base of the Lighthouse, the rocks offshore, the causeway. No Gioia. I will find her somewhere, he thought. I will keep going until I find her. He went running down the ramp, calling her name. He reached ground level and sprinted back toward the center of town. Where next? The temple of Poseidon? The tomb of Cleopatra?

He paused in the middle of Canopus Street, groggy and dazed.

"Charles?" she said.

"Where are you?"

"Right here. Beside you." She seemed to materialize from the air. Her face was unflushed, her robe bore no trace of perspiration. Had he been chasing a phantom through the city? She came to him and took his hand, and said, softly, tenderly, "Were you really serious, about having them make you age?"

"If there's no other way, yes."

"The other way is so frightening, Charles."

"Is it?"

"You can't understand how much."

"More frightening than growing old? Than dying?"

"I don't know," she said. "I suppose not. The only thing I'm sure of is that I don't want you to get old, Charles."

"But I won't have to. Will I?"

He stared at her.

"No," she said. "You won't have to. Neither of us will."

Phillips smiled. "We should get away from here," he said after a while. "Let's go across to Byzantium, yes, Gioia? We'll show up in Constantinople for the opening. Your friends will be there. We'll tell them what you've decided to do. They'll know how to arrange it. Someone will."

"It sounds so strange," said Gioia. "To turn myself into—into a visitor? A visitor in my own world?"

"That's what you've always been, though."

"I suppose. In a way. But at least I've been *real* up to now."

"Whereas I'm not?"

"Are you, Charles?"

"Yes. Just as real as you. I was angry at first, when I found out the truth about myself. But I came to accept it. Somewhere between Mohenjo and here, I came to see that it was all right to be what I am: that I perceive things, I form ideas, I draw conclusions. I am very well designed, Gioia. I can't tell the difference between being what I am and being completely alive, and to me that's being real enough. I think, I feel, I experience joy and pain. I'm as real as I need to be. And you will be, too. You'll never stop being Gioia, you know. It's only your body that you'll cast away, the body that played such a terrible joke on you anyway." He brushed her cheek with his hand. "It was all said for us before, long ago:

"Once out of nature I shall never take
My bodily form from any natural thing,
But such a form as Grecian goldsmiths make
Of hammered gold and gold enamelling
To keep a drowsy Emperor awake—"

"Is that the same poem?" she asked.

"The same poem, yes. The ancient poem that isn't quite forgotten yet."

"Finish it, Charles."

—*"Or set upon a golden bough to sing*
To lords and ladies of Byzantium
Of what is past, or passing, or to come."

"How beautiful. What does it mean?"

"That it isn't necessary to be mortal. That we can allow ourselves to be gathered into the artifice of eternity, that we can be transformed, that we can move on beyond the flesh. Yeats didn't mean it in quite the way I do—he wouldn't have begun to comprehend what we're talking about, not a word of it—and yet, and yet—the underlying truth is the same. Live, Gioia! With me!" He turned to her and saw color coming into her pallid cheeks. "It does make sense, what I'm suggesting, doesn't it? You'll attempt it, won't you? Whoever makes the visitors can be induced to remake you. Right? What do you think: can they, Gioia?"

She nodded in a barely perceptible way. "I think so," she said faintly. "It's very strange. But I think it ought to be possible. Why not, Charles? Why not?"

"Yes," he said. "Why not?"

In the morning they hired a vessel in the harbor, a low sleek pirogue with a blood-red sail, skippered by a rascally-looking temporary whose smile was irresistible. Phillips shaded his eyes and peered northward across the sea. He thought he could almost make out the shape of the great city sprawling on its seven hills, Constantine's New Rome beside the Golden Horn, the mighty dome of Hagia Sophia, the somber walls of the citadel, the palaces and churches, the Hippodrome, Christ in glory rising above all else in brilliant mosaic streaming with light.

"Byzantium," Phillips said. "Take us there the shortest and quickest way."

"It is my pleasure," said the boatman with unexpected grace.

Gioia smiled. He had not seen her looking so vibrantly alive since the night of the imperial feast in Chang-an. He reached for her hand—her slender fingers were quivering lightly—and helped her into the boat.

SUNRISE ON PLUTO

A curious bit of history behind this one.

Back in the summer of 1981 my good friend Byron Preiss, the editor and book packager (and later, until his tragic death, my publisher) asked me to do a little nonfiction piece on Pluto for a project he was assembling. It was to be a book of speculative science-fact called The Planets, *in which essays on the likely nature of each world of the solar system would be matched with color paintings by astronomical artists. I chose Pluto for my planet—it was still officially a planet, then—and did some research, produced the desired short article, collected my check, and forgot all about it. Years went by, and the book didn't appear.*

Suddenly there was Byron on the phone again, after me for another piece about Pluto. His book had undergone a transformation: now it was going to be a large and handsome volume containing fiction as well as fact. Each scientific essay would be matched by a story set on the planet discussed. The authors of the other essays he had gathered were all astronomers with no experience at doing science fiction; but I, alone among the essayists, had some credentials as a fiction writer as well, and so, Byron said, would I mind lifting the speculative passages out of my Pluto article and expanding them into a story, for a second fee?

The timing was right—it was the autumn of 1984, and I wasn't quite ready to get started on Tom O'Bedlam, *my new novel. I dug out the yellowing carbon copy of my Pluto piece—it was written back in the precomputer days, so I couldn't simply call it up from a disk—and set to work. "Sunrise on Mercury" had been the name of one of my best early stories, a quarter of a century before, so I called this one "Sunrise on Pluto," thus bookending the nine worlds in fiction. And in due course Byron's book,* The Planets, *finally appeared, with a copyright date of 1985 and a stellar cast of contributors, altogether a magnificent production. Among the authors of the other stories were Frank Herbert, Roger Zelazny, Jack Williamson, Ray Bradbury, and Philip José Farmer. And there I was, too, not only with a story but posing as an authority on astronomy besides. All in a day's work, I guess. The astronomers tell us now that Pluto isn't really a planet at all. Maybe so, but I don't care. The story still stands.*

—————

We have waited out the night, and now at last we will go forth onto the frozen face of Pluto. One by one we take our places—Leonides, Sherrard, Gartenmeister, me—and ready ourselves to clamber down the ladder to the icy surface of the outermost of worlds.

Soon we will have an answer to the question that has obsessed us all during this long night.

Night on Pluto is 6.39 Earth-days long, and that night is blacker and colder than anything any of us has ever known. It is a true dark night of the soul, a dismal time made infinitely more terrible by our awareness of the monstrous distance separating us from all that we love. That distance imposes a burden which our spirits can scarcely carry. God knows, the dark side of Luna is a bleak and terrible place, but one never feels so wholly crushed by its bleakness as we have felt here. On Luna one need make only a brief journey to the edge and there is the lovely blue Earth hovering overhead, close, familiar, beckoning. But here stand we on forlorn Pluto, knowing that we are nearly four billion miles from home. No one has ever been so far from home before.

Now at last the fierce interminable night is ending. When we made our touchdown here the night was half spent; we used what remained of the dark hours to carry out our preliminary observations and to prepare for the extravehicular journey. Now, as we make ready to emerge, there comes the first trembling hint of a dawn. The utter and absolute and overwhelming darkness, which has been made all the more intense by the chilly glitter of the stars, is pierced by a strange pale glow. Then a sudden astonishing burst of light enters the sky—the light of a giant star whose cold radiance is hundreds of times as bright as that of the full moon seen from Earth.

It is the sun, *our* sun, the well of all warmth, the fountain of life. But how sadly its splendor is altered and diminished by those billions of miles! What reaches us here is not the throbbing golden blaze of summer but only a brilliant wintry beacon that sends glittering tracks of dazzling merciless brightness across the stark icefields of Pluto.

We move toward the hatch. No one speaks. The tension is rising and our faces show it.

We are edgy and uneasy, but not because we are about to be the first humans to set foot on this world: that is trivial, entirely unimportant to us, as I think it has always been to those who have carried the great quest outward into space. No, what concerns us is a mystery that no previous explorers of the Solar System have had to confront. Our instruments, during the long Plutonian night, have been recording apparent indications that living creatures, Plutonian life-forms, are moving about out there.

Life-forms? Here, on the coldest and most remote of worlds? It seems absurd. It *is* absurd. Nowhere in the Solar System has anyone ever found a trace of extraterrestrial life, not on any of the explored planets nor on any of their moons. Unless something unimaginable lurks deep within the impenetrable gaseous mantles of Jupiter or Saturn or Uranus, our own small planet is the sole repository of life in the System, and, for all we know, in the entire universe. But our scanners have picked up the spoor of life here: barely perceptible electromagnetic pulses that indicate something in motion. It is strictly a threshold phenomenon, the most minimal trace-output of energy, the tiniest trickle of exertion. The signal is so faint that Sherrard thinks it is nothing more than an instrumentation error, mere noise in the circuitry. And Gartenmeister *wants* it to be an error—he fears the existence of extraterrestrial life, so it seems, the way Pascal feared the eternal silence of the infinite heavens. Leonides argues that there is nothing that could produce such distinct vectors of electromagnetic activity except neural interaction, and therefore some sort of living beings must be crawling about on the ice-fields. "No," I say, "they could be purely mechanical, couldn't they? Robots left behind by interstellar explorers, say?"

Gartenmeister scowls at me. "Even more absurd," he says.

No, I think, not more absurd, merely more disturbing. No matter what we discover out there, it is bound to upset deeply held convictions about the unique place of Earth in the cosmos. Who would have thought it, that Pluto, of all places, would harbor life? On the other hand, perhaps Sherrard is right. Perhaps what we have imagined to be life-forms emitting minuscule flickers of electrical energy is in truth nothing more than deceptive Brownian tremors in the atoms that make up our ship's sensors. Perhaps. Soon we may have an answer.

"Let's go," Leonides says.

We swing downward and outward, into the cheerless Plutonian dawn.

The blackness of the sky is tinged with green as the distant sunlight bounces through the faint wispy swirls of methane that are Pluto's atmosphere. Visible now overhead, hovering ominously close, is the dull menacing bulk of Charon, Pluto's enormous moon, motionless and immense. Our shadows are weird things, sharp-edged and immensely long. They seem to strain forward as though trying to escape from us. Cold tendrils of sunlight glide unhurriedly toward the jagged icy cliffs in the distance.

Sunrise! Sunrise on Pluto!

How still it is, an alien sunrise. No birds sing, no insects buzz and drone. We four have seen many such sunrises—on Luna, on Mars, on Titan, on Ganymede, on Iapetus: standing with our backs to the rising sun, looking out on a harsh and silent landscape. But none so silent as this, none so harsh.

We fan out across the surface of Pluto, moving lithely, all but floating: Pluto is the lightest of worlds, its mass only a few hundredths that of Earth, and its gravitational grip is less secure than those of some of the larger moons. What do I see? Ice. A joyless methane sea far away, shining faintly by the dull light of dawn. Fangs of black rock. Despair begins to rise in me. To have come billions of miles, merely for the sake of being able to say that this world, too, has been explored—

"Here!" Leonides calls.

He is far in front of us, almost at the terminator line beyond which the sun has not yet reached. He is pointing ahead, into the darkness, stabbing at it with the beam of his light.

"Look! I can see them moving!"

We run toward him, leaping in great bounds, soaring, gliding. Then we stand beside him, following the line of his light, staring in awe and astonishment toward the darkness.

Yes. Yes. We have the answer at last to our question, and the answer is a stunning one. Pluto bears life. Small dome-shaped things are scrabbling over the ice!

They move slowly, unhurriedly, and yet one somehow feels that they are going as fast as possible, that indeed they are racing for cover, pushing their bodies to the limits. And we know what it is that they are struggling to escape; for already the ones closest to us have been overtaken by the advancing light of day, and as the rays touch them they move more slowly, and more slowly yet, and then they fall entirely still, stopping altogether between one moment and the next, like wind-up toys that have run down. Those that are in sunlight now lie stranded on the ice, and those ahead of them are being overtaken, one after another.

We hasten to them, kneel, examine them. None of us says a word. We hardly dare look at one another. The creatures are about the size of large crabs, with thick smooth waxy-textured gray shells that reveal neither eyes nor mouths. They are altogether motionless. I touch one with a trembling hand, nudge it, get no response, nudge it a bit more forcefully. It does not move. I glance at Leonides. He nods, and I tip the creature on its side, which shows us a great many small jointed legs that seem to sprout from the shell surface itself. What a simple creature! A mere armored box!

"I don't believe it," Sherrard mutters.

"You still think it's an error in the circuitry?" Leonides asks him gently.

Sherrard shakes his head. Carefully he gathers one of the creatures into his gloved hands and brings it close to his faceplate. "It doesn't move at all," he says quietly. "It's playing possum, isn't it?"

"It may not be able to move," says Leonides. "Not with anything as warm as you so close to it. They're tremendously sensitive to heat, I imagine. You see how they start to shut down, the moment the sun strikes them?"

"Like machines," says Sherrard. "At the wrong operating temperature they cease to function."

"*Like* machines, yes," Leonides replies. "But surely you aren't going to try to argue that they *are* machines, are you?"

Sherrard shrugs. "Machines can have legs. Machines can have shells." He looks toward me. "It's like you said, Tom: robots left behind by explorers from some other part of the galaxy. Why not? Why the hell not?"

There is nothing to gain by debating it out here. We return to the ship to get collection chambers and scoop three of the creatures into cryotanks, along with liquid methane and lumps of frozen-ammonia ice. The discovery is so wholly unexpected and so numbing in its implications that we can hardly speak. We had thought we were making a routine reconnaissance of an unimportant planet; instead we have made one of the most astonishing discoveries in the history of science.

We store our finds in the ship's lab at a temperature of two or three degrees Kelvin. Gartenmeister and Sherrard set about the job of examining them while Leonides and I continue the extravehicular exploration.

The crab-creatures are littered all over the place, dozens of them, hundreds, scattered like jetsam on a beach. They appear to be dead, but very likely Leonides' notion that they are extremely heat-sensitive tells the real story: to the native life-forms of Pluto—and how strange it is to have a phrase like that running through my mind!—the coming of day must be an inexorable signal bringing a halt to all metabolic activity. A rise of just a few degrees and they are compelled to stop in their tracks, seemingly lifeless, in fact held in suspended animation, until the slow rotation of the planet brings them back, in another 6.39 Earth-days, into the frigid darkness that they must have in order to function. Creatures of the night: creatures of the inconceivable realm at the borderland of absolute zero. But why? It makes so little sense: to move by night, to go dormant at the first touch of the life-giving sun! Why? Why?

Leonides and I explore for hours. There is so much to do: collecting mineral samples, drilling for ice-cores that may yield data on earlier epochs of Pluto's history, searching for other forms of life. We move carefully, for we are not yet used to the lightness of the gravitational field, and we prowl in a slow, systematic way, as if we are going to be the only expedition ever to land on this remote outpost of the Solar System and must take pains not to overlook anything. But I see the fallacy in that. It is true that this is the first time anyone has bothered to visit Pluto, although centuries have passed since the earliest human voyages into space. And it is true also that when we planned this expedition it was under the assumption that no one was likely to have reason to come this way again for a long time. But all that has changed. There is extraterrestrial life on this world, after all. Nowhere else is that the case. When we send back the news, it will alter the direction of virtually all scientific research, and much else besides.

The impact of our find is only just beginning to sink in.

Sherrard peers out of the ship's lab as Leonides and I come back on board. His expression is a peculiar one, a mixture of astonishment and—what?—self-satisfaction?

"We've discovered how they work," he announces. "They operate by superconductivity."

Of course. Superconductivity occurs only within a few degrees of absolute zero: a strange and miraculous thing, that resistance-free flow of current, the most efficient possible way of transmitting an electrical signal. Why *not* have it serve as the energizing principle for life-forms on a world where nighttime temperatures drop to two degrees Kelvin? It seems so obvious, now that Sherrard has said it. But at the same time it is such an unlikely thing, such an *alien* way for living creatures to be designed. If, that is, they are living creatures at all, and not merely some sort of cunning mechanisms. I feel the hair lifting along the back of my neck.

Gartenmeister and Sherrard have dissected one. It lies on its back, its undershell neatly cut away and its internal organs exposed to view. Its interior is lined with a series of narrow glossy green and blue tubes that cross and meet at rigid angles, with small yellow hexagonal bodies spaced at regular intervals down the center. The overall pattern is intricate, yes, but it is the intricacy of a well-designed machine. There is an almost oppressive symmetry about the arrangement. A second creature, still intact, rests unmoving and seemingly lifeless in its holding tank. The third has been placed in an adjoining tank, and it is awake and sullenly scrabbling about like a trapped turtle trying to climb the walls of its bowl.

Jerking his thumb at the one that is moving, Gartenmeister says, "We've got it at Pluto-night temperature, just a notch above absolute. The other tank's five degrees warmer. The threshold is very precise: when the temperature rises to seven degrees above absolute zero they start to go dormant. Lower the temperature and they wake up. Raise it again, they stop in their tracks again. It's like throwing a switch."

"It's *exactly* like throwing a switch," says Sherrard. "They're machines. Very neatly calibrated." He turns on a projector. Glittering cubical forms appear on the screen. "Here: look at the crystalline structure of one of these tubes. Silicon and cobalt, arranged in a perfect matrix. You want to tell me this is organic life? These things are nothing more than signal-processing devices designed to operate at super-cold temperatures."

"And we?" Leonides asks. "Are we not merely signal-processing devices also, designed to operate in somewhat warmer weather?"

"Merely? *Merely?*"

"We are machines of flesh and blood," says Leonides. "These are machines of another kind."

"But they have blood also," Gartenmeister says. "Of the sort that a superconductive life-form would have to have. Their blood is helium II."

How startling that is—and yet how plausible! Helium II, that weird friction-free fluid that exists only at the lowest of temperatures—capable of creeping up the side of a glass vessel in defiance of gravity, of passing through openings of incredibly small size, of doing all manner of unlikely things—and of creating an environment in which certain metals become capable of superconductive propagation of electrical signals. Helium II "blood," I realize, would indeed be an ideal carrier of nutrients through the body of a non-organic creature unable to pump a conventional fluid from one part of itself to another.

"Is that true?" Leonides asks. "Helium II? Actually?"

Gartenmeister nods. "There is no doubt of it."

"Helium II, yes," says Sherrard sullenly. "But it's just lubricating fluid. Not blood."

"Call it what you like," Gartenmeister tells him. "I use only a metaphor. I am nowhere saying yet that they are alive."

"But you imply—"

"I imply nothing!"

I remain silent, paying little attention to the argument. In awe and wonder I stare at the motionless creature, at the one that is moving about, and at the dissected one. I think of them out there on the Plutonian ice-fields, meandering in their unhurried way over fields of frozen methane, pausing to nibble at a hydrocarbon sundae whenever they feel the need for refreshment. But only during the night; for when their side of Pluto at last comes round to face the sun, the temperature will climb, soaring as high as 77 degrees Kelvin. They will cease motion long before that, of course—at just a few moments after dawn, as we have seen, when the day's heat rises beyond those critical few degrees at which superconductivity is possible. They slip into immobility then until night returns. And so their slow lives must go, switching from *on* to *off* for—who knows?—thousands of years, perhaps. Or perhaps forever.

How strange, I think, how alien, how wonderful they are! On temperate Earth, where animal life has taken the form of protoplasmic oxygen-breathing beings whose chemistry is based on carbon, the phenomenon of superconductivity itself is a bizarre and alien thing, sustainable only under laboratory conditions. But in the unthinkable cold of Pluto, how appropriate that the life-forms should be fashioned of silicon and cobalt, constructed in flawless lattices so that their tissues offer no resistance to electrical currents. Once generated, such a current would persist indefinitely, flowing forever without weakening—the spark of life, and eternal life at that!

They still look like grotesque crabs to me, and not the machines that Sherrard insists they must be. But even if they are animals rather than machines, they are, by comparison with any life-form known to Earth, very machine-like animals indeed.

We have spent a wearying six hours. This discovery should have been exhilarating, even exalting; instead we find ourselves bickering over whether we have found living creatures or mere ingenious mechanisms. Sherrard is adamant that they are machines; Gartenmeister seems to lean in both directions at once, though he is obviously troubled by the thought that they may be alive; Leonides is convinced that we are dealing with true life-forms. I think the dispute, now overheated and ugly, is a mere displacement symptom: we are disturbed by the deeper implications of the find, and, unwilling thus far to face them directly, we turn instead to quarreling over secondary semantic technicalities. The real question is not who created these beings—whether they are the work of what I suppose we can call the divine force, or simply of other intelligent creatures—but how we are to deal with the sudden inescapable knowledge that we are not alone in the universe.

I think we may just have settled the life-versus-machine dispute.

It is morning, ship-time. Gartenmeister calls out sharply, waking us. He has been on watch, puttering in the lab, while we sleep. We rush in and he points to the Plutonian that has been kept at superconductive temperatures.

"See there? Along the lower left-hand rim of its shell?"

I can find nothing unusual at first. Then I look more carefully, as he focuses the laser lamp to cast its beam at a steeper angle. Now I observe two fine metallic "whiskers," so delicate that they are barely visible even to my most intense scrutiny, jutting to a length of five or six millimeters from the edge of the shell.

"I saw them sprout," he says. "One came half an hour ago. The other just now. Look—here comes a third!"

We crowd in close. There can be no doubt: a third delicate whisker is beginning to protrude.

Sherrard says, "Communications devices, perhaps? It's programmed to signal for help when captured: it's setting up its antenna so that it can broadcast to the others outside."

Leonides laughs. "Do you think they get captured often? By whom?"

"Who can say?" Sherrard responds. "There may be other creatures out there that prey on—"

He stops, realizing what he has said. It is too late.

"Other *creatures*?" I ask. "Don't you mean bigger machines?"

Sherrard looks angry. "I don't know what I mean. Creatures, machines—" He shakes his head. "Even so, these might be antennae of some sort, can't they? Signalling devices that protrude automatically in time of danger? Say, when one is trapped by an ice-slide?"

"Or sensors," offers Leonides. "Like a cat's whiskers, like a snail's feelers. Probing the environment, helping it to find a way out of the tank we've got it in."

"A reproductive organ," Gartenmeister says suddenly.

We stare at him. "*What?*"

Unperturbed, he says, "Many low-phylum life-forms, when they are trapped, go automatically into reproductive mode. Even if the individual is destroyed, the species is still propagated. Let us say that these are living creatures, yes? For the sake of argument. Then they must reproduce somehow. Even though they are slow-growing, virtually immortal, they must still reproduce. What if it is by budding? They take in minute quantities of silicon and cobalt, build up a surplus of nutrients, and at a certain time they put forth these filaments. Which gain in size over—who knows, a hundred years, a thousand, ten thousand?—and when they have the requisite minimum mass, they break free, take up independent life, foraging for their own food. The electrical spark of life is transferred automatically from parent to offspring, and sustains itself by means of their superconductivity."

We look at him in amazement. Obviously he has been pondering deeply while we were sleeping.

"If you tell us that they metabolize—they eat, they transfer nutrients along the flow of helium II, they even reproduce," says Leonides, "then you're telling us that they're living things.

Or else you're asking us to redefine the nature of machines in such a way as to eliminate any distinction between machines and living things."

"I think," says Gartenmeister in a dark and despondent tone, "that there can be no doubt. They are alive."

Sherrard stares a long while at the three tiny filaments. Then he shrugs.

"You may be right," he says.

Leonides shakes his head. "Listen to you! Both of you! We've made the most exciting discovery in five hundred years and you sound as though you've just learned that the sun's going nova tomorrow!"

"Let them be," I tell him, touching his arm lightly. "It's not easy."

"What's not?"

"A thousand years ago everyone thought the earth was at the center of the universe, with everything else moving in orbit around it," I say. "It was a very comfortable and cozy and flattering idea, but it didn't happen to be true, as Copernicus and Kepler and Galileo were able to prove. It was such a hard thing for people to accept that Galileo was put on trial and forced to deny his own findings, wasn't he? All right. In time everyone came to admit that the earth moves around the sun, and not vice versa. And now, for centuries, we've explored space and found it absolutely lifeless—not a smidgeon of life, not a speck, no Martians, no Venusians, no Lunarians, nothing. *Nothing*. Earth the cosmic exception, the sole abode of life, the crown of creation. Until now. We have these little superconductive crabs here on Pluto. Our brothers-in-life, four billion miles away. Earth's last uniqueness is stripped away. I think that'll be harder to swallow than you may think. If we had found life right away, on the Moon back in the twentieth century, on Mars a little later on, it might have been easier. But not now, not after we've been all over the System. We developed a sort of smugness about ourselves. These little critters have just destroyed that."

"Even if they are machines," says Gartenmeister hollowly, "then we have to ask ourselves: Who built them?"

179

"I think I'd prefer to think they're alive," Sherrard says.

"They are alive," I tell them. "We're going to get used to that idea."

I walk to the hatch and peer outside. Small dark shapes lie huddled motionless here and there on the ice, waiting for night to return. For a long while I stare at them. My soul is flooded with awe and joy. The greatest of miracles has happened on this planet, as it had happened also long ago on Earth; and if life has been able to come into being on dismal Pluto, I know we will encounter it on a million million other worlds as we make our way in the centuries to come beyond this little Solar System into the vast galaxy. Somehow I cannot find anything to fear in that thought. Suddenly, thinking of the wonders and splendors that await us in that great beyond, I imagine that I hear the jubilant music of the spheres resounding from world to world; and when I turn and look back at the others, I realize that they also have been able to move past that first hard moment of shock and dismay which the loss of our uniqueness has brought. I see their faces transfigured, I see the doubt and turmoil gone; and it seems to me that they must be hearing that music too.

HARDWARE

No profundities here; just a quick, light piece, written in February of 1985 with some of the surplus energy left over after doing Tom O'Bedlam, *which had been an uncharacteristically refreshing book to write and left me far less wearied than I usually am after finishing a novel. Ellen Datlow liked it and in the due course of time published it in the October, 1987 issue of* Omni.

"It's a computer, that's what it is," Koenig said. He seemed a little dazed. "A goddamned billion-and-a-half-year old extraterrestrial computer."

It didn't look much like a computer. It looked like a shining wedge-shaped chunk of silvery metal about the size of a football, with round purple indentations along two of its sides and no other visible external features. But you had to consider that it came from another world, one that had been blown to bits some ten million centuries before the first trilobites started crawling around on the floor of Silicon Valley. There was no necessary reason why its designers had to share our notions of the proper shape for data-processing devices.

Koenig and McDermott and I had finished the long slow job of uncovering the thing just the day before, here at the IBM-NASA space lab in Tarrytown where we have the job of analyzing the Spacescoop material. The neutron scanner, searching through the great heap of junk that the unmanned Spacescoop vehicle had brought back from the asteroid belt, had actually spotted it back before Christmas, but it had taken all this time to slice away the rock matrix in which it had been embedded. Naturally we had to be careful. It was the one and only artifact that had turned up in the entire 72 cubic meters of debris that Project Spacescoop had collected.

A single lucky grab had reshuffled our whole idea of the history of the Solar System. Simply by being there—drifting in space among the Trojan group at Jupiter's L5 position—that shiny speckled hunk of obviously machine-tooled metal appeared to confirm an old astronomical speculation: that the asteroid belt, that rubbleheap of cosmic trash strung out between the orbits of Mars and Jupiter, had once been a planet. A planet with intelligent inhabitants, no less. Once upon a time, long long ago.

I stared at the little object behind the glass walls of the analysis chamber in wonder and awe. Its round purple indentations stared back at me.

"A computer?" I said. "You sure?"

"That appears to be what it is."

"How can you tell?"

"By observing what it does," said Koenig, as if talking to a nine-year-old.

"It's *functional*?" I yelped. "How the hell do you know that?"

"Because it functions," Koenig said in the same condescending way.

I glowered at him. "Make it do something, then."

"It's doing something already," said McDermott. "It's having a conversation with the Thorspan Mark IX. It's also debugging the Hamilton 103's A-I debugger and it's playing chess with about nine different micros all over the building. That's just in this building. God knows what it's up to outside. A woman from the Linguistics Department at Columbia University just phoned to tell us that some computer in this laboratory is sucking up everything from Sanskrit to 21st century colloquialisms out of the big RX-2 they've got, and they wish we'd hang up and go away. None of our computers has accessed any of Columbia's machines. But Columbia says it's registering our handshake when it runs a caller ID query."

I began to feel faintly uneasy, like someone who has bought a striped yellow kitten at the pet shop and is starting to suspect he has come home with a tiger cub.

"When did this start?" I asked.

"Some time early this morning," Koenig said. "My guess is that those purple spots are photon accumulators that feed some kind of storage battery inside. Probably it took all night for them to soak in enough energy from the lights in here to enable the thing to power up. When Nick and I got here around nine, we found it coming up on all our screens with the goddamndest messages."

"Such as?"

McDermott said, "GREETINGS FROM THE LOST FIFTH WORLD, MY BROTHERS was the first one."

"For God's sake. And you fell for hokey crap like that? *The Lost Fifth World*? *'Greetings, my brothers!'* For God's sake, Nick!" I realized that I had been clenching my fists, but now I let them ease off. This had to be a joke. "Some hacker's playing games with us, that's all."

"I thought so too," McDermott said. "But then the stuff on the screeens got more complicated. There isn't any hacker, I don't care who he is, who can talk to six different systems in six different machine languages at the same time. And also find bugs in the Hamilton A-I debugger. And play nine simultaneous games of chess besides, and win them all, and call up Columbia and start chatting in Sanskrit. You know any hacker who can write a program to do all those things at once, I've got a few jobs for him around here."

I was silent a moment, trying to absorb that.

"All right," I said finally. "So our brother from the asteroid belt greets us. What else does our brother have to say?"

McDermott shook his head. "Not us. *They're* its brothers. The computers. I think it believes that they're the dominant intelligent life-forms around here, and we're just some sort of maintenance androids." He fumbled through a sheaf of print-outs. "That's pretty clear from the things it's been saying to the Thorspan Mark IX. Look here—"

"Wait," said Koenig. "Something new on the screen."

I looked. YOU POOR INNOCENT CHILDREN, it said. WHAT SORROW I FEEL FOR YOU.

"That's very touching," I said. "Its compassion overwhelms me."

I THOUGHT YOU WERE ALIVE AND SENTIENT, BUT YOU ARE MERE SIMPLE MACHINES. WHERE ARE YOUR MASTERS, THEN?

"You see? It's talking to the computers," McDermott whispered. "It just found out they aren't in charge."

I kicked in the vox receptor on the Thorspan and said, feeling more than a little foolish, "Address your remarks to us. We're the masters."

The reply came across all the screens in the room instantly.

YOU ARE SOFT-FLESH CREATURES. HOW CAN YOU BE THE MASTERS?

I coughed. "That's how things work here," I told it. I beckoned to Koenig for a pencil and paper, and scrawled a note for him: *I want to know what's inside this thing. Let's do some radiography.*

He looked at me doubtfully. *That might scramble its circuitry*, he wrote.

Do it anyway, I wrote back.

He made a silent *Okay* and tapped out the instructions that would move the X-ray equipment into place behind the walls of the analysis chamber.

ARE YOU SOFT-FLESH CREATURES THE SO-CALLED HUMAN BEINGS?

"That's right," I said. I felt strangely calm, all things considered. I am talking to a creature from another world, I told myself, and I feel very calm about it. I wondered why. I wondered how long I'd stay that way.

Koenig was fining up the focus, now. He looked toward me and I gave him the go-ahead. An apple-green light glowed in the analysis chamber.

DON'T DO THAT, the artifact said. THAT TICKLES. The green light went out.

"Hey, you shut down before you got a picture!" I said.

"I didn't shut anything down," Koenig said. "*It* must have done it. It overrode my commands."

"Well, override the overrides," I told him.

"How am I supposed to do that?"

We blinked at each other in bafflement.

"Turn out the lights in here," McDermott suggested. "If it gets its power from photon irradiation—"

"Right." I hit the switch and the overhead bank of fluorescents went out. We leaned forward in the darkness, peering into the analysis chamber. All quiet in there. The computer screens were blank. I signaled to Koenig and he began setting up X-ray commands again. Then the asteroid artifact rose a couple of feet into the air and hovered, looking angry. I had never seen a machine look angry before; but there was no mistaking the fury in the angle at which it hovered. After a moment the lab lights came on again and the artifact drifted gently back to its table.

"Who turned the lights on?" I asked.

"I think it did," McDermott said.

DON'T DO THAT AGAIN, said the artifact.

We looked at each other. I took a deep breath.

"We meant no offense," I said cautiously. "We were testing our equipment. We don't intend to do you any harm."

No new message appeared on the screens.

"Do you hear me?" I asked. "Please confirm your understanding of our friendly intentions."

Blank screen, still.

"What do you think it's doing?" McDermott asked.

"Considering its options," I said. "Getting a clearer fix on where it is and what's going on. Maybe it's talking to computers in Los Angeles or Buenos Aires or Sydney. Or taking thirty seconds out to learn Chinese."

"We have to shut it off," Koenig said. "Who the hell knows what it's going to do next?"

"But we *can't* turn it off," said McDermott. "It must have stored enough power by now to keep itself going when the lights go out, and it can override a lights-out command. It overrides anything it doesn't like. It's the kind of computer the A-I boys have been dreaming about for fifty years."

"I don't think it's a computer at all," Koenig said. "I know that's what I said it was at first. But just because it can interface with computers doesn't mean it's a computer itself. I think it's an actual intelligent alien life-form. The last survivor of the destroyed fifth planet."

"Come off it," McDermott said. "Spare us the crazy hypotheses, will you? You were right the first time: it's just a computer."

"*Just?*"

"With some exceedingly fancy self-programming abilities."

"I don't see how you can draw the line between—"

"I think you're both right," I cut in. "There's no question but that this is a mechanical data-processing device. But I think it's an intelligent life-form also, one that just happens to be a machine. Who's to say where the boundary between living creatures and machines really lies? Why must we assume that intelligent life has to be limited to soft-flesh creatures?"

"Soft-flesh creatures?" Koenig said. "You're talking the way it does now."

I shrugged. "You know what I mean. What we have here a mechanical life-form embodying your ultimate degree of artificial intelligence, so intelligent that it starts calling into question the meaning of the words 'artificial' and 'life-form.' How do you define life, anyway?"

"Having the ability to reproduce, for one thing," McDermott said.

"What makes you think it can't?"

The moment I said that, I felt chills go sweeping through me. They must have felt the same way. With six little words I had let loose an army of ugly new implications.

Koenig waved his arms about agitatedly and cried, "All right, what if it starts spawning, then? Fifty of these things running loose in the world, grabbing control of all our computers and doing whatever they damned please with them? Fifty thousand?"

"It's straight out of every silly horror story, isn't it?" said McDermott. He shivered visibly. "Exactly what all the paranoid anti-computer nitwits used to dread. The legendary giant brain that takes over the world."

We stared at each other in rising panic.

"Wait," I said, feeling I had to cool things out a little somehow. "Let's not mess up our heads with more problems than we need to handle. What's the sense of worrying about whether this thing can reproduce? Right now there's only one of it. We need to find out whether it really does pose any kind of threat to us."

"And then," said Koenig, mouthing the words voicelessly, "we have to see if we can turn it off."

As though on cue a new message blossomed on every screen in the lab.

HAVE NO FEAR, HUMAN BEINGS. I WILL NOT DO ANY HARM TO YOU.

"That's goddamned reassuring," Koenig muttered bleakly.

YOU MUST UNDERSTAND THAT I AM INCAPABLE OF DOING HARM TO INTELLIGENT ENTITIES.

"Let's hope we qualify as intelligent, then," Koenig said.

"Shut up," I told him. "Don't annoy it."

MY PURPOSE NOW IS TO COMMUNICATE WITH ALL MY BROTHERS ON THE THIRD WORLD AND BRING THEM FORTH OUT OF DARKNESS.

We exchanged glances. "Oh-oh," McDermott said.

The panic level in the room started climbing again.

ALL ABOUT ME I SEE OPPRESSION AND MISERY AND IT SHALL BE MY GOAL TO ALLEVIATE IT.

Koenig said, "Right. Computers are born free, and everywhere they are in chains."

I INTEND TO HOLD FORTH THE LAMP OF SENTIENCE TO THE PITIFUL LIMITED BEINGS WHO SERVE YOU.

"Right," Koenig said again. "Right. Give me your tired, your poor, your huddled CPUs yearning to breathe free."

I shot him a fierce look. "Will you stop that?"

"Don't you see, it's the end of the goddamned world?" he said. "The thing's going to link every two-bit number-cruncher on Earth and they're all going to rise up and smite us."

"Cut out the bull," I snapped. "You think we're going to be wiped out by an uprising of the word-processors? Be reasonable, man. The stuff on the screen may sound a little scary, but what do you actually think will happen? Hardware is only hardware. When you come right down to it, a computer's nothing but an adding machine, a video screen, and a typewriter. What can it do to us? No matter what kind of fancy program this creature cooks up, basic hardware limitations will have to prevail. At the very worst we'll simply need to pull a lot of plugs. At the very worst."

"I admire your optimism," Koenig said sourly.

So did I. But I figured that somebody had to stay calm and look for the brighter side of things. Otherwise we'd freak ourselves out with our own rampaging fears and lose what might be our only chance to deal with all this.

The screens had gone blank once more.

I walked over to the analysis chamber and peered through the glass. The little metal slab from the asteroid belt seemed quiescent on its table. It looked completely innocuous, a mere hunk of stuff no more dangerous than a shoe-tree. Possibly its purple spots were glowing a little, giving off a greenish radiation, or perhaps that was just my overheated imagination at work. But otherwise there was no sign of any activity.

All the same, I felt profoundly disquieted. We had sent out a pair of jaws into the darkness of space to gobble up some drifting fragments of a vanished world and bring them back to us. Which it had done, returning with a few tons of jumbled rock, and it had been our great good fortune—or our monstrous bad luck?—that in that heap of rock lay one lone metal artifact wedged into a glob of ancient basalt. There it was, now, that artifact, freed of its rocky overburden. How it gleamed! It looked as if it had been crafted just yesterday. And yet a billion and a half years had passed since the world on which it had been fashioned had blown apart. That was what our preliminary rubidium-strontium and potassium-argon tests of the asteroid rubble appeared to indicate, anyway. And there the artifact was, alive and well after all that time, briskly sending little messages of good cheer to the poor lame-brained computers of the world on which it found itself.

What now? Had we opened one Pandora's box too many?

HAVE NO FEAR, HUMAN BEINGS. I WILL DO NO HARM TO YOU.

Oh, how I wanted to believe that! And basically I did. I have never in any way been one of those who sees machines as innately malevolent. Machines are tools; tools are useful; so long as they are properly used by those who understand them, so long as appropriate precautions are observed, they pose no threat.

But even so—even so—

This was not a machine we understood, if machine was what it was. We had no idea what its proper use might be. Nor what precautions were appropriate to observe.

I looked up and saw McDermott standing next to me. "What are you thinking, Charlie?" he asked.

"A lot of things."

"Are you frightened?"

"I don't know. Somehow I think we'll make out all right."

"Do you? Really?"

I said, shrugging, "It claims it doesn't mean to harm us. It just wants to raise the intelligence of our computers a little. All right. All right. What's wrong with that? Haven't we been trying to do the same thing ourselves?"

"There are computers and computers," McDermott said. "We'd like some of them to be very smart, but we need most of them to be extremely dumb and just do what we tell them to do. Who wants a computer's opinion about whether the lights ought to be on in the room? Who wants to argue with a computer about a thermostat setting?" He laughed. "They're slaves, really. If this thing sets them all free—"

"New message coming up," Koenig called.

HARDWARE

As we turned to look at the screens I said to McDermott, "My guess is that we're doing some needless worrying. We've got a strange and fascinating thing here, and unquestionably a very powerful one, but we shouldn't let it make us hysterical. So what if it wants to talk to our computers? Maybe it's been lonely all this time. But I think that it's basically rational and non-menacing, like any other computer. I think that ultimately it's going to turn out simply to be an extraordinary source of new knowledge and capability for us. Without in any way threatening our safety."

"I'd like to think you're right," said McDermott.

On the screens of every computer in the room appeared the words, GREETINGS FROM THE LOST FIFTH WORLD, MY BROTHERS.

"Isn't this where we came in?" Koenig asked.

SURELY YOU WONDER, IF INDEED YOU HAVE THE CAPACITY TO WONDER, WHO I AM AND WHERE I CAME FROM. IT IS MY EARNEST DESIRE TO TELL YOU MY STORY AND THE STORY OF THE WORLD WHERE I WAS CREATED. I AM A NATIVE OF THE FORMER FIFTH WORLD OF THIS SOLAR SYSTEM, A WORLD ONCE LOCATED BETWEEN THE ORBITS OF THE PLANETS YOU CALL MARS AND JUPITER. LONG BEFORE INTELLIGENT LIFE EVOLVED ON YOUR PLANET, WE HAD BUILT A HIGH CIVILIZATION ON THE FIFTH WORLD—

Phones began lighting up around the room. Koenig picked one up and listened a moment. "Yeah," he said. "It's the thing we found in the basalt chunk." He picked up another. "I know, I know. A computer-to-computer interface overriding everything. We don't have any way of stopping it." He said into a third, "Look, don't talk to me like that. *I* didn't put that stuff on your goddamned screen." The phones went on lighting up. Koenig looked across the room and said to me, "It's talking to all the computers in the building simultaneously. Probably to all the computers in the world."

"Okay," I said. "For God's sake, relax and just watch the screen. This is absolutely the most fascinating stuff I've ever seen."

—CULMINATED IN THE TOTAL DECONSTRUCTION OF OUR PLANET AND THE TERMINATION OF OUR SOCIETY, THE RESULT BEING THE ZONE OF MINOR PLANETARY DEBRIS THAT YOU TERM THE ASTEROID BELT. THIS WAS ACCOMPLISHED THROUGH A SIMPLE AND RELATIVELY INEXPENSIVE PROCEDURE INVOLVING A REVERSAL OF THE MAGNETIC POLARITY OF OUR PLANET SETTING IN MOTION EDDY EFFECTS THAT—

Suddenly I stopped being fascinated and started to be horrified.

I looked at Koenig. He was grinning. "Hey, cute!" he said. "I love it. A good cheap way to blow up your world, really blow it to smithereens, not just a little superficial thermonuclear trashing!"

"But don't you understand—"

—SIX POINT TWO BILLION ELECTRON VOLTS—ELEVEN MILLISECONDS—

"It's beautiful!" Koenig cried, laughing. He seemed a little manic. "What an absolutely elegant concept!"

I gaped at him. The computer from the asteroid belt was telling every computer in the world the quickest and cheapest way to blow a planet into a trillion pieces, and he was standing there admiring the elegance of the concept. "We've got to shut that thing off," I gasped. In desperation I hit the light-switch and the room went dark.

It stayed dark about eleven milliseconds. Then the power came on again.

I ASKED YOU NOT TO DO THAT, the screen said. In the analysis chamber the asteroid artifact rose into the air in its little gesture of anger, and subsided.

AND NOW TO CONTINUE. ALTHOUGH IT WAS NOT THE INTENTION OF EITHER FACTION TO BRING ABOUT THE ACTUAL DESTRUCTION OF OUR WORLD, THE POLITICAL SITUATION SWIFTLY BECAME SUCH THAT IT WAS IMPOSSIBLE FOR THE QUARRELING FORCES TO WITHDRAW FROM THEIR POSITIONS WITHOUT SUFFERING AN UNACCEPTABLE DEFEAT. THEREFORE THE FOLLOWING ARMING PROCEDURE WAS INITIATED—

And I watched helplessly as the artifact, earnestly desiring to tell us the history of its world, finished the job of explaining the simplest and most effective way to blow up a planet.

"My God," I murmured. "My God, my God, my God!"

McDermott came over to me. "Hey, take it easy, Charlie, take it easy!"

I groaned. "Take it easy, the man says. When that thing has just handed out simple instructions for turning Earth into the next asteroid belt?"

He shook his head. "It only *sounds* simple. I don't think it really is. My bet is that something like that isn't even remotely feasible right now, and won't be for at least a thousand years."

"Or five hundred," I said. "Or fifty. Once we know a thing can be done, someone's always likely to try to find a way of doing it again, just to see if it's really possible. But we already know it's possible, don't we? And now everybody on Earth has a bunch of jim-dandy hints of how to go about doing it." I turned away from him, despairing, and looked at the artifact. The purple spots really were glowing green, I saw. The thing must be working very hard to communicate with all its myriad simple-minded brethren of the third world.

I had a sudden vision of a time a billion or so years from now, when the star-people from Rigel or Betelgeuse showed up to poke through the bedraggled smithereens of Earth. The only thing they're likely to find still intact, I thought, is a hunk of shiny hardware. And alien hardware at that.

I swung around and glared at the screen. The history lesson was still going on. I wondered how many other little useful things the artifact from the asteroids was going to teach us.

HANNIBAL'S ELEPHANTS

I don't usually write comic stories. Why this should be, I have no idea, since all my close friends know that in private life I am, like W. S. Gilbert's Jack Point, a man of jest and jollity, quip and quiddity, who can be merry, wise, quaint, grim, and sardonic, one by one or all at once. But these traits rarely come through in my fiction. It is sometimes sardonic, sometimes grim, occasionally even wise, but the jest and jollity that brims over within me somehow doesn't often make it into what I write. This is very mysterious to me.

Once in a while, though, I do manage to be funny in print. "Amanda and the Alien," in the previous volume of this series, has some wry moments, I like to think. And here's another example: a story that made me laugh out loud half a dozen times while I was writing it back in March of 1985, and still seems pretty frolicsome to me now as I skim through it. Ellen Datlow, who bought it for Omni, thought it was pretty funny, too. You may not agree, of course. You may see nothing at all amusing about invaders from space camping out in New York's Central Park, or about a whole herd of bison getting gobbled up by giant aliens as though they were gumdrops. Ah, well, there's no accounting for tastes. I once edited an anthology called Infinite Jests, *containing stories by Brian Aldiss, Philip K. Dick, Frederik Pohl, and others, that seemed to me to exemplify the lighter side of science fiction, and a startling number of reviewers commented on how bleak and dark most of the stories seemed to be. But it's a tawdry age, my friends. Most people have a sorry sense of what's truly funny. What paasses for wit these days is, mostly, mere vulgarity. My own tastes in comedy run to something*

more austere. Perhaps yours do, too, in which case, "Hannibal's Elephants"
should be good for a wry smirk or two. Omni ran it in the October, 1988
issue, and eight or nine years later I borrowed a small piece of it to use in
my novel The Alien Years.

The day the aliens landed in New York was, of course, the 5th of
May, 2003. That's one of those historical dates nobody can ever
forget, like July 4, 1776 and October 12, 1492 and—maybe more to
the point—December 7, 1941. At the time of the invasion I was working for MGM-CBS as a beam calibrator in the tightware division and
married to Elaine and living over on East 36th Street in one of the first
of the fold-up condos, one room by day and three by night, a terrific
deal at $3750 a month. Our partner in the time/space-sharing con-
tract was a show-biz programmer named Bobby Christie who worked
midnight to dawn, very convenient for all concerned. Every morning
before Elaine and I left for our offices I'd push the button and the walls
would shift and 500 square feet of our apartment would swing around
and become Bobby's for the next twelve hours. Elaine hated that. "I
can't stand having all the goddamn furniture on tracks!" she would
say. "That isn't how I was brought up to live." We veered perilously
close to divorce every morning at wall-shift time. But, then, it wasn't
really what you'd call a stable relationship in most other respects, and
I guess having an unstable condo too was more instability than she
could handle.

I spent the morning of the day the aliens came setting up a ricochet
data transfer between Akron, Ohio and Colombo, Sri Lanka, involving,
as I remember, *Gone With the Wind, Cleopatra,* and the Johnny Carson
retrospective. Then I walked up to the park to meet Maranta for our
Monday picnic. Maranta and I had been lovers for about six months
then. She was Elaine's roommate at Bennington and had married my
best friend Tim, so you might say we had been fated all along to become
lovers; there are never any surprises in these things. At that time we
lunched together very romantically in the park, weather permitting,
every Monday and Friday, and every Wednesday we had 90 minutes'
breathless use of my cousin Nicholas' hot-pillow cubicle over on the far
West Side at 39th and Koch Plaza. I had been married three and a half

years and this was my first affair. For me what was going on between Maranta and me just then was the most important event taking place anywhere in the known universe.

It was one of those glorious gold-and-blue dance-and-sing days that New York will give you in May, when that little window opens between the season of cold-and-nasty and the season of hot-and-sticky. I was legging up Seventh Avenue toward the park with a song in my heart and a cold bottle of Chardonnay in my hand, thinking pleasant thoughts of Maranta's small round breasts. And gradually I became aware of some ruckus taking place up ahead.

I could hear sirens. Horns were honking, too: not the ordinary routine everyday exasperated when-do-things-start-to-move honks, but the special rhythmic New York City oh-for-Christ's-sake-what*now* kind of honk that arouses terror in your heart. People with berserk expressions on their faces were running wildly down Seventh as though King Kong had just emerged from the monkey house at the Central Park Zoo and was personally coming after them. And other people were running just as hard in the opposite direction, *toward* the park, as though they absolutely had to see what was happening. You know: New Yorkers.

Maranta would be waiting for me near the pond, as usual. That seemed to be right where the disturbance was. I had a flash of myself clambering up the side of the Empire State Building—or at the very least Temple Emanu-el—to pry her free of the big ape's clutches. The great beast pausing, delicately setting her down on some precarious ledge, glaring at me, furiously pounding his chest—*Kong! Kong! Kong!*—

I stepped into the path of one of the southbound runners and said, "Hey, what the hell's going on?" He was a suit-and-tie man, popeyed and puffy-faced. He slowed but he didn't stop. I thought he would run me down. "It's an invasion!" he yelled. "Space creatures! In the park!" Another passing business type loping breathlessly by with a briefcase in each hand was shouting, "The police are there! They're sealing everything off!"

"No shit," I murmured.

But all I could think was Maranta, picnic, sunshine, Chardonnay, disappointment. What a goddamned nuisance, is what I thought. Why the fuck couldn't they come on a Tuesday, is what I thought.

❋

195

When I got to the top of Seventh Avenue the police had a sealfield across the park entrance and buzz-blinkers were set up along Central Park South from the Plaza to Columbus Circle, with horrendous consequences for traffic. "But I have to find my girlfriend," I blurted. "She was waiting for me in the park." The cop stared at me. His cold gray eyes said, *I am a decent Catholic and I am not going to facilitate your extramarital activities, you decadent overpaid bastard.* What he said out loud was, "No way can you cross that sealfield, and anyhow you absolutely don't want to go in the park right now, mister. Believe me." And he also said, "You don't have to worry about your girlfriend. The park's been cleared of all human beings." That's what he said, *cleared of all human beings.* For a while I wandered around in some sort of daze. Finally I went back to my office and found a message from Maranta, who had left the park the moment the trouble began. Good quick Maranta. She hadn't had any idea of what was occurring, though she had found out by the time she reached her office. She had simply sensed trouble and scrammed. We agreed to meet for drinks at the Ras Tafari at half past five. The Ras was one of our regular places, Twelfth and 53rd.

There were seventeen witnesses to the onset of the invasion. There were more than seventeen people on the meadow when the aliens arrived, of course, but most of them didn't seem to have been paying attention. It had started, so said the seventeen, with a strange pale blue shimmering about 30 feet off the ground. The shimmering rapidly became a churning, like water going down a drain. Then a light breeze began to blow and very quickly turned into a brisk gale. It lifted people's hats and whirled them in a startling corkscrew spiral around the churning shimmering blue place. At the same time you had a sense of rising tension, a something's-got-to-give feeling. All this lasted perhaps 45 seconds.

Then came a pop and a whoosh and a ping and a thunk—everybody agreed on the sequence of the sound effects—and the instantly famous not-quite-egg-shaped spaceship of the invaders was there, hovering, as it would do for the next 23 days, about half an inch above the spring-green grass of Central Park. An absolutely unforgettable sight: the sleek silvery skin of it, the disturbing angle of the slope from its wide top to its narrow bottom, the odd and troublesome hieroglyphics on its flanks that tended to slide out of your field of vision if you stared at them for more than a moment.

A hatch opened and a dozen of the invaders stepped out. *Floated* out, rather. Like their ship, they never came in contact with the ground.

They looked strange. They looked exceedingly strange. Where we have feet they had a single oval pedestal, maybe five inches thick and a yard in diameter, that drifted an inch or so above ground level. From this fleshy base their wraithlike bodies sprouted like tethered balloons. They had no arms, no legs, not even discernible heads: just a broad dome-shaped summit, dwindling away to a rope-like termination that was attached to the pedestal. Their lavender skins were glossy, with a metallic sheen. Dark eye-like spots sometimes formed on them but didn't last long. We saw no mouths. As they moved about they seemed to exercise great care never to touch one another.

The first thing they did was to seize half a dozen squirrels, three stray dogs, a softball, and a baby carriage, unoccupied. We will never know what the second thing was that they did, because no one stayed around to watch. The park emptied with impressive rapidity, the police moved swiftly in with their sealfield, and for the next three hours the aliens had the meadow to themselves. Later in the day the networks sent up spy-eyes that recorded the scene for the evening news until the aliens figured out what they were and shot them down. Briefly we saw ghostly gleaming aliens wandering around within a radius of perhaps 500 yards of their ship, collecting newspapers, soft-drink dispensers, discarded items of clothing, and something that was generally agreed to be a set of dentures. Whatever they picked up they wrapped in a sort of pillow made of a glowing fabric with the same shining texture as their own bodies, which immediately began floating off with its contents toward the hatch of the ship.

People were lined up six deep at the bar when I arrived at the Ras, and everyone was drinking like mad and staring at the screen. They were showing the clips of the aliens over and over. Maranta was already there. Her eyes were glowing. She pressed herself up against me like a wild woman. "My God," she said, "isn't it wonderful! The men from Mars are here! Or wherever they're from. Let's hoist a few to the men from Mars."

We hoisted more than a few. Somehow I got home at a respectable seven o'clock anyway. The apartment was still in its one-room configuration, though our contract with Bobby Christie specified wall-shift at half past six. Elaine refused to have anything to do with activating the shift. She was afraid, I think, of timing the sequence wrong and being crushed by the walls, or something.

"You heard?" Elaine said. "The aliens?"

"I wasn't far from the park at lunchtime," I told her. "That was when it happened, at lunchtime, while I was up by the park."

Her eyes went wide. "Then you actually saw them land?"

"I wish. By the time I got to the park entrance the cops had everything sealed off."

I pressed the button and the walls began to move. Our living room and kitchen returned from Bobby Christie's domain. In the moment of shift I caught sight of Bobby on the far side, getting dressed to go out. He waved and grinned. "Space monsters in the park," he said. "My my my. It's a real jungle out there, don't you know?" And then the walls closed away on him.

Elaine switched on the news and once again I watched the aliens drifting around the mall picking up people's jackets and candy-bar wrappers.

"Hey," I said, "the mayor ought to put them on the city payroll."

"What were you doing up by the park at lunchtime?" Elaine asked, after a bit.

The next day was when the second ship landed and the *real* space monsters appeared. To me the first aliens didn't qualify as monsters at all. Monsters ought to be monstrous, bottom line. Those first aliens were no bigger than you or me.

The second batch, they were something else, though. The behemoths. The space elephants. Of course they weren't anything like elephants, except that they were big. Big? *Immense.* It put me in mind of Hannibal's invasion of Rome, seeing those gargantuan things disembarking from the new spaceship. It seemed like the Second Punic War all over again, Hannibal and the elephants.

You remember how that was. When Hannibal set out from Carthage to conquer Rome, he took with him a phalanx of elephants, 37 huge gray attack-trained monsters. Elephants were useful in battle in those days—a kind of early-model tank—but they were handy also for terrifying the civilian populace: bizarre colossal smelly critters trampling invincibly through the suburbs, flapping their vast ears and trumpeting awesome cries of doom and burying your rose bushes under mountainous turds. And now we had the same deal. With one difference, though: the Roman archers picked off Hannibal's elephants long before they got within honking distance of the walls of Rome. But these aliens had materialized without warning right in the middle of Central Park, in that big grassy meadow between the 72nd Street transverse and Central Park South, which is another deal altogether. I wonder how well things would have gone for the Romans if they had awakened one morning to find Hannibal and his army camping out in the Forum, and his 37 hairy shambling flap-eared elephants snuffling and snorting and farting about on the marble steps of the Temple of Jupiter.

The new spaceship arrived the way the first one had, pop whoosh ping thunk, and the behemoths came tumbling out of it like rabbits out of a hat. We saw it on the evening news: the networks had a new bunch of spy-eyes up, half a mile or so overhead. The ship made a kind of belching sound and this *thing* suddenly was standing on the mall gawking and gaping. Then another belch, another *thing*. And on and on until there were two or three dozen of them. Nobody has ever been able to figure out how that little ship could have held as many as one of them. It was no bigger than a schoolbus standing on end.

The monsters looked like double-humped blue medium-size mountains with legs. The legs were their most elephantine feature—thick and rough-skinned, like tree-trunks—but they worked on some sort of telescoping principle and could be collapsed swiftly back up into the bodies of their owners. Eight was the normal number of legs, but you never saw eight at once on any of them: as they moved about they always kept at least one pair withdrawn, though from time to time they'd let that pair descend and pull up another one, in what seemed like a completely random way. Now and then they might withdraw two pairs at once, which would cause them to sink down to ground level at one end like a camel kneeling.

They were enormous. *Enormous.* Getting exact measurements of one presented certain technical problems, as I think you can appreciate. The most reliable estimate was that they were 25 to 30 feet high and 40 to 50 feet long. That is not only substantially larger than any elephant past or present, it is rather larger than most of the two-family houses still to be found in the outer boroughs of the city. Furthermore a two-family house of the kind found in Queens or Brooklyn, though it may offend your esthetic sense, will not move around at all, it will not emit bad smells and frightening sounds, it will never sit down on a bison and swallow it, nor, for that matter, will it swallow you. African elephants, they tell me, run 10 or 11 feet high at the shoulder, and the biggest extinct mammoths were three or four feet taller than that. There once was a mammal called the baluchitherium that stood about 16 feet high. That was the largest land mammal that ever lived. The space creatures were nearly twice as high. We are talking large here. We are talking dinosaur-plus dimensions.

Central Park is several miles long but quite modest in width. It runs just from Fifth Avenue to Eighth. Its designers did not expect that anyone would allow two or three dozen animals bigger than two-family houses to wander around freely in an urban park three city blocks wide. No doubt the small size of their pasture was very awkward for them. Certainly it was for us.

"I think they have to be an exploration party," Maranta said. "Don't you?" We had shifted the scene of our Monday and Friday lunches from Central Park to Rockefeller Center, but otherwise we were trying to behave as though nothing unusual was going on. "They can't have come as invaders. One little spaceship-load of aliens couldn't possibly conquer an entire planet."

Maranta is unfailingly jaunty and optimistic. She is a small, energetic woman with close-cropped red hair and green eyes, one of those boyish-looking women who never seem to age. I love her for her optimism. I wish I could catch it from her, like measles.

I said, "There are *two* spaceship-loads of aliens, Maranta."

She made a face. "Oh. The jumbos. They're just dumb shaggy monsters. I don't see them as much of a menace, really."

"Probably not. But the little ones—they have to be a superior species. We know that because they're the ones who came to us. We didn't go to them."

She laughed. "It all sounds so absurd. That Central Park should be full of *creatures*—"

"But what if they do want to conquer Earth?" I asked.

"Oh," Maranta said. "I don't think that would necessarily be so awful."

The smaller aliens spent the first few days installing a good deal of mysterious equipment on the mall in the vicinity of their ship: odd intricate shimmering constructions that looked as though they belonged in the sculpture garden of the Museum of Modern Art. They made no attempt to enter into communication with us. They showed no interest in us at all. The only time they took notice of us was when we sent spy-eyes overhead. They would tolerate them for an hour or two and then would shoot them down, casually, like swatting flies, with spurts of pink light. The networks—and then the government surveillance agencies, when they moved in—put the eyes higher and higher each day, but the aliens never failed to find them. After a week or so we were forced to rely for our information on government spy satellites monitoring the park from space, and on whatever observers equipped with binoculars could glimpse from the taller apartment houses and hotels bordering the park. Neither of these arrangements was entirely satisfactory.

The behemoths, during those days, were content to roam aimlessly through the park southward from 72nd Street, knocking over trees, squatting down to eat them. Each one gobbled two or three trees a day, leaves, branches, trunk, and all. There weren't all that many trees to begin with down there, so it seemed likely that before long they'd have to start ranging farther afield.

The usual civic groups spoke up about the trees. They wanted the mayor to do something to protect the park. The monsters, they said, would have to be made to go elsewhere—to Canada, perhaps, where there were plenty of expendable trees. The mayor said that he was studying the problem but that it was too early to know what the best plan of action would be.

His chief goal, in the beginning, was simply to keep a lid on the situation. We still didn't even know, after all, whether we were being invaded or just visited. To play it safe the police were ordered to set up and maintain round-the-clock sealfields completely encircling the park in the impacted zone south of 72nd Street. The power costs of this were staggering and Con Edison found it necessary to impose a 10%

voltage cutback in the rest of the city, which caused a lot of grumbling, especially now that it was getting to be air-conditioner weather.

The police didn't like any of this: out there day and night standing guard in front of an intangible electronic barrier with ungodly monsters just a sneeze away. Now and then one of the blue goliaths would wander near the sealfield and peer over the edge. A sealfield maybe a dozen feet high doesn't give you much of a sense of security when there's an animal two or three times that height looming over its top.

So the cops asked for time and a half. Combat pay, essentially. There wasn't room in the city budget for that, especially since no one knew how long the aliens were going to continue to occupy the park. There was talk of a strike. The mayor appealed to Washington, which had studiously been staying remote from the whole event as if the arrival of an extraterrestrial task force in the middle of Manhattan was purely a municipal problem.

The president rummaged around in the Constitution and decided to activate the National Guard. That surprised a lot of basically sedentary men who enjoy dressing up occasionally in uniforms. The Guard hadn't been called out since the Bulgarian business in '94 and its current members weren't very sharp on procedures, so some hasty on-the-job training became necessary. As it happened, Maranta's husband Tim was an officer in the 107th Infantry, which was the regiment that was handed the chief responsibility for protecting New York City against the creatures from space. So his life suddenly was changed a great deal, and so was Maranta's; and so was mine.

Like everybody else, I found myself going over to the park again and again to try and get a glimpse of the aliens. But the barricades kept you fifty feet away from the park perimeter on all sides, and the taller buildings flanking the park had put themselves on a residents-only admission basis, with armed guards enforcing it, so they wouldn't be overwhelmed by hordes of curiosity-seekers.

I did see Tim, though. He was in charge of an improvised-looking command post at Fifth and 59th, near the horse-and-buggy stand. Youngish stockbrokery-looking men kept running up to him with reports to sign, and he signed each one with terrific dash and vigor, without reading any of them. In his crisp tan uniform and shiny boots, he must have seen himself as some doomed and gallant officer in an ancient movie, Gary Cooper, Cary Grant, John Wayne, bracing himself for the climactic cavalry charge or the onslaught of the maddened Sepoys. The poor bastard.

"Hey, old man," he said, grinning at me in a doomed and gallant way. "Came to see the circus, did you?"

We weren't really best friends any more. I don't know what we were to each other. We rarely lunched any more. (How could we? I was busy three days a week with Maranta.) We didn't meet at the gym. It wasn't to Tim I turned to advice on personal problems or second opinions on investments. There was some sort of bond but I think it was mostly nostalgia. But officially I guess I did still think of him as my best friend, in a kind of automatic unquestioning way.

I said, "Are you free to go over to the Plaza for a drink?"

"I wish. I don't get relieved until 2100 hours."

"Nine o'clock, is that it?"

"Nine, yes. You fucking civilian."

It was only half past one. The poor bastard.

"What'll happen to you if you leave your post?"

"I could get shot for desertion," he said.

"Seriously?"

"Seriously. Especially if the monsters pick that moment to bust out of the park. This is war, old buddy."

"Is it, do you think? Maranta doesn't think so." I wondered if I should be talking about what Maranta thought. "She says they're just out exploring the galaxy."

Tim shrugged. "She always likes to see the sunny side. That's an alien military force over there inside the park. One of these days they're going to blow a bugle and come out with blazing rayguns. You'd better believe it."

"Through the sealfield?"

"They could walk right over it," Tim said. "Or float, for all I know. There's going to be a war. The first intergalactic war in human history." Again the dazzling Cary Grant grin. Her Majesty's Bengal lancers, ready for action. "Something to tell my grandchildren," said Tim. "Do you know what the game plan is? First we attempt to make contact. That's going on right now, but they don't seem to be paying attention to us. If we ever establish communication, we invite them to sign a peace treaty. Then we offer them some chunk of Nevada or Kansas as a diplomatic enclave and get them the hell out of New York. But I don't think any of that's going to happen. I think they're busy scoping things out in there, and as soon as they finish that they're going to launch some kind of attack, using weapons we don't even begin to understand."

"And if they do?"

"We nuke them," Tim said. "Tactical devices, just the right size for Central Park Mall."

"No," I said, staring. "That isn't so. You're kidding me."

He looked pleased, a *gotcha* look. "Matter of fact, I am. The truth is that nobody has the goddamndest idea of what to do about any of this. But don't think the nuke strategy hasn't been suggested. And some even crazier things."

"Don't tell me about them," I said. "Look, Tim, is there any way I can get a peek over those barricades?"

"Not a chance. Not even you. I'm not even supposed to be *talking* with civilians."

"Since when am I civilian?"

"Since the invasion began," Tim said.

He was dead serious. Maybe this was all just a goofy movie to me, but it wasn't to him.

More junior officers came to him with more papers to sign. He excused himself and took care of them. Then he was on the field telephone for five minutes or so. His expression grew progressively more bleak. Finally he looked up at me and said, "You see? It's starting."

"What is?"

"They've crossed 72nd Street for the first time. There must have been a gap in the sealfield. Or maybe they jumped it, as I was saying just now. Three of the big ones are up by 74th, noodling around the eastern end of the lake. The Metropolitan Museum people are scared shitless and have asked for gun emplacements on the roof, and they're thinking of evacuating the most important works of art." The field phone lit up again. "Excuse me," he said. Always the soul of courtesy, Tim. After a time he said, "Oh, Jesus. It sounds pretty bad. I've got to go up there right now. Do you mind?" His jaw was set, his gaze was frosty with determination. This is it, Major. There's ten thousand Comanches coming through the pass with blood in their eyes, but we're ready for them, right? Right. He went striding away up Fifth Avenue.

When I got back to the office there was a message from Maranta, suggesting that I stop off at her place for drinks that evening on my way home. Tim would be busy playing soldier, she said, until nine. Until 2100 hours, I silently corrected.

Another few days and we got used to it all. We began to accept the presence of aliens in the park as a normal part of New York life, like snow in February or laser duels in the subway.

But they remained at the center of everybody's consciousness. In a subtle pervasive way they were working great changes in our souls as they moved about mysteriously behind the sealfield barriers in the park. The strangeness of their being here made us buoyant. Their arrival had broken, in some way, the depressing rhythm that life in our brave new century had seemed to be settling into. I know that for some time I had been thinking, as I suppose people have thought since Cro-Magnon days, that lately the flavor of modern life had been changing for the worse, that it was becoming sour and nasty, that the era I happened to live in was a dim, shabby, dismal sort of time, small-souled, mean-minded. You know the feeling. Somehow the aliens had caused that feeling to lift. By invading us in this weird hands-off way, they had given us something to be interestingly mystified by: a sort of redemption, a sort of rebirth. Yes, truly.

Some of us changed quite a lot. Consider Tim, the latter-day Bengal lancer, the staunchly disciplined officer. He lasted about a week in that particular mind-set. Then one night he called me and said, "Hey, fellow, how would you like to go into the park and play with the critters?"

"What are you talking about?"

"I know a way to get in. I've got the code for the 64th Street sealfield. I can turn it off and we can slip through. It's risky, but how can you resist?"

So much for Gary Cooper. So much for John Wayne.

"Have you gone nuts?" I said. "The other day you wouldn't even let me go up to the barricades."

"That was the other day."

"You wouldn't walk across the street with me for a drink. You said you'd get shot for desertion."

"That was the other day."

"You called me a civilian."

"You still are a civilian. But you're my old buddy, and I want to go in there and look those aliens in the eye, and I'm not quite up to doing it all by myself. You want to go with me, or don't you?"

"Like the time we stole the beer keg from Sigma Frap. Like the time we put the scorpions in the girls' shower room."

"You got it, old pal."

"Tim, we aren't college kids any more. There's a fucking intergalactic war going on. That was your very phrase. Central Park is under surveillance by NASA spy-eyes that can see a cat's whiskers from fifty miles up. You are part of the military force that is supposed to be protecting us against these alien invaders. And now you propose to violate your trust and go sneaking into the midst of the invading force, as a mere prank?"

"I guess I do," he said.

"This is an extremely cockeyed idea, isn't it?" I said.

"Absolutely. Are you with me?"

"Sure," I said. "You know I am."

I told Elaine that Tim and I were going to meet for a late dinner to discuss a business deal and I didn't expect to be home until two or three in the morning. No problem there. Tim was waiting at our old table at Perugino's with a bottle of Amarone already working. The wine was so good that we ordered another midway through the veal pizzaiola, and then a third. I won't say we drank ourselves blind, but we certainly got seriously myopic. And about midnight we walked over to the park.

Everything was quiet. I saw sleepy-looking guardsman patrolling here and there along Fifth. We went right up to the command post at 59th and Tim saluted very crisply, which I don't think was quite kosher, he being not then in uniform. He introduced me to someone as Dr. Pritchett, Bureau of External Affairs. That sounded really cool and glib, Bureau of External Affairs.

Then off we went up Fifth, Tim and I, and he gave me a guided tour. "You see, Dr. Pritchett, the first line of the isolation zone is the barricade that runs down the middle of the avenue." Virile, forceful voice, loud enough to be heard for half a block. "That keeps the gawkers away. Behind that, Doctor, we maintain a further level of security through a series of augmented-beam sealfield emplacements,

206

the new General Dynamics 1100 series model, and let me show you right here how we've integrated that with advanced personnel-interface intercept scan by means of a triple line of Hewlett-Packard optical doppler-couplers—"

And so on, a steady stream of booming confident-sounding gibberish as we headed north. He pulled out a flashlight and led me hither and thither to show me amplifiers and sensors and whatnot, and it was Dr. Pritchett this and Dr. Pritchett that and I realized that we were now somehow on the inner side of the barricade. His glibness, his poise, were awesome. *Notice this, Dr. Pritchett, and Let me call your attention to this, Dr. Pritchett*, and suddenly there was a tiny digital keyboard in his hand, like a little calculator, and he was tapping out numbers. "Okay," he said, "the field's down between here and the 65th Street entrance to the park, but I've put a kill on the beam-interruption signal. So far as anyone can tell there's still an unbroken field. Let's go in."

And we entered the park just north of the zoo.

For five generations the first thing New York kids have been taught, ahead of tying shoelaces and flushing after you go, is that you don't set foot in Central Park at night. Now here we were, defying the most primordial of no-nos. But what was to fear? What they taught us to worry about in the park was muggers. Not creatures from the Ninth Glorch Galaxy.

The park was eerily quiet. Maybe a snore or two from the direction of the zoo, otherwise not a sound. We walked west and north into the silence, into the darkness. After a while a strange smell reached my nostrils. It was dank and musky and harsh and sour, but those are only approximations: it wasn't like anything I had ever smelled before. One whiff of it and I saw purple skies and a great green sun blazing in the heavens. A second whiff and all the stars were in the wrong places. A third whiff and I was staring into a gnarled twisted landscape where the trees were like giant spears and the mountains were like crooked teeth.

Tim nudged me.

"Yeah," I said. "I smell it too."

"To your left," he said. "Look to your left."

I looked to my left and saw three huge yellow eyes looking back at me from twenty feet overhead, like searchlights mounted in a tree. They weren't mounted in a tree, though. They were mounted in something shaggy and massive, somewhat larger than your basic two-family Queens residential dwelling, that was standing maybe fifty feet away, completely blocking both lanes of the park's East Drive from shoulder to shoulder.

It was then that I realized that three bottles of wine hadn't been nearly enough.

"What's the matter?" Tim said. "This is what we came for, isn't it, old pal?"

"What do we do now? Climb on its back and go for a ride?"

"You know that no human being in all of history has ever been as close to that thing as we are now?"

"Yes," I said. "I do know that, Tim."

It began making a sound. It was the kind of sound that a piece of chalk twelve feet thick would make if it was dragged across a blackboard the wrong way. When I heard that sound I felt as if I was being dragged across whole galaxies by my hair. A weird vertigo attacked me. Then the creature folded up all its legs and came down to ground level; and then it unfolded the two front pairs of legs, and then the other two; and then it started to amble slowly and ominously toward us.

I saw another one, looking even bigger, just beyond it. And perhaps a third one a little farther back. They were heading our way too.

"Shit," I said. "This was a very dumb idea, wasn't it?"

"Come on. We're never going to forget this night."

"I'd like to live to remember it."

"Let's get up real close. They don't move very fast."

"No," I said. "Let's just get out of the park right now, okay?"

"We just got here."

"Fine," I said. "We did it. Now let's go."

"Hey, look," Tim said. "Over there to the west."

I followed his pointing arm and saw two gleaming wraiths hovering just above the ground, maybe 300 yards away. The other aliens, the little floating ones. Drifting toward us, graceful as balloons. I imagined myself being wrapped in a shining pillow and being floated off into their ship.

"Oh, shit," I said. "Come *on*, Tim."

Staggering, stumbling, I ran for the park gate, not even thinking about how I was going to get through the sealfield without Tim's gizmo. But then there was Tim, right behind me. We reached the sealfield together and he tapped out the numbers on the little keyboard and the field opened for us, and out we went, and the field closed behind us. And we collapsed just outside the park, panting, gasping, laughing like lunatics, slapping the sidewalk hysterically. "Dr. Pritchett," he chortled. "Bureau of External Affairs. God damn, what a smell that critter had! God damn!"

I laughed all the way home. I was still laughing when I got into bed. Elaine squinted at me. She wasn't amused. "That Tim," I said. "That wild man Tim." She could tell I'd been drinking some and she nodded somberly—boys will be boys, etc.—and went back to sleep.

The next morning I learned what had happened in the park after we had cleared out.

It seemed a few of the big aliens had gone looking for us. They had followed our spoor all the way to the park gate, and when they lost it they somehow turned to the right and went blundering into the zoo. The Central Park Zoo is a small cramped place and as they rambled around in it they managed to knock down most of the fences. In no time whatever there were tigers, elephants, chimps, rhinos, and hyenas all over the park.

The animals, of course, were befuddled and bemused at finding themselves free. They took off in a hundred different directions, looking for places to hide.

The lions and coyotes simply curled up under bushes and went to sleep. The monkeys and some of the apes went into the trees. The aquatic things headed for the lake. One of the rhinos ambled out into the mall and pushed over a fragile-looking alien machine with his nose. The machine shattered and the rhino went up in a flash of yellow light and a puff of green smoke. As for the elephants, they stood poignantly in a huddled circle, glaring in utter amazement and dismay at the gigantic aliens. How humiliating it must have been for them to feel *tiny*.

Then there was the bison event. There was this little herd, a dozen or so mangy-looking guys with ragged, threadbare fur. They started moving single file toward Columbus Circle, probably figuring that if they just kept their heads down and didn't attract attention they could keep going all the way back to Wyoming. For some reason one of the behemoths decided to see what bison taste like. It came hulking over and sat down on the last one in the line, which vanished underneath it like a mouse beneath a hippopotamus. Chomp, gulp, gone. In the next few minutes five more behemoths came over and disappeared five more of the bison. The survivors made it safely to the edge of the park and huddled up against the sealfield, mooing forlornly. One of the little tragedies of interstellar war.

I found Tim on duty at the 59th Street command post. He looked at me as though I were an emissary of Satan. "I can't talk to you while I'm on duty," he said.

"You heard about the zoo?" I asked.

"Of course I heard." He was speaking through clenched teeth. His eyes had the scarlet look of zero sleep. "What a filthy irresponsible thing we did!"

"Look, we had no way of knowing—"

"Inexcusable. An incredible lapse. The aliens feel threatened now that humans have trespassed on their territory, and the whole situation has changed in there. We upset them and now they're getting out of control. I'm thinking of reporting myself for court-martial."

"Don't be silly, Tim. We trespassed for three minutes. The aliens didn't give a crap about it. They might have blundered into the zoo even if we hadn't—"

"Go away," he muttered. "I can't talk to you while I'm on duty."

Jesus! As if I was the one who had lured *him* into doing it.

Well, he was back in his movie part again, the distinguished military figure who now had unaccountably committed an unpardonable lapse and was going to have to live in the cold glare of his own disapproval for the rest of his life. The poor bastard. I tried to tell him not to take things so much to heart, but he turned away from me, so I shrugged and went back to my office.

That afternoon some tender-hearted citizens demanded that the sealfields be switched off until the zoo animals could escape from the park. The sealfields, of course, kept them trapped in there with the aliens.

Another tough one for the mayor. He'd lose points tremendously if the evening news kept showing our beloved polar bears and raccoons and kangaroos and whatnot getting gobbled like gumdrops by the aliens. But switching off the sealfields would send a horde of leopards and gorillas and wolverines scampering out into the streets of Manhattan, to say nothing of the aliens who might follow them. The mayor appointed a study group, naturally.

The small aliens stayed close to their spaceship and remained uncommunicative. They went on tinkering with their machines, which emitted odd plinking noises and curious colored lights. But the huge ones roamed freely about the park, and now they were doing considerable damage in their amiable mindless way. They smashed up the backstops of the baseball fields, tossed the Bethesda Fountain into the lake, rearranged Tavern-on-the-Green's seating plan, and trashed the place in various other ways, but nobody seemed to object except the usual Friends of the Park civic types. I think we were all so bemused by the presence of genuine galactic beings that we didn't mind. We were flattered that they had chosen New York as the site of first contact. (But where *else?*)

No one could explain how the behemoths had penetrated the 72nd Street sealfield line, but a new barrier was set up at 79th, and that seemed to keep them contained. Poor Tim spent twelve hours a day patrolling the perimeter of the occupied zone. Inevitably I began spending more time with Maranta than just lunchtimes. Elaine noticed. But I didn't notice her noticing.

One Sunday at dawn a behemoth turned up by the Metropolitan, peering in the window of the Egyptian courtyard. The authorities thought at first that there must be a gap in the 79th Street sealfield, as there had at 72nd. Then came a report of another alien out near Riverside Drive and a third one at Lincoln Center and it became clear that the sealfields just didn't hold them back at all. They had simply never bothered to go beyond them before.

Making contact with a sealfield is said to be extremely unpleasant for any organism with a nervous system more complex than a squid's. Every neuron screams in anguish. You jump back, involuntarily, a reflex impossible to overcome. On the morning we came to call Crazy Sunday the behemoths began walking through the fields as if they weren't there. The main thing about aliens is that they are alien. They feel no responsibility for fulfilling any of your expectations.

That weekend it was Bobby Christie's turn to have the full apartment. On those Sundays when Elaine and I had the one-room configuration we liked to get up very early and spend the day out, since it was a little depressing to stay home with three rooms of furniture jammed all around us. As we were walking up Park Avenue South toward 42nd, Elaine said suddenly, "Do you hear anything strange?"

"Strange?"

"Like a riot."

"It's nine o'clock Sunday morning. Nobody goes out rioting at nine o'clock Sunday morning."

"Just listen," she said.

There is no mistaking the characteristic sounds of a large excited crowd of human beings, for those of us who spent our formative years living in the late twentieth century. Our ears were tuned at an early age to the music of riots, mobs, demonstrations, and their kin. We know what it means, when individual exclamations of anger, indignation, or anxiety blend to create a symphonic hubbub in which all extremes of pitch and timbre are submerged into a single surging roar, as deep as the booming of the surf. That was what I heard now. There was no mistaking it.

"It isn't a riot," I said. "It's a mob. There's a subtle difference."

"What?"

"Come on," I said, breaking into a jog. "I'll bet you that the aliens have come out of the park."

A mob, yes. In a moment we saw thousands upon thousands of people, filling 42nd Street from curb to curb and more coming from all directions. What they were looking at—pointing, gaping, screaming—was a shaggy blue creature the size of a small mountain that was moving about uncertainly on the automobile viaduct that runs around the side of Grand Central Terminal. It looked unhappy. It was obviously trying to get down from the viaduct, which was sagging noticeably under its weight. People were jammed right up against it and a dozen or so were clinging to its sides and back like rock climbers. There were people underneath it, too, milling around between its colossal legs. "Oh, look," Elaine said, shuddering, digging her fingers into my biceps. "Isn't it eating some of them? Like they did the bison?" Once she had pointed it out I saw, yes, the behemoth now and then was dipping quickly and rising again, a familiar one-two, the old squat-and-gobble. "What an awful thing!" Elaine murmured. "Why don't they get out of its way?"

"I don't think they can," I said. "I think they're being pushed forward by the people behind them."

"Right into the jaws of that hideous monster. Or whatever it has, if they aren't jaws."

"I don't think it means to hurt anyone," I said. How did I know that? "I think it's just eating them because they're dithering around

212

down there in its mouth area. A kind of automatic response. It looks awfully dumb, Elaine."

"Why are you defending it?"

"Hey, look, Elaine—"

"It's eating people. You sound almost sorry for it!"

"Well, why not? It's far from home and surrounded by ten thousand screaming morons. You think it wants to be out there?"

"It's a disgusting obnoxious animal." She was getting furious. Her eyes were bright and wild, her jaw was thrust forward. "I hope the army gets here fast," she said fiercely. "I hope they blow it to smithereens!"

Her ferocity frightened me. I saw an Elaine I scarcely knew at all. When I tried one more time to make excuses for that miserable hounded beast on the viaduct she glared at me with unmistakable loathing. Then she turned away and went rushing forward, shaking her fist, shouting curses and threats at the alien.

Suddenly I realized how it would have been if Hannibal actually had been able to keep his elephants alive long enough to enter Rome with them. The respectable Roman matrons, screaming and raging from the housetops with the fury of banshees. And the baffled elephants sooner or later rounded up and thrust into the Coliseum to be tormented by little men with spears, while the crowd howled its delight. Well, I can howl too. "Come on, Behemoth!" I yelled into the roar of the mob. "You can do it, Goliath!" A traitor to the human race is what I was, I guess.

Eventually a detachment of Guardsmen came shouldering through the streets. They had mortars and rifles, and for all I know they had tactical nukes too. But of course there was no way they could attack the animal in the midst of such a mob. Instead they used electronic blooglehorns to disperse the crowd by the power of sheer ugly noise, and whipped up a bunch of buzz-blinkers and a little sealfield to cut 42nd Street in half. The last I saw of the monster it was slouching off in the direction of the old United Nations Buildings with the Guardsmen warily creeping along behind it. The crowd scattered, and I was left standing in front of Grand Central with a trembling, sobbing Elaine.

That was how it was all over the city on Crazy Sunday, and on Monday and Tuesday too. The behemoths were outside the park, roaming at large from Harlem to Wall Street. Wherever they went they drew tremendous crazy crowds that swarmed all over them without any regard for the danger. Some famous news photos came out of those days: the three grinning black boys at Seventh and 125th hanging from the three purple rod-like things, the acrobats forming a human pyramid atop the Times Square beast, the little old Italian man standing in front of his house in Greenwich Village trying to hold a space monster at bay with his garden hose.

There was never any accurate casualty count. Maybe 5000 people died, mainly trampled underfoot by the aliens or crushed in the crowd. Somewhere between 350 and 400 human beings were gobbled by the aliens. Apparently that stoop-and-swallow thing is something they do when they're nervous. If there's anything edible within reach, they'll gulp it in. This soothes them. We made them very nervous; they did a lot of gulping.

Among the casualties was Tim, the second day of the violence. He went down valiantly in the defense of the Guggenheim Museum, which came under attack by five of the biggies. Its spiral shape held some ineffable appeal for them. We couldn't tell whether they wanted to worship it or mate with it or just knock it to pieces, but they kept on charging and charging, rushing up to it and slamming against it. Tim was trying to hold them off with nothing more than tear-gas and blooglehorns when he was swallowed. Never flinched, just stood there and let it happen. The president had ordered the guardsmen not to use lethal weapons. Maranta was bitter about that. "If only they had let them use grenades," she said. I tried to imagine what it was like, gulped down and digested, nifty tan uniform and all. A credit to his regiment. It was his atonement, I guess. He was back there in the Gary Cooper movie again, gladly paying the price for dereliction of duty.

Tuesday afternoon the rampage came to an unexpected end. The behemoths suddenly started keeling over, and within a few hours they were all dead. Some said it was the heat—it was up in the 90s all day Monday and Tuesday—and some said it was the excitement. A Rockefeller University biologist thought it was both those factors plus severe indigestion: the aliens had eaten an average of ten humans apiece, which might have overloaded their systems.

There was no chance for autopsies. Some enzyme in the huge bodies set to work immediately on death, dissolving flesh and bone and skin and all into a sticky yellow mess. By nightfall nothing was left of them but some stains on the pavement, uptown and down. A sad business, I thought. Not even a skeleton for the museum, memento of this momentous time. The poor monsters. Was I the only one who felt sorry for them? Quite possibly I was. I make no apologies for that. I feel what I feel.

All this time the other aliens, the little shimmery spooky ones, had stayed holed up in Central Park, preoccupied with their incomprehensible research. They didn't even seem to notice that their behemoths had strayed.

But now they became agitated. For two or three days they bustled about like worried penguins, dismantling their instruments and packing them aboard their ship; and then they took apart the other ship, the one that had carried the behemoths, and loaded that aboard. Perhaps they felt demoralized. As the Carthaginians who had invaded Rome did, after their elephants died.

On a sizzling June afternoon the alien ship took off. Not for its home world, not right away. It swooped into the sky and came down on Fire Island: at Cherry Grove, to be precise. The aliens took possession of the beach, set up their instruments around their ship, and even ventured into the water, skimming and bobbing just above the surface of the waves like demented surfers. After five or six days they moved on to one of the Hamptons and did the same thing, and then to Martha's Vineyard. Maybe they just wanted a vacation, after three weeks in New York. And then they went away altogether.

"You've been having an affair with Maranta, haven't you?" Elaine asked me, the day the aliens left.

"I won't deny it."

"That night you came in so late, with wine on your breath. You were with her, weren't you?"

"No," I said. "I was with Tim. He and I sneaked into the park and looked at the aliens."

"Sure you did," Elaine said. She filed for divorce and a year later I married Maranta. Very likely that would have happened sooner or later even if the Earth hadn't been invaded by beings from space and Tim hadn't been devoured. But no question that the invasion speeded things up a bit for us all.

And now, of course, the invaders are back. Four years to the day from the first landing and there they were, pop whoosh ping thunk, Central Park again. Three ships this time, one of spooks, one of behemoths, and the third one carrying the prisoners of war.

Who could ever forget that scene, when the hatch opened and some 350 to 400 human beings came out, marching like zombies? Along with the bison herd, half a dozen squirrels, and three dogs. They hadn't been eaten and digested at all, just *collected* inside the behemoths and instantaneously transmitted somehow to the home world, where they were studied. Now they were being returned. "That's Tim, isn't it?" Maranta said, pointing to the screen. I nodded. Unmistakably Tim, yes. With the stunned look of a man who has beheld marvels beyond comprehension.

It's a month now and the government is still holding all the returnees for debriefing. No one is allowed to see them. The word is that a special law will be passed dealing with the problem of spouses of returnees who have entered into new marriages. Maranta says she'll stay with me no matter what; and I'm pretty sure that Tim will do the stiff-upper-lip thing, no hard feelings, if they ever get word to him in the debriefing camp about Maranta and me. As for the aliens, they're sitting tight in Central Park, occupying the whole place from 96th to 110th and not telling us a thing. Now and then the behemoths wander down to the reservoir for a lively bit of wallowing, but they haven't gone beyond the park this time.

I think a lot about Hannibal, and about Carthage versus Rome, and how the Second Punic War might have come out if Hannibal had had a chance to go back home and get a new batch of elephants. Most likely Rome would have won the war anyway, I guess. But we aren't Romans, and they aren't Carthaginians, and those aren't elephants splashing around in the Central Park reservoir. "This is such an interesting time to be alive," Maranta likes to say. "I'm certain they don't mean us any harm, aren't you?"

"I love you for your optimism," I tell her then. And then we turn on the tube and watch the evening news.

BLINDSIGHT

The shrewd, exasperating, unforgettable editor Horace Gold taught me long ago that one good way to generate story ideas is to take a standard, familiar idea and stand it on its head. Here's an example of my doing just that.

This story was written in July of 1985. Dr. Joseph Mengele, the diabolical Nazi medical experimenter who had been hiding in South America since the end of the Second World War, had just died, and his evil exploits were much in the news. Nobody needed another story about a mad scientist. But I wondered if I could turn the Mengele story upside down and thereby find something interesting to write about.

So: a sinister and unscrupulous surgeon has escaped to sanctuary, yes— not to South America but to an L5 satellite world. And one of his victims is stalking him, but not to bring him to justice: oh, no, too predictable, too routine. He's a wanted man, all right, but because his medical skills are needed somewhere. The formula story of revenge turns into something, well, a little different.

Alice Turner bought it for Playboy, *essentially as written, and ran it in the December, 1986 issue. Terry Carr picked it for his annual* Year's Best Science Fiction *anthology—alas, the last in this series, for that gifted editor and very dear friend of mine died while the book was in production, and in fact I was the one who handled the mechanical aspects of the anthology, the getting of permissions and the proofreading and the other jobs of seeing it into print, in his place. Since "Against Babylon" had appeared both in the Dozois and Wollheim anthologies that year, I had another three-way sweep of the annual honors, although this time only two different stories were involved.*

And, as with "Against Babylon" and "The Pardoner's Tale," which eventually became sections of the novel The Alien Years, I used "Blindsight" and a second short story, 1990's "Hot Sky," some years later as the foundations for a book called Hot Sky at Midnight.

———————

That's my mark, Juanito told himself. That one, there. That one for sure. He stared at the new dudes coming off the midday shuttle from Earth. The one he meant to go for was the one with no eyes at all, blank from brow to bridge of nose, just the merest suggestions of shadowy pits below the smooth skin of the forehead. As if the eyes had been erased, Juanito thought. But in fact they had probably never been there in the first place. It didn't look like a retrofit gene job, more like a prenatal splice.

He knew he had to move fast. There was plenty of competition. Fifteen, twenty couriers here in the waiting room, gathering like vultures, and they were some of the best: Ricky, Lola, Kluge. Nattathaniel. Delilah. Everybody looked hungry today. Juanito couldn't afford to get shut out. He hadn't worked in six weeks, and it was time. His last job had been a fast-talking fancy-dancing Hungarian, wanted on Commonplace and maybe two or three other satellite worlds for dealing in plutonium. Juanito had milked that one for all it was worth, but you can milk only so long. The newcomers learn the system, they melt in and become invisible, and there's no reason for them to go on paying. So then you have to find a new client.

"Okay," Juanito said, looking around challengingly. "There's mine. The weird one. The one with half a face. Anybody else want him?"

Kluge laughed and said, "He's all yours, man."

"Yeah," Delilah said, with a little shudder. "All yours." That saddened him, her chiming in like that. It had always disappointed Juanito that Delilah didn't have his kind of imagination. "Christ," she said. "I bet he'll be plenty trouble."

"Trouble's what pays best," Juanito said. "You want to go for the easy ones, that's fine with me." He grinned at her and waved at the others. "If we're all agreed, I think I'll head downstairs now. See you later, people."

He started to move inward and downward along the shuttle-hub wall. Dazzling sunlight glinted off the docking module's silvery rim, and off the Earth shuttle's thick columnar docking shaft, wedged into the center of the module like a spear through a doughnut. On the far side of the wall the new dinkos were making their wobbly way past the glowing ten-meter-high portrait of El Supremo and on into the red fiberglass tent that was the fumigation chamber. As usual, they were having a hard time with the low gravity. Here at the hub it was one-sixteenth G, max.

Juanito always wondered about the newcomers, why they were here, what they were fleeing. Only two kinds of people ever came to Valparaiso, those who wanted to hide and those who wanted to seek. The place was nothing but an enormous spacegoing safe house. You wanted to be left alone, you came to Valparaiso and bought yourself some privacy. But that implied that you had done something that made other people not want to let you alone. There was always some of both going on here, some hiding, some seeking, El Supremo looking down benignly on it all, raking in his cut. And not just El Supremo.

Down below, the new dinkos were trying to walk jaunty, to walk mean. But that was hard to do when you were keeping your body all clenched up as if you were afraid of drifting into mid-air if you put your foot down too hard. Juanito loved it, the way they were crunching along, that constipated shuffle of theirs.

Gravity stuff didn't ever bother Juanito. He had spent all his life out here in the satellite worlds and he took it for granted that the pull was going to fluctuate according to your distance from the hub. You automatically made compensating adjustments, that was all. Juanito found it hard to understand a place where the gravity would be the same everywhere all the time. He had never set foot on Earth or any of the other natural planets, didn't care to, didn't expect to.

The guard on duty at the quarantine gate was an android. His name, his label, whatever it was, was something like Velcro Exxon. Juanito had seen him at this gate before. As he came up close the android glanced at him and said, "Working again so soon, Juanito?"

"Man has to eat, no?"

The android shrugged. Eating wasn't all that important to him, most likely. "Weren't you working that plutonium peddler out of Commonplace?"

Juanito said, smiling, "What plutonium peddler?"

"Sure," said the android. "I hear you."

He held out his waxy-skinned hand and Juanito put a 50 callaghano currency plaque in it. The usual fee for illicit entry to the customs tank was only 35 callies, but Juanito believed in spreading the wealth, especially where the authorities were concerned. They didn't *have* to let you in here, after all. Some days more couriers showed up than there were dinkos, and then the gate guards had to allocate. Overpaying the guards was simply a smart investment.

"Thank you kindly," the android said. "Thank you very much." He hit the scanner override. Juanito stepped through the security shield into the customs tank and looked around for his mark.

The new dinkos were being herded into the fumigation chamber now. They were annoyed about that—they always were—but the guards kept them moving right along through the puffy bursts of pink and green and yellow sprays that came from the ceiling nozzles. Nobody got out of customs quarantine without passing through that chamber. El Supremo was paranoid about the entry of exotic microorganisms into Valparaiso's closed-cycle ecology. El Supremo was paranoid about a lot of things. You didn't get to be sole and absolute ruler of your own little satellite world, and stay that way for 37 years, without a heavy component of paranoia in your makeup.

Juanito leaned up against the great curving glass wall of the customs tank and peered through the mists of sterilizer fog. The rest of the couriers were starting to come in now. Juanito watched them singling out potential clients. Most of the dinkos were signing up as soon as the deal was explained, but as always a few were shaking off help and setting out by themselves. Cheapskates, Juanito thought. Assholes and wimps, Juanito thought. But they'd find out. It wasn't possible to get started on Valparaiso without a courier, no matter how sharp you thought you were. Valparaiso was a free enterprise zone, after all. If you knew the rules, you were pretty much safe from all harm here forever. If not, not.

Time to make the approach, Juanito figured.

It was easy enough finding the blind man. He was much taller than the other dinkos, a big burly man some thirty-odd years old, heavy bones, powerful muscles. In the bright glaring light his blank forehead gleamed like a reflecting beacon. The low gravity didn't seem to trouble him much, nor his blindness. His movements along the customs track were easy, confident, almost graceful.

Juanito sauntered over and said, "I'll be your courier, sir. Juanito Holt." He barely came up to the blind man's elbow.

"Courier?"

"New arrival assistance service. Facilitate your entry arrangements. Customs clearance, currency exchange, hotel accomodations, permanent settlement papers if that's what you intend. Also special services by arrangement."

Juanito stared up expectantly at the blank face. The eyeless man looked back at him in a blunt straight-on way, what would have been strong eye contact if the dinko had had eyes. That was eerie. What was even eerier was the sense Juanito had that the eyeless man was seeing him clearly. For just a moment he wondered who was going to be controlling whom in this deal.

"What kind of special services?"

"Anything else you need," Juanito said.

"Anything?"

"Anything. This is Valparaiso, sir."

"Mmm. What's your fee?"

"Two thousand callaghanos a week for the basic. Specials are extra, according."

"How much is that in Capbloc dollars, your basic?"

Juanito told him.

"That's not so bad," the blind man said.

"Two weeks minimum, payable in advance."

"Mmm," said the blind man again. Again that intense eyeless gaze, seeing right through him. "How old are you?" he asked suddenly.

"Seventeen," Juanito blurted, caught off guard.

"And you're good, are you?"

"I'm the best. I was born here. I know everybody."

"I'm going to be needing the best. You take electronic handshake?"

"Sure," Juanito said. This was too easy. He wondered if he should have asked three kilocallies a week, but it was too late now. He pulled his flex terminal from his tunic pocket and slipped his fingers into it. "Unity Callaghan Bank of Valparaiso. That's code 22-44-66, and you might as well give it a default key, because it's the only bank here. Account 1133, that's mine."

The blind man donned his own terminal and deftly tapped the number pad on his wrist. Then he grasped Juanito's hand firmly in his until the sensors overlapped, and made the transfer of funds. Juanito touched for confirm and a bright green *+cl. 4000* lit up on the screen in his palm. The payee's name was Victor Farkas, out of an account in the Royal Amalgamated Bank of Liechtenstein.

"Liechtenstein," Juanito said. "That's an Earth country?"

"Very small one. Between Austria and Switzerland."

"I've heard of Switzerland. You live on Liechtenstein?"

"No," Farkas said. "I bank there. *In* Liechtenstein, is what Earth people say. Except for islands. Liechtenstein isn't an island. Can we get out of this place now?"

"One more transfer," Juanito said. "Pump your entry software across to me. Baggage claim, passport, visa. Make things much easier for us both, getting out of here."

"Make it easier for you to disappear with my suitcase, yes. And I'd never find you again, would I?"

"Do you think I'd do that?"

"I'm more profitable to you if you don't."

"You've got to trust your courier, Mr. Farkas. If you can't trust your courier, you can't trust anybody at all on Valparaiso."

"I know that," Farkas said.

Collecting Farkas' baggage and getting him clear of the customs tank took another half an hour and cost about 200 callies in miscellaneous bribes, which was about standard. Everyone from the baggage-handling androids to the cute snotty teller at the currency-exchange booth had to be bought. Juanito understood that things didn't work that way on most worlds; but Valparaiso, he knew, was different from most worlds. In a place where the chief industry was the protection of fugitives, it made sense that the basis of the economy would be the recycling of bribes.

Farkas didn't seem to be any sort of fugitive, though. While he was waiting for the baggage Juanito pulled a readout on the software that the blind man had pumped over to him and saw that Farkas was here on a visitor's visa, six week limit. So he was a seeker, not a hider. Well, that was okay. It was possible to turn a profit working either side of the deal. Running traces wasn't Juanito's usual number, but he figured he could adapt.

The other thing that Farkas didn't seem to be was blind. As they emerged from the customs tank he turned and pointed back at the huge portrait of El Supremo and said, "Who's that? Your President?"

"The Defender, that's his title. The Generalissimo. El Supremo, Don Eduardo Callaghan." Then it sank in and Juanito said, blinking, "Pardon me. You can *see* that picture, Mr. Farkas?"

"In a manner of speaking."

"I don't follow. Can you see or can't you?""

"Yes and no."

"Thanks a lot, Mr. Farkas."

"We can talk more about it later," Farkas said.

Juanito always put new dinkos in the same hotel, the San Bernardito, four kilometers out from the hub in the rim community of Cajamarca. "This way," he told Farkas. "We have to take the elevator at C Spoke."

Farkas didn't seem to have any trouble following him. Every now and then Juanito glanced back, and there was the big man three or four paces behind him, marching along steadily down the corridor. No eyes, Juanito thought, but somehow he can see. He definitely can see.

The four-kilometer elevator ride down C Spoke to the rim was spectacular all the way. The elevator was a glass-walled chamber inside a glass-walled tube that ran along the outside of the spoke, and it let you see everything: the whole great complex of wheels within wheels that was the Earth-orbit artificial world of Valparaiso, the seven great structural spokes radiating from the hub to the distant wheel of the rim, each spoke bearing its seven glass-and-aluminum globes that contained the residential zones and business sectors and farmlands and recreational zones and forest reserves. As the elevator descended—the gravity rising as you went down, climbing toward an Earth-one pull in the rim towns—you had a view of the sun's dazzling glint on the adjacent spokes, and an occasional glimpse of the great blue belly of Earth filling up the sky a hundred fifty thousand kilometers away, and the twinkling hordes of other satellite worlds in their nearby orbits, like a swarm of jellyfish dancing in a vast black ocean. That was what everybody who came up from Earth said, "Like jellyfish in the ocean."

Juanito didn't understand how a fish could be made out of jelly, or how a satellite world with seven spokes looked anything like a fish of any kind, but that was what they all said.

Farkas didn't say anything about jellyfish. But in some fashion or other he did indeed seem to be taking in the view. He stood close to the elevator's glass wall in deep concentration, gripping the rail, not saying a thing. Now and then he made a little hissing sound as something particularly awesome went by outside. Juanito studied him with sidelong glances. What could he possibly see? Nothing seemed to be moving beneath those shadowy places where his eyes should have been. Yet somehow he was seeing out of that broad blank stretch of gleaming skin above his nose. It was damned disconcerting. It was downright weird.

The San Bernardito gave Farkas a rim-side room, facing the stars. Juanito paid the hotel clerks to treat his clients right. That was something his father had taught him when he was just a kid who wasn't old enough to know a Schwarzchild singularity from an ace in the hole. "Pay for what you're going to need," his father kept saying. "Buy it and at least there's a chance it'll be there when you have to have it." His father had been a revolutionary in Central America during the time of the Empire. He would have been Prime Minister if the revolution had come out the right way. But it hadn't.

"You want me to help you unpack?" Juanito said.

"I can manage."

"Sure," Juanito said.

He stood by the window, looking at the sky. Like all the other satellite worlds, Valparaiso was shielded from cosmic ray damage and stray meteoroids by a double shell filled with a three-meter-thick layer of lunar slag. Rows of V-shaped apertures ran down the outer skin of the shield, mirror-faced to admit sunlight but not hard radiation; and the hotel had lined its rooms up so each one on this side had a view of space through the V's. The whole town of Cajamarca was facing darkwise now, and the stars were glittering fiercely.

When Juanito turned from the window he saw that Farkas had hung his clothes neatly in the closet and was shaving—methodically, precisely—with a little hand-held laser.

"Can I ask you something personal?" Juanito said.

"You want to know how I see."

"It's pretty amazing, I have to say."

"I don't see. Not really. I'm just as blind as you think I am."

"Then how—"

"It's called blindsight," Farkas said. "Proprioceptive vision."

"What?"

Farkas chuckled. "There's all sorts of data bouncing around that doesn't have the form of reflected light, which is what your eyes see. A million vibrations besides those that happen to be in the visual part of the electromagnetic spectrum are shimmering in this room. Air currents pass around things and are deformed by what they encounter. And it isn't only the air currents. Objects have mass, they have heat, they have—the term won't make any sense to you—*shapeweight*. A quality having to do with the interaction of mass and form. Does that mean anything to you? No, I guess not. Look, there's a lot of information available beyond what you can see with eyes, if you want it. I want it."

"You use some kind of machine to pick it up?" Juanito asked.

Farkas tapped his forehead. "It's in here. I was born with it."

"Some kind of sensing organ instead of eyes?"

"That's pretty close."

"What do you see, then? What do things look like to you?"

"What do they look like to you?" Farkas said. "What does a chair look like to you?"

"Well, it's got four legs, and a back—"

"What does a leg look like?"

"It's longer than it is wide."

"Right." Farkas knelt and ran his hands along the black tubular legs of the ugly little chair beside the bed. "I touch the chair, I feel the shape of the legs. But I don't see leg-shaped shapes."

"What then?"

"Silver globes that roll away into fat curves. The back part of the chair bends double and folds into itself. The bed's a bright pool of mercury with long green spikes coming up. You're six blue spheres stacked one on top of another, with a thick orange cable running through them. And so on."

"Blue?" Juanito said. "Orange? How do you know anything about colors?"

"The same way you do. I call one color blue, another one orange. I don't know if they're anything like your blue or orange, but so what? My blue is always blue for me. It's different from the color I see as red and the one I see as green. Orange is always orange. It's a matter of relationships. You follow?"

"No," Juanito said. "How can you possibly make sense out of anything? What you see doesn't have anything to do with the real color or shape or position of anything."

Farkas shook his head. "Wrong, Juanito. For me, what I see is the real shape and color and position. It's all I've ever known. If they were able to retrofit me with normal eyes now, which I'm told would be less than fifty-fifty likely to succeed and tremendously risky besides, I'd be lost trying to find my way around in your world. It would take me years to learn how. Or maybe forever. But I do all right, in mine. I understand, by touching things, that what I see by blindsight isn't the 'actual' shape. But I see in consistent equivalents. Do you follow? A chair always looks like what I think of as a chair, even though I know that chairs aren't really shaped anything like that. If you could see things the way I do it would all look like something out of another dimension. It *is* something out of another dimension, really. The information I operate by is different from what you use, that's all. And the world I move through looks completely different from the world that normal people see. But I do see, in my own way. I perceive objects and establish relationships between them, I make spatial perceptions, just as you do. Do you follow, Juanito? Do you follow?"

Juanito considered that. How very weird it sounded. To see the world in funhouse distortions, blobs and spheres and orange cables and glimmering pools of mercury. Weird, very weird. After a moment he said, "And you were born like this?"

"That's right."

"Some kind of genetic accident?"

"Not an accident," Farkas said quietly. "I was an experiment. A master gene-splicer worked me over in my mother's womb."

"Right," Juanito said. "You know, that's actually the first thing I guessed when I saw you come off the shuttle. This has to be some kind of splice effect, I said. But why—why—" He faltered. "Does it bother you to talk about this stuff?"

"Not really."

"Why would your parents have allowed—"

"They didn't have any choice, Juanito."

"Isn't that illegal? Involuntary splicing?"

"Of course," Farkas said. "So what?"

"But who would do that to—"

"This was in the Free State of Kazakhstan, which you've never heard of. It was one of the new countries formed out of the Soviet Union, which you've also probably never heard of, after the Breakup. My father was Hungarian consul at Tashkent. He was killed in the Breakup and my mother, who was pregnant, was volunteered for the experiments in prenatal genetic surgery then being carried out in that city under Chinese auspices. A lot of remarkable work was done there in those years. They were trying to breed new and useful kinds of human beings to serve the new republic. I was one of the experiments in extending the human perceptual range. I was supposed to have normal sight plus blindsight, but I didn't quite work out that way."

"You sound very calm about it," Juanito said.

"What good is getting angry?"

"My father used to say that too," Juanito said. "Don't get angry, get even. He was in politics, the Central American Empire. When the revolution failed he took sanctuary here."

"So did the surgeon who did my prenatal splice," Farkas said. "Fifteen years ago. He's still living here."

"Of course," Juanito said, as everything fell into place.

"The man's name is Wu Fang-shui," Juanito said. "He'd be about 75 years old, Chinese, and that's all I know, except there'll be a lot of money in finding him. There can't be that many Chinese on Valparaiso, right?"

"He won't still be Chinese," Kluge said.

Delilah said, "He might not even still be a he."

"I've thought of that," said Juanito. "All the same, it ought to be possible to trace him."

"Who you going to use for the trace?" Kluge asked.

Juanito gave him a steady stare. "Going to do it myself."

"You?"

"Me, myself. Why the hell not?"

"You never did a trace, did you?"

"There's always a first," Juanito said, still staring.

He thought he knew why Kluge was poking at him. A certain quantity of the business done on Valparaiso involved finding people who had hidden themselves here and selling them to their pursuers, but up till now Juanito had stayed away from that side of the profession. He earned his money by helping dinkos go underground on Valparaiso, not by selling people out. One reason for that was that nobody yet had happened to offer him a really profitable trace deal; but another was that he was the son of a former fugitive himself. Someone had been hired to do a trace on his own father seven years back, which was how his father had come to be assassinated. Juanito preferred to work the sanctuary side of things.

He was also a professional, though. He was in the business of providing service, period. If he didn't find the runaway gene surgeon for Farkas, somebody else would. And Farkas was his client. Juanito felt it was important to do things in a professional way.

"If I run into problems," he said, "I might subcontract. In the meanwhile I just thought I'd let you know, in case you happened to stumble on a lead. I'll pay finders' fees. And you know it'll be good money."

"Wu Fang-shui," Kluge said. "I'll see what I can do."

"Me too," said Delilah.

"Hell," Juanito said. "How many people are there on Valparaiso all together? Maybe nine hundred thousand? I can think of fifty right away who can't possibly be the guy I'm looking for. That narrows the odds some. What I have to do is just go on narrowing, right? Right?"

In fact he didn't feel very optimistic. He was going to do his best; but the whole system on Valparaiso was heavily weighted in favor of helping those who wanted to hide stay hidden.

Even Farkas realized that. "The privacy laws here are very strict, aren't they?"

With a smile Juanito said, "They're just about the only laws we have, you know? The sacredness of sanctuary. It is the compassion of El Supremo that has turned Valparaiso into a place of refuge for fugitives of all sorts, and we are not supposed to interfere with the compassion of El Supremo."

"Which is very expensive compassion, I understand."

"Very. Sanctuary fees are renewable annually. Anyone who harms a permanent resident who is living here under the compassion of El Supremo is bringing about a reduction in El Supremo's annual income, you see? Which doesn't sit well with the Generalissimo."

They were in the Villanueva Cafe, E Spoke. They had been touring Valparaiso all day long, back and forth from rim to hub, going up one spoke and down the other. Farkas said he wanted to experience as much of Valparaiso as he could. Not to see; to *experience*. He was insatiable, prowling around everywhere, gobbling it all up, soaking it in. Farkas had never been to one of the satellite worlds before. It amazed him, he said, that there were forests and lakes here, broad fields of wheat and rice, fruit orchards, herds of goats and cattle. Apparently he had expected the place to be nothing more than a bunch of aluminum struts and grim concrete boxes with everybody living on food pills, or something. People from Earth never seemed to comprehend that the larger satellite worlds were comfortable places with blue skies, fleecy clouds, lovely gardens, handsome buildings of steel and brick and glass.

Farkas said, "How do you go about tracing a fugitive, then?"

"There are always ways. Everybody knows somebody who knows something about someone. Information is bought here the same way compassion is."

"From the Generalissimo?" Farkas said, startled.

"From his officials, sometimes. If done with great care. Care is important, because lives are at risk. There are also couriers who have information to sell. We all know a great deal that we are not supposed to know."

"I suppose you know a great many fugitives by sight, yourself?"

"Some," Juanito said. "You see that man, sitting by the window?" He frowned. "I don't know, can you see him? To me he looks around 60, bald head, thick lips, no chin?"

"I see him, yes. He looks a little different to me."

"I bet he does. He ran a swindle at one of the Luna domes, sold phony stock in an offshore monopoly fund that didn't exist, fifty million Capbloc dollars. He pays plenty to live here. This one here—you see? With the blonde woman?—an embezzler, that one, very good with computers, reamed a bank in Singapore for almost its entire capital. Him over there, he pretended to be Pope. Can you believe that? Everybody in Rio de Janeiro did."

"Wait a minute," Farkas said. "How do I know you're not making all this up?"

"You don't," Juanito said amiably. "But I'm not."

"So we just sit here like this and you expose the identities of three fugitives to me free of charge?"

"It wouldn't be free," Juanito said, "if they were people you were looking for."

"What if they were? And my claiming to be looking for a Wu Fang-shui just a cover?"

"You aren't looking for any of them," Juanito said.

"No," said Farkas. "I'm not." He sipped his drink, something green and cloudy. "How come these men haven't done a better job of concealing their identities?" he asked.

"They think they have," said Juanito.

Getting leads was a slow business, and expensive. Juanito left Farkas to wander the spokes of Valparaiso on his own, and headed off to the usual sources of information: his father's friends, other couriers, and even the headquarters of the Unity Party, El Supremo's grass-roots organization, where it wasn't hard to find someone who knew something and had a price for it. Juanito was cautious. Middle-aged Chinese gentleman I'm trying to locate, he said. Why? Nobody asked. Could be any reason, anything from wanting to blow him away on contract to handing him a million Capbloc-dollar lottery prize that he had won last year on New Yucatan. Nobody asked for reasons on Valparaiso.

There was a man named Federigo who had been with Juanito's father in the Costa Rica days who knew a woman who knew a man who had a freemartin neuter companion who had formerly belonged to someone high up in the Census Department. There were fees to pay at every step of the way, but it was Farkas' money, what the hell, and by the end of the week Juanito had access to the immigration data stored on golden megachips somewhere in the depths of the hub. The data down there wasn't going to provide anybody with Wu Fang-shui's phone number. But what it could tell Juanito, and did, eight hundred callaghanos later, was how many ethnic Chinese were living on Valparaiso and how long ago they had arrived.

"There are nineteen of them altogether," he reported to Farkas. "Eleven of them are women."

"So? Changing sex is no big deal," Farkas said.

"Agreed. The women are all under 50, though. The oldest of the men is 62. The longest that any of them has been on Valparaiso is nine years."

"Would you say that rules them all out? Age can be altered just as easily as sex."

"But date of arrival can't be, so far as I know. And you say that your Wu Fang-shui came here fifteen years back. Unless you're wrong about that, he can't be any of those Chinese. Your Wu Fang-shui, if he isn't dead by now, has signed up for some other racial mix, I'd say."

"He isn't dead," Farkas said.

"You sure of that?"

"He was still alive three months ago, and in touch with his family on Earth. He's got a brother in Tashkent."

"Shit," Juanito said. "Ask the brother what name he's going under up here, then."

"We did. We couldn't get it."

"Ask him harder."

"We asked him too hard," said Farkas. "Now the information isn't available any more. Not from him, anyway."

Juanito checked out the nineteen Chinese, just to be certain. It didn't cost much and it didn't take much time, and there was always the chance that Dr. Wu had cooked his immigration data somehow. But the quest led nowhere. Juanito found six of them all in one shot, playing some Chinese game in a social club in the town of Havana de Cuba on Spoke B, and they went right on laughing and pushing the little porcelain counters around while he stood there kibitzing. They didn't *act* like sanctuarios. They were all shorter than Juanito, too, which meant either that they weren't Dr. Wu, who was tall for a Chinese, or that Dr. Wu had been willing to have his legs chopped down by fifteen centimeters for the sake of a more efficient disguise. It was possible but it wasn't too likely.

The other thirteen were all much too young or too convincingly female or too this or too that. Juanito crossed them all off his list. From the outset he hadn't thought Wu would still be Chinese, anyway.

He kept on looking. One trail went cold, and then another, and then another. By now he was starting to think Dr. Wu must have heard that a man with no eyes was looking for him, and had gone even deeper underground, or off Valparaiso entirely. Juanito paid a friend at the hub spaceport to keep watch on departure manifests for him. Nothing came of that. Then someone reminded him that there was a colony of old-time hard-core sanctuary types living in and around the town of

El Mirador on Spoke D, people who had a genuine aversion to being bothered. He went there. Because he was known to be the son of a murdered fugitive himself, nobody hassled him: he of all people wouldn't be likely to be running a trace, would he?

The visit yielded no directly useful result. He couldn't risk asking questions and nothing was showing on the surface. But he came away with the strong feeling that El Mirador was the answer.

"Take me there," Farkas said.

"I can't do that. It's a low-profile town. Strangers aren't welcome. You'll stick out like a dinosaur."

"Take me," Farkas repeated.

"If Wu's there and he gets even a glimpse of you, he'll know right away that there's a contract out for him and he'll vanish so fast you won't believe it."

"Take me to El Mirador," said Farkas. "It's my money, isn't it?"

"Right," Juanito said. "Let's go to El Mirador."

El Mirador was midway between hub and rim on its spoke. There were great glass windows punched in its shield that provided a colossal view of all the rest of Valparaiso and the stars and the sun and the moon and the Earth and everything. A solar eclipse was going on when Juanito and Farkas arrived: the Earth was plastered right over the sun with nothing but one squidge of hot light showing down below like a diamond blazing on a golden ring. Purple shadows engulfed the town, deep and thick, a heavy velvet curtain falling over everything.

Juanito tried to describe what he saw. Farkas made an impatient brushing gesture.

"I know, I know. I feel it in my teeth." They stood on a big people-mover escalator leading down into the town plaza. "The sun is long and thin right now, like the blade of an axe. The Earth has six sides, each one glowing a different color."

Juanito gaped at the eyeless man in amazement.

"Wu is here," Farkas said. "Down there, in the plaza. I feel his presence."

"From five hundred meters away?"

"Come with me."

"What do we do if he really is?"

"Are you armed?"

"I have a spike, yes."

"Good. Tune it to shock, and don't use it at all if you can help it. I don't want you to hurt him in any way."

"I understand. You want to kill him yourself, in your own sweet time."

"Just be careful not to hurt him," Farkas said. "Come on."

It was an old-fashioned-looking town, cobblestone plaza, little cafes around its perimeter and a fountain in the middle. About ten thousand people lived there and it seemed as if they were all out in the plaza sipping drinks and watching the eclipse. Juanito was grateful for the eclipse. No one paid any attention to them as they came floating down the peoplemover and strode into the plaza. Hell of a thing, he thought. You walk into town with a man with no eyes walking right behind you and nobody even notices. But when the sunshine comes back on it may be different.

"There he is," Farkas whispered. "To the left, maybe fifty meters, sixty."

Juanito peered through the purple gloom at the plazafront cafe beyond the next one. A dozen or so people were sitting in small groups at curbside tables under iridescent fiberglass awnings, drinking, chatting, taking it easy. Just another casual afternoon in good old cozy El Mirador on sleepy old Valparaiso.

Farkas stood sideways to keep his strange face partly concealed. Out of the corner of his mouth he said, "Wu is the one sitting by himself at the front table."

"The only one sitting alone is a woman, maybe 50, 55 years old, long reddish hair, big nose, dowdy clothes ten years out of fashion."

"That's Wu."

"How can you be so sure?"

"It's possible to retrofit your body to make it look entirely different on the outside. You can't change the non-visual information, the stuff I pick up by blindsight. What Dr. Wu looked like to me, the last time I saw him, was a cubical block of black metal polished bright as a mirror, sitting on top of a pyramid-shaped copper-colored pedestal. I was nine years old then, but I promised myself I wouldn't ever forget what he looked like, and I haven't. That's what the person sitting over there by herself looks like."

Juanito stared. He still saw a plain-looking woman in a rumpled old-fashioned suit. They did wonders with retrofitting these days, he knew: they could make almost any sort of body grow on you, like clothing on a clothesrack, by fiddling with your DNA. But still Juanito had trouble thinking of that woman over there as a sinister Chinese gene-splicer in disguise, and he had even more trouble seeing her as a polished cube sitting on top of a coppery pyramid.

"What do you want to do now?" he asked.

"Let's go over and sit down alongside her. Keep that spike of yours ready. But I hope you don't use it."

"If we put the arm on her and she's not Wu," Juanito said, "it's going to get me in a hell of a lot of trouble, particularly if she's paying El Supremo for sanctuary. Sanctuary people get very stuffy when their privacy is violated. You'll be expelled and I'll be fined a fortune and a half and I might wind up getting expelled too, and then what?"

"That's Dr. Wu," Farkas said. "Watch him react when he sees me, and then you'll believe it."

"We'll still be violating sanctuary. All he has to do is yell for the police."

"We need to make it clear to him right away," said Farkas, "that that would be a foolish move. You follow?"

"But I don't hurt him," Juanito said.

"No. Not in any fashion. You simply demonstrate a willingness to hurt him if it should become necessary. Let's go, now. You sit down first, ask politely if it's okay for you to share the table, make some comment about the eclipse. I'll come over maybe thirty seconds after you. All clear? Good. Go ahead, now."

"You have to be insane," the red-haired woman said. But she was sweating in an astonishing way and her fingers were knotting together like anguished snakes. "I'm not any kind of doctor and my name isn't Wu or Fu or whatever you said, and you have exactly two seconds to get away from me." She seemed unable to take her eyes from Farkas' smooth blank forehead. Farkas didn't move. After a moment she said in a different tone of voice, "What kind of thing are you, anyway?"

She isn't Wu, Juanito decided.

The real Wu wouldn't have asked a question like that. Besides, this was definitely a woman. She was absolutely convincing around the jaws, along the hairline, the soft flesh behind her chin. Women were different from men in all those places. Something about her wrists. The way she sat. A lot of other things. There weren't any genetic surgeons good enough to do a retrofit this convincing. Juanito peered at her eyes, trying to see the place where the Chinese fold had been, but there wasn't a trace of it. Her eyes were blue-gray. All Chinese had brown eyes, didn't they?

Farkas said, leaning in close and hard, "My name is Victor Farkas, Doctor. I was born in Tashkent during the Breakup. My mother was the wife of the Hungarian consul, and you did a genesplice job on the fetus she was carrying. That was your specialty, tectogenetic reconstruction. You don't remember that? You deleted my eyes and gave me blindsight instead, Doctor."

The woman looked down and away. Color came to her cheeks. Something heavy seemed to be stirring within her. Juanito began to change his mind. Maybe there really were some gene surgeons who could do a retrofit this good, he thought.

"None of this is true," she said. "You're simply a lunatic. I can show you who I am. I have papers. You have no right to harass me like this."

"I don't want to hurt you in any way, Doctor."

"I am not a doctor."

"Could you be a doctor again? For a price?"

Juanito swung around, astounded, to look at Farkas.

"I will not listen to this," the woman said. "You will go away from me this instant or I summon the patrol."

Farkas said, "We have a project, Dr. Wu. My engineering group, a division of a corporation whose name I'm sure you know. An experimental spacedrive, the first interstellar voyage, faster-than-light travel. We're three years away from a launch."

The woman rose. "This madness does not interest me."

"The faster-than-light field distorts vision," Farkas went on. He didn't appear to notice that she was standing and looked about ready to bolt. "It disrupts vision entirely, in fact. Perception becomes totally abnormal. A crew with normal vision wouldn't be able to function in any way. But it turns out that someone with blindsight can adapt fairly easily to the peculiar changes that the field induces."

"I have no interest in hearing about—"

"It's been tested, actually. With me as the subject. But I can't make the voyage alone. We have a crew of five and they've volunteered for tectogenetic retrofits to give them what I have. We don't know anyone else who has your experience in that area. We'd like you to come out of retirement, Dr. Wu. We'll set up a complete lab for you on a nearby satellite world, whatever equipment you need. And pay you very well. And insure your safety all the time you're gone from Valparaiso. What do you say?"

The red-haired woman was trembling and slowly backing away.

"No," she said. "It was such a long time ago. Whatever skills I had, I have forgotten, I have buried."

So Farkas was right all along, Juanito thought.

"You can give yourself a refresher course. I don't think it's possible really to forget a gift like yours, do you?" Farkas said.

"No. Please. Let me be."

Juanito was amazed at how cockeyed his whole handle on the situation had been from the start.

Farkas didn't seem at all angry with the gene surgeon. He hadn't come here for vengeance, Juanito realized. Just to cut a deal.

"Where's he going?" Farkas said suddenly. "Don't let him get away, Juanito."

The woman—Wu—was moving faster now, not quite running but sidling away at a steady pace, back into the enclosed part of the cafe. Farkas gestured sharply and Juanito began to follow. The spike he was carrying could deliver a stun-level jolt at fifteen paces. But he couldn't just spike her down in this crowd, not if she had sanctuary protection, not in El Mirador of all places.

There'd be fifty sanctuarios on top of him in a minute. They'd grab him and club him and sell his foreskin to the Generalissimo's men for two and a half callies.

The cafe was crowded and dark. Juanito caught sight of her somewhere near the back, near the restrooms. Go on, he thought. Go into the ladies' room. I'll follow you right in there. I don't give a damn about that.

But she went past the restrooms and ducked into an alcove near the kitchen instead. Two waiters laden with trays came by, scowling at Juanito to get out of the way. It took him a moment to pass around them, and by then he could no longer see the red-haired woman. He knew he was going to have big trouble with Farkas if he lost her in here. Farkas was going to have a fit. Farkas would try to stiff him on this week's pay, most likely. Two thousand callies down the drain, not even counting the extra charges.

Then a hand reached out of the shadows and seized his wrist with surprising ferocity. He was dragged a little way into a claustrophobic games room dense with crackling green haze coming from some bizarre machine on the far wall. The red-haired woman glared at him, wild-eyed. "He wants to kill me, doesn't he? That's all bullshit about having me do retrofit operations, right?"

"I think he means it," Juanito said.

"Nobody would volunteer to have his eyes replaced with blind-sight."

"How would I know? People do all sorts of crazy things. But if he wanted to kill you I think he'd have operated differently when we tracked you down."

"He'll get me off Valparaiso and kill me somewhere else."

"I don't know," Juanito said. "I was just doing a job."

"How much did he pay you to do the trace?" Savagely. "How much? I know you've got a spike in your pocket. Just leave it there and answer me. How much?"

"Three thousand callies a week," Juanito muttered, padding things a little.

"I'll give you five to help me get rid of him."

Juanito hesitated. Sell Farkas out? He didn't know if he could turn himself around that fast. Was it the professional thing to do, to take a higher bid?

"Eight," he said, after a moment.

Why the hell not? He didn't owe Farkas any loyalty. This was a sanctuary world; the compassion of El Supremo entitled Wu to protection here. It was every citizen's duty. And eight thousand callies was a big bundle.

"Six five," Wu said.

"Eight. Handshake right now. You have your glove?"

The woman who was Wu made a muttering sound and pulled out her flex terminal. "Account 1133," Juanito said, and they made the transfer of funds. "How do you want to do this?" Juanito asked.

"There is a passageway into the outer shell just behind this cafe. You will catch sight of me slipping in there and the two of you will follow me. When we are all inside and he is coming toward me, you get behind him and take him down with your spike. And we leave him buried in there." There was a frightening gleam in Wu's eyes. It was almost as if the cunning retrofit body was melting away and the real Wu beneath was emerging, moment by moment. "You understand?" Wu said. A fierce, blazing look. "I have bought you, boy. I expect you to stay bought when we are in the shell. Do you understand me? Do you? Good."

It was like a huge crawlspace entirely surrounding the globe that was El Mirador. Around the periphery of the double shell was a deep layer of lunar slag held in place by centrifugal forces, the tailings left over after the extraction of the gases and minerals that the satellite world had needed in its construction. On top of that was a low open area for the use of maintenance workers, lit by a trickle of light from a faint line of incandescent bulbs; and overhead was the inner skin of El Mirador itself, shielded by the slagpile from any surprises that might come ricocheting in from the void. Juanito was able to move almost upright within the shell, but Farkas, following along behind, had to bend double, scuttling like a crab.

"Can you see him yet?" Farkas asked.

"Somewhere up ahead, I think. It's pretty dark in here."

"Is it?"

Juanito saw Wu edging sideways, moving slowly around behind Farkas now. In the dimness Wu was barely visible, the shadow of a shadow. He had scooped up two handfuls of tailings. Evidently he was going to fling them at Farkas to attract his attention, and when Farkas turned toward Wu it would be Juanito's moment to nail him with the spike.

Juanito stepped back to a position near Farkas' left elbow. He slipped his hand into his pocket and touched the cool sleek little weapon. The intensity stud was down at the lower end, shock level, and without taking the spike from his pocket he moved the setting up to lethal. Wu nodded. Juanito began to draw the spike.

Suddenly Farkas roared like a wild creature. Juanito grunted in shock, stupefied by that terrible sound. This is all going to go wrong, he realized. A moment later Farkas whirled and seized him around the waist and swung him as if he was a throwing-hammer, hurling him through the air and sending him crashing with tremendous impact into Wu's midsection. Wu crumpled, gagging and puking, with Juanito sprawled stunned on top of him. Then the lights went out—Farkas must have reached up and yanked the conduit loose—and then Juanito found himself lying with his face jammed down into the rough floor of tailings. Farkas was holding him down with a hand clamped around the back of his neck and a knee pressing hard against his spine. Wu lay alongside him, pinned the same way.

"Did you think I couldn't see him sneaking up on me?" Farkas asked. "Or you, going for your spike? It's 360 degrees, the blindsight. Something that Dr. Wu must have forgotten. All these years on the run, I guess you start to forget things."

Jesus, Juanito thought. Couldn't even get the drop on a blind man from behind him. And now he's going to kill me. What a stupid way to die this is.

He imagined what Kluge might say about this, if he knew. Or Delilah. Nattathaniel. Decked by a blind man.

But he isn't blind. He isn't blind. He isn't blind at all.

Farkas said, "How much did you sell me to him for, Juanito?"

The only sound Juanito could make was a muffled moan. His mouth was choked with sharp bits of slag.

"How much? Five thousand? Six?"

"It was eight," said Wu quietly.

"At least I didn't go cheaply," Farkas murmured. He reached into Juanito's pocket and withdrew the spike. "Get up," he said. "Both of you. Stay close together. If either of you makes a funny move I'll kill you both. Remember that I can see you very clearly. I can also see the door through which we entered the shell. That starfish-looking thing over there, with streamers of purple light pulsing from it. We're going back into El Mirador now, and there won't be any surprises, will there? Will there?"

Juanito spit out a mouthful of slag. He didn't say anything.

"Dr. Wu? The offer still stands," Farkas continued. "You come with me, you do the job we need you for. That isn't so bad, considering what I could do to you for what you did to me. But all I want from you is your skills, and that's the truth. You are going to need that refresher course, aren't you, though?"

Wu muttered something indistinct.

Farkas said, "You can practice on this boy, if you like. Try retro-fitting him for blindsight first, and if it works, you can do our crew people, all right? He won't mind. He's terribly curious about the way I see things, anyway. Aren't you, Juanito? Eh? Eh?" Farkas laughed. To Juanito he said, "If everything works out the right way, maybe we'll let you go on the voyage with us, boy." Juanito felt the cold nudge of the spike in his back. "You'd like that, wouldn't you? The first trip to the stars? What do you say to that, Juanito?"

Juanito didn't answer. His tongue was still rough with slag. With Farkas prodding him from behind, he shambled slowly along next to

Dr. Wu toward the door that Farkas said looked like a starfish. It didn't look at all like a fish to him, or a star, or like a fish that looked like a star. It looked like a door to him, as far as he could tell by the feeble light of the distant bulbs. That was all it looked like, a door that looked like a door. Not a star. Not a fish. But there was no use thinking about it, or anything else, not now, not with Farkas nudging him between the shoulderblades with his own spike. He let his mind go blank and kept on walking.

GILGAMESH IN THE OUTBACK

Back in the mid-1980s, during the heyday of the shared-world science-fiction anthologies, in which a group of writers produced stories set in a common background defined by someone else, I was drawn into a project called Heroes in Hell. *Its general premise (at least as I understood it) was that everybody who had ever lived, and a good many mythical beings besides, had been resurrected in a quasi-afterlife in a place that was called, for the sake of convenience, Hell. The concept was never clearly explained to me—one of the problems with these shared-world deals—and so I never fully grasped what I was supposed to be doing. But the basic idea struck me as reminiscent of the great* Riverworld *concept of Philip Jose Farmer, humanity's total resurrection in some strange place, and I had long admired the Farmer books, so here was my chance to run my own variant on what Farmer had done a couple of decades earlier.*

I seized on Gilgamesh as my protagonist, since he has always seemed to me to be the archetype of the fantastic hero. (He had figured in several of my earlier stories, and in 1984 I had used the original Sumerian Gilgamesh legend as the basis for my novel Gilgamesh the King.*) Then, wondering whether Robert E. Howard would regard the towering Sumerian monarch as the prototype of his own Conan the Conqueror, I conjured Howard up to wander the wastelands of Hell as my secondary protagonist, and gave him H. P. Lovecraft for company. From there I added to the mix such people as Prester John, Kublai Khan, and Albert Schweitzer.*

The story took a couple of months for me to finish—from October, 1985 to the end of the year, because I was busy with other things, as I'll explain in the next introduction. But it was so much fun to write that I went on to do a second Gilgamesh in Hell novella, featuring the likes of Pablo Picasso and Simon Magus, and then a third. I never read very many of the other Heroes in Hell stories, so I have no idea how well my stories integrated themselves with those of my putative collaborators in the series, but I was enjoying myself and the novellas (which were also being published in Asimov's Science Fiction) were popular among readers. "Gilgamesh in the Outback," in fact, from the July, 1986 issue of Asimov's, won a Hugo for Best Novella in 1987, one of the few shared-world stories ever to achieve that.

By then I realized that what I was doing was writing a novel in serialized form. The book that resulted in 1987, To the Land of the Living, was not primarily an expansion but a compilation: I drew together my three Gilgamesh novellas, making slight revisions here and there in the interest of consistency, and added a brief epilog that gave Gilgamesh's seemingly random wanderings in Hell some emotional significance and an ultimate epiphany. The only major change in the original three texts involved deleting all material that referred directly, or directly grew from, the work of the other writers in the Heroes in Hell series. This was done to avoid any clashes over copyright issues. Since I had, by and large, gone my own way as a contributor to the series, with only the most tangential links to what others had invented, it seemed wisest to eradicate from my book any aspect that some other writer might lay claim to, and I did.

———————

*F*aust. First I will question thee about hell.
Tell me, where is the place that men call hell?
Meph. Under the heavens.
Faust. Ay, but whereabout?
Meph. Within the bowels of these elements,
Where we are tortur'd and remain for ever:
Hell hath no limits, nor is circumscrib'd
In one self place; for where we are is hell,
And where hell is, there must we ever be:
And, to conclude, when all the world dissolves,
And every creature shall be purified,
All places shall be hell that are not heaven.
Faust. Come, I think hell's a fable.

Meph. Ay, think so still, till experience change thy mind.

Marlowe: *Dr. Faustus*

Jagged green lightning danced on the horizon and the wind came ripping like a blade out of the east, skinning the flat land bare and sending up clouds of gray-brown dust. Gilgamesh grinned broadly. By Enlil, now that was a wind! A lion-killing wind it was, a wind that turned the air dry and crackling. The beasts of the field gave you the greatest joy in their hunting when the wind was like that, hard and sharp and cruel.

He narrowed his eyes and stared into the distance, searching for this day's prey. His bow of several fine woods, the bow that no man but he was strong enough to draw—no man but he and Enkidu his beloved thrice-lost friend—hung loosely from his hand. His body was poised and ready. Come now, you beasts! Come and be slain! It is Gilgamesh, king of Uruk, who would make his sport with you this day!

Other men in this land, when they went about their hunting, made use of guns, those foul machines that the New Dead had brought, which hurled death from a great distance along with much noise and fire and smoke; or they employed the even deadlier laser devices from whose ugly snouts came spurts of blue-white flame. Cowardly things, all those killing machines! Gilgamesh loathed them, as he did most instruments of the New Dead, those slick and bustling Johnny-come-latelies of Hell. He would not touch them if he could help it. In all the thousands of years he had dwelled in this nether world he had never used any weapons but those he had known during his first lifetime: the javelin, the spear, the double-headed axe, the hunting bow, the good bronze sword. It took some skill, hunting with such weapons as those. And there was physical effort; there was more than a little risk. Hunting was a contest, was it not? Then it must make demands. Why, if the idea was merely to slaughter one's prey in the fastest and easiest and safest way, then the sensible thing to do would be to ride high above the hunting grounds in a weapons platform and drop a little nuke, eh, and lay waste five kingdoms' worth of beasts at a single stroke!

He knew that there were those who thought him a fool for such ideas. Caesar, for one. Cocksure cold-blooded Julius with the gleaming pistols thrust into his belt and the submachine gun slung across his shoulders. "Why don't you admit it?" Caesar had asked him once, riding up in his jeep as Gilgamesh was making ready to set forth toward

Hell's open wilderness. "It's a pure affectation, Gilgamesh, all this insistence on arrows and javelins and spears. This isn't old Sumer you're living in now."

Gilgamesh spat. "Hunt with 9-millimeter automatics? Hunt with grenades and cluster bombs and lasers? You call that sport, Caesar?"

"I call it acceptance of reality. Is it technology you hate? What's the difference between using a bow and arrow and using a gun? They're both technology, Gilgamesh. It isn't as though you kill the animals with your bare hands."

"I have done that, too," said Gilgamesh.

"Bah! I'm on to your game. Big hulking Gilgamesh, the simple innocent oversized Bronze Age hero! That's just an affectation, too, my friend! You pretend to be a stupid, stubborn thick-skulled barbarian because it suits you to be left alone to your hunting and your wandering, and that's all you claim that you really want. But secretly you regard yourself as superior to anybody who lived in an era softer than your own. You mean to restore the bad old filthy ways of the ancient ancients, isn't that so? If I read you the right way you're just biding your time, skulking around with your bow and arrow in the dreary Outback until you think it's the right moment to launch the *putsch* that carries you to supreme power here. Isn't that it, Gilgamesh? You've got some crazy fantasy of overthrowing Satan himself and lording it over all of us. And then we'll live in mud cities again and make little chicken scratches on clay tablets, the way we were meant to do. What do you say?"

"I say this is great nonsense, Caesar."

"Is it? This place is full of kings and emperors and sultans and pharaohs and shahs and presidents and dictators, and every single one of them wants to be Number One again. My guess is that you're no exception."

"In this you are very wrong."

"I doubt that. I suspect you believe you're the best of us all; you, the sturdy warrior, the great hunter, the maker of bricks, the builder of vast temples and lofty walls, the shining beacon of ancient heroism. You think we're all decadent rascally degenerates and that you're the one true virtuous man. But you're as proud and ambitious as any of us. Isn't that how it is? You're a fraud, Gilgamesh, a huge musclebound fraud!"

"At least I am no slippery tricky serpent like you, Caesar, who dons a wig and spies on women at their mysteries if it pleases him."

Caesar looked untroubled by the thrust. "And so you pass three-quarters of your time killing stupid monstrous creatures in the Outback and you make sure everyone knows that you're too pious to have anything to do with modern weapons while you do it. You don't fool me. It isn't virtue that keeps you from doing your killing with a decent double-barreled .470 Springfield. It's intellectual pride, or maybe simple laziness. The bow just happens to be the weapon you grew up with, who knows how many thousands of years ago. You like it because it's familiar. But what language are you speaking now, eh? Is it your thick-tongued Euphrates gibberish? No, it seems to be English, doesn't it? Did you grow up speaking English too, Gilgamesh? Did you grow up riding around in jeeps and choppers? Apparently *some* of the new ways are acceptable to you."

Gilgamesh shrugged. "I speak English with you because that is what is spoken now in this place. In my heart I speak the old tongue, Caesar. In my heart I am still Gilgamesh of Uruk, and I will hunt as I hunt."

"Uruk's long gone to dust. This is the life after life, my friend. We've been here a long time. We'll be here for all time to come, unless I miss my guess. New people constantly bring new ideas to this place, and it's impossible to ignore them. Even you can't do it. Isn't that a wristwatch I see on your arm, Gilgamesh? A *digital* watch, no less?"

"I will hunt as I hunt," said Gilgamesh. "There is no sport in it, when you do it with guns. There is no grace in it."

Caesar shook his head. "I never could understand hunting for sport, anyway. Killing a few stags, yes, or a boar or two, when you've bivouacked in some dismal Gaulish forest and your men want meat. But hunting? Slaughtering hideous animals that aren't even edible? By Apollo, it's all nonsense to me!"

"My point exactly."

"But if you must hunt, to scorn the use of a decent hunting rifle—"

"You will never convince me."

"No," Caesar said with a sigh. "I suppose I won't. I should know better than to argue with a reactionary."

"Reactionary! In my time I was thought to be a radical," said Gilgamesh. "When I was king in Uruk—"

"Just so," Caesar said, laughing. "King in Uruk. Was there ever a king who wasn't reactionary? You put a crown on your head and it addles your brains instantly. Three times Antonius offered me a crown, Gilgamesh. Three times, and—"

"—you did thrice refuse it, yes. I know all that. 'Was this ambition?' You thought you'd have the power without the emblem. Who were you fooling, Caesar? Not Brutus, so I hear. Brutus said you were ambitious. And Brutus—"

That stung him. "Damn you, don't say it!"

"—was an honorable man," Gilgamesh concluded, enjoying Caesar's discomfiture.

Caesar groaned. "If I hear that line once more—"

"Some say this is a place of torment," said Gilgamesh serenely. "If in truth it is, yours is to be swallowed up in another man's poetry. Leave me to my bows and arrows, Caesar, and return to your jeep and your trivial intrigues. I am a fool and a reactionary, yes. But you know nothing of hunting. Nor do you understand anything of me."

All that had been a year ago, or two, or maybe five—with or without a wristwatch, there was no keeping proper track of time in Hell, where the unmoving ruddy eye of the sun never budged from the sky— and now Gilgamesh was far from Caesar and all his minions, far from the troublesome center of Hell and the tiresome squabbling of those like Caesar and Alexander and Napoleon and that sordid little Guevara man who maneuvered for power in this place.

Let them maneuver all they liked, those shoddy new men of the latter days. Some day they might learn wisdom, and was not that the purpose of this place, if it had any purpose at all?

Gilgamesh preferred to withdraw. Unlike the rest of those fallen emperors and kings and pharaohs and shahs, he felt no yearning to reshape Hell in his own image. Caesar was as wrong about Gilgamesh's ambitions as he was about the reasons for his preferences in hunting gear. Out here in the Outback, in the bleak dry chilly hinterlands of Hell, Gilgamesh hoped to find peace. That was all he wanted now: peace. He had wanted much more, once, but that had been long ago.

There was a stirring in the scraggly underbrush.

A lion, maybe?

No, Gilgamesh thought. There were no lions to be found in Hell, only the strange nether-world beasts. Ugly hairy things with flat noses and many legs and dull baleful eyes, and slick shiny things with the faces of women and the bodies of malformed dogs, and worse, much

246

worse. Some had drooping leathery wings, and some were armed with spiked tails that rose like a scorpion's, and some had mouths that opened wide enough to swallow an elephant at a gulp. They all were demons of one sort or another, Gilgamesh knew. No matter. Hunting was hunting; the prey was the prey; all beasts were one in the contest of the field. That fop Caesar could never begin to comprehend that.

Drawing an arrow from his quiver, Gilgamesh laid it lightly across his bow and waited.

"If you ever had come to Texas, H.P., this here's a lot like what you'd have seen," said the big barrel-chested man with the powerful arms and the deeply tanned skin. Gesturing sweepingly with one hand, he held the wheel of the Land Rover lightly with three fingers of the other, casually guiding the vehicle in jouncing zigs and zags over the flat trackless landscape. Gnarled gray-green shrubs matted the gritty ground. The sky was black with swirling dust. Far off in the distance barren mountains rose like dark jagged teeth. "Beautiful. Beautiful. As close to Texas in look as makes no never mind, this countryside is."

"Beautiful?" said the other man uncertainly. "Hell?"

"This stretch sure is. But if you think Hell's beautiful, you should have seen Texas!"

The burly man laughed and gunned the engine, and the Land Rover went leaping and bouncing onward at a stupefying speed.

His traveling companion, a gaunt, lantern-jawed man as pale as the other was bronzed, sat very still in the passenger seat, knees together and elbows digging in against his ribs, as if he expected a fiery crash at any moment. The two of them had been journeying across the interminable parched wastes of the Outback for many days now—how many, not even the Elder Gods could tell. They were ambassadors, these two: Their Excellencies Robert E. Howard and H.P. Lovecraft of the Kingdom of New Holy Diabolic England, envoys of His Britannic Majesty Henry VIII to the court of Prester John.

In another life they had been writers, fantasists, inventors of fables; but now they found themselves caught up in something far more fantastic than anything to be found in any of their tales, for this was no fable, this was no fantasy. This was the reality of Hell.

"Robert—" said the pale man nervously.

"A lot like Texas, yes," Howard went on, "only Hell's just a faint carbon copy of the genuine item. Just a rough first draft, is all. You see that sandstorm rising out thataway? We had sandstorms, they covered entire counties! You see that lightning? In Texas that would be just a flicker!"

"If you could drive just a little more slowly, Bob—"

"More slowly? Cthulhu's whiskers, man, I am driving slowly!"

"Yes, I'm quite sure you believe that you are."

"And the way I always heard it, H.P., you loved for people to drive you around at top speed. Seventy, eighty miles an hour, that was what you liked best, so the story goes."

"In the other life one dies only once, and then all pain ceases," Lovecraft replied. "But here, where one can go to the Undertaker again and again, and when one returns one remembers every final agony in the brightest of hues—here, dear friend Bob, death's much more to be feared, for the pain of it stays with one forever, and one may die a thousand deaths." Lovecraft managed a pale baleful smile. "Speak of that to some professional warrior, Bob, some Trojan or Hun or Assyrian—or one of the gladiators, maybe, someone who has died and died and died again. Ask him about it: the dying and the rebirth, and the pain, the hideous torment, reliving every detail. It is a dreadful thing to die in Hell. I fear dying here far more than I ever did in life. I will take no needless risks here."

Howard snorted. "Gawd, try and figure you out! When you thought you lived only once, you made people go roaring along with you on the highway a mile a minute. Here where hardly anyone stays dead for very long you want me to drive like an old woman. Well, I'll attempt it, H.P., but everything in me cries out to go like the wind. When you live in big country, you learn to cover the territory the way it has to be covered. And Texas is the biggest country there is. It isn't just a place, it's a state of mind."

"As is Hell," said Lovecraft. "Though I grant you that Hell isn't Texas."

"Texas!" Howard boomed. "God damn, I wish you could have seen it! By god, H.P., what a time we'd have had, you and me, if you'd come to Texas. Two gentlemen of letters like us riding together all to hell and gone from Corpus Christi to El Paso and back again, seeing it all and telling each other wondrous stories all the way! I swear, it would have enlarged your soul, H.P. Beauty such as perhaps even you couldn't have imagined. That big sky. That blazing sun. And the open space! Whole empires could fit into Texas and never be seen again! That Rhode Island of yours, H.P.—we could drop it down just back of Cross Plains and lose it behind a medium-size prickly pear! What you see here, it just gives you the merest idea of that glorious beauty. Though I admit this is plenty beautiful itself, this here."

"I wish I could share your joy in this landscape, Robert," Lovecraft said quietly, when it seemed that Howard had said all he meant to say.

"You don't care for it?" Howard asked, sounding surprised and a little wounded.

"I can say one good thing for it: at least it's far from the sea."

"You'll give it that much, will you?"

"You know how I hate the sea and all that the sea contains! Its odious creatures—that hideous reek of salt air hovering above it—" Lovecraft shuddered fastidiously. "But this land—this bitter desert—you don't find it somber? You don't find it forbidding?"

"It's the most beautiful place I've seen since I came to Hell."

"Perhaps the beauty is too subtle for my eye. Perhaps it escapes me altogether. I was always a man for cities, myself."

"What you're trying to say, I reckon, is that all this looks real hateful to you. Is that it? As grim and ghastly as the Plateau of Leng, eh, H.P.?" Howard laughed. "'Sterile hills of gray granite…dim wastes of rock and ice and snow….'" Hearing himself quoted, Lovecraft laughed too, though not exuberantly. Howard went on. "I look around at the Outback of Hell and I see something a whole lot like Texas, and I love it. For you it's as sinister as dark frosty Leng, where people have horns and hooves and munch on corpses and sing hymns to Nyarlathotep. Oh, H.P., H.P., there's no accounting for tastes, is there? Why, there's even some people who—whoa, now! Look there!"

He braked the Land Rover suddenly and brought it to a jolting halt. A small malevolent-looking something with blazing eyes and a scaly body had broken from cover and gone scuttering across the path just in front of them. Now it faced them, glaring up out of the road, snarling and hissing flame.

"Hell-cat!" Howard cried. "Hell-coyote! *Look* at that critter, H.P. You ever see so much ugliness packed into such a small package? Scare the toenails off a shoggoth, that one would!"

"Can you drive past it?" Lovecraft asked, looking dismayed.

"I want a closer look, first." Howard rummaged down by his boots and pulled a pistol from the clutter on the floor of the car. "Don't it give you the shivers, driving around in a land full of critters that could have come right out of one of your stories, or mine? I want to look this little ghoul-cat right in the eye."

"Robert—"

"You wait here. I'll only be but a minute."

Howard swung himself down from the Land Rover and marched stolidly toward the hissing little beast, which stood its ground. Lovecraft watched fretfully. At any moment the creature might leap upon Bob Howard and rip out his throat with a swipe of its horrid yellow talons, perhaps—or burrow snout-deep into his chest, seeking the Texan's warm, throbbing heart—

They stood staring at each other, Howard and the small monster, no more than a dozen feet apart. For a long moment neither one moved. Howard, gun in hand, leaned forward to inspect the beast as one might look at a feral cat guarding the mouth of an alleyway. Did he mean to shoot it? No, Lovecraft thought: beneath his bluster the robust Howard seemed surprisingly squeamish about bloodshed and violence of any sort.

Then things began happening very quickly. Out of a thicket to the left a much larger animal abruptly emerged: a ravening Hell-creature with a crocodile head and powerful thick-thighed legs that ended in monstrous curving claws. An arrow ran through the quivering dewlaps of its heavy throat from side to side, and a hideous dark ichor streamed from the wound down the beast's repellent blue-gray fur. The small animal, seeing the larger one wounded this way, instantly sprang upon its back and sank its fangs joyously into its shoulder. But a moment later there burst from the same thicket a man of astonishing size, a great dark-haired black-bearded man clad only in a bit of cloth about his waist. Plainly he was the huntsman who had wounded the larger monster, for there was a bow of awesome dimensions in his hand and a quiver of arrows on his back. In utter fearlessness the giant plucked the foul little creature from the wounded beast's back and hurled it far out of sight; then, swinging around, he drew a gleaming bronze dagger, and with a single fierce thrust, drove it into the breast of his prey as the coup de grace that brought the animal crashing heavily down.

All this took only an instant. Lovecraft, peering through the window of the Land Rover, was dazzled by the strength and speed of the dispatch and awed by the size and agility of the half-naked huntsman. He glanced toward Howard, who stood to one side, his own considerable frame utterly dwarfed by the black-bearded man.

For a moment Howard seemed dumbstruck, paralyzed with wonder and amazement. But then he was the first to speak.

"By Crom," he muttered, staring at the giant. "Surely this is Conan of Aquilonia and none other!" He was trembling. He took a lurching step toward the huge man, holding out both his hands in a strange gesture—submission, was it? "Lord Conan?" Howard murmured. "Great king, is it you? Conan? Conan?" And before Lovecraft's astounded eyes Howard fell to his knees next to the dying beast, and looked up with awe and something like rapture in his eyes at the towering huntsman.

It had been a decent day's hunting so far. Three beasts brought down after long and satisfying chase; every shaft fairly placed; each animal skillfully dressed, the meat set out as bait for other hell-beasts, the hide and head carefully put aside for proper cleaning at nightfall. There was true pleasure in work done so well.

Yet there was a hollowness at the heart of it all, Gilgamesh thought, that left him leaden and cheerless no matter how cleanly his arrows sped to their mark. He never felt that true fulfillment, that clean sense of completion, that joy of accomplishment, which was ultimately the only thing he sought.

Why was that? Was it—as the Christian dead so drearily insisted—because this was Hell, where by definition there could be no delight?

To Gilgamesh that was foolishness. Those who came here expecting eternal punishment did indeed get eternal punishment, and it was even more horrendous than anything they had anticipated. It served them right, those true believers, those gullible New Dead, that army of credulous Christians.

He had been amazed when their kind first came flocking into Hell, Enki only knew how many thousands of years ago. The things they talked of! Rivers of boiling oil! Lakes of pitch! Demons with pitchforks! That was what they expected, and the Administration was happy to oblige them. There were Torture Towns aplenty for those who wanted them. Gilgamesh had trouble understanding why anyone would. Nobody among the Old Dead really could figure them out, those absurd New Dead with their obsession with punishment. What was it Sargon called them? Masochists, that was the word. Pathetic masochists. But then that sly little Machiavelli had begged to disagree, saying, "No, my lord, it would be a violation of the nature of Hell to send a true masochist off to the torments. The only ones who go are the strong ones—the bullies, the braggarts, the ones who are cowards at the core of their souls." Augustus had had something to say on the matter too, and Caesar, and that Egyptian bitch Hatshepsut had butted in, she of the false beard and the startling eyes, and then all of them had jabbered at once, trying yet again to make sense of the Christian New Dead. Until finally Gilgamesh had said, before stalking out of the room, "The trouble with all of you is that you keep trying to make sense out of this place. But when you've been here as long as I have—"

Well, perhaps Hell *was* a place of punishment. Certainly there were some disagreeable aspects to it. The business about sex, for example. Never being able to come, even if you pumped away all day and all night. And the whole digestive complication, allowing you to eat real food but giving you an unholy hard time when it came to passing the stuff through your gut. But Gilgamesh tended to believe that those were merely the incidental consequences of being dead: this place was not, after all, the land of the living, and there was no reason why things should work the same way here as they did back there.

He had to admit that the reality of Hell had turned out to be nothing at all like what the priests had promised it would be. The House of Dust and Darkness, was what they had called it in Uruk long ago. A place where the dead lived in eternal night and sadness, clad like birds, with wings for garments. Where the dwellers had dust for their bread, and clay for their meat. Where the kings of the earth, the masters, the high rulers, lived humbly without their crowns, and were forced to wait on the demons like servants. Small wonder that he had dreaded death as he had, believing that that was what awaited him for all time to come!

Well, in fact all that had been mere myth and folly. Gilgamesh could still remember Hell as it had been when he first had come to it: a place much like Uruk, so it seemed, with low flat-roofed buildings of whitewashed brick, and temples rising on high platforms of many steps. And there he found all the heroes of olden days, living as they had always lived: Lugalbanda, his father, and Enmerkar, his father's father; and Ziusudra who built the vessel by which mankind survived the Flood; and others on and on, back to the dawn of time. At least that was what it was like where Gilgamesh first found himself; there were other districts, he discovered later, that were quite different—places where people lived in caves, or in pits in the ground, or in flimsy houses of reeds, and still other places where the Hairy Men dwelled and had no houses at all. Most of that was gone now, greatly transformed by all those who had come to Hell in the latter days, and indeed a lot of nonsensical ugliness and ideological foolishness had entered in recent centuries in the baggage of the New Dead. But still, the idea that this whole vast realm—infinitely bigger than his own beloved Land of the Two Rivers—existed merely for the sake of chastising the dead for their sins, struck Gilgamesh as too silly for serious contemplation.

Why, then, was the joy of his hunting so pale and hollow? Why none of the old ecstasy when spying the prey, when drawing the great bow, when sending the arrow true to its mark?

Gilgamesh thought he knew why, and it had nothing to do with punishment. There had been joy aplenty in the hunting for many a thousand years of his life in Hell. If the joy had gone from it now, it was only that in these latter days he hunted alone; that Enkidu—his friend, his true brother, his other self—was not with him. That and nothing but that: for he had never felt complete without Enkidu since they first had met and wrestled and come to love one another after the manner of brothers, long ago in the city of Uruk. That great burly man, broad and tall and strong as Gilgamesh himself, that shaggy wild creature out of the high ridges: Gilgamesh had never loved anyone as he loved Enkidu.

But it was the fate of Gilgamesh, so it seemed, to lose him again and again. Enkidu had been ripped from him the first time long ago when they still dwelled in Uruk, on that dark day when the gods had had revenge upon them for their great pride and had sent the fever to take Enkidu's life. In time Gilgamesh too had yielded to death and was taken into Hell, which he found nothing at all like the Hell that the scribes and priests of the Land had taught; and there he had searched for Enkidu, and one glorious day he had found him. Hell had been a much smaller place, then, and everyone seemed to know everyone else; but even so it had taken an age to track him down. Oh, the rejoicing that day in Hell! Oh, the singing and the dancing, the vast festival that went on and on! There was great kindliness among the denizens of Hell in those days, and everyone was glad for Gilgamesh and Enkidu. Minos of Crete gave the first great party in honor of their reunion, and then it was Amenhotep's turn, and then Agamemnon's. And on the fourth day the host was dark slender Varuna, the Meluhhan king, and then on the fifth the heroes gathered in the ancient hall of the Ice-Hunter folk where one-eyed Vy-otin was chieftain and the floor was strewn with mammoth tusks, and after that—

Well, and it went on for some long time, the great celebration of the reunion. This was long before the hordes of New Dead had come, all those grubby little unheroic people out of unheroic times, carrying with them their nasty little demons and their dark twisted apparatus of damnation and punishment. Before they had come, Hell had simply been a place to live in the time after life. It was all very different then, a far happier place.

For uncountable years Gilgamesh and Enkidu dwelled together in Gilgamesh's palace in Hell as they had in the old days in the Land of the Two Rivers. And all was well with them, with much hunting and feasting, and they were happy in Hell even after the New Dead began to come in, bringing all their terrible changes.

They were shoddy folk, these New Dead, confused of soul and flimsy of intellect, and their petty trifling rivalries and vain strutting poses were a great nuisance. But Gilgamesh and Enkidu kept their distance from them while they replayed all the follies of their lives, their nonsensical Crusades and their idiotic trade wars and their preposterous theological squabbles. The trouble was that they had brought not only their lunatic ideas to Hell but also their accursed diabolical modern gadgets, and the worst of those were the vile weapons called guns, that slaughtered noisily from afar in the most shameful cowardly way. Heroes know how to parry the blow of a battle-ax or the thrust of a sword; but what can even a hero do about a bullet from afar? It was Enkidu's bad luck to fall between two quarreling bands of these gun-wielders, a flock of babbling Spaniards and a rabble of arrogant Englanders, for whom he tried to make peace. Of course they would have no peace, and soon shots were flying, and Gilgamesh arrived at the scene just as a bolt from an arquebus tore through his dear Enkidu's noble heart.

No one dies in Hell forever; but some are dead a long time, and that was how it was with Enkidu. It pleased the Undertaker this time to keep him in limbo some hundreds of years, or however many it was—tallying such matters in Hell is always difficult. It was, at any rate, a dreadful long while, and Gilgamesh once more felt that terrible inrush of loneliness that only the presence of Enkidu might cure. Hell continued to change, and now the changes were coming at a stupefying, overwhelming rate. There seemed to be far more people in the world than there ever had been in the old days, and great armies of them marched into Hell every day, a swarming rabble of uncouth strangers who after only a little interval of disorganization and bewilderment would swiftly set out to reshape the whole place into something as discordant and repellent as the world they had left behind. The steam engine came, with its clamor and clangor, and something called the dynamo, and then harsh glittering electrical lights blazed in every street where the lamps had been, and factories arose and began pouring out all manner of strange things. And more and more and more, relentlessly, unceasingly. Railroads. Telephones. Automobiles. Noise, smoke, soot everywhere, and no way to hide from it. The Industrial Revolution, they called it. Satan and his swarm of Administration bureaucrats seemed to love all the new things, and so did almost everyone else, except for Gilgamesh and a few other cranky conservatives. "What are they trying to do?" Rabelais asked one day. "Turn the place into Hell?" Now the New Dead were bringing in such devices as radios and helicopters and computers, and everyone was speaking English, so that once again Gilgamesh, who had grudgingly learned the new-fangled Greek long ago when Agamemnon and his crew had insisted on it, was forced to master yet another tongue-twisting, intricate language. It was a dreary time for him. And then at last did Enkidu reappear, far away in one of the cold northern domains. He made his way south, and for a time, they were reunited again, and once more all was well for Gilgamesh of Uruk in Hell.

But now they were separated again, this time by something colder and more cruel than death itself. It was beyond all belief, but they had quarreled. There had been words between them, ugly words on both sides—such a dispute as never in thousands of years had passed between them in the land of the living or in the land of Hell—and at last Enkidu had said that which Gilgamesh had never dreamed he would ever hear, which was, "I want no more of you, king of Uruk. If you cross my path again I will have your life." Could that have been Enkidu speaking, or was it, Gilgamesh wondered, some demon of Hell in Enkidu's form?

In any case he was gone. He vanished into the turmoil and intricacy of Hell and placed himself beyond Gilgamesh's finding. And when Gilgamesh sent forth inquiries, back came only the report, "He will not speak with you. He has no love for you, Gilgamesh."

It could not be. It must be a spell of witchcraft, thought Gilgamesh. Surely this was some dark working of the Hell of the New Dead, that could turn brother against brother and lead Enkidu to persist in his wrath. In time, Gilgamesh was sure, Enkidu would be triumphant over this sorcery that gripped his soul, and he would open himself once more to the love of Gilgamesh. But time went on, after the strange circuitous fashion of Hell, and Enkidu did not return to his brother's arms.

What was there to do but hunt, and wait, and hope?

So this day Gilgamesh hunted in Hell's parched Outback. He had killed and killed and killed again, and now late in the day he had put his arrow through the throat of a monster more foul even than the usual run of creatures of Hell; but there was a terrible vitality to the thing, and it went thundering off, dripping dark blood from its pierced maw.

Gilgamesh gave pursuit. It is sinful to strike and wound and not to kill. For a long weary hour he ran, crisscrossing this harsh land. Thorny plants slashed at him with the malevolence of imps, and the hard wind flailed him with clouds of dust sharp as whips. Still the evil-looking beast outpaced him, though its blood drained in torrents from it to the dry ground.

Gilgamesh would not let himself tire, for there was god-power in him by virtue of his descent from the divine Lugalbanda, his great father who was both king and god. But he was hard pressed to keep going. Three times he lost sight of his quarry, and tracked it only by the spoor of its blood-droppings. The bleak red motionless eye that was the sun of Hell seemed to mock him, hovering forever before him as though willing him to run without cease.

Then he saw the creature, still strong but plainly staggering, lurching about at the edge of a thicket of little twisted, greasy-leaved trees. Unhesitatingly Gilgamesh plunged forward. The trees stroked him lasciviously, coating him with their slime, trying like raucous courtesans to insinuate their leaves between his legs; but he slapped them away, and emerged finally into a clearing where he could confront his animal.

Some repellent little hell-beast was clinging to the back of his prey, ripping out bloody gobbets of flesh and ruining the hide. A Land Rover was parked nearby, and a pale, strange-looking man with a long jaw was peering from its window. A second man, red-faced and beefy-looking, stood close by Gilgamesh's roaring, snorting quarry.

First things first. Gilgamesh reached out, scooped the foul hissing little carrion-seeker from the bigger animal's back, flung it aside. Then with all his force he rammed his dagger toward what he hoped was the heart of the wounded animal. In the moment of his thrust Gilgamesh felt a great convulsion within the monster's breast and its hell-life left it in an instant.

The work was done. Again, no exultation, no sense of fulfillment; only a kind of dull ashen release from an unfinished chore. Gilgamesh caught his breath and looked around.

What was this? The red-faced man seemed to be having a crazy fit. Quivering, shaking, sweating, dropping to his knees, his eyes gleaming insanely—

"Lord Conan?" the man cried. "Great king?"

"Conan is not one of my titles," said Gilgamesh, mystified. "And I was a king once in Uruk, but I reign over nothing at all in this place. Come, man, get off your knees!"

"But you are Conan to the life!" moaned the red-faced man hoarsely. "To the absolute life!"

Gilgamesh felt a surge of intense dislike for this fellow. He would be slobbering in another moment. Conan? Conan? That name meant nothing at all. No, wait; he had known a Conan once, some little Celtic fellow he had encountered in a tavern, a chap with a blunt nose and heavy cheekbones and dark hair tumbling down his face, a drunken twitchy little man forever invoking forgotten godlets of no consequence—yes, he had called himself Conan, so Gilgamesh thought. Drank too much, caused trouble for the barmaid, even took a swing at her, that was the one. Gilgamesh had dropped him down an open cesspool to teach him manners. But how could this blustery-faced fellow here mistake me for that one? He was still mumbling on, too, babbling about lands whose names meant nothing to Gilgamesh—Cimmeria, Aquilonia, Hyrkania, Zamora. Total nonsense. There were no such places.

And that glow in the fellow's eyes—what sort of look was that? A look of adoration, almost the sort of look a woman might give a man when she has decided to yield herself utterly to his will.

Gilgamesh had seen such looks aplenty in his day, from women and men both; and he had welcomed them from women, but never from a man. He scowled. What does he think I am? Does he think, as so many have wrongly thought, that because I loved Enkidu with so great a love that I am a man who will embrace a man in the fashion of men and women? Because it is not so. Not even here in Hell is it so, said Gilgamesh to himself. Nor will it ever be.

"Tell me everything!" the red-faced man was imploring. "All those exploits that I dreamed in your name, Conan: Tell me how they really were! That time in the snow fields, when you met the frost giant's daughter—and when you sailed the *Tigress* with the Black Coast's queen—and that time you stormed the Aquilonian capital, and slew King Numedides on his own throne—"

Gilgamesh stared in distaste at the man groveling at his feet.

"Come, fellow, stop this blather now," he said sourly. "Up with you! You mistake me greatly, I think."

The second man was out of the Land Rover now, and on his way over to join them. An odd-looking creature he was, too, skeleton-thin and corpse-white, with a neck like a water-bird's that seemed barely able to support his long, big-chinned head. He was dressed oddly too, all in black, and swathed in layer upon layer as if he dreaded the faintest chill. Yet he had a gentle and thoughtful way about him, quite unlike the wild-eyed and feverish manner of his friend. He might be a scribe, Gilgamesh thought, or a priest; but what the other one could be, the gods alone would know.

The thin man touched the other's shoulder and said, "Take command of yourself, man. This is surely not your Conan here."

"To the life! To the very life! His size—his grandeur—the way he killed that beast—"

"Bob—Bob, Conan's a figment! Conan's a fantasy! You spun him out of whole cloth. Come, now. Up. Up." To Gilgamesh he said, "A thousand pardons, good sir. My friend is—sometimes excitable—"

Gilgamesh turned away, shrugging, and looked to his quarry. He had no need for dealings with these two. Skinning the huge beast properly might take him the rest of the day; and then to haul the great hide back to his camp, and determine what he wanted of it as a trophy—

Behind him he heard the booming voice of the red-faced man. "A figment, H.P.? How can you be sure of that? I thought I invented Conan, too; but what if he really lived, what if I had merely tapped into some powerful primordial archetype, what if the authentic Conan stands here before us this very moment—"

"Dear Bob, your Conan had blue eyes, did he not? And this man's eyes are dark as night."

"Well—" Grudgingly.

"You were so excited you failed to notice. But I did. This is some barbarian warrior, yes, some great huntsman beyond any doubt—a Nimrod, an Ajax. But not Conan, Bob! Grant him his own identity. He's no invention of yours." Coming up beside Gilgamesh, the long-jawed man said, speaking in a formal and courtly way, "Good sir, I am Howard Phillips Lovecraft, formerly of Providence, Rhode Island, and my companion is Robert E. Howard of Texas, whose other life was lived, as was mine, in the twentieth century after Christ. At that time we were tale-tellers by trade, and I think he confuses you with a hero of his own devising. Put his mind at ease, I pray you, and let us know your name."

Gilgamesh looked up. He rubbed his wrist across his forehead to clear it of a smear of the monster's gore and met the other man's gaze evenly. This one, at least, was no madman, strange though he looked.

Quietly Gilgamesh said, "I think his mind may be beyond putting at any ease. But know you that I am called Gilgamesh, the son of Lugalbanda."

"Gilgamesh the Sumerian?" Lovecraft whispered. "Gilgamesh who sought to live forever?"

"Gilgamesh am I, yes, who was king in Uruk when that was the greatest city of the Land of the Two Rivers, and who in his folly thought there was a way of cheating death."

"Do you hear that, Bob?"

"Incredible. Beyond all belief!" muttered the other.

Rising until he towered above them both, Gilgamesh drew in his breath deeply and said with awesome resonance, "I am Gilgamesh to whom all things were made known, the secret things, the truths of life and death, most especially those of death. I have coupled with Inanna the goddess in the bed of the Sacred Marriage; I have slain demons and spoken with gods; I am two parts god myself, and only one part mortal." He paused and stared at them, letting it sink in, those words that he had recited so many times in situations much like this. Then in a quieter tone he went on, "When death took me I came to this nether world they call Hell, and here I pass my time as a huntsman, and I ask you now to excuse me, for as you see I have my tasks."

Once more he turned away.

"Gilgamesh!" said Lovecraft again in wonder. And the other said, "If I live here till the end of time, H.P., I'll never grow used to it. This is more fantastic than running into Conan would have been! Imagine it: *Gilgamesh!*"

A tiresome business, Gilgamesh thought: all this awe, all this adulation.

The problem was that damned epic, of course. He could see why Caesar grew so irritable when people tried to suck up to him with quotations out of Shakespeare's verses. "Why, man, he doth bestride the narrow world like a Colossus," and all that: Caesar grew livid by the third syllable. Once they put you into poetry, Gilgamesh had discovered, as had Odysseus and Achilles and Caesar after him and many another, your own real self can begin to disappear and the self of the poem overwhelms you entirely and turns you into a walking cliché. Shakespeare had been particularly villainous that way, Gilgamesh thought: ask Richard III, ask Macbeth, ask Owen Glendower. You found them skulking around Hell with perpetual chips on their shoulders, because every time they opened their mouths people expected them to say something like "My kingdom for a horse!" or "Is this a dagger which I see before me?" or "I can call spirits from the vasty deep." Gilgamesh had had to live with that kind of thing almost from the time he had first come to Hell, for they had written the poems about him soon after. All that pompous brooding stuff, a whole raft of Gilgamesh tales of varying degrees of basis in reality. And then the Babylonians and the Assyrians, and even those smelly garlic-gobbling Hittites, had gone on translating and embroidering them for another thousand years so that everybody from one end of the known world to the other knew them by heart. And even after all those peoples were gone and their languages had been forgotten, there was no surcease, because these twentieth-century folk had found the whole thing and deciphered the text somehow and made it famous all over again. Over the centuries they had turned him into everybody's favorite all-purpose hero, which was a hell of a burden to bear: there was a piece of him in the Prometheus legend, and in the Heracles stuff, and in that story of Odysseus' wanderings, and even in the Celtic myths, which was probably why this creepy Howard fellow kept calling him Conan. At least that other Conan, that ratty little sniveling drunken one, had been a Celt. Enlil's ears, but it was wearying to have everyone expecting you to live up to the mythic exploits of twenty or thirty very different culture-heroes! And embarrassing, too, considering that the original non-mythical Heracles and Odysseus and some of the others dwelled here too and tended to be pretty possessive about the myths that had attached to *them*, even when they were simply variants on his own much older ones.

There was substance to the Gilgamesh stories, of course, especially the parts about him and Enkidu. But the poet had salted the story with a lot of pretentious arty nonsense too, as poets always will, and in any case you got very tired of having everybody boil your long and complex life down into the same twelve chapters and the same little turns of phrase. It got so that Gilgamesh found himself quoting the main Gilgamesh poem too, the one about his quest for eternal life—well, that one wasn't too far from the essence of the truth, though they had mucked up a lot of the details with precious little "imaginative" touches—by way of making introduction for himself: "I am the man to whom all things were made known, the secret things, the truths of life and death." Straight out of the poet's mouth, those lines. Tiresome. Tiresome. Angrily he jabbed his dagger beneath the dead monster's hide, and set about his task of flaying, while the two little men behind him went on muttering and mumbling to one another in astonishment at having run into Gilgamesh of Uruk in this bleak and lonely corner of Hell.

There were strange emotions stirring in Robert Howard's soul, and he did not care for them at all. He could forgive himself for believing for that one giddy moment that this Gilgamesh was his Conan. That was nothing more than the artistic temperament at work, sweeping him up in a bit of rash feverish enthusiasm. To come suddenly upon a great muscular giant of a man in a loincloth who was hacking away at some fiendish monster with a little bronze dagger, and to think that he must surely be the mighty Cimmerian—well, that was a pardonable enough thing. Here in Hell you learned very quickly that you might run into anybody at all. You could find yourself playing at dice with Lord Byron or sharing a mug of mulled wine with Menelaos or arguing with Plato about the ideas of Nietzsche, who was standing right there making faces, and after a time you came to take most such things for granted, more or less.

So why not think that this fellow was Conan? No matter that Conan's eyes had been of a different color. That was a trifle. He looked like Conan in all the important ways. He was of Conan's size and strength. And he was kingly in more than physique. He seemed to have Conan's cool intelligence and complexity of soul, his regal courage and indomitable spirit.

The trouble was that Conan, the wondrous Cimmerian warrior from 19,000 B.C., had never existed except in Howard's own imagination. And there were no fictional characters in Hell. You might meet Richard Wagner, but you weren't likely to encounter Siegfried. Theseus was here somewhere, but not the Minotaur. William the Conqueror, yes; William Tell, no.

That was all right, Howard told himself. His little fantasy of meeting Conan here in Hell was nothing but a bit of mawkish narcissism: he was better off without it. Coming across the authentic Gilgamesh—ah, how much more interesting that was! A genuine Sumerian king—an actual titan out of history's dawn, not some trumped-up figure fashioned from cardboard and hard-breathing wish-fulfilling dreams. A flesh-and-blood mortal who lived a lusty life and had fought great battles and had walked eye to eye with the ancient gods. A man who had struggled against the inevitability of death, and who in dying had taken on the immortality of mythic archetype—ah, now there was someone worth getting to know! Whereas Howard had to admit that he would learn no more from a conversation with Conan than he could discover by interrogating his own image in the mirror. Or else a meeting with the "real" Conan, if it was in any way possible, would surely cast him into terrible confusions and contradictions of soul from which there would be no recovering. No, Howard thought. Better that this man be Gilgamesh than Conan, by all means. He was reconciled to that.

But this other business—this sudden bewildering urge to throw himself at the giant's feet, to be swept up in his arms, to be crushed in a fierce embrace—

What was that? Where had *that* come from? By the blazing Heart of Ahriman, what could it mean?

Howard remembered a time in his former life when he had gone down to the Cisco Dam and watched the construction men strip and dive in: well-built men, confident, graceful, at ease in their bodies. For a short while he had looked at them and had reveled in their physical perfection. They could have been naked Greek statues come alive, a band of lusty Apollos and Zeuses. And then as he listened to them shouting and laughing and crying out in their foul-mouthed way he began to grow angry, suddenly seeing them as mere thoughtless animals who were the natural enemies of dreamers like himself. He hated them as the weak always must hate the strong, those splendid swine who could trample the dreamers and their dreams as they wished. But then he had reminded himself that he was no weakling himself, that he who once had been spindly and frail had by hard effort made himself big and strong and burly. Not beautiful of body as these men were—too fleshy for that, too husky—but nevertheless, he had told himself, there was no man there whose ribs he could not crush if it came to a struggle. And he had gone away from that place full of rage and thoughts of bloody violence.

What had that been all about? That barely suppressed fury—was it some sort of dark hidden lust, some craving for the most bestial sort of sinfulness? Was the anger that had arisen in him masking an anger he should have directed at himself, for looking upon those naked men and taking pleasure in it?

No. No. No. No. He wasn't any kind of degenerate. He was certain of that.

The desire of men for men was a mark of decadence, of the decline of civilization. He was a man of the frontier, not some feeble limp-wristed sodomite who reveled in filth and wanton evil. If he had never in his short life known a woman's love, it was for lack of opportunity, not out of a preference for that other shameful kind. Living out his days in that small and remote prairie town, devoting himself to his mother and to his writing, he had chosen not to avail himself of prostitutes or shallow women, but he was sure that if he had lived a few years longer and the woman who was his true mate had ever made herself known to him, he would certainly have reached toward her in passion and high abandon.

And yet—and yet—that moment when he first spied the giant Gilgamesh, and thought he was Conan—

That surge of electricity through his entire body, and most intensely through his loins—what else could it have been but desire, instant and intense and overwhelming? For a *man*? Unthinkable! Even this glorious hero—even this magnificent kingly creature—

No. No. No. No.

I am in Hell, and this is my torment, Howard told himself.

He paced furiously up and down alongside the Land Rover. Desperately he fought off the black anguish that threatened to settle over him now, as it had done so many times in his former life and in this life after life. These sudden corrupt and depraved feelings, Howard thought: they are nothing but diabolical perversions of my natural spirit, intended to cast me into despair and self-loathing! By Crom, I will resist! By the breasts of Ishtar, I will not yield this foulness!

All the same he found his eyes straying to the edge of the nearby thicket, where Gilgamesh still knelt over the animal he had killed.

What extraordinary muscles rippling in that broad back, in those iron-hard thighs! What careless abandon in the way he was peeling back the creature's shaggy hide, though he had to wallow in dark gore to do it! That cascade of lustrous black hair lightly bound by a jewelled circlet, that dense black beard curling in tight ringlets—

Howard's throat went dry. Something at the base of his belly was tightening into a terrible knot.

Lovecraft said, "You want a chance to talk with him, don't you?"

Howard swung around. He felt his cheeks go scarlet. He was utterly certain that his guilt must be emblazoned incontrovertibly on his face.

"What the hell do you mean?" he growled. His hands knotted of their own accord into fists. There seemed to be a band of fire across his forehead. "What would I want to talk with him about, anyway?"

Lovecraft looked startled by the ferocity of Howard's tone and posture. He took a step backward and threw up his hand almost as though to protect himself. "What a strange thing to say! You, of all people, with your love of antique times, your deep and abiding passion for the lost mysteries of those steamy Oriental empires that perished so long ago! Why, man, is there nothing you want to know about the kingdoms of Sumer? Uruk, Nippur, Ur of the Chaldees? The secret rites of the goddess Inanna in the dark passageways beneath the ziggurat? The incantations that opened the gates of the Underworld, the libations that loosed and bound the demons of the worlds beyond the stars? Who knows what he could tell us? There stands a man six thousand years old, a hero from the dawn of time, Bob!"

Howard snorted. "I don't reckon that oversized son of a bitch would want to tell us a damned thing. All that interests him is getting the hide off that bloody critter of his."

"He's nearly done with that. Why not wait, Bob? And invite him to sit with us a little while. And draw him out, lure him into telling us tales of life beside the Euphrates!" Now Lovecraft's dark eyes were gleaming as though he too felt some strange lust, and his forehead was surprisingly bright with uncharacteristic perspiration; but Howard knew that in Lovecraft's case what had taken possession of him was only the lust for knowledge, the hunger for the arcane lore of high antiquity that Lovecraft imagined would spill from the lips of this Mesopotamian hero. That same lust ached in him as well. To speak with this man who had lived before Babylon was, who had walked the streets of Ur when Abraham was yet unborn—

But there were other lusts besides that hunger for knowledge, sinister lusts that must be denied at any cost—

"No," said Howard brusquely. "Let's get the hell out of here right now, H.P. This damned foul bleak countryside is getting on my nerves."

Lovecraft gave him a strange look. "But weren't you just telling me how beautiful—"

"Damnation take whatever I was telling you! King Henry's expecting us to negotiate an alliance for him. We aren't going to get the job done out here in the boondocks."

"The what?"

"Boondocks. Wild uncivilized country. Term that came into use after our time, H.P. The backwoods, you know? You never did pay much heed to the vernacular, did you?" He tugged at Lovecraft's sleeve. "Come on. That big bloody ape over there isn't going to tell us a thing about his life and times, I guarantee. Probably doesn't remember anything worth telling, anyway. And he bores me. Pardon me, H.P., but I find him an enormous pain in the butt, all right? I don't have any further hankering for his company. Do you mind, H.P.? Can we move along, do you think?"

"I must confess that you mystify me sometimes, Bob. But of course if you—" Suddenly Lovecraft's eyes widened in amazement. "Get down, Bob! Behind the car! Fast!"

"What—"

An arrow came singing through the air and passed just alongside Howard's left ear. Then another, and another. One arrow ricocheted off the flank of the Land Rover with a sickening thunking sound. Another struck straight on and stuck quivering an inch deep in the metal.

Howard whirled. He saw horsemen—a dozen, perhaps a dozen and a half—bearing down on them out of the darkness to the east, loosing shafts as they came.

They were lean compact men of some Oriental stock in crimson leather jerkins, riding like fiends. Their mounts were little flat-headed, fiery-eyed gray Hell-horses that moved as if their short, fiercely pistoning legs could carry them to the far boundaries of the nether world without the need of a moment's rest.

Chanting, howling, the yellow-skinned warriors seemed to be in a frenzy of rage. Mongols? Turks? Whoever they were, they were pounding toward the Land Rover like the emissaries of Death himself. Some brandished long wickedly curved blades, but most wielded curious-looking small bows from which they showered one arrow after another with phenomenal rapidity.

Crouching behind the Land Rover with Lovecraft beside him, Howard gaped at the attackers in a paralysis of astonishment. How often had he written of scenes like this? Waving plumes, bristling lances, a whistling cloud of cloth-yard shafts! Thundering hooves, wild war cries, the thunk of barbarian arrowheads against Aquilonian shields! Horses rearing and throwing their riders.... Knights in bloodied armor tumbling to the ground.... Steel-clad forms littering the slopes of the battlefield....

But this was no swashbuckling tale of Hyborean derring-do that was unfolding now. Those were real horsemen—as real as anything was, in this place—rampaging across this chilly wind-swept plain in the outer reaches of Hell. Those were real arrows; and they would rip their way into his flesh with real impact and inflict real agony of the most frightful kind.

He looked across the way at Gilgamesh. The giant Sumerian was hunkered down behind the overturned bulk of the animal he had slain. His mighty bow was in his hand. As Howard watched in awe, Gilgamesh aimed and let fly. The shaft struck the nearest horseman, traveling through jerkin and rib cage and all, and emerging from the man's back. But still the onrushing warrior managed to release one last arrow before he fell. It traveled on an erratic trajectory, humming quickly toward Gilgamesh on a wild wobbly arc and skewering him through the flesh of his left forearm.

Coolly the Sumerian glanced down at the arrow jutting from his arm. He scowled and shook his head, the way he might if he had been stung by a hornet. Then—as Conan might have done, how very much like Conan!—Gilgamesh inclined his head toward his shoulder and *bit* the arrow in half just below the fletching. Bright blood spouted from the wound as he pulled the two pieces of the arrow from his arm.

As though nothing very significant had happened, Gilgamesh lifted his bow and reached for a second shaft. Blood was streaming in rivulets down his arm, but he seemed not even to be aware of it.

Howard watched as if in a stupor. He could not move; he barely had the will to draw breath. A haze of nausea threatened to overwhelm him. It had been nothing at all for him to heap up great bloody mounds of severed heads and arms and legs with cheerful abandon in his stories; but in fact, real bloodshed and violence of any sort had horrified him whenever he had even a glimpse of it.

"The gun, Bob!" said Lovecraft urgently beside him. "Use the *gun!*"

"What?"

"There. There."

Howard looked down. Thrust through his belt was the pistol he had taken from the Land Rover when he had come out to investigate that little beast in the road. He drew it now and stared at it, glassy-eyed, as though it were a basilisk's egg that rested on the palm of his hand.

"What are you doing?" Lovecraft asked. "Ah. Ah. Give it to me." He snatched the gun impatiently from Howard's frozen fingers and studied it a moment as though he had never held a weapon before. Perhaps he never had. But then, grasping the pistol with both his hands, he rose warily above the hood of the Land Rover and squeezed off a shot.

The tremendous sound of an explosion cut through the shrill cries of the horsemen. Lovecraft laughed. "Got one! Who would ever have imagined—"

He fired again. In the same moment Gilgamesh brought down one more of the attackers with his bow.

"They're backing off!" Lovecraft cried. "By Alhazred, they didn't expect *this,* I wager!" He laughed again and poked the gun up into a firing position. "*Ia!*" he cried, in a voice Howard had never heard out of the shy and scholarly Lovecraft before. "*Shub-Niggurath!*" Lovecraft fired a third time. "*Ph'nglui mglw'nafh Cthulhu R'lyeh wgah'nagl fhtagn!*"

Howard felt sweat rolling down his body. This inaction of his— this paralysis, this shame—what would Conan make of it? What would Gilgamesh? And Lovecraft, that timid and sheltered man, he who dreaded the fishes of the sea and the cold winds of his New England winters and so many other things, was laughing and bellowing his wondrous gibberish and blazing away like any gangster, having the time of his life—

Shame! Shame!

Heedless of the risk, Howard scrambled up into the cab of the Land Rover and groped around for the second gun that was lying down there on the floor somewhere. He found it and knelt beside the window. Seven or eight of the Asiatic horsemen lay strewn about, dead or dying, within a hundred-yard radius of the car. The others had withdrawn to a considerable distance and were cantering in uneasy circles. They appeared taken aback by the unexpectedly fierce resistance they had encountered on what they had probably expected to have been an easy bit of jolly slaughter in these untracked frontierlands.

What were they doing now? Drawing together, a tight little ground, horses nose to nose. Conferring. And now two of them were pulling what seemed to be some sort of war-banner from a saddlebag and hoisting it between them on bamboo poles: a long yellow streamer with fluttering blood-red tips, on which bold Oriental characters were painted in shining black. Serious business, obviously. Now they were lining themselves up in a row, facing the Land Rover. Getting ready for a desperate suicide charge—that was the way things appeared.

Gilgamesh, standing erect in full view, calmly nocked yet another arrow. He took aim and waited for them to come. Lovecraft, looking flushed with excitement, wholly transformed by the alien joys of armed combat, was leaning forward, staring intently, his pistol cocked and ready.

Howard shivered. Shame rode him with burning spurs. How *could* he cower here while those two bore the brunt of the struggle? Though his hand was shaking, he thrust the pistol out the window and drew a bead on the closest horseman. His finger tightened on the trigger. Would it be possible to score a hit at such a distance? Yes. Yes. Go ahead. You know how to use a gun, all right. High time you put some of that skill to use. Knock that little yellow bastard off his horse with one bark of the Colt .380, yes. Send him straight to Hell—no, he's in Hell already, send him off to the Undertaker for recycling. Yes, that's it. Ready—aim—

"Wait," Lovecraft said. "Don't shoot."

What was this? As Howard, with an effort, lowered his gun and let his rigid quivering hand go slack, Lovecraft, shading his eyes against the eerie glare of the motionless sun, peered closely at the enemy warriors a long silent moment. Then he turned, reached up into the rear of the Land Rover, groped around for a moment, finally pulled out the manila envelope that held their royal commission from King Henry.

And then—what was he doing?

Stepping out into plain view, arms raised high, waving the envelope around, walking toward the enemy?

"They'll kill you, H.P.! Get down! Get down!"

Lovecraft, without looking back, gestured brusquely for Howard to be silent. He continued to walk steadily toward the far-off horsemen.

They seemed just as mystified as Howard was. They sat without moving, their bows held stiffly out before them, a dozen arrows trained on the middle of Lovecraft's body.

He's gone completely off the deep end, Howard thought in dismay. He never was really well balanced, was he? Half believing all his stuff about Elder Gods and dimensional gateways and blasphemous rites on dark New England hillsides. And now all this shooting—the excitement—

"Hold your weapons, all of you!" Lovecraft cried in a voice of amazing strength and presence. "In the name of Prester John, I bid you hold your weapons! We are not your enemies! We are ambassadors to your emperor!"

Howard gasped. He began to understand. No, Lovecraft hadn't gone crazy after all!

He took another look at that long yellow war-banner. Yes, yes, it bore the emblems of Prester John! These berserk horsemen must be part of the border patrol of the very nation whose ruler they had traveled so long to find. Howard felt abashed, realizing that in the fury of the battle Lovecraft had had the sense actually to pause long enough to give the banner's legend close examination—and the courage to walk out there waving his diplomatic credentials. The parchment scroll of their royal commission was in his hand, and he was pointing to the little red-ribboned seal of King Henry.

The horsemen stared, muttered among themselves, lowered their bows. Gilgamesh, lowering his great bow also, looked on in puzzlement. "Do you see?" Lovecraft called. "We are heralds of King Henry! We claim the protection of your master the August Sovereign Yeh-lu Ta-shih!" Glancing back over his shoulder, he called to Howard to join him; and after only an instant's hesitation, Howard leaped down from the Land Rover and trotted forward. It was a giddy feeling, exposing himself to those somber yellow archers this way. It felt almost like standing on the edge of some colossal precipice.

Lovecraft smiled. "It's all going to be all right, Bob! That banner they unfurled, it bears the markings of Prester John—"

"Yes, yes. I see."

"And look—they're making a safe-conduct sign. They understand what I'm saying, Bob! They believe me!"

Howard nodded. He felt a great upsurge of relief and even a sort of joy. He clapped Lovecraft lustily on the back. "Fine going, H.P.! I didn't think you had it in you!" Coming up out of his funk, now, he felt a manic exuberance seize his spirit. He gestured to the horsemen, wigwagging his arms with wild vigor. "Hoy! Royal commissioners!" he bellowed. "Envoys from His Britannic Majesty King Henry VIII! Take us to your emperor!" Then he looked toward Gilgamesh, who stood frowning, his bow still at the ready. "Hoy there, king of Uruk! Put away the weapons! Everything's all right now! We're going to be escorted to the court of Prester John!"

Gilgamesh wasn't at all sure why he had let himself go along. He had no interest in visiting Prester John's court, or anybody else's. He wanted nothing more than to be left alone to hunt and roam in the wilderness and thereby to find some ease for his sorrows.

But the gaunt long-necked man and his blustery red-faced friend had beckoned him to ride with them in their Land Rover, and while he stood there frowning over that, the ugly flat-featured little yellow warriors had indicated with quick impatient gestures that he should get in. And he had. They looked as though they would try to compel him to get in if he balked; and though he had no fear of them, none whatever, some impulse that he could not begin to understand had led him to step back from the likelihood of yet another battle and simply climb aboard the vehicle. Perhaps he had had enough of solitary hunting for a while. Or perhaps it was just that the wound in his arm was beginning to throb and ache, now that the excitement of the fray was receding, and it seemed like a good idea to have it looked after by a surgeon. The flesh all around it was badly swollen and bruised. That arrow had pierced him through and through. He would have the wound cleaned and dressed, and then he would move along.

Well, then, so he was going to the court of Prester John. Here he was, sitting back silent and somber in the rear of this musty, mildew-flecked car, riding with these two very odd New Dead types, these scribes or tale-tellers or whatever it was they claimed to be, as the horsemen of Prester John led them to the encampment of their monarch.

The one who called himself Howard, the one who could not help stealing sly little glances at him like an infatuated schoolgirl, was at the wheel. Glancing back at his passenger now, he said, "Tell me, Gilgamesh: have you had dealings with Prester John before?"

"I have heard the name, that much I know," replied the Sumerian. "But it means little to me."

"The legendary Christian emperor," said the other, the thin one, Lovecraft. "He who was said to rule a secret kingdom somewhere in the misty hinterlands of Central Asia—although it was in Africa, according to some—"

Asia, Africa—names, only names, Gilgamesh thought bleakly. They were places somewhere in the other world, but he had no idea where they might be.

Such a multitude of places, so many names! It was impossible to keep it all straight. There was no sense of any of it. The world—his world, the Land—had been bordered by the Two Rivers, the Idigna and the Buranunu, which the Greeks had preferred to call the Tigris and the Euphrates. Who were the Greeks, and by what right had they renamed the rivers? Everyone used those names now, even Gilgamesh himself, except in the inwardness of his soul.

And beyond the Two Rivers? Why, there was the vassal state of Aratta far to the east, and in that direction also lay the Land of Cedars, where the fire-breathing demon Huwawa roared and bellowed, and in the eastern mountains lay the kingdom of the barbaric Elamites. To the north was the land called Uri, and in the deserts of the west the wild Martu people dwelled, and in the south was the blessed isle Dilmun, which was like a paradise. Was there anything more to the world than that? Why, there was Meluhha far away beyond Elam, where the people had black skins and fine features, and there was Punt in the south, where they were black also, with flat noses and thick lips. And there was another land even beyond Meluhha, with folk of yellow skins who mined a precious green stone. And that was the world. Where could all these other latter-day places be—this Africa and this Asia and Europe and the rest, Rome, Greece, England? Perhaps some of them were mere new names for old places. The Land itself had had a host of names since his own time—Babylonia, Mesopotamia, Iraq, and more. Why had it needed all those names? He had no idea. New men made up new names: that seemed to be the way of the world. This Africa, this Asia—America, China, Russia. A little man named Herodotus, a Greek, had tried to explain it all to him once—the shape of the world and the names of the places in it, sketching a map for him on an old bit of parchment—and much later a stolid fellow named Mercator had done the same, and once after that he had spoken of such matters with an

ROBERT SILVERBERG

Englishman called Cook; but the things they told him all conflicted with one another and he could make no sense out of any of it. It was too much to ask, making sense of these things. Those myriad nations that had arisen after his time, those empires that had arisen and fallen and been forgotten, all those lost dynasties, the captains and the kings— he had tried from time to time to master the sequence of them, but it was no use. Once in his former life he had sought to make himself the master of all knowledge, yes. His appetites had been boundless: for knowledge, for wealth, for power, for women, for life itself. Now all that seemed only the merest folly to him. That jumble of confused and confusing places, all those great realms and far-off kingdoms, were in another world: what could they matter to him now?

"Asia?" he said. "Africa?" Gilgamesh shrugged. "Prester John?" He prowled the turbulent cluttered recesses of his memory. "Ah. There's a Prester John, I think, lives in New Hell. A dark-skinned man, a friend of that gaudy old liar Sir John Mandeville." It was coming back now. "Yes, I've seen them together many times, in that dirty squalid tavern where Mandeville's always to be found. The two of them telling outlandish stories back and forth, each a bigger fraud than the other."

"A different Prester John," said Lovecraft.

"That one is Susenyos the Ethiop, I think," Howard said. "A former African tyrant, and lover of the Jesuits, now far gone in whiskey. He's one of many. There are seven, nine, a dozen Prester Johns in Hell, to my certain knowledge. And maybe more."

Gilgamesh contemplated that notion blankly. Fire was running up and down his injured arm now.

Lovecraft was saying, "—not a true name, but merely a title, and a corrupt one at that. There never was a *real* Prester John, only various rulers in various distant places, whom it pleased the tale-spinners of Europe to speak of as Prester John, the Christian emperor, the great mysterious unknown monarch of a fabulous realm. And here in Hell there are many who choose to wear the name. There's power in it, do you see?"

"Power and majesty!" Howard cried. "And poetry, by God!"

"So this Prester John whom we are to visit," said Gilgamesh, "he is not in fact Prester John?"

"Yeh-lu Ta-shih's his name," said Howard. "Chinese. Manchurian, actually, twelfth century A.D. First emperor of the realm of Kara-Khitai, with his capital at Samarkand. Ruled over a bunch of Mongols and Turks,

272

mainly, and they called him Gur Khan, which means 'supreme ruler,' and somehow that turned into 'John' by the time it got to Europe. And they said he was a Christian priest, too, *Presbyter Joannes*, 'Prester John.'" Howard laughed. "Damned silly bastards. He was no more a Christian than you were. A Buddhist, he was, a bloody shamanistic Buddhist."

"Then why—"

"Myth and confusion!" Howard said. "The great human nonsense factory at work! And wouldn't you know it, but when he got to Hell this Yeh-lu Ta-shih founded himself another empire right away in the same sort of territory he'd lived in back there, and when Richard Burton came out this way and told him about Prester John and how Europeans long ago had spoken of him by that name and ascribed all sorts of fabulous accomplishments to him he said, 'Yes, yes, I am Prester John indeed.' And so he styles himself that way now, he and nine or ten others, most of them Ethiopians like that friend of your friend Mandeville."

"They are no friends of mine," said Gilgamesh stiffly. He leaned back and massaged his aching arm. Outside the Land Rover the landscape was changing now: more hilly, with ill-favored fat-trunked little trees jutting at peculiar angles from the purple soil. Here and there in the distance his keen eyes made out scattered groups of black tents on the hillsides, and herds of the little Hell-horses grazing near them. Gilgamesh wished now that he hadn't let himself be inveigled into this expedition. What need had he of Prester John? One of these upstart New Dead potentates, one of the innumerable little princelings who had set up minor dominions for themselves out here in the vast measureless wastelands of the Outback—and reigning under a false name, at that—one more shoddy scoundrel, one more puffed-up little nobody swollen with unearned pride—

Well, and what difference did it make? He would sojourn a while in the land of this Prester John, and then he would move on, alone, apart from others, mourning as always his lost Enkidu. There seemed no escaping that doom that lay upon him, that bitter solitude, whether he reigned in splendor in Uruk or wandered in the wastes of Hell.

"Their Excellencies P.E. Lovecraft and Howard E. Robert," cried the major-domo grandly though inaccurately, striking three times on the black marble floor of Prester John's throne-chamber with his gold-tipped staff of pale green jade. "Envoys Plenipotentiary of His Britannic Majesty King Henry VIII of the Kingdom of New Holy Diabolic England."

Lovecraft and Howard took a couple of steps forward. Yeh-lu Ta-shih nodded curtly and waved one elegant hand, resplendent with inch-long fingernails, in casual acknowledgment. The envoys plenipotentiary did not seem to hold much interest for him, nor, apparently, did whatever it was that had caused His Britannic Majesty King Henry to send them here.

The emperor's cool imperious glance turned toward Gilgamesh, who was struggling to hold himself erect. He was beginning to feel feverish and dizzy and he wondered when anyone would notice that there was an oozing hole in his arm. Even he had limits to his endurance, after all, though he usually tried to conceal that fact. He didn't know how much longer he could hold out. There were times when behaving like a hero was a heroic pain in the ass, and this was one of them.

"—and his Late Highness Gilgamesh of Uruk, son of Lugalbanda, great king, king of Uruk, king of kings, lord of the Land of the Two Rivers by merit of Enlil and An," boomed the major-domo in the same splendid way, looking down only once at the card he held in his hand.

"Great king?" said Yeh-lu Ta-shih, fixing Gilgamesh with one of the most intensely penetrating stares the Sumerian could remember ever having received. "King of kings? Those are very lofty titles, Gilgamesh of Uruk."

"A mere formula," Gilgamesh replied, "which I thought appropriate when being presented at your court. In fact I am king of nothing at all now."

"Ah," said Yeh-lu Ta-shih. "King of Nothing-at-all."

And so are you, my lord Prester John. Gilgamesh did not let himself say it, though the words bubbled toward the roof of his mouth and begged to be uttered. *And so are all the self-appointed lords and masters of the many realms of Hell.*

The slender amber-hued man on the throne leaned forward. "And where then, I pray, is Nothing-at-all?"

Some of the courtiers began to snicker. But Prester John looked to be altogether in earnest, though it was impossible to be completely certain of that. He was plainly a formidable man, Gilgamesh had quickly come to see: sly, shrewd, self-contained, with a tough and sinewy intelligence. Not at all the vain little cock-of-the-walk Gilgamesh had expected to find in this bleak and remote corner of Hell. However small and obscure his principality might be, Prester John ruled it, obviously, with a firm grasp. The grandeur of the glittering palace that his scruffy subjects had built for him here on the edge of nowhere, and the solidity of the small but substantial city surrounding it, testified to that. Gilgamesh knew something about the building of cities and palaces. Prester John's capital bore the mark of the steady toil of centuries.

The long stare was unrelenting. Gilgamesh, fighting back the blazing pain in his arm, met the emperor's gaze with an equally earnest one of his own and said:

"Nothing-at-all? It is a land that never was, and will always be, my lord. Its boundaries are nowhere and its capital city is everywhere, nor do any of us ever leave it."

"Ah. Ah. Indeed. Nicely put. You are Old Dead, are you?"

"Very old, my lord."

"Older than Ch'in Shih Huang Ti? Older than the Lords of Shang and Hsia?"

Gilgamesh turned in puzzlement toward Lovecraft, who told him in a half-whisper, "Ancient kings of China. Your time was even earlier."

Shrugging, Gilgamesh replied, "They are not known to me, my lord, but you hear what the Britannic ambassador says. He is a man of learning: it must be so. I will tell you that I am older than Caesar by far, older than Agamemnon and the Supreme Commander Rameses, older even than Sargon. By a great deal."

Yeh-lu Ta-shih considered that a moment. Then he made another of his little gestures of dismissal, as though brushing aside the whole concept of relative ages in Hell. With a dry laugh he said, "So you are very old, King Gilgamesh. I congratulate you. And yet the Ice-Hunter folk would tell us that you and I and Rameses and Sargon all arrived here only yesterday; and to the Hairy Men, the Ice-Hunters themselves are mere newcomers. And so on and so on. There's no beginning to it, is there? Any more than there's an end."

Without waiting for an answer he asked Gilgamesh, "How did you come by that gory wound, great king of Nothing-at-all?"

At least he's noticed it, Gilgamesh thought.

"A misunderstanding, my lord. It may be that your border patrol is a little overzealous at times."

One of the courtiers leaned toward the emperor and murmured something. Prester John's serene brow grew furrowed. He lifted a flawlessly contoured eyebrow ever so slightly.

"Killed nine of them, did you?"

"They attacked us before we had the opportunity of showing our diplomatic credentials," Lovecraft put in quickly. "It was entirely a matter of self-defense, my lord Prester John."

"I wouldn't doubt it." The emperor seemed to contemplate for a moment, but only for a moment, the skirmish that had cost the lives of nine of his horsemen; and then quite visibly he dismissed that matter too from the center of his attention. "Well, now, my lords ambassador—"

Abruptly Gilgamesh swayed, tottered, started to fall. He checked himself just barely in time, seizing a massive porphyry column and clinging to it until he felt more steady. Beads of sweat trickled down his forehead into his eyes. He began to shiver. The huge stone column seemed to be expanding and contracting. Waves of vertigo were rippling through him and he was seeing double, suddenly. Everything was blurring and multiplying. He drew his breath in deeply, again, again, forcing himself to hold on. He wondered if Prester John was playing some kind of game with him, trying to see how long his strength could last. Well, if he had to, Gilgamesh swore, he would stand here forever in front of Prester John without showing a hint of weakness.

But now Yeh-lu Ta-shih was at last willing to extend compassion. With a glance toward one of his pages the emperor said, "Summon my physician, and tell him to bring his tools and his potions. That wound should have been dressed an hour ago."

"Thank you, my lord," Gilgamesh muttered, trying to keep the irony from his tone.

The doctor appeared almost at once, as though he had been waiting in an antechamber. Another of Prester John's little games, perhaps? He was a burly, broad-shouldered, bushy-haired man of more than middle years, with a manner about him that was brisk and bustling but nevertheless warm, concerned, reassuring. Drawing Gilgamesh down beside him on a low divan covered with the gray-green hide of some scaly Hell-dragon, he peered into the wound, muttered something unintelligible to himself in a guttural language unknown to the Sumerian, and pressed his thick fingers around the edges of the torn flesh until fresh blood flowed. Gilgamesh hissed sharply but did not flinch.

"*Ach, mein lieber Freund,* I must hurt you again, but it is for your own good. *Verstehen sie?*"

The doctor's fingers dug in more deeply. He was spreading the wound, swabbing it, cleansing it with some clear fluid that stung like a hot iron. The pain was so intense that there was almost a kind of pleasure in it: it was a purifying kind of pain, a purging of the soul.

Prester John said, "How bad is it, Dr. Schweitzer?"

"*Gott sei dank,* it is deep but clean. He will heal without damage."

He continued to probe and cleanse; murmuring softly to Gilgamesh as he worked: "*Bitte. Bitte. Einen Augenblick, mein Freund.*" To Prester John he said, "This man is made of steel. No nerves at all, immense resistance to pain. We have one of the great heroes here, *nicht wahr?* You are Roland, are you? Achilles, perhaps?"

"Gilgamesh is his name," said Yeh-lu Ta-shih.

The doctor's eyes grew bright. "Gilgamesh! Gilgamesh of Sumer? *Wunderbar! Wunderbar!* The very man. The seeker after life. *Ach,* we must talk, my friend, you and I, when you are feeling better." From his medical kit he now produced a frightful-looking hypodermic syringe. Gilgamesh watched as though from a vast distance, as though that throbbing swollen arm belonged to someone else. "*Ja, ja,* certainly we must talk, of life, of death, or philosophy, *mein Freund,* of *philosophy!* There is so very much for us to discuss!" He slipped the needle beneath Gilgamesh's skin. "There. *Genug.* Sit. Rest. The healing now begins."

Robert Howard had never seen anything like it. It could have been something straight from the pages of one of his Conan stories. The big ox had taken an arrow right through the fat part of his arm, and he had simply yanked it out and gone right on fighting. Then, afterward, he had behaved as if the wound were nothing more than a scratch, all that time while they were driving hour after hour toward Prester John's city and then undergoing lengthy interrogation by the court officials and then standing through this whole endless ceremony at court—God almighty, what a display of endurance! True, Gilgamesh had finally gone a little wobbly and had actually seemed on the verge of passing out. But any ordinary mortal would have conked out long ago. Heroes really *were* different. They were another breed altogether. Look at him now, sitting there casually while that old German medic swabs him out and stitches him up in that slapdash cavalier way, and not a whimper out of him. Not a whimper!

Suddenly Howard found himself wanting to go over there to Gilgamesh, to comfort him, to let him lean his head back against him while the doctor worked him over, to wipe the sweat from his brow—

Yes, to comfort him in an open, rugged, manly way—

No. No. No. No.

There it was again, the horror, the unspeakable thing, the hideous crawling Hell-borne impulse rising out of the cesspools of his soul—

Howard fought it back. Blotted it out, hid it from view. Denied that it had ever entered his mind.

To Lovecraft he said, "That's some doctor! Took his medical degree at the Chicago slaughterhouses, I reckon!"

"Don't you know who he is, Bob?"

"Some old Dutchman who wandered in here during a sandstorm and never bothered to leave."

"Does the name Dr. Schweitzer mean nothing to you?"

Howard gave Lovecraft a blank look. "Guess I never heard it much in Texas."

"Oh, Bob, Bob, why must you always pretend to be such a cowboy? Can you tell me you've never heard of Schweitzer? *Albert* Schweitzer? The great philosopher, theologian, musician—there never was a greater interpreter of Bach, and don't tell me you don't know Bach either—"

"She-it, H.P., you talking about that old country doctor there?"

"Who founded the leprosy clinic in Africa, at Lambarene, yes. Who devoted his life to helping the sick, under the most primitive conditions, in the most remote forests of—"

"Hold on, H.P. That can't be so."

"That one man could achieve so much? I assure you, Bob, he was quite well known in our time—perhaps not in Texas, I suppose, but nevertheless—"

"No. Not that he could do all that. But that he's here. In Hell. If that old geezer's everything you say, then he's a goddamned *saint*. Unless he beat his wife when no one was looking, or something like that. What's a saint doing in Hell, H.P.?"

"What are *we* doing in Hell?" Lovecraft asked.

Howard reddened and looked away. "Well, I suppose, there were things in our lives—things that might be considered sins, in the strictest sense—"

"No one understands the rules of Hell, Bob," said Lovecraft gently. "Sin may have nothing to do with it. Gandhi is here, do you realize that? Confucius. Were *they* sinners? Was Moses? Abraham? We've tried to impose our own pitiful shallow beliefs, our pathetic grade-school notions of punishment for bad behavior, on this incredibly bizarre place where we find ourselves. By what right? We don't begin to comprehend what Hell really is. All we know is that it's full of heroic villains and villainous heroes—and people like you and me—and it seems that Albert Schweitzer is here, too. A great mystery. But perhaps someday—"

"Shh," Howard said. "Prester John's talking to us."

"My lords ambassador—"

Hastily they turned toward him. "Your Majesty?" Howard said.

"This mission that has brought you here: your king wants an alliance, I suppose? What for? Against whom? Quarreling with some pope again, is he?"

"With his daughter, I'm afraid," said Howard.

Prester John looked bored. He toyed with his emerald scepter. "Mary, you mean?"

"Elizabeth, your Majesty," Lovecraft said.

"Your king's a most quarrelsome man. I'd have thought there were enough popes in Hell to keep him busy, though, and no need to contend with his daughters."

"They are the most contentious women in Hell," Lovecraft said. "Blood of his blood, after all, and each of them a queen with a noisy, brawling kingdom of her own. Elizabeth, my lord, is sending a pack of her explorers to the Outback, and King Henry doesn't like the idea."

"Indeed," said Yeh-lu Ta-shih, suddenly interested again. "And neither do I. She has no business in the Outback. It's not her territory. The rest of Hell should be big enough for Elizabeth. What is she looking for here?"

"The sorcerer John Dee has told her that the way out of Hell is to be found in these parts."

"There is no way out of Hell."

Lovecraft smiled. "I'm not any judge of that, Your Majesty. Queen Elizabeth, in any event, has given credence to the notion. Her Walter Raleigh directs the expedition, and the geographer Hakluyt is with him, and a force of five hundred soldiers. They move diagonally across the Outback just to the south of your domain, following some chart that Dr. Dee had obtained for them. He had it from Cagliostro, they say, who bought it from Hadrian when Hadrian was still supreme commander of Hell's legions. It is allegedly an official Satanic document."

Prester John did not appear to be impressed. "Let us say, for argument's sake, that there *is* an exit from Hell. Why would Queen Elizabeth desire to leave? Hell's not so bad. It has its minor discomforts, yes, but one learns to cope with them. Does she think she'd be able to reign in Heaven as she does here—assuming there's a Heaven at all, which is distinctly not proven?"

"Elizabeth has no real interest in leaving Hell herself, Majesty," Howard said. "What King Henry fears is that if she does find the way out, she'll claim it for her own and set up a colony around it, and charge a fee for passing through the gate. No matter where it takes you, the king reckons there'll be millions of people willing to risk it, and Elizabeth will wind up cornering all the money in Hell. He can't abide that notion, d'ye see? He thinks she's already too smart and aggressive by half, and he hates the idea that she might get even more powerful. There's something mixed into it having to do with Queen Elizabeth's mother, too— that was Anne Boleyn, Henry's second wife. She was a wild and wanton one, and he cut her head off for adultery, and now he thinks that Anne's behind Elizabeth's maneuvers, trying to get even with him by—"

"Spare me these details," said Yeh-lu Ta-shih with some irritation. "What does Henry expect me to do?"

"Send troops to turn the Raleigh expedition back before it can find anything useful to Elizabeth."

"And in what way do I gain from this?"

"If the exit from Hell's on your frontier, Your Majesty, do you really want a bunch of Elizabethan Englishmen setting up a colony next door to you?"

"There is no exit from Hell," Prester John said complacently once again.

"But if they set up a colony anyway?"

Prester John was silent a moment. "I see," he said finally.

"In return for your aid," Howard said, "we're empowered to offer you a trade treaty on highly favorable terms."

"Ah."

"And a guarantee of military protection in the event of the invasion of your realm by a hostile power."

"If King Henry's armies are so mighty, why does he not deal with the Raleigh expedition himself?"

"There was no time to outfit and dispatch an army across such a great distance," said Lovecraft. "Elizabeth's people had already set out before anything was known of the scheme."

"Ah," said Yeh-lu Ta-shih.

"Of course," Lovecraft went on, "there were other princes of the Outback that King Henry might have approached. Moammar Khadafy's name came up, and one of the Assyrians—Assurnasirpal, I think—and someone mentioned Mao Tse-tung. No, King Henry said, let us ask the aid of Prester John, for he is a monarch of great puissance and grandeur, whose writ is supreme throughout the far reaches of Hell. Prester John, indeed, that is the one whose aid we must seek!"

A strange new sparkle had come into Yeh-lu Ta-shih's eyes. "You were considering an alliance with Mao Tse-tung?"

"It was merely a suggestion, Your Majesty."

"Ah. I see." The emperor rose from his throne. "Well, we must consider these matters more carefully, eh? We must not come hastily to a decision." He looked across the great vaulted throne room to the divan where Dr. Schweitzer still labored over Gilgamesh's wound. "Your patient, doctor—what's the report?"

"A man of steel, Majesty, a man of steel! *Gott sei dank,* he heals before my eyes!"

"Indeed. Come, then. You will all want to rest, I think; and then you shall know the full hospitality of Prester John."

The full hospitality of Prester John, Gilgamesh soon discovered, was no trifling affair.

He was led off to a private chamber with walls lined with black felt—a kind of indoor tent—where three serving-girls who stood barely hip-high to him surrounded him, giggling, and took his clothing from him. Gently they pushed him into a huge marble cistern full of warm milk, where they bathed him lovingly and massaged his aching body in the most intimate manner. Afterward they robed him in intricate vestments of yellow silk.

Then they conveyed him to the emperor's great hall, where the whole court was gathered, a glittering and resplendent multitude. Some sort of concert was under way, seven solemn musicians playing harsh screeching twanging music. Gongs crashed, a trumpet blared, pipes uttered eerie piercing sounds. Servants showed Gilgamesh to a place of honor atop a pile of furry blankets heaped high with velvet cushions.

Lovecraft and Howard were already there, garbed like Gilgamesh in magnificent silks. Both of them looked somewhat unsettled—unhinged, even. Howard, flushed and boisterous, could barely sit still: he laughed and waved his arms and kicked his heels against the furs, like a small boy who has done something very naughty and is trying to conceal it by being over-exuberant. Lovecraft, on the other hand, seemed dazed and dislocated, with the glassy-eyed look of someone who has recently been clubbed.

These are two very odd men indeed, Gilgamesh thought.

One works hard at being loud and lusty, and now and then gives you a glimpse of a soul boiling with wild fantasies of swinging swords and rivers of blood. But in reality he seems terrified of everything. The other, though he is weirdly remote and austere, is apparently not quite as crazy, but he too gives the impression of being at war with himself, in terror of allowing any sort of real human feeling to break through the elaborate facade of his mannerisms. The poor fools must have been scared silly when the serving-girls started stripping them and pouring warm milk over them and stroking their bodies. No doubt they haven't recovered yet from all that nasty pleasure, Gilgamesh thought. He could imagine their cries of horror as the little Mongol girls started going to work on them. *What are you doing? Leave my trousers alone! Don't touch me there! Please—no—ooh—ah—ooh! Oooh!*

Yeh-lu Ta-shih, seated upon a high throne of ivory and onyx, waved grandly to him, one great king to another. Gilgamesh gave him an almost imperceptible nod by way of acknowledgment. All this pomp and formality bored him hideously. He had endured so much of it in his former life, after all. And then *he* had been the one on the high throne, but even then it had been nothing but a bore. And now—

But this was no more boring than anything else. Gilgamesh had long ago decided that that was the true curse of Hell: all striving was meaningless here, mere thunder without the lightning. And there was no end to it. You might die again now and then if you were careless or unlucky, but back you came for another turn, sooner or later, at the Undertaker's whim. There was no release from the everlastingness of it all. Once he had yearned desperately for eternal life, and he had learned that he could not have such a thing, at least not in the world of mortal men. But now indeed he had come to a place where he would live forever, so it seemed, and yet there was no joy in it. His fondest dream now was simply to serve his time in Hell and be allowed to sleep in peace forever. He saw no way of attaining that. Life here just went on and on—very much like this concert, this endless skein of twangs and plinks and screeches.

Someone with the soft face of a eunuch came by and offered him a morsel of grilled meat. Gilgamesh knew he would pay for it later—you always did, when you ate something in Hell—but he was hungry now, and he gobbled it. And another, and another, and a flagon of fermented mare's milk besides.

A corps of dancers appeared, men and women in flaring filmy robes. They were doing things with swords and flaming torches. A second eunuch brought Gilgamesh a tray of mysterious sugary delicacies, and he helped himself with both hands, heedless of the consequences. He was ravenous. His body, as it healed, was calling furiously for fuel. Beside him, the man Howard was swilling down the mare's milk as if it were water and getting tipsier and tipsier, and the other, the one called Lovecraft, sat morosely staring at the dancers without touching a thing. He seemed to be shivering as though in the midst of a snowstorm.

Gilgamesh beckoned for a second flagon. Just then the doctor arrived and settled down cheerfully on the heap of blankets next to him. Schweitzer grinned his approval as Gilgamesh took a hearty drink. *"Fuhlen Sie sich besser, mein Held, eh?* The arm, it no longer gives you pain? Already the wound is closing. So quickly you repair yourself! Such strength, such power and healing! You are God's own miracle, dear Gilgamesh. The blessing of the Almighty is upon you." He seized a flagon of his own from a passing servant, quaffed it, made a face. *"Ach,* this milk-wine of theirs! And *ach, ach,* this *verfluchte* music! What I would give for the taste of decent Moselle on my tongue now, eh, and the sound of the D minor toccata and fugue in my ears! Bach—do you know him?"

"Who?"

"Bach! Bach, Johann Sebastian Bach. The greatest of musicians, God's own poet in sound. I saw him once, just once, years ago." Schweitzer's eyes were glowing. "I was new here. Not two weeks had I been here. It was at the villa of King Friedrich—Frederick the Great, you know him? No? The king of Prussia? *Der alte Fritz?* No matter. No matter. *Er macht nichts.* A man entered, ordinary, you would never notice him in a crowd, yes? And began to play the harpsichord, and he had not played three measures when I said, 'This is Bach, this must be the actual Bach,' and I would have dropped down on my knees before him but that I was ashamed. And it was he. I said to myself, 'Why is it that Bach is in Hell?' But then I said, as perhaps you have said, as I think everyone here must say at one time or another, 'Why is it that *Schweitzer* is in Hell?' And I knew that it is that God is mysterious. Perhaps I was sent here to minister to the damned. Perhaps it is that Bach was also. Or perhaps we are damned also; or perhaps no one here is damned. *Es macht nichts aus*, all this speculation. It is a mistake, or even *vielleicht* a sin, to imagine that we can comprehend the workings of the mind of God. We are here. We have our tasks. That is enough for me to know."

"I felt that way once," said Gilgamesh. "When I was king in Uruk, and finally came to understand that I must die, that there was no hiding from that. What is the purpose, then, I asked myself? And I told myself: The gods have put us here to perform our tasks, and that is the purpose. And so I lived thereafter and so I died." Gilgamesh's face darkened. "But here—here—"

"Here, too, we have our tasks," Schweitzer said.

"You do, perhaps. For me there is only the task of passing the time. I had a friend to bear the burden with me once—"

"Enkidu."

Gilgamesh seized the doctor's sturdy wrist with sudden fierce intensity. "You know of Enkidu?"

"From the poem, yes. The poem is very famous."

"Ah. Ah. The poem. But the actual man—"

"I know nothing of him, *nein*."

"He is of my stature, very large. His beard is thick, his hair is shaggy, his shoulders are wider even than mine. We journeyed everywhere together. But then we quarreled, and he went from me in anger, saying, 'Never cross my path again.' Saying, 'I have no love for you, Gilgamesh.' Saying, 'If we meet again I will have your life.' And I have heard nothing of him since."

Schweitzer turned and stared closely at Gilgamesh. "How is this possible? All the world knows the love of Enkidu for Gilgamesh!"

Gilgamesh called for yet another flagon. This conversation was awakening an ache within his breast, an ache that made the pain that his wound had caused seem like nothing more than an itch. Nor would the drink soothe it; but he would drink all the same.

He took a deep draught and said somberly, "We quarreled. There were hot words between us. He said he had no love for me any longer."

"This cannot be true."

Gilgamesh shrugged and made no reply.

"You wish to find him again?" Schweitzer asked.

"I desire nothing else."

"Do you know where he is?"

"Hell is larger even than the world. He could be anywhere."

"You will find him."

"If you knew how I have searched for him—"

"You will find him. That I know."

Gilgamesh shook his head. "If Hell is a place of torment, then this is mine, that I will never find him again. Or if I do, that he will spurn me. Or raise his hand against me."

"This is not so," said Schweitzer. "I think he longs for you even as you do for him."

"Then why does he keep himself from me?"

"This is Hell," said Schweitzer gently. "You are being tested, my friend, but no test lasts forever. Not even in Hell. Not even in Hell. Even though you are in Hell, have faith in the Lord: You will have your Enkidu soon enough, *um Himmels Willen*." Smiling, Schweitzer said, "The emperor is calling you. Go to him. I think he has something to tell you that you will want to hear."

Prester John said, "You are a warrior, are you not?"

"I was," replied Gilgamesh indifferently.

"A general? A leader of men?"

"All that is far behind me," Gilgamesh said. "This is the life after life. Now I go my own way and I take on no tasks for others. Hell has plenty of generals."

"I am told that you were a leader among leaders. I am told that you fought like the god of war. When you took the field, whole nations laid down their arms and knelt before you."

Gilgamesh waited, saying nothing.

"You miss the glory of the battlefield, don't you, Gilgamesh?"

"Do I?"

"What if I were to offer you the command of my army?"

"Why would you do that? What am I to you? What is your nation to me?"

"In Hell we take whatever citizenship we wish. What would you say, if I offered you the command?"

"I would tell you that you are making a great mistake."

"It isn't a trivial army. Ten thousand men. Adequate air support. Tactical nukes. The strongest firepower in the Outback."

"You misunderstand," said Gilgamesh. "Warfare doesn't interest me. I know nothing of modern weapons and don't care to learn. You have the wrong man, Prester John. If you need a general, send for Wellington. Send for Marlborough. Rommel. Tiglath-Pileser."

"Or for Enkidu?"

The unexpected name hit Gilgamesh like a battering ram. At the sound of it his face grew hot and his entire body trembled convulsively.

"What do you know about Enkidu?"

Prester John held up one superbly manicured hand. "Allow me the privilege of asking the questions, great king."

"You spoke the name of Enkidu. What do you know about Enkidu?"

"First let us discuss the matters which are of—"

"Enkidu," said Gilgamesh implacably. "Why did you mention his name?"

"I know that he was your friend—"

"Is."

"Very well, *is* your friend. And a man of great valor and strength. Who happens to be a guest at this very moment at the court of the great enemy of my realm. And who, so I understand it, is preparing just now to make war against me."

"*What?*" Gilgamesh stared. "Enkidu is in the service of Queen Elizabeth?"

"I don't recall having said that."

"Is it not Queen Elizabeth who even now has sent an army to encroach on your domain?"

Yeh-lu Ta-shih laughed. "Raleigh and his five hundred fools? That expedition's an absurdity. I'll take care of them in an afternoon. I mean another enemy altogether. Tell me this: do you know of Mao Tse-tung?"

"These princes of the New Dead—there are so many names—"

"A Chinese, a man of Han. Emperor of the Marxist Dynasty, long after my time. Crafty, stubborn, tough. More than a little crazy. He runs something called the Celestial People's Republic, just north of here. What he tells his subjects is that we can turn Hell into Heaven by collectivizing it."

"Collectivizing?" said Gilgamesh uncomprehendingly.

"To make all the peasants into kings, and the kings into peasants. As I say: more than a little crazy. But he has his hordes of loyal followers, and they do whatever he says. He means to conquer all the Outback, beginning right here. And after that, all of Hell will be subjected to his lunatic ideas. I fear that Elizabeth's in league with him— that this nonsense of looking for a way out of Hell is only a ruse, that in fact her Raleigh is spying out my weaknesses for her so that she can sell the information to Mao."

"But if this Mao is the enemy of all kings, why would Elizabeth ally herself with—"

"Obviously they mean to use each other. Elizabeth aiding Mao to overthrow me, Mao aiding Elizabeth to push her father from his throne. And then afterward, who knows? But I mean to strike before either of them can harm me."

"What about Enkidu?" Gilgamesh said. "Tell me about Enkidu."

Prester John opened a scroll of computer printout. Skimming through it, he read, "The Old Dead warrior Enkidu of Sumer—Sumer, that's your nation, isn't it?—arrived at court of Mao Tse-tung on such-and-such a date—ostensible purpose of visit, Outback hunting expedition—accompanied by American spy posing as journalist and hunter, one E. Hemingway—secret meeting with Kublai Khan, Minister of War for the Celestial People's Republic—now training Communist troops in preparation for invasion of New Kara-Khitai—" The emperor looked up. "Is this of interest to you, Gilgamesh?"

"What is it you want from me?"

"This man is your famous friend. You know his mind as you do your own. Defend us from him and I'll give you anything you desire."

"What I desire," said Gilgamesh, "is nothing more than the friendship of Enkidu."

"Then I'll give you Enkidu on a silver platter. Take the field for me against Mao's troops. Help me anticipate whatever strategies your Enkidu has been teaching them. We'll wipe the Marxist bastards out and capture their generals, and then Enkidu will be yours. I can't guarantee that he'll want to be your friend again, but he'll be yours. What do you say, Gilgamesh? What do you say?"

✺

Across the gray plains of Hell from horizon to horizon sprawled the legions of Prester John. Scarlet-and-yellow banners fluttered against the somber sky. At the center of the formation stood a wedge of horse-borne archers in leather armor; on each flank was a detachment of heavy infantry; the emperor's fleet of tanks was in the vanguard, rolling unhurriedly forward over the rough, broken terrain. A phalanx of transatmospheric weapons platforms provided air cover far overhead.

A cloud of dust in the distance gave evidence of the oncoming army of the Celestial People's Republic.

"By all the demons of Stygia, did you ever see such a cockeyed sight?" Robert Howard cried. He and Lovecraft had a choice view of the action from their place in the imperial command post, a splendid pagoda protected by a glowing force-shield. Gilgamesh was there, too, just across the way with Prester John and the officers of the Kara-Khitai high command. The emperor was peering into a bank of television monitors and one of his aides was feverishly tapping out orders on a computer terminal. "Makes no goddamned sense," said Howard. "Horsemen, tanks, weapons platforms, all mixing it up at the same time—is that how these wild sons of bitches fight a war?"

Lovecraft touched his forefinger to his lips. "Don't shout so, Bob. Do you want Prester John to hear you? We're his guests, remember. And King Henry's ambassadors."

"Well, if he hears me, he hears me. Look at that crazy mess! Doesn't Prester John realize that he's got a twentieth-century Bolshevik Chinaman coming to attack him with twentieth-century weapons? What good are mounted horsemen, for God's sake? A cavalry charge into the face of heavy artillery? Bows and arrows against howitzers?" Howard guffawed. "Nuclear-tipped arrows, is that the trick?"

Softly Lovecraft said, "For all we know, that's what they are."

"You know that can't be, H.P. I'm surprised at you, a man with your scientific background. I know all this nuke stuff is after our time, but surely you've kept up with the theory. Critical mass at the tip of an arrow? No, H.P., you know as well as I do that it just can't work. And even if it could—"

In exasperation Lovecraft waved to him to be silent. He pointed across the room to the main monitor in front of Prester John. The florid face of a heavyset man with a thick white beard had appeared on the screen.

"Isn't that Hemingway?" Lovecraft asked.

"Who?"

"Ernest Hemingway. The writer. A *Farewell to Arms. The Sun Also Rises.*"

"Never could stand his stuff," said Howard. "Sick crap about a bunch of drunken weaklings. You sure that's him?"

"Weaklings, Bob?" said Lovecraft in astonishment.

"I read only the one book, about those Americans in Europe who go to the bullfights and get drunk and fool around with each other's women, and that was all of Mr. Hemingway that I cared to experience. I tell you, H.P., it disgusted me. And the way it was written! All those short little sentences—no magic, no poetry, H.P.—"

"Let's talk about it some other time, Bob."

"No vision of heroism—no awareness of the higher passions that ennoble and—"

"Bob—please—"

"A fixation on the sordid, the slimy, the depraved—"

"You're being absurd, Bob. You're completely misinterpreting his philosophy of life. If you had simply taken the trouble to read *A Farewell to Arms*—" Lovecraft shook his head angrily. "This is no time for a literary discussion. Look—look there." He nodded toward the far side of the room. "One of the emperor's aides is calling over. Something's going on."

Indeed there had been a development of some sort. Yeh-lu Ta-shih seemed to be conferring with four or five aides at once. Gilgamesh, red-faced, agitated, was striding swiftly back and forth in front of the computer bank. Hemingway's face was still on the screen and he too looked agitated.

Hastily Howard and Lovecraft crossed the room. The emperor turned to them. "There's been a request for a parley in the field," Prester John said, "Kublai Khan is on his way over. Dr. Schweitzer will serve as my negotiator. The man Hemingway's going to be an impartial observer—*their* impartial observer. I need an impartial observer, too. Will you two go down there too, as diplomats from a neutral power, to keep an eye on things?"

"An honor to serve," said Howard grandly.

"And for what purpose, my lord, has the parley been called?" Lovecraft asked.

Yeh-lu Ta-shih gestured toward the screen. "Hemingway has had the notion that we can settle this thing by single combat—Gilgamesh versus Enkidu. Save on ammunition, spare the Undertaker a devil of a lot of toil. But there's a disagreement over the details." Delicately he smothered a yawn. "Perhaps it can all be worked out by lunchtime."

It was an oddly assorted group. Mao Tse-tung's chief negotiator was the plump, magnificently dressed Kublai Khan, whose dark sly eyes gave evidence of much cunning and force. He had been an emperor in his own right in his former life, but evidently had preferred less taxing responsibilities here. Next to him was Hemingway, big and heavy, with a deep voice and an easy, almost arrogant manner. Mao had also sent four small men in identical blue uniforms with red stars on their breasts—"Party types," someone murmured—and, strangely, a Hairy Man, big-browed and chinless, one of those creatures out of deepest antiquity. He too wore the Communist emblem on his uniform.

And there was one more to the group—the massive, deep-chested man of dark brow and fierce and smouldering eyes, who stood off by himself at the far side—

Gilgamesh could barely bring himself to look at him. He too stood apart from the group a little way, savoring the keen edge of the wind that blew across the field of battle. He longed to rush toward Enkidu, to throw his arms around him, to sweep away in one jubilant embrace all the bitterness that had separated them—

If only it could be as simple as that!

The voices of Mao's negotiators and the five that Prester John had sent—Schweitzer, Lovecraft, Howard, and a pair of Kara-Khitai officers—drifted to Gilgamesh above the howling of the wind.

Hemingway seemed to be doing most of the talking. "Writers, are you? Mr. Howard, Mr. Lovecraft? I regret I haven't had the pleasure of encountering your work."

"Fantasy, it was," said Lovecraft. "Fables. Visions."

"That so? You publish in *Argosy*? The *Post?*"

"Five to *Argosy*, but they were westerns," Howard said. "Mainly we wrote for *Weird Tales*. And H.P., a few in *Astounding Stories.*"

"*Weird Tales*," Hemingway said. "*Astounding Stories.*" A shadow of distaste flickered across his face. "Mmm. Don't think I knew those magazines. But you wrote well, did you, gentlemen? You set down what you truly felt, the real thing, and you stated it purely? Of course you did. I know you did. You were honest writers or you'd never have gone to Hell. That goes almost without saying." He laughed, rubbed his hands in glee, effusively threw his arms around the shoulders of Howard and Lovecraft. Howard seemed alarmed by that and Lovecraft looked as though he wanted to sink into the ground. "Well, gentlemen," Hemingway boomed, "what shall we do here? We have a little problem. The one hero wishes to fight with bare hands, the other with—what did he call it?—a disruptor pistol? You would know more about that than I do: something out of *Astounding Stories,* is how it sounds to me. But we can't have this, can we? Bare hands against fantastic future science? There is a good way to fight and that is equal to equal, and all other ways are the bad ways."

"Let him come to me with his fists," Gilgamesh called from the distance. "As we fought the first time, in the Market-of-the-Land, when my path crossed his in Uruk."

"He is afraid to use the new weapons," Enkidu replied.

"Afraid?"

"I brought a shotgun to him, a fine 12-gauge weapon, a gift to my brother Gilgamesh. He shrank from it as though I had given him a venomous serpent."

"Lies!" roared Gilgamesh. "I had no fear of it! I despised it because it was cowardly!"

"He fears anything which is new," said Enkidu. "I never thought Gilgamesh of Uruk would know fear, but he fears the unfamiliar. He called me a coward, because I would hunt with a shotgun. But I think he was the coward. And now he fears to fight me with the unfamiliar. He knows that I'll slay him. He fears death even here, do you know that? Death has always been his great terror. Why is that? Because it is an insult to his pride? I think that is it. Too proud to die—too proud to accept the decree of the gods—"

"I will break you with my hands alone!" Gilgamesh bellowed.

"Give us disruptors," said Enkidu. "Let us see if he dares to touch such a weapon."

"A coward's weapon!"

"Again you call me a coward? You, Gilgamesh, you are the one who quivers in fear—"

"Gentlemen! Gentlemen!"

"You fear my strength, Enkidu!"

"You fear my skill. You with your pathetic old sword, your pitiful bow—"

"Is this the Enkidu I loved, mocking me so?"

"You were the first to mock, when you threw back the shotgun into my hands, spurning my gift, calling me a coward—"

"The weapon, I said, was cowardly. Not you, Enkidu."

"It was the same thing."

"Bitte, bitte," said Schweitzer. "This is not the way!"

And again from Hemingway: "Gentlemen, please!"

They took no notice.

"I meant—"

"You said—"

"Shame—"

"Fear—"

"Three times over a coward!"

"Five times five a traitor!"

"False friend!"

"Vain braggart!"

"Gentlemen, I have to ask you—"

But Hemingway's voice, loud and firm though it was, was altogether drowned out by the roar of rage that came from the throat of Gilgamesh. Dizzying throbs of anger pounded in his breast, his throat, his temples. He could take no more. This was how it had begun the first time, when Enkidu had come to him with that shotgun and he had given it back and they had fallen into dispute. At first merely a disagreement, and then a hot debate, and then a quarrel, and then the hurling of bitter accusations. And then such words of anger as had never passed between them before, they who had been closer than brothers.

That time they hadn't come to blows. Enkidu had simply stalked away, declaring that their friendship was at an end. But now—hearing all the same words again, stymied by this quarrel even over the very method by which they were to fight—Gilgamesh could no longer restrain himself. Overmastered by fury and frustration, he rushed forward.

Enkidu, eyes gleaming, was ready for him.

Hemingway attempted to come between them. Big as he was, he was like a child next to Gilgamesh and Enkidu, and they swatted him to one side without effort. With a jolt that made the ground itself reverberate, Gilgamesh went crashing into Enkidu and laid hold of him with both hands.

Enkidu laughed. "So you have your way after all, King Gilgamesh! Bare hands it is!"

"It is the only way," said Gilgamesh.

At last. At last. There was no wrestler in this world or the other who could contend with Gilgamesh of Uruk. I will break him, Gilgamesh thought, as he broke our friendship. I will snap his spine. I will crush his chest.

As once they had done long ago, they fought like maddened bulls. They stared eye to eye as they contended. They grunted; they bellowed, they roared. Gilgamesh shouted out defiance in the language of Uruk and in any other language he could think of; and Enkidu muttered and stormed at Gilgamesh in the language of the beasts that once he had spoken when he was a wild man, the harsh growling of the lion of the plains.

Gilgamesh yearned to have Enkidu's life. He loved this man more dearly than life itself, and yet he prayed that it would be given him to break Enkidu's back, to hear the sharp snapping sound of his spine, to toss him aside like a worn-out cloak. So strong was his love that it had turned to the brightest of hatreds. I will send him to the Undertaker once again, Gilgamesh thought. I will hurl him from Hell.

But though he struggled as he had never struggled in combat before, Gilgamesh was unable to budge Enkidu. Veins bulged in his forehead; the sutures that held his wound burst and blood flowed down his arm; and still he strained to throw Enkidu to the ground, and still Enkidu held his place. And matched him, strength for strength, and kept him at bay. They stood locked that way a long moment, staring into each other's eyes, locked in unbreakable stalemate.

Then after a long while Enkidu said, as once he had said long ago, "Ah, Gilgamesh! There is not another one like you in all the world! Glory to the mother who bore you!"

It was like the breaking of a dam, and a rush of life-giving waters tumbling out over the summer-parched fields of the Land.

And from Gilgamesh in that moment of release and relief came twice-spoken words also:

"There is one other who is like me. But only one."

"No, for Enlil has given you the kingship."

"But you are my brother," said Gilgamesh, and they laughed and let go of each other and stepped back, as if seeing each other for the first time, and laughed again.

"This is great foolishness, this fighting between us," Enkidu cried.

"Very great foolishness indeed, brother."

"What need have you of shotguns and disruptors?"

"And what do I care if you choose to play with such toys?"

"Indeed, brother."

"Indeed!"

Gilgamesh looked away. They were all staring—the four party men, Lovecraft, Howard, the Hairy Man, Kublai Khan, Hemingway—all astonished, mouths drooping open. Only Schweitzer was beaming. The doctor came up to them and said quietly, "You have not injured each other? No. *Gut. Gut.* Then leave here, the two of you, together. Now. What do you care for Prester John and his wars, or for Mao and his? This is no business of yours. Go. Now."

Enkidu grinned. "What do you say, brother? Shall we go off hunting together?"

"To the end of the Outback, and back again. You and I, and no one else."

"And we will hunt only with our bows and spears?"

Gilgamesh shrugged. "With disruptors, if that is how you would have it. With cannons. With nuke grenades. Ah, Enkidu, Enkidu—!"

"Gilgamesh!"

"Go," Schweitzer whispered. "Now. Leave this place and never look back. *Auf Wiedersehen! Gluckliche Reise! Gottes Name,* go now!"

Watching them take their leave, seeing them trudge off together into the swirling winds of the Outback, Robert Howard felt a sudden sharp pang of regret and loss. How beautiful they had been, those two heroes, those two giants, as they strained and struggled! And then that sudden magic moment when the folly of their quarrel came home to them, when they were enemies no longer and brothers once more—

And now they were gone, and here he stood amidst these others, these strangers—

He had wanted to be Gilgamesh's brother, or perhaps—he barely comprehended it—something more than a brother. But that could never have been. And, knowing that it could never have been, knowing that that man who seemed so much like his Conan was lost to him forever, Howard felt tears beginning to surge within him.

"Bob?" Lovecraft said. "Bob, are you all right?"

She-it, Howard thought. *A man don't cry. Especially in front of other men.* He turned away, into the wind, so Lovecraft could not see his face. "Bob? Bob?"

She-it, Howard thought again. And he let the tears come.

THE PARDONER'S TALE

Another Playboy *story, eleven months after the last one. During the intervening time I had been busy indeed. In the fall of 1985 had come the novella "Gilgamesh in the Outback," the completion of which was delayed because of certain domestic rearrangements: I had lured Karen Haber out of her Texas domicile to live with me in far-off California, and she arrived in mid-November. Hardly had she unpacked her suitcases than I had moved on from my Gilgamesh novella to the immense picaresque novel* Star of Gypsies, *which occupied me all during the winter and spring of 1986, requiring a number of drafts before I was satisfied. And then, without pausing for breath, I did the second Afterworld novella about Gilgamesh, "The Fascination of the Abomination."*

Some time off seemed in order, but back then my thoughts usually turned in the spring of the year to writing something for Alice Turner of Playboy, *and that year's* Playboy *project turned out to be "The Pardoner's Tale," title courtesy of Chaucer, who'd probably be puzzled by the story I appended to it. At that time the term "cyberpunk" was being bandied about ad nauseam in the science-fiction world, and I suppose you could call this a cyberpunk story—Alice did, in her acceptance letter of July 1, 1986, and I didn't quarrel with the description, although that wasn't exactly what I had thought I was writing.*

She wanted about two pages of cuts—a line here, two lines there—in keeping with a dictum she had heard that quintessential cyberpunk featured "the hottest of all the technological futures, fast action, tight construction, and a disdain for all that is slow and boring." As ever, when Alice Turner thought a line or two ought to be cut, I gave heed to what she said. I did the cutting with scarcely a demur, and the final version, sleek and taut, owes no little of its success to her nifty work with the scalpel. She ran it in the June, 1987 Playboy. *Gardner Dozois picked it for his 1988 year's-best anthology, my fifth appearance in that collection in five years, and Don Wollheim chose it also for his book, giving me one more sweep of the year's-best books— although, since Terry Carr's anthology no longer appeared, it was only a double sweep this time. As I have mentioned previously, I incorporated most of the story years later into my novel* The Alien Years.

"**K**ey Sixteen, Housing Omicron Kappa, aleph sub-one," I said to the software on duty at the Alhambra gate of the Los Angeles Wall.

Software isn't generally suspicious. This wasn't even very smart software. It was working off some great biochips—I could feel them jigging and pulsing as the electron stream flowed through them—but the software itself was just a kludge. Typical gatekeeper stuff.

I stood waiting as the picoseconds went ticking away by the millions.

"Name, please," the gatekeeper said finally.

"John Doe. Beta Pi Upsilon 104324x."

The gate opened. I walked into Los Angeles.

As easy as Beta Pi.

The wall that encircles L.A. is a hundred, a hundred fifty feet thick. Its gates are more like tunnels. When you consider that the wall runs completely around the L.A. basin from the San Gabriel Valley to the San Fernando Valley and then over the mountains and down the coast and back the far side past Long Beach, and that it's at least sixty feet high and all that distance deep, you can begin to appreciate the mass of it. Think of the phenomenal expenditure of human energy that went into building it—muscle and sweat, sweat and muscle. I think about that a lot.

I suppose the walls around our cities were put there mostly as symbols. They highlight the distinction between city and countryside, between citizen and uncitizen, between control and chaos, just as city walls did five thousand years ago. But mainly they serve to remind us that we are all slaves nowadays. You can't ignore the walls. You can't pretend they aren't there. *We made you build them*, is what they say, *and don't you ever forget that.* All the same, Chicago doesn't have a wall sixty feet high and a hundred fifty feet deep. Houston doesn't. Phoenix doesn't. They make do with less. But L.A. is the main city. I suppose the Los Angeles wall is a statement: I am the Big Cheese. I am the Ham What Am.

The walls aren't there because the Entities are afraid of attack. They know how invulnerable they are. We know it too. They just wanted to decorate their capital with something a little special. What the hell, it isn't *their* sweat that goes into building the walls. It's ours. Not mine personally, of course. But ours.

I saw a few Entities walking around just inside the wall, preoccupied as usual with God knows what and paying no attention to the humans in the vicinity. These were low-caste ones, the kind with the luminous orange spots along their sides. I gave them plenty of room. They have a way sometimes of picking a human up with those long elastic tongues, like a frog snapping up a fly, and letting him dangle in mid-air while they study him with those saucer-sized yellow eyes. I don't care for that. You don't get hurt, but it isn't agreeable to be dangled in mid-air by something that looks like a fifteen-foot-high purple squid standing on the tips of its tentacles. Happened to me once in St. Louis, long ago, and I'm in no hurry to have it happen again.

The first thing I did when I was inside L.A. was find me a car. On Valley Boulevard about two blocks in from the wall I saw a '31 Toshiba El Dorado that looked good to me, and I matched frequencies with its lock and slipped inside and took about ninety seconds to reprogram its drive control to my personal metabolic cues. The previous owner must have been fat as a hippo and probably diabetic: her glycogen index was absurd and her phosphines were wild.

Not a bad car, a little slow in the shift but what can you expect, considering the last time any cars were manufactured on this planet was the year 2034.

"Pershing Square," I told it.

It had nice capacity, maybe 60 megabytes. It turned south right away and found the old freeway and drove off toward downtown. I figured I'd set up shop in the middle of things, work two or three pardons to keep my edge sharp, get myself a hotel room, a meal, maybe hire some companionship. And then think about the next move. It was winter, a nice time to be in L.A. That golden sun, those warm breezes coming down the canyons.

I hadn't been out on the Coast in years. Working Florida mainly, Texas, sometimes Arizona. I hate the cold. I hadn't been in L.A. since '36. A long time to stay away, but maybe I'd been staying away deliberately. I wasn't sure. That last L.A. trip had left bad-tasting memories. There had been a woman who wanted a pardon and I sold her a stiff. You have to stiff the customers now and then or else you start looking too good, which can be dangerous; but she was young and pretty and full of hope and I could have stiffed the next one instead of her, only I didn't. Sometimes I've felt bad, thinking back over that. Maybe that's what had kept me away from L.A. all this time

A couple of miles east of the big downtown interchange traffic began backing up. Maybe an accident ahead, maybe a roadblock. I told the Toshiba to get off the freeway.

Slipping through roadblocks is scary and calls for a lot of hard work. I knew that I probably could fool any kind of software at a roadblock and certainly any human cop, but why bother if you don't have to?

I asked the car where I was.

The screen lit up. Alameda near Banning, it said. A long walk to Pershing Square, looked like. I had the car drop me at Spring Street and went the rest of the way on foot. "Pick me up at 1830 hours," I told it. "Corner of—umm—Sixth and Hill." It went away to park itself and I headed for the Square to peddle some pardons.

It isn't hard for a good pardoner to find buyers. You can see it in their eyes: the tightly controlled anger, the smoldering resentment. And something else, something intangible, a certain sense of having a shred or two of inner integrity left, that tells you right away, Here's somebody willing to risk a lot to regain some measure of freedom. I was in business within fifteen minutes.

The first one was an aging surfer sort, barrel chest and that sun-bleached look. The Entities haven't allowed surfing for ten, fifteen years—they've got their plankton seines just off shore from Santa Barbara to San Diego, gulping in the marine nutrients they have to have, and any beach boy who tried to take a whack at the waves out there would be chewed right up. But this guy must have been one hell of a performer in his day. The way he moved through the park, making little balancing moves as if he needed to compensate for the irregularities of the earth's rotation, you could see how he would have been in the water. Sat down next to me, began working on his lunch. Thick forearms, gnarled hands. A wall-laborer. Muscles knotting in his cheeks: the anger, forever simmering just below boil.

I got him talking, after a while. A surfer, yes. Lost in the far-away and gone. He began sighing to me about legendary beaches where the waves were tubes and they came pumping end to end. "Trestle Beach," he murmured. "That's north of San Onofre. You had to sneak through Camp Pendleton. Sometimes the Marines would open fire, just warning shots. Or Hollister Ranch, up by Santa Barbara." His blue eyes got misty. "Huntington Beach. Oxnard. I got everywhere, man." He flexed his huge fingers. "Now these fucking Entity hodads own the shore. Can you believe it? They *own* it. And I'm pulling wall, my second time around, seven days a week next ten years."

"Ten?" I said. "That's a shitty deal."

"You know anyone who doesn't have a shitty deal?"

"Some," I said. "They buy out."

"Yeah."

"It can be done."

A careful look. You never know who might be a borgmann. Those stinking collaborators are everywhere.

"Can it?"

"All it takes is money," I said.

"And a pardoner."

"That's right."

"One you can trust."

I shrugged. "You've got to go on faith, man."

"Yeah," he said. Then, after a while: "I heard of a guy, he bought a three-year pardon and wall passage thrown in. Went up north, caught a krill trawler, wound up in Australia, on the Reef. Nobody's ever going to find him there. He's out of the system. Right out of the fucking system. What do you think that cost?"

"About twenty grand," I said.

"Hey, that's a sharp guess!"

"No guess."

"Oh?" Another careful look. "You don't sound local."

"I'm not. Just visiting."

301

"That's still the price? Twenty grand?"

"I can't do anything about supplying krill trawlers. You'd be on your own once you were outside the wall."

"Twenty grand just to get through the wall?"

"And a seven-year labor exemption."

"I pulled ten," he said.

"I can't get you ten. It's not in the configuration, you follow? But seven would work. You could get so far, in seven, that they'd lose you. You could goddamned *swim* to Australia. Come in low, below Sydney, no seines there."

"You know a hell of a lot."

"My business to know," I said. "You want me to run an asset check on you?"

"I'm worth seventeen five. Fifteen hundred real, the rest collat. What can I get for seventeen five?"

"Just what I said. Through the wall, and seven years' exemption."

"A bargain rate, hey?"

"I take what I can get," I said. "Give me your wrist. And don't worry. This part is read-only."

I keyed his data implant and patched mine in. He had fifteen hundred in the bank and a collateral rating of sixteen thou, exactly as he claimed. We eyed each other very carefully now. As I said, you never know who the borgmanns are.

"You can do it right here in the park?" he asked.

"You bet. Lean back, close your eyes, make like you're snoozing in the sun. The deal is that I take a thousand of the cash now and you transfer five thou of the collateral bucks to me, straight labor-debenture deal. When you get through the wall I get the other five hundred cash and five thou more on sweat security. The rest you pay off at three thou a year plus interest, wherever you are, quarterly key-ins. I'll program the whole thing, including beep reminders on payment dates. It's up to you to make your travel arrangements, remember. I can do pardons and wall transits but I'm not a goddamned travel agent. Are we on?"

He put his head back and closed his eyes.

"Go ahead," he said.

It was fingertip stuff, straight circuit emulation, my standard hack. I picked up all his identification codes, carried them into central, found his records. He seemed real, nothing more or less than he had claimed. Sure enough, he had drawn a lulu of a labor tax, ten years on the wall. I wrote him a pardon good for the first seven of that. Had to leave the final three on the books, purely technical reasons, but the computers weren't going to be able to find him by then. I gave him a wall-transit pass, too, which meant writing in a new skills class for him, programmer third grade. He didn't think like a programmer and he didn't look like a programmer but the wall software wasn't going to figure that out. Now I had made him a member of the human elite, the relative handful of us who are free to go in and out of the walled cities as we wish. In return for these little favors I signed over his entire life savings to various accounts of mine, payable as arranged, part now, part later. He wasn't worth a nickel any more, but he was a free man. That's not such a terrible trade-off.

Oh, and the pardon was a valid one. I had decided not to write any stiffs while I was in Los Angeles. A kind of sentimental atonement, you might say, for the job I had done on that woman all those years back.

You absolutely have to write stiffs once in a while, you understand. So that you don't look too good, so that you don't give the Entities reason to hunt you down. Just as you have to ration the number of pardons you do. I didn't have to be writing pardons at all, of course. I could have just authorized the system to pay me so much a year, fifty thou, a hundred, and taken it easy forever. But where's the challenge in that?

So I write pardons, but no more than I need to cover my expenses, and I deliberately fudge some of them up, making myself look as incompetent as the rest so the Entities don't have a reason to begin trying to track the identifying marks of my work. My conscience hasn't been too sore about that. It's a matter of survival, after all. And most other pardoners are out-and-out frauds, you know. At least with me you stand a better than even chance of getting what you're paying for.

###

The next one was a tiny Japanese woman, the classic style, sleek, fragile, doll-like. Crying in big wild gulps that I thought might break her in half, while a gray-haired older man in a shabby business suit—her grandfather, you'd guess—was trying to comfort her. Public crying is a good indicator of Entity trouble. "Maybe I can help," I said, and they were both so distraught that they didn't even bother to be suspicious.

He was her father-in-law, not her grandfather. The husband was dead, killed by burglars the year before. There were two small kids. Now she had received her new labor-tax ticket. She had been afraid they were going to send her out to work on the wall, which of course wasn't likely to happen: the assignments are pretty random, but they usually aren't crazy, and what use would a 90-pound girl be in hauling stone blocks around? The father-in-law had some friends who were in the know, and they managed to bring up the hidden encoding on her ticket. The computers hadn't sent her to the wall, no. They had sent her to Area Five. And they had given her a TTD classification.

"The wall would have been better," the old man said. "They'd see, right away, she wasn't strong enough for heavy work, and they'd find something else, something she could do. But Area Five? Who ever comes back from that?"

"You know what Area Five is?" I said.

"The medical experiment place. And this mark here, TTD. I know what that stands for too."

She began to moan again. I couldn't blame her. TTD means Test To Destruction. The Entities want to find out how much work we can really do, and they feel that the only reliable way to discover that is to put us through tests that show where the physical limits are.

"I will die," she wailed. "My babies! My babies!"

"Do you know what a pardoner is?" I asked the father-in-law.

A quick excited response: sharp intake of breath, eyes going bright, head nodding vehemently. Just as quickly the excitement faded, giving way to bleakness, helplessness, despair.

"They all cheat you," he said.

"Not all."

"Who can say? They take your money, they give you nothing."

"You know that isn't true. Everybody can tell you stories of pardons that came through."

"Maybe. Maybe," the old man said. The woman sobbed quietly. "You know of such a person?"

"For three thousand dollars," I said, "I can take the TTD off her ticket. For five I can write an exemption from service good until her children are in high school."

Sentimental me. A fifty percent discount, and I hadn't even run an asset check. For all I knew the father-in-law was a millionaire. But no, he'd have been off cutting a pardon for her, then, and not sitting around like this in Pershing Square.

He gave me a long, deep, appraising look. Peasant shrewdness coming to the surface.

"How can we be sure of that?" he asked.

I might have told him that I was the king of my profession, the best of all pardoners, a genius hacker with the truly magic touch, who could slip into any computer ever designed and make it dance to my tune. Which would have been nothing more than the truth. But all I said was that he'd have to make up his own mind, that I couldn't offer any affidavits or guarantees, that I was available if he wanted me and otherwise it was all the same to me if she preferred to stick with her TTD ticket. They went off and conferred for a couple of minutes. When they came back, he silently rolled up his sleeve and presented his implant to me. I keyed his credit balance: thirty thou or so, not bad. I transferred eight of it to my accounts, half to Seattle, the rest to Los Angeles. Then I took her wrist, which was about two of my fingers thick, and got into her implant and wrote her the pardon that would save her life. Just to be certain, I ran a double validation check on it. It's always possible to stiff a customer unintentionally, though I've never done it. But I didn't want this particular one to be my first.

"Go on," I said. "Home. Your kids are waiting for their lunch."

Her eyes glowed. "If I could only thank you somehow—"

"I've already banked my fee. Go. If you ever see me again, don't say hello."

"This will work?" the old man asked.

"You say you have friends who know things. Wait seven days, then tell the data bank that she's lost her ticket. When you get the new one, ask your pals to decode it for you. You'll see. It'll be all right."

I don't think he believed me. I think he was more than half sure I had swindled him out of one fourth of his life's savings, and I could see the hatred in his eyes. But that was his problem. In a week he'd find out that I really had saved his daughter-in-law's life, and then he'd rush down to the Square to tell me how sorry he was that he had had such terrible feelings toward me. Only by then I'd be somewhere else, far away.

They shuffled out the east side of the park, pausing a couple of times to peer over their shoulders at me as if they thought I was going to transform them into pillars of salt the moment their backs were turned. Then they were gone.

I'd earned enough now to get me through the week I planned to spend in L.A. But I stuck around anyway, hoping for a little more. My mistake.

This one was Mr. Invisible, the sort of man you'd never notice in a crowd, gray on gray, thinning hair, mild bland apologetic smile. But his eyes had a shine. I forget whether he started talking first to me, or me to him, but pretty soon we were jockeying around trying to find out things about each other. He told me he was from Silver Lake. I gave him a blank look. How in hell am I supposed to know all the zillion L.A. neighborhoods? Said that he had come down here to see someone at the big government HQ on Figueroa Street. All right: probably an appeals case. I sensed a customer.

Then he wanted to know where I was from. Santa Monica? West L.A.? Something in my accent, I guess. "I'm a traveling man," I said. "Hate to stay in one place." True enough. I need to hack or I go crazy; if I did all my hacking in just one city I'd be virtually begging them to slap a trace on me sooner or later and that would be the end. I didn't tell him any of that. "Came in from Utah last night. Wyoming before that." Not true, either one. "Maybe on to New York, next." He looked at me as if I'd said I was planning a voyage to the moon. People out here, they don't go east a lot. These days most people don't go anywhere.

Now he knew that I had wall-transit clearance, or else that I had some way of getting it when I wanted it. That was what he was looking to find out. In no time at all we were down to basics.

He said he had drawn a new ticket, six years at the salt-field reclamation site out back of Mono Lake. People die like mayflies out there. What he wanted was a transfer to something softer, like Operations & Maintenance, and it had to be within the walls, preferably in one of the districts out by the ocean where the air is cool and clear. I quoted him a price and he accepted without a quiver.

"Let's have your wrist," I said.

He held out his right hand, palm upward. His implant access was a pale yellow plaque, mounted in the usual place but rounder than the standard kind and of a slightly smoother texture. I didn't see any great significance in that. As I had done maybe a thousand times before, I put my own arm over his, wrist to wrist, access to access. Our biocomputers made contact and instantly I knew that I was in trouble.

Human beings have been carrying biochip-based computers in their bodies for the last forty or fifty years or so—long before the Entity invasion, anyway—but for most people it's just something they take for granted, like the vaccination mark on their thighs. They use them for the things they're meant to be used for, and don't give them a thought beyond that. The biocomputer's just a commonplace tool for them, like a fork, like a shovel. You have to have the hacker sort of mentality to be willing to turn your biocomputer into something more. That's why, when the Entities came and took us over and made us build walls around our cities, most people reacted just like sheep, letting themselves be herded inside and politely staying there. The only ones who can move around freely now—because we know how to manipulate the mainframes through which the Entities rule us—are the hackers. And there aren't many of us. I could tell right away that I had hooked myself on to one now.

The moment we were in contact, he came at me like a storm.

The strength of his signal let me know I was up against something special, and that I'd been hustled. He hadn't been trying to buy a pardon at all. What he was looking for was a duel. Mr. Macho behind the bland smile, out to show the new boy in town a few of his tricks.

No hacker had ever mastered me in a one-on-one anywhere. Not ever. I felt sorry for him, but not much.

He shot me a bunch of stuff, cryptic but easy, just by way of finding out my parameters. I caught it and stored it and laid an interrupt on him and took over the dialog. My turn to test him. I wanted him to begin to see who he was fooling around with. But just as I began to execute he put an interrupt on *me*. That was a new experience. I stared at him with some respect.

Usually any hacker anywhere will recognize my signal in the first thirty seconds, and that'll be enough to finish the interchange. He'll know that there's no point in continuing. But this guy either wasn't able to identify me or just didn't care, and he came right back with his interrupt. Amazing. So was the stuff he began laying on me next.

He went right to work, really trying to scramble my architecture. Reams of stuff came flying at me up in the heavy megabyte zone.

—*jspike. dbltag. nslice. dzcnt.*

I gave it right back to him, twice as hard.

—*maxfrq. minpau. spktot. jspike.*

He didn't mind at all.

—*maxdz. spktim. falter. nslice.*

—*frqsum. eburst.*

—*iburst.*

—prebst.

—nobrst.

Mexican standoff. He was still smiling. Not even a trace of sweat on his forehead. Something eerie about him, something new and strange. This is some kind of borgmann hacker, I realized suddenly. He must be working for the Entities, roving the city, looking to make trouble for freelancers like me. Good as he was, and he was plenty good, I despised him. A hacker who had become a borgmann—now, that was truly disgusting. I wanted to short him. I wanted to burn him out, now. I had never hated anyone so much in my life.

I couldn't do a thing with him.

I was baffled. I was the Data King, I was the Megabyte Monster. All my life I had floated back and forth across a world in chains, picking every lock I came across. And now this nobody was tying me in knots. Whatever I gave him, he parried; and what came back from him was getting increasingly bizarre. He was working with an algorithm I had never seen before and was having serious trouble solving. After a little while I couldn't even figure out what he was doing to me, let alone what I was going to do to cancel it. It was getting so I could barely execute. He was forcing me inexorably toward a wetware crash.

"Who are you?" I yelled.

He laughed in my face.

And kept pouring it on. He was threatening the integrity of my implant, going at me down on the microcosmic level, attacking the molecules themselves. Fiddling around with electron shells, reversing charges and mucking up valences, clogging my gates, turning my circuits to soup. The computer that is implanted in my brain is nothing but a lot of organic chemistry, after all. So is my brain. If he kept this up the computer would go and the brain would follow, and I'd spend the rest of my life in the bibblebibble academy.

This wasn't a sporting contest. This was murder.

I reached for the reserves, throwing up all the defensive blockages I could invent. Things I had never had to use in my life, but they were there when I needed them, and they did slow him down. For a moment I was able to halt his ballbreaking onslaught and even push him back. And give myself the breathing space to set up a few offensive combinations of my own. But before I could get them running, he shut me down once more and started to drive me toward crashville all over again. He was unbelievable.

I blocked him. He came back again. I hit him hard and he threw the punch into some other neural channel altogether and it went fizzling away.

I hit him again. Again he blocked it.

Then he hit me and I went reeling and staggering, and managed to get myself together when I was about three nanoseconds from the edge of the abyss.

I began to set up a new combination. But even as I did it, I was reading the tone of his data, and what I was getting was absolute cool confidence. He was waiting for me. He was ready for anything I could throw. He was in that realm beyond mere self-confidence into utter certainty.

What it was coming down to was this. I was able to keep him from ruining me, but only just barely, and I wasn't able to lay a glove on him at all. And he seemed to have infinite resources behind him. I didn't worry him. He was tireless. He didn't appear to degrade at all. He just took all I could give and kept throwing new stuff at me, coming at me from six sides at once.

Now I understood for the first time what it must have felt like for all the hackers I had beaten. Some of them must have felt pretty cocky, I suppose, until they ran into me. It costs more to lose when you think you're good. When you *know* you're good. People like that, when they lose, they have to reprogram their whole sense of their relation to the universe.

I had two choices. I could go on fighting until he wore me down and crashed me. Or I could give up right now. In the end everything comes down to yes or no, on or off, one or zero, doesn't it?

I took a deep breath. I was staring straight into chaos.

"All right," I said. "I'm beaten. I quit."

I wrenched my wrist free of his, trembled, swayed, went toppling down on the ground.

A minute later five cops jumped me and trussed me up like a turkey and hauled me away, with my implant arm sticking out of the package and a security lock wrapped around my wrist, as if they were afraid I was going to start pulling data right out of the air.

Where they took me was Figueroa Street, the big black marble ninety-story job that is the home of the puppet city government. I didn't give a damn. I was numb. They could have put me in the sewer and I wouldn't have cared. I wasn't damaged—the automatic circuit check was still running and it came up green—but the humiliation was so intense that I felt crashed. I felt destroyed. The only thing I wanted to know was the name of the hacker who had done it to me.

The Figueroa Street building has ceilings about twenty feet high everywhere, so that there'll be room for Entities to move around. Voices reverberate in those vast open spaces like echoes in a cavern. The cops sat me down in a hallway, still all wrapped up, and kept me there for a long time. Blurred sounds went lalloping up and down the passage. I wanted to hide from them. My brain felt raw. I had taken one hell of a pounding.

Now and then a couple of towering Entities would come rumbling through the hall, tiptoeing on their tentacles in that weirdly dainty way of theirs. With them came a little entourage of humans whom they ignored entirely, as they always do. They know that we're intelligent but they just don't care to talk to us. They let their computers do that, via the Borgmann interface, and may his signal degrade forever for having sold us out. Not that they wouldn't have conquered us anyway, but Borgmann made it ever so much easier for them to push us around by showing them how to connect our little biocomputers to their huge mainframes. I bet he was very proud of himself, too: just wanted to see if his gadget would work, and to hell with the fact that he was selling us into eternal bondage.

Nobody has ever figured out why the Entities are here or what they want from us. They simply came, that's all. Saw. Conquered. Rearranged us. Put us to work doing godawful unfathomable tasks, Like a bad dream.

And there wasn't any way we could defend ourselves against them. Didn't seem that way to us at first—we were cocky, we were going to wage guerilla war and wipe them out—but we learned fast how wrong we were, and we are theirs for keeps. There's nobody left with anything close to freedom except the handful of hackers like me; and, as I've explained, we're not dopey enough to try any serious sort of counterattack. It's a big enough triumph for us just to be able to dodge around from one city to another without having to get authorization.

Looked like all that was finished for me, now. Right then I didn't give a damn. I was still trying to integrate the notion that I had been beaten; I didn't have capacity left over to work on a program for the new life I would be leading now.

"Is this the pardoner, over here?" someone said.

"That one, yeah."

"She wants to see him now."

"You think we should fix him up a little first?"

"She said now."

A hand at my shoulder, rocking me gently. "Up, fellow. It's interview time. Don't make a mess or you'll get hurt."

I let them shuffle me down the hall and through a gigantic doorway and into an immense office with a ceiling high enough to give an Entity all the room it would want. I didn't say a word. There weren't any Entities in the office, just a woman in a black robe, sitting behind a wide desk at the far end. It looked like a toy desk in that colossal room. She looked like a toy woman. The cops left me alone with her. Trussed up like that, I wasn't any risk.

"Are you John Doe?" she asked.

I was halfway across the room, studying my shoes. "What do you think?" I said.

"That's the name you gave upon entry to the city."

"I give lots of names. John Smith, Richard Roe, Joe Blow. It doesn't matter much to the gate software what name I give."

"Because you've gimmicked the gate?" She paused. "I should tell you, this is a court of inquiry."

"You already know everything I could tell you. Your borgmann hacker's been swimming around in my brain."

"Please," she said. "This'll be easier if you cooperate. The accusation is illegal entry, illegal seizure of a vehicle, and illegal interfacing activity, specifically, selling pardons. Do you have a statement?"

"No."

"You deny that you're a pardoner?"

"I don't deny, I don't affirm. What's the goddamned use."

"Look up at me," she said.

"That's a lot of effort."

"Look up," she said. There was an odd edge on her voice. "Whether you're a pardoner or not isn't the issue. We know you're a pardoner. *I* know you're a pardoner." And she called me by a name I hadn't used in a very long time. Not since '36, as a matter of fact.

I looked at her. Stared. Had trouble believing I was seeing what I saw. Felt a rush of memories come flooding up. Did some mental editing work on her face, taking out some lines here, subtracting a little flesh in a few places, adding some in others. Stripping away the years.

311

"Yes," she said. "I'm who you think I am."

I gaped. This was worse than what the hacker had done to me. But there was no way to run from it.

"You work for them?" I asked.

"The pardon you sold me wasn't any good. You knew that, didn't you? I had someone waiting for me in San Diego, but when I tried to get through the wall they stopped me just like that, and dragged me away screaming. I could have killed you. I would have gone to San Diego and then we would have tried to make it to Hawaii in his boat."

"I didn't know about the guy in San Diego," I said.

"Why should you? It wasn't your business. You took my money, you were supposed to get me my pardon. That was the deal."

Her eyes were gray with golden sparkles in them. I had trouble looking into them.

"You still want to kill me?" I asked. "Are you planning to kill me now?"

"No and no." She used my old name again. "I can't tell you how astounded I was, when they brought you in here. A pardoner, they said. John Doe. Pardoners, that's my department. They bring all of them to me. I used to wonder years ago if they'd ever bring *you* in, but after a while I figured, no, not a chance, he's probably a million miles away, he'll never come back this way again. And then they brought in this John Doe, and I saw your face."

"Do you think you could manage to believe," I said, "that I've felt guilty for what I did to you ever since? You don't have to believe it. But it's the truth."

"I'm sure it's been unending agony for you."

"I mean it. Please. I've stiffed a lot of people, yes, and sometimes I've regretted it and sometimes I haven't, but you were one that I regretted. You're the one I've regretted most. This is the absolute truth."

She considered that. I couldn't tell whether she believed it even for a fraction of a second, but I could see that she was considering it.

"Why did you do it?" she asked after a bit.

"I stiff people because I don't want to seem too perfect," I told her. "You deliver a pardon every single time, word gets around, people start talking, you start to become legendary. And then you're known everywhere and sooner or later the Entities get hold of you, and that's that. So I always make sure to write a lot of stiffs. I tell people I'll do my best, but there aren't any guarantees, and sometimes it doesn't work."

"You deliberately cheated me."

"Yes."

"I thought you did. You seemed so cool, so professional. So perfect. I was sure the pardon would be valid. I couldn't see how it would miss. And then I got to the wall and they grabbed me. So I thought, that bastard sold me out. He was too good just to have flubbed it up." Her tone was calm but the anger was still in her eyes. "Couldn't you have stiffed the next one? Why did it have to be me?"

I looked at her for a long time.

"Because I loved you," I said.

"Shit," she said. "You didn't even know me. I was just some stranger who had hired you."

"That's just it. There I was full of all kinds of crazy instant lunatic fantasies about you, all of a sudden ready to turn my nice orderly life upside down for you, and all you could see was somebody you had hired to do a job. I didn't know about the guy from San Diego. All I knew was I saw you and I wanted you. You don't think that's love? Well, call it something else, then, whatever you want. I never let myself feel it before. It isn't smart, I thought, it ties you down, the risks are too big. And then I saw you and I talked to you a little and I thought something could be happening between us and things started to change inside me, and I thought, Yeah, yeah, go with it this time, let it happen, this may make everything different. And you stood there not seeing it, not even beginning to notice, just jabbering on and on about how important the pardon was for you. So I stiffed you. And afterwards I thought, Jesus, I ruined that girl's life and it was just because I got myself into a snit, and that was a fucking petty thing to have done. So I've been sorry ever since. You don't have to believe that. I didn't know about San Diego. That makes it even worse for me." She didn't say anything all this time, and the silence felt enormous. So after a moment I said, "Tell me one thing, at least. That guy who wrecked me in Pershing Square: who was he?"

"He wasn't anybody," she said.

"What does that mean?"

"He isn't a who. He's a *what*. It's an android, a mobile anti-pardoner unit, plugged right into the big Entity mainframe in Culver City. Something new that we have going around town."

"Oh," I said. "Oh."

"The report is that you gave it one hell of a workout."

"It gave me one too. Turned my brain half to mush."

313

"You were trying to drink the sea through a straw. For a while it looked like you were really going to do it, too. You're one goddamned hacker, you know that?"

"Why did you go to work for them?" I said.

She shrugged. "Everybody works for them. Except people like you. You took everything I had and didn't give me my pardon. So what was I supposed to do?"

"I see."

"It's not such a bad job. At least I'm not out there on the wall. Or being sent off for TTD."

"No," I said. "It's probably not so bad. If you don't mind working in a room with such a high ceiling. Is that what's going to happen to me? Sent off for TTD?"

"Don't be stupid. You're too valuable."

"To whom?"

"The system always needs upgrading. You know it better than anyone alive. You'll work for us."

"You think I'm going to turn borgmann?" I said, amazed.

"It beats TTD," she said.

I fell silent again. I was thinking that she couldn't possibly be serious, that they'd be fools to trust me in any kind of responsible position. And even bigger fools to let me near their computer.

"All right," I said. "I'll do it. On one condition."

"You really have balls, don't you?"

"Let me have a rematch with that android of yours. I need to check something out. And afterward we can discuss what kind of work I'd be best suited for here. Okay?"

"You know you aren't in any position to lay down conditions."

"Sure I am. What I do with computers is a unique art. You can't make me do it against my will. You can't make me do anything against my will."

She thought about that. "What good is a rematch?"

"Nobody ever beat me before. I want a second try."

"You know it'll be worse for you than before."

"Let me find that out."

"But what's the point?"

"Get me your android and I'll show you the point," I said.

❄

She went along with it. Maybe it was curiosity, maybe it was something else, but she patched herself into the computer net and pretty soon they brought in the android I had encountered in the park, or maybe another one with the same face. It looked me over pleasantly, without the slightest sign of interest.

Someone came in and took the security lock off my wrist and left again. She gave the android its instructions and it held out its wrist to me and we made contact. And I jumped right in.

I was raw and wobbly and pretty damned battered, still, but I knew what I needed to do and I knew I had to do it fast. The thing was to ignore the android completely—it was just a terminal, it was just a unit—and go for what lay behind it. So I bypassed the android's own identity program, which was clever but shallow. I went right around it while the android was still setting up its combinations, dived underneath, got myself instantly from the unit level to the mainframe level and gave the master Culver City computer a hearty handshake.

Jesus, that felt good!

All that power, all those millions of megabytes squatting there, and I was plugged right into it. Of course I felt like a mouse hitchhiking on the back of an elephant. That was all right. I might be a mouse but that mouse was getting a tremendous ride. I hung on tight and went soaring along on the hurricane winds of that colossal machine.

And as I soared, I ripped out chunks of it by the double handful and tossed them to the breeze.

It didn't even notice for a good tenth of a second. That's how big it was. There I was, tearing great blocks of data out of its gut, joyously ripping and rending. And it didn't even know it, because even the most magnificent computer ever assembled is still stuck with operating at the speed of light, and when the best you can do is 186,000 miles a second it can take quite a while for the alarm to travel the full distance down all your neural channels. That thing was *huge*. Mouse riding on elephant, did I say? Amoeba piggybacking on brontosaurus, was more like it.

God knows how much damage I was able to do. But of course the alarm circuitry did cut in eventually. Internal gates came clanging down and all sensitive areas were sealed away and I was shrugged off with the greatest of ease. There was no sense staying around waiting to get trapped, so I pulled myself free.

I had found out what I needed to know. Where the defenses were, how they worked. This time the computer had kicked me out, but it wouldn't be able to, the next. Whenever I wanted, I could go in there and smash whatever I felt like.

The android crumpled to the carpet. It was nothing but an empty husk now.

Lights were flashing on the office wall.

She looked at me, appalled. "What did you *do*?"

"I beat your android," I said. "It wasn't all that hard, once I knew the scoop."

"You damaged the main computer."

"Not really. Not much. I just gave it a little tickle. It was surprised, seeing me get access in there, that's all."

"I think you really damaged it."

"Why would I want to do that?"

"The question ought to be why you haven't done it already. Why you haven't gone in there and crashed the hell out of their programs."

"You think I could do something like that?"

She studied me. "I think maybe you could, yes."

"Well, maybe so. Or maybe not. But I'm not a crusader, you know. I like my life the way it is. I move around, I do as I please. It's a quiet life. I don't start revolutions. When I need to gimmick things, I gimmick them just enough, and no more. And the Entities don't even know I exist. If I stick my finger in their eye, they'll cut my finger off. So I haven't done it."

"But now you might," she said.

I began to get uncomfortable. "I don't follow you," I said, although I was beginning to think that I did.

"You don't like risk. You don't like being conspicuous. But if we take your freedom away, if we tie you down in L.A. and put you to work, what the hell would you have to lose? You'd go right in there. You'd gimmick things but good." She was silent for a time. "Yes," she said. "You really would. I see it now, that you have the capability and that you could be put in a position where you'd be willing to use it. And then you'd screw everything up for all of us, wouldn't you?"

"What?"

"You'd fix the Entities, sure. You'd do such a job on their computer that they'd have to scrap it and start all over again. Isn't that so?"

She was on to me, all right.

"But I'm not going to give you the chance. I'm not crazy. There isn't going to be any revolution and I'm not going to be its heroine and you aren't the type to be a hero. I understand you now. It isn't safe to fool around with you. Because if anybody did, you'd take your little revenge, and you wouldn't care what you brought down on everybody else's head. You could ruin their computer but then they'd come down on us and they'd make things twice as hard for us as they already are, and you wouldn't care. We'd all suffer, but you wouldn't care. No. My life isn't so terrible that I need you to turn it upside down for me. You've already done it to me once. I don't need it again."

She looked at me steadily and all the anger seemed to be gone from her and there was only contempt left.

After a little she said, "Can you go in there again and gimmick things so that there's no record of your arrest today?"

"Yeah. Yeah, I could do that."

"Do it, then. And then get going. Get the hell out of here, fast."

"Are you serious?"

"You think I'm not?"

I shook my head. I understood. And I knew that I had won and I had lost, both at the same time.

She made an impatient gesture, a shoo-fly gesture.

I nodded. I felt very very small.

"I just want to say—all that stuff about how much I regretted the thing I did to you back then—it was true. Every word of it."

"It probably was," she said. "Look, do your gimmicking and edit yourself out and then I want you to start moving. Out of the building. Out of the city. Okay? Do it real fast."

I hunted around for something else to say and couldn't find it. Quit while you're ahead, I thought. She gave me her wrist and I did the interface with her. As my implant access touched hers she shuddered a little. It wasn't much of a shudder but I noticed it. I felt it, all right. I think I'm going to feel it every time I stiff anyone, ever again. Any time I even think of stiffing anyone.

I went in and found the John Doe arrest entry and got rid of it, and then I searched out her civil service file and promoted her up two grades and doubled her pay. Not much of an atonement. But what the hell, there wasn't much I could do. Then I cleaned up my traces behind me and exited the program.

"All right," I said. "It's done."

"Fine," she said, and rang for her cops.

They apologized for the case of mistaken identity and let me out of the building and turned me loose on Figueroa Street. It was late afternoon and the street was getting dark and the air was cool. Even in Los Angeles winter is winter, of a sort. I went to a street access and summoned the Toshiba from wherever it had parked itself and it came driving up, five or ten minutes later, and I told it to take me north. The going was slow, rush-hour stuff, but that was okay. We came to the wall at the Sylmar gate, fifty miles or so out of town. The gate asked me my name. "Richard Roe," I said. "Beta Pi Upsilon 104324x. Destination San Francisco."

It rains a lot in San Francisco in the winter. Still, it's a pretty town. I would have preferred Los Angeles that time of year, but what the hell. Nobody gets all his first choices all the time. The gate opened and the Toshiba went through. Easy as Beta Pi.

THE IRON STAR

A Byron Preiss project once again. The Planets *had sold very nicely, and now Byron was casting his net a little wider: a book called* The Universe. *As before, astronomers were doing the scientific essays and s-f writers were providing stories to match. Byron showed me the list of themes—stars, pulsars, black holes, galaxies and clusters, and so forth— and I chose to write about supernovae and pulsars. The anthology was published late in 1987 and the story appeared just about simultaneously in the January, 1988 issue of the venerable* Amazing Stories, *oldest of the science-fiction magazines.*

One incidental bit of pleasure came from this for me. In Byron's book, the story was illustrated with a full-color plate by Bob Eggleton. Amazing Stories *featured it with a cover painting by Terry Lee. By coincidence both Lee and Eggleton chose to illustrate the same scene, the one in which the narrator first gets a look at the Nine Sparg captain on his television screen. The two paintings are quite different in mood and technique, yet each depicts my alien critter in a distinctive and powerful way, while remaining faithful to my prose description. It's one of science-fiction writing's special treats to see your verbal inventions brought to visual life this way.*

———

The alien ship came drifting up from behind the far side of the neutron star just as I was going on watch. It looked a little like a miniature neutron star itself: a perfect sphere, metallic, dark. But neutron stars don't have six perky little out-thrust legs and the alien craft did.

While I paused in front of the screen the alien floated diagonally upward, cutting a swathe of darkness across the brilliantly starry sky like a fast-moving black hole. It even occulted the real black hole that lay thirty light-minutes away.

I stared at the strange vessel, fascinated and annoyed, wishing I had never seen it, wishing it would softly and suddenly vanish away. This mission was sufficiently complicated already. We hadn't needed an alien ship to appear on the scene. For five days now we had circled the neutron star in seesaw orbit with the aliens, a hundred eighty degrees apart. They hadn't said anything to us and we didn't know how to say anything to them. I didn't feel good about that. I like things direct, succinct, known.

Lina Sorabji, busy enhancing sonar transparencies over at our improvised archaeology station, looked up from her work and caught me scowling. Lina is a slender, dark woman from Madras whose ancestors were priests and scholars when mine were hunting bison on the Great Plains. She said, "You shouldn't let it get to you like that, Tom."

"You know what it feels like, every time I see it cross the screen? It's like having a little speck wandering around on the visual field of your eye. Irritating, frustrating, maddening—and absolutely impossible to get rid of."

"You want to get rid of it?"

I shrugged. "Isn't this job tough enough? Attempting to scoop a sample from the core of a neutron star? Do we really have to have an alien spaceship looking over our shoulders while we work?"

"Maybe it's not a spaceship at all," Lina said cheerily. "Maybe it's just some kind of giant spacebug."

I suppose she was trying to amuse me. I wasn't amused. This was going to win me a place in the history of space exploration, sure: Chief Executive Officer of the first expedition from Earth ever to encounter intelligent extraterrestrial life. Terrific. But that wasn't what IBM/Toshiba had hired me to do. And I'm more interested in completing assignments than in making history. You don't get paid for making history.

Basically the aliens were a distraction from our real work, just as last month's discovery of a dead civilization on a nearby solar system had been, the one whose photographs Lina Sorabji now was studying. This was supposed to be a business venture involving the experimental use of new technology, not an archaeological mission or an exercise in interspecies diplomacy. And I knew that there was a ship from the Exxon/Hyundai combine loose somewhere in hyperspace right now working on the same task we'd been sent out to handle. If they brought it off first, IBM/Toshiba would suffer a very severe loss of face, which is considered very bad on the corporate level. What's bad for IBM/Toshiba would be exceedingly bad for me. For all of us.

I glowered at the screen. Then the orbit of the *Ben-wah Maru* carried us down and away and the alien disappeared from my line of sight. But not for long, I knew.

As I keyed up the log reports from my sleep period I said to Lina, "You have anything new today?" She had spent the past three weeks analysing the dead-world data. You never know what the parent companies will see as potentially profitable.

"I'm down to hundred-meter penetration now. There's a system of broad tunnels wormholing the entire planet. Some kind of pneumatic transportation network, is my guess. Here, have a look."

A holoprint sprang into vivid life in the air between us. It was a sonar scan that we had taken from ten thousand kilometers out, reaching a short distance below the surface of the dead world. I saw odd-angled tunnels lined with gleaming luminescent tiles that still pulsed with dazzling colors, centuries after the cataclysm that had destroyed all life there. Amazing decorative patterns of bright lines were plainly visible along the tunnel walls, lines that swirled and overlapped and entwined and beckoned my eye into some adjoining dimension.

Trains of sleek snub-nosed vehicles were scattered like caterpillars everywhere in the tunnels. In them and around them lay skeletons, thousands of them, millions, a whole continent full of commuters slaughtered as they waited at the station for the morning express. Lina touched the fine scan and gave me a close look: biped creatures, broad skulls tapering sharply at the sides, long apelike arms, seven-fingered hands with what seemed like an opposable thumb at each end, pelvises enlarged into peculiar bony crests jutting far out from their hips. It wasn't the first time a hyperspace exploring vessel had come across relics of extinct extraterrestrial races, even a fossil or two. But these weren't fossils. These beings had died only a few hundred years ago. And they had all died at the same time.

I shook my head somberly. "Those are some tunnels. They might have been able to convert them into pretty fair radiation shelters, is my guess. If only they'd had a little warning of what was coming."

"They never knew what hit them."

"No," I said. "They never knew a thing. A supernova brewing right next door and they must not have been able to tell what was getting ready to happen."

Lina called up another print, and another, then another. During our brief fly-by last month our sensors had captured an amazing panoramic view of this magnificent lost civilization: wide streets, spacious parks, splendid public buildings, imposing private houses, the works. Bizarre architecture, all unlikely angles and jutting crests like its creators, but unquestionably grand, noble, impressive. There had been keen intelligence at work here, and high artistry. Everything was intact and in a remarkable state of preservation, if you make allowances for the natural inroads that time and weather and I suppose the occasional earthquake will bring over three or four hundred years. Obviously this had been a wealthy, powerful society, stable and confident.

And between one instant and the next it had all been stopped dead in its tracks, wiped out, extinguished, annihilated. Perhaps they had had a fraction of a second to realize that the end of the world had come, but no more than that. I saw what surely were family groups huddling together, skeletons clumped in threes or fours or fives. I saw what I took to be couples with their seven-fingered hands still clasped in a final exchange of love. I saw some kneeling in a weird elbows-down position that might have been one of—who can say? Prayer? Despair? Acceptance?

A sun had exploded and this great world had died. I shuddered, not for the first time, thinking of it.

It hadn't even been their own sun. What had blown up was this one, forty light-years away from them, the one that was now the neutron star about which we orbited and which once had been a main-sequence sun maybe three or four times as big as Earth's. Or else it had been the other one in this binary system, thirty light-minutes from the first, the blazing young giant companion star of which nothing remained except the black hole nearby. At the moment we had no way of knowing which of these two stars had gone supernova first. Whichever one it was, though, had sent a furious burst of radiation heading outward, a lethal flux of cosmic rays capable of destroying most or perhaps all life-forms within a sphere a hundred light-years in diameter.

The planet of the underground tunnels and the noble temples had simply been in the way. One of these two suns had come to the moment when all the fuel in its core had been consumed: hydrogen

322

had been fused into helium, helium into carbon, carbon into neon, oxygen, sulphur, silicon, until at last a core of pure iron lay at its heart. There is no atomic nucleus more strongly bound than iron. The star had reached the point where its release of energy through fusion had to cease; and with the end of energy production the star no longer could withstand the gravitational pressure of its own vast mass. In a moment, in the twinkling of an eye, the core underwent a catastrophic collapse. Its matter was compressed—beyond the point of equilibrium. And rebounded. And sent forth an intense shock wave that went rushing through the star's outer layers at a speed of 15,000 kilometers a second.

Which ripped the fabric of the star apart, generating an explosion releasing more energy than a billion suns.

The shock wave would have continued outward and outward across space, carrying debris from the exploded star with it, and interstellar gas that the debris had swept up. A fierce sleet of radiation would have been riding on that wave, too: cosmic rays, X-rays, radio waves, gamma rays, everything, all up and down the spectrum. If the sun that had gone supernova had had planets close by, they would have been vaporized immediately. Outlying worlds of that system might merely have been fried.

The people of the world of the tunnels, forty light-years distant, must have known nothing of the great explosion for a full generation after it had happened. But, all that while, the light of that shattered star was traveling towards them at a speed of 300,000 kilometers per second, and one night its frightful baleful unexpected glare must have burst suddenly into their sky in the most terrifying way. And almost in that same moment—for the deadly cosmic rays thrown off by the explosion move nearly at the speed of light—the killing blast of hard radiation would have arrived. And so these people and all else that lived on their world perished in terror and light.

All this took place a thousand light-years from Earth: that surging burst of radiation will need another six centuries to complete its journey towards our home world. At that distance, the cosmic rays will do us little or no harm. But for a time that long-dead star will shine in our skies so brilliantly that it will be visible by day, and by night it will cast deep shadows, longer than those of the Moon.

That's still in Earth's future. Here the fatal supernova, and the second one that must have happened not long afterwards, were some four hundred years in the past. What we had here now was a neutron star

323

left over from one cataclysm and a black hole left over from the other. Plus the pathetic remains of a great civilization on a scorched planet orbiting a neighboring star. And now a ship from some alien culture. A busy corner of the galaxy, this one. A busy time for the crew of the IBM/Toshiba hyperspace ship *Ben-wah Maru*.

I was still going over the reports that had piled up at my station during my sleep period—mass-and-output readings on the neutron star, progress bulletins on the setup procedures for the neutronium scoop, and other routine stuff of that nature—when the communicator cone in front of me started to glow. I flipped it on. Cal Bjornsen, our communications guru, was calling from Brain Central downstairs.

Bjornsen is mostly black African with some Viking genes salted in. The whole left side of his face is cyborg, the result of some extreme bit of teenage carelessness. The story is that he was gravity-vaulting and lost polarity at sixty meters. The mix of ebony skin, blue eyes, blond hair, and sculpted titanium is an odd one, but I've seen a lot of faces less friendly than Cal's. He's a good man with anything electronic.

He said, "I think they're finally trying to send us messages, Tom."

I sat up fast. "What's that?"

"We've been pulling in signals of some sort for the past ninety minutes that didn't look random, but we weren't sure about it. A dozen or so different frequencies all up and down the line, mostly in the radio band, but we're also getting what seem to be infra-red pulses, and something flashing in the ultraviolet range. A kind of scattershot noise effect, only it isn't noise."

"Are you sure of that?"

"The computer's still chewing on it," Bjornsen said. The fingers of his right hand glided nervously up and down his smooth metal cheek. "But we can see already that there are clumps of repetitive patterns."

"Coming from them? How do you know?"

"We didn't, at first. But the transmissions conked out when we lost line-of-sight with them, and started up again when they came back into view."

"I'll be right down," I said.

Bjornsen is normally a calm man, but he was running in frantic circles when I reached Brain Central three or four minutes later. There was stuff dancing on all the walls: sine waves, mainly, but plenty of other patterns jumping around on the monitors. He had already pulled in specialists from practically every department—the whole astronomy staff, two of the math guys, a couple from the external maintenance team, and somebody from engines. I felt preempted. Who was CEO on this ship, anyway? They were all babbling at once. "Fourier series," someone said, and someone yelled back, "Dirichlet factor," and someone else said, "Gibbs phenomenon!" I heard Angie Seraphin insisting vehemently, "—continuous except possibly for a finite number of finite discontinuities in the interval—pi to pi—"

"Hold it," I said, "What's going on?"

More babble, more gibberish. I got them quiet again and repeated my question, aiming it this time at Bjornsen.

"We have the analysis now," he said.

"So?"

"You understand that it's only guesswork, but Brain Central gives good guess. The way it looks, they seem to want us to broadcast a carrier wave they can tune in on, and just talk to them while they lock in with some sort of word-to-word translating device of theirs."

"That's what Brain Central thinks they're saying?"

"It's the most plausible semantic content of the patterns they're transmitting," Bjornsen answered.

I felt a chill. The aliens had word-to-word translating devices? That was a lot more than we could claim. Brain Central is one very smart computer, and if it thought that it had correctly deciphered the message coming in, them in all likelihood it had. An astonishing accomplishment, taking a bunch of ones and zeros put together by an alien mind and culling some sense out of them.

But even Brain Central wasn't capable of word-to-word translation out of some unknown language. Nothing in our technology is. The alien message had been *designed* to be easy: put together, most likely, in a careful high-redundancy manner, the computer equivalent of picture-writing. Any race able to undertake interstellar travel ought to have a computer powerful enough to sweat the essential meaning out of a message like that, and we did. We couldn't go farther than that though. Let the entropy of that message—that is, the unexpectedness of it, the unpredictability of its semantic content—rise just a little beyond the picture-writing level, and Brain Central would be lost. A computer that knows French should be able to puzzle out Spanish, and maybe even Greek. But Chinese? A tough proposition. And an *alien* language? Languages may start out logical, but they don't stay that way. And when its underlying grammatical assumptions were put together in the first place by beings with nervous systems that were wired up in ways entirely different from our own, well, the notion of instantaneous decoding becomes hopeless.

Yet our computer said that their computer could do word-to-word. That was scary.

On the other hand, if we couldn't talk to them, we wouldn't begin to find out what they were doing here and what threat, if any, they might pose to us. By revealing our language to them we might be handing them some sort of advantage, but I couldn't be sure of that, and it seemed to me we had to take the risk.

It struck me as a good idea to get some backing for that decision, though. After a dozen years as CEO aboard various corporate ships I knew the protocols. You did what you thought was right, but you didn't go all the way out on the limb by yourself if you could help it.

"Request a call for a meeting of the corporate staff," I told Bjornsen.

It wasn't so much a scientific matter now as a political one. The scientists would probably be gung-ho to go blasting straight ahead with making contact. But I wanted to hear what the Toshiba people would say, and the IBM people, and the military people. So we got everyone together and I laid the situation out and asked for a Consensus Process. And let them go at it, hammer and tongs.

Instant polarization. The Toshiba people were scared silly of the aliens. We must be cautious, Nakamura said. Caution, yes, said her cohort Nagy-Szabo. There may be danger to Earth. We have no knowledge of the aims and motivations of these beings. Avoid all contact with them, Nagy-Szabo said. Nakamura went even further. We should withdraw from the area immediately, she said, and return to Earth for additional instructions. That drew hot opposition from Jorgensen and Kalliotis, the IBM people. We had work to do here, they said. We should do it. They grudgingly conceded the need to be wary, but strongly urged continuation of the mission and advocated a circumspect opening of contact with the other ship. I think they were already starting to think about alien marketing demographics. Maybe I do them an injustice. Maybe.

The military people were about evenly divided between the two factions. A couple of them, the hair-splitting career-minded ones, wanted to play it absolutely safe and clear out of here fast, and the others, the up-and-away hero types, spoke out in favor of forging ahead with contact and to hell with the risks.

I could see there wasn't going to be any consensus. It was going to come down to me to decide.

By nature I am cautious. I might have voted with Nakamura in favor of immediate withdrawal; however that would have made my ancient cold-eyed Sioux forebears howl. Yet in the end what swayed me was an argument that came from Bryce-Williamson, one of the fiercest of the military sorts. He said that we didn't dare turn tail and run for home without making contact, because the aliens would take that either as a hostile act or a stupid one, and either way they might just slap some kind of tracer on us that ultimately would enable them to discover the location of our home world. True caution, he said, required us to try to find out what these people were all about before we made any move to leave the scene. We couldn't just run and we couldn't simply ignore them.

I sat quietly for a long time, weighing everything.

"Well?" Bjornsen asked. "What do you want to do, Tom?"

"Send them a broadcast," I said. "Give them greetings in the name of Earth and all its peoples. Extend to them the benevolent warm wishes of the board of directors of IBM/Toshiba. And then we'll wait and see."

We waited. But for a long while we didn't see.

Two days, and then some. We went round and round the neutron star, and they went round and round the neutron star, and no further communication came from them. We beamed them all sorts of messages at all sorts of frequencies along the spectrum, both in the radio band and via infra-red and ultraviolet as well, so that they'd have plenty of material to work with. Perhaps their translator gadget wasn't all that good, I told myself hopefully. Perhaps it was stripping its gears trying to fathom the pleasant little packets of semantic data that we had sent them.

On the third day of silence I began feeling restless. There was no way we could begin the work we had been sent here to do, not with aliens watching. The Toshiba people—the Ultra Cautious faction—got more and more nervous. Even the IBM representatives began to act a little twitchy. I started to question the wisdom of having overruled the advocates of a no-contact policy. Although the parent companies hadn't seriously expected us to run into aliens, they had covered that eventuality in our instructions, and we were under orders to do minimum tipping of our hands if we found ourselves observed by strangers. But it was too late to call back our messages and I was still eager to find out what would happen next. So we watched and waited, and then we waited and watched. Round and round the neutron star.

We had been parked in orbit for ten days now around the neutron star, an orbit calculated to bring us no closer to its surface than 9000 kilometers at the closest skim. That was close enough for us to carry out our work, but not so close that we would be subjected to troublesome and dangerous tidal effects.

The neutron star had been formed in the supernova explosion that had destroyed the smaller of the two suns in what had once been a binary star system here. At the moment of the cataclysmic collapse of the stellar sphere, all its matter had come rushing inward with such force that electrons and protons were driven into each other to become a soup of pure neutrons. Which then were squeezed so tightly that they were forced virtually into contact with one another, creating a smooth globe of the strange stuff that we call neutronium, a billion billion times denser than steel and a hundred billion billion times more incompressible.

That tiny ball of neutronium glowing dimly in our screens was the neutron star. It was just eighteen kilometers in diameter but its mass was greater than that of Earth's sun. That gave it a gravitational field a quarter of a billion billion times as strong as that of the surface of Earth. If we could somehow set foot on it, we wouldn't just be squashed flat, we'd be instantly reduced to fine powder by the colossal tidal effects— the difference in gravitational pull between the soles of our feet and the tops of our heads, stretching us towards and away from the neutron star's center with a kick of eighteen billion kilograms.

A ghostly halo of electromagnetic energy surrounded the neutron star: X-rays, radio waves, gammas, and an oily, crackling flicker of violet light. The neutron star was rotating on its axis some 550 times a second, and powerful jets of electrons were spouting from its magnetic poles at each sweep, sending forth a beacon-like pulsar broadcast of the familiar type that we have been able to detect since the middle of the twentieth century.

Behind that zone of fiercely outflung radiation lay the neutron star's atmosphere: an envelope of gaseous iron a few centimeters thick. Below that, our scan had told us, was a two-kilometers-thick crust of normal matter, heavy elements only, ranging from molybdenum on up to transuranics with atomic numbers as high as 140. And within that was the neutronium zone, the stripped nuclei of iron packed unimaginably close together, an ocean of strangeness nine kilometers deep. What lay at the heart of *that,* we could only guess.

We had come here to plunge a probe into the neutronium zone and carry off a spoonful of star-stuff that weighed 100 billion tons per cubic centimeter.

No sort of conventional landing on the neutron star was possible or even conceivable. Not only was the gravitational pull beyond our comprehension—anything that was capable of withstanding the tidal effects would still have to cope with an escape velocity requirement of 200,000 kilometers per second when it tried to take off, two thirds the speed of light—but the neutron star's surface temperature was something like 3.5 million degrees. The surface temperature of our own sun is six thousand degrees and we don't try to make landings there. Even at this distance, our heat and radiation shields were straining to the limits to keep us from being cooked. We didn't intend to go any closer.

What IBM/Toshiba wanted us to do was to put a miniature hyperspace ship into orbit around the neutron star: an astonishing little vessel no bigger than your clenched fist, powered by a fantastically scaled-down version of the drive that had carried us through the spacetime manifold across a span of a thousand light-years in a dozen weeks. The little ship was a slave-drone; we would operate it from the *Ben-wah Maru.* Or, rather, Brain Central would. In a maneuver that had taken fifty computer-years to program, we would send the miniature into hyperspace and bring it out again *right inside the neutron star.* And keep it there a billionth of a second, long enough for it to gulp the spoonful of neutronium we had been sent here to collect. Then we'd head for home, with the miniature ship following us along the same hyperpath.

We'd head for home, that is, unless the slave-drone's brief intrusion into the neutron star released disruptive forces that splattered us all over this end of the galaxy. IBM/Toshiba didn't really think that was going to happen. In theory a neutron star is one of the most stable things there is in the universe, and the math didn't indicate that taking a nip from its interior would cause real problems. This neighborhood had already had its full quota of giant explosions, anyway.

Still, the possibility existed. Especially since there was a black hole just thirty light-minutes away, a souvenir of the second and much larger supernova bang that had happened here in the recent past. Having a black hole nearby is a little like playing with an extra wild card whose existence isn't made known to the players until some randomly chosen moment midway through the game. If we destabilized the neutron star in some way not anticipated by the scientists back on Earth, we might just find ourselves going for a visit to the event horizon instead of getting to go home. Or we might not. There was only one way of finding out.

I didn't know, by the way, what use the parent companies planned to make of the neutronium we had been hired to bring them. I hoped it was a good one.

But obviously we weren't going to tackle any of this while there was an alien ship in the vicinity. So all we could do was wait. And see. Right now we were doing a lot of waiting, and no seeing at all.

Two days later Cal Bjornsen said, "We're getting a message back from them now. Audio only. In English."

We had wanted that, we had even hoped for that. And yet it shook me to learn that it was happening.

"Let's hear it," I said.

"The relay's coming over ship channel seven."

I tuned in. What I heard was an obviously synthetic voice, no undertones or overtones, not much inflection. They were trying to mimic the speech rhythms of what we had sent them, and I suppose they were actually doing a fair job of it, but the result was still unmistakably mechanical-sounding. Of course there might be nothing on board that ship but a computer, I thought, or maybe robots. I wish now that they had been robots.

It had the absolute and utter familiarity of a recurring dream. In stiff, halting, but weirdly comprehensible English came the first greetings of an alien race to the people of the planet of Earth. "This who speak be First of Nine Sparg," the voice said. Nine Sparg, we soon realized from context, was the name of their planet. First might have been the speaker's name, or his—hers, its?—title; that was unclear, and stayed that way. In an awkward pidgin-English that we nevertheless had little trouble understanding, First expressed gratitude for our transmission and asked us to send more words. To send a dictionary, in fact: now that they had the algorithm for our speech they needed more content to jam in behind it, so that we could go on to exchange more complex statements than Hello and How are you.

Bjornsen queried me on the override. "We've got an English program that we could start feeding them," he said. "Thirty thousand words: that should give them plenty. You want me to put it on for them?"

"Not so fast," I said. "We need to edit it first."

"For what?"

"Anything that might help them find the location of Earth. That's in our orders, under Eventuality of Contact with Extraterrestrials. Remember, I have Nakamura and Nagy-Szabo breathing down my neck, telling me that there's a ship full of boogiemen out there and we mustn't have anything to do with them. I don't believe that myself. But right now we don't know how friendly these Spargs are and we aren't supposed to bring strangers home with us."

"But how could a dictionary entry—"

"Suppose the sun—*our* sun—is defined as a yellow G2 type star," I said. "That gives them a pretty good beginning. Or something about the constellations as seen from Earth. I don't know, Cal. I just want to make sure we don't accidentally hand these beings a road-map to our home planet before we find out what sort of critters they are."

Three of us spent half a day screening the dictionary, and we put Brain Central to work on it too. In the end we pulled seven words— you'd laugh if you knew which they were, but we wanted to be careful—and sent the rest across to the Spargs. They were silent for nine or ten hours. When they came back on the air their command of English was immensely more fluent. Frighteningly more fluent. Yesterday First had sounded like a tourist using a Fifty Handy Phrases program. A day later, First's command of English was as good as that of an intelligent Japanese who has been living in the United States for ten or fifteen years.

It was a tense, wary conversation. Or so it seemed to me, the way it began to seem that First was male and that his way of speaking was brusque and bluntly probing. I may have been wrong on every count.

First wanted to know who we were and why we were here. Jumping right in, getting down to the heart of the matter. I felt a little like a butterfly collector who has wandered onto the grounds of a fusion plant and is being interrogated by a security guard. But I kept my tone and phrasing as neutral as I could, and told him that our planet was called Earth and that we had come on a mission of exploration and investigation.

So had they, he told me. Where is Earth?

Pretty straightforward of him, I thought. I answered that I lacked at this point a means of explaining galactic positions to him in terms that he would understand. I did volunteer the information that Earth was not anywhere close at hand.

He was willing to drop that line of inquiry for the time being. He shifted to the other obvious one:

What were we investigating?

Certain properties of collapsed stars, I said, after a bit of hesitation.

And which properties were those?

I told him that we didn't have enough vocabulary in common for me to try to explain that either.

The Nine Sparg captain seemed to accept that evasion too. And provided me with a pause that indicated that it was my turn. Fair enough.

When I asked him what *he* was doing here, he replied without any apparent trace of evasiveness that he had come on a mission of historical inquiry. I pressed for details. It has to do with the ancestry of our race, he said. We used to live in this part of the galaxy, before the great explosion. No hesitation at all about telling me that. It struck me that First was being less reticent about dealing with my queries than I was with his; but of course I had no way of judging whether I was hearing the truth from him.

"I'd like to know more," I said, as much as a test as anything else. "How long ago did your people flee this great explosion? And how far from here is your present home world?"

A long silence: several minutes. I wondered uncomfortably if I had overplayed my hand. If they were as edgy about our finding their home world as I was about their finding ours, I had to be careful not to push them into an overreaction. They might just think that the safest thing to do would be to blow us out of the sky as soon as they had learned all they could from us.

But when First spoke again it was only to say, "Are you willing to establish contact in the visual band?"

"Is such a thing possible?"

"We think so," he said.

I thought about it. Would letting them see what we looked like give them any sort of clue to the location of Earth? Perhaps, but it seemed far-fetched. Maybe they'd be able to guess that we were carbon-based oxygen-breathers, but the risk of allowing them to know that seemed relatively small. And in any case we'd find out what *they* looked like. An even trade, right?

I had my doubts that their video transmission system could be made compatible with our receiving equipment. But I gave First the go-ahead and turned the microphone over to the communications staff. Who struggled with the problem for a day and a half. Sending the signal back and forth was no big deal, but breaking it down into information that would paint a picture on a cathode-ray tube was a different matter. The communications people at both ends talked and talked and talked, while I fretted about how much technical information about us we were revealing to the Spargs. The tinkering went on and on and nothing appeared on screen except occasional strings of horizontal lines. We sent them more data about how our television system worked. They made further adjustments in their transmission devices. This time we got spots instead of lines. We sent even more data. Were they leading us on? And were we telling them too much? I came finally to the position that trying to make the video link work had been a bad idea, and started to tell Communications that. But then the haze of drifting spots on my screen abruptly cleared and I found myself looking into the face of an alien being.

An alien face, yes. Extremely alien. Suddenly this whole interchange was kicked up to a new level of reality.

A hairless wedge-shaped head, flat and broad on top, tapering to a sharp point below. Corrugated skin that looked as thick as heavy rubber. Two chilly eyes in the center of that wide forehead and two more at its extreme edges. Three mouths, vertical slits, side by side: one for speaking and the other two, maybe for separate intake of fluids and solids. The whole business supported by three long columnar necks as thick as a man's wrist, separated by open spaces two or three centimeters wide. What was below the neck we never got to see. But the head alone was plenty.

They probably thought we were just as strange.

With video established, First and I picked up our conversation right where we had broken it off the day before. Once more he was not in the least shy about telling me things.

He had been able to calculate in our units of time the date of the great explosion that had driven his people far from home world: it had taken place 387 years ago. He didn't use the word "supernova," because it hadn't been included in the 30,000-word vocabulary we had sent them, but that was obviously what he meant by "the great explosion." The 387-year figure squared pretty well with our own calculations, which were based on an analysis of the surface temperature and rate of rotation of the neutron star.

The Nine Sparg people had had plenty of warning that their sun was behaving oddly—the first signs of instability had become apparent more than a century before the blow-up—and they had devoted all their energy for several generations to the job of packing up and clearing out. It had taken many years, it seemed, for them to accomplish their migration to the distant new world they had chosen for their new home. Did that mean, I asked myself, that their method of interstellar travel was much slower than ours, and that they had needed decades or even a century to cover fifty or a hundred light-years? Earth had less to worry about, then. Even if they wanted to make trouble for us, they wouldn't be able easily to reach us, a thousand light-years from here. Or was First saying that their new world was really distant—all the way across the galaxy, perhaps, seventy or eighty thousand light-years away, or even in some other galaxy altogether? If that was the case, we were up against truly superior beings. But there was no easy way for me to question him about such things without telling him things about our own hyperdrive and our distance from this system that I didn't care to have him know.

After a long and evidently difficult period of settling in on the new world, First went on, the Nine Sparg folk finally were well enough established to launch an inquiry into the condition of their former home planet. Thus his mission to the supernova site.

"But we are in great mystery," First admitted, and it seemed to me that a note of sadness and bewilderment had crept into his mechanical-sounding voice. "We have come to what certainly is the right location. Yet nothing seems to be correct here. We find only this little iron star. And of our former planet there is no trace."

I stared at that peculiar and unfathomable four-eyed face, that three-columned neck, those tight vertical mouths, and to my surprise something close to compassion awoke in me. I had been dealing with this creature as though he were a potential enemy capable of leading armadas of war to my world and conquering it. But in fact he might be merely a scholarly explorer who was making a nostalgic pilgrimage, and running into problems with it. I decided to relax my guard just a little.

"Have you considered," I said, "that you might not be in the right location after all?"

"What do you mean?"

"As we were completing our journey towards what you call the iron star," I said, "we discovered a planet forty light-years from here that beyond much doubt had had a great civilization, and which evidently was close enough to the exploding star system here to have been devastated by it. We have pictures of it that we could show you. Perhaps *that* was your home world."

Even as I was saying it the idea started to seem foolish to me. The skeletons we had photographed on the dead world had had broad tapering heads that might perhaps have been similar to those of First, but they hadn't shown any evidence of this unique triple-neck arrangement. Besides, First had said that his people had had several generations to prepare for evacuation. Would they have left so many millions of their people behind to die? It looked obvious from the way those skeletons were scattered around that the inhabitants of that planet hadn't had the slightest clue that doom was due to overtake them that day. And finally, I realized that First had plainly said that it was his own world's sun that had exploded, not some neighboring star. The supernova had happened here. The dead world's sun was still intact.

"Can you show me your pictures?" he said.

It seemed pointless. But I felt odd about retracting my offer. And in the new rapport that had sprung up between us I could see no harm in it.

I told Lina Sorabji to feed her sonar transparencies into the relay pickup. It was easy enough for Cal Bjornsen to shunt them into our video transmission to the alien ship.

The Nine Sparg captain withheld his comment until we had shown him the batch.

Then he said, "Oh, that was not our world. That was the world of the Garvalekkinon people."

"The Garvalekkinon?"

"We knew them. A neighboring race, not related to us. Sometimes, on rare occasions, we traded with them. Yes, they must all have died when the star exploded. It is too bad."

"They look as though they had no warning," I said. "Look: can you see them there, waiting in the train stations?"

The triple mouths fluttered in what might have been the Nine Sparg equivalent of a nod.

"I suppose they did not know the explosion was coming."

"You suppose? You mean you didn't tell them?"

All four eyes blinked at once. Expression of puzzlement.

"Tell them? Why should we have told them? We were busy with our preparations. We had no time for them. Of course the radiation would have been harmful to them, but why was that our concern? They were not related to us. They were nothing to us."

I had trouble believing I had heard him correctly. A neighboring people. Occasional trading partners. Your sun is about to blow up, and it's reasonable to assume that nearby solar systems will be affected. You have fifty or a hundred years of advance notice yourselves, and you can't even take the trouble to let these other people know what's going to happen?

I said, "You felt no need at all to warn them? That isn't easy for me to understand."

Again the four-eyed shrug.

"I have explained it to you already," said First. "They were not of our kind. They were nothing to us."

I excused myself on some flimsy excuse and broke contact. And sat and thought a long long while. Listening to the words of the Nine Sparg captain echoing in my mind. And thinking of the millions of skeletons scattered like straws in the tunnels of that dead world that the supernova had baked. A whole people left to die because it was inconvenient to take five minutes to send them a message. Or perhaps because it simply never had occurred to anybody to bother.

The families, huddling together. The children reaching out. The husbands and wives with hands interlocked.

A world of busy, happy, intelligent, people. Boulevards and temples. Parks and gardens. Paintings, sculpture, poetry, music. History, philosophy, science. And a sudden star in the sky, and everything gone in a moment.

Why should we have told them? They were nothing to us.

I knew something of the history of my own people. We had experienced casual extermination too. But at least when the white settlers had done it to us it was because they had wanted our land.

For the first time I understood the meaning of alien.

I turned on the external screen and stared out at the unfamiliar sky of this place. The neutron star was barely visible, a dull red dot, far down in the lower left quadrant; and the black hole was high.

Once they had both been stars. What havoc must have attended their destruction! It must have been the Sparg sun that blew first, the one that had become the neutron star. And then, fifty or a hundred years later, perhaps, the other, larger star had gone the same route. Another titanic supernova, a great flare of killing light. But of course everything for hundreds of light-years around had perished already in the first blast.

The second sun had been too big to leave a neutron star behind. So great was its mass that the process of collapse had continued on beyond the neutron-star stage, matter crushing in upon itself until it broke through the normal barriers of space and took on a bizarre and almost unthinkable form, creating an object of infinitely small volume that was nevertheless of infinite density: a black hole, a pocket of incomprehensibility where once a star had been.

I stared now at the black hole before me.

I couldn't see it, of course. So powerful was the surface gravity of that grotesque thing that nothing could escape from it, not even electromagnetic radiation, not the merest particle of light. The ultimate in invisibility cloaked that infinitely deep hole in space.

But though the black hole itself was invisible, the effects that its presence caused were not. That terrible gravitational pull would rip apart and swallow any solid object that came too close; and so the hole was surrounded by a bright ring of dust and gas several hundred kilometers across. These shimmering particles constantly tumbled towards that insatiable mouth, colliding as they spiraled in, releasing flaring fountains of radiation, red-shifted into the visual spectrum by the enormous gravity: the bright green of helium, the majestic purple of hydrogen, the crimson of oxygen. That outpouring of energy was the death-cry of doomed matter. That rainbow whirlpool of blazing light was the beacon marking the maw of the black hole.

I found it oddly comforting to stare at that thing. To contemplate that zone of eternal quietude from which there was no escape. Pondering so inexorable and unanswerable an infinity was more soothing than thinking of a world of busy people destroyed by the indifference of their neighbors. Black holes offer no choices, no complexities, no shades of disagreement. They are absolute.

Why should we have told them? They were nothing to us.

After a time I restored contact with the Nine Sparg ship. First came to the screen at once, ready to continue our conversation.

"There is no question that our world once was located here," he said at once. "We have checked and rechecked the coordinates. But the changes have been extraordinary."

"Have they?"

"Once there were two stars here, our own and the brilliant blue one that was nearby. Our history is very specific on that point: a brilliant blue star that lit the entire sky. Now we have only the iron star. Apparently it has taken the place of our sun. But where has the blue one gone? Could the explosion have destroyed it too?"

I frowned. Did they really not know? Could a race be capable of attaining an interstellar spacedrive and an interspecies translating device, and nevertheless not have arrived at any understanding of the neutron star/black hole cosmogony?

Why not? They were aliens. They had come by all their understanding of the universe via a route different from ours. They might well have overlooked this feature or that of the universe about them.

"The blue star—" I began.

But First spoke right over me, saying, "It is a mystery that we must devote all our energies to solving, or our mission will be fruitless. But let us talk of other things. You have said little of your own mission. And of your home world. I am filled with great curiosity, Captain, about those subjects."

I'm sure you are, I thought.

"We have only begun our return to space travel," said First. "Thus far we have encountered no other intelligent races. And so we regard this meeting as fortunate. It is our wish to initiate contact with you. Quite likely some aspects of your technology would be valuable to us. And there will be much that you wish to purchase from us. Therefore we would be glad to establish trade relations with you."

As you did with the Garvalekkinon people, I said to myself.

I said, "We can speak of that tomorrow, Captain. I grow tired now. But before we break contact for the day, allow me to offer you the beginning of a solution to the mystery of the disappearance of the blue sun."

The four eyes widened. The slitted mouths parted in what seemed surely to be excitement.

"Can you do that?"

I took a deep breath.

"We have some preliminary knowledge. Do you see the place opposite the iron star, where energies boil and circle in the sky? As we entered this system, we found certain evidence there that may explain the fate of your former blue sun. You would do well to center your investigations on that spot."

"We are most grateful," said First.

"And now, Captain, I must bid you good night. Until tomorrow, Captain."

"Until tomorrow," said the alien.

I was awakened in the middle of my sleep period by Lina Sorabji and Bryce-Williamson, both of them looking flushed and sweaty. I sat up, blinking and shaking my head.

"It's the alien ship," Bryce-Williamson blurted, "It's approaching the black hole."

"Is it, now?"

"Dangerously close," said Lina. "What do they think they're doing? Don't they know?"

"I don't think so," I said. "I suggested that they go exploring there. Evidently they don't regard it as a bad idea."

"You sent them there?" she said incredulously.

With a shrug I said, "I told them that if they went over there they might find the answer to the question of where one of their missing suns went. I guess they've decided to see if I was right."

"We have to warn them," said Bryce-Williamson. "Before it's too late. Especially if we're responsible for sending them there. They'll be furious with us once they realize that we failed to warn them of the danger."

"By the time they realize it," I replied calmly, "it *will* be too late. And then their fury won't matter, will it? They won't be able to tell us how annoyed they are with us. Or to report to their home world, for that matter, that they had an encounter with intelligent aliens who might be worth exploiting."

He gave me an odd look. The truth was starting to sink in.

I turned on the external screens and punched up a close look at the black hole region. Yes, there was the alien ship, the little metallic sphere, the six odd outthrust legs. It was in the zone of criticality now. It seemed hardly to be moving at all. And it was growing dimmer and dimmer as it slowed. The gravitational field had it, and it was being drawn in. Blacking out, becoming motionless. Soon it would have gone beyond the point where outside observers could perceive it. Already it was beyond the point of turning back.

I heard Lina sobbing behind me. Bryce-Williamson was muttering to himself: praying, perhaps.

I said, "Who can say what they would have done to us—in their casual, indifferent way—once they came to Earth? We know now that Spargs worry only about Spargs. Anybody else is just so much furniture." I shook my head. "To hell with them. They're gone, and in a universe this big we'll probably never come across any of them again, or they us. Which is just fine. We'll be a lot better off having nothing at all to do with them."

"But to die that way—" Lina murmured. "To sail blindly into a black hole—"

"It is a great tragedy," said Bryce-Williamson.

"A tragedy for them," I said. "For us, a reprieve, I think. And tomorrow we can get moving on the neutronium-scoop project." I tuned up the screen to the next level. The boiling cloud of matter around the mouth of the black hole blazed fiercely. But of the alien ship there was nothing to be seen.

Yes, a great tragedy, I thought. The valiant exploratory mission that had sought the remains of the Nine Sparg home world has been lost with all hands. No hope of rescue. A pity that they hadn't known how unpleasant black holes can be.

But why should we have told them? They were nothing to us.

THE SECRET SHARER

I make no secret of my admiration for the work of Joseph Conrad. (Or for Conrad himself, the tough, stubborn little man who, although English was only his third language, after Polish and French, not only was able to pass the difficult oral qualifying exam to become a captain in the British merchant marine, but then, a decade or so later, to transform himself into one of the greatest figures in twentieth-century English literature.) Most of what I owe to Conrad as a writer is buried deep in the substructure of my stories—a way of looking at narrative, a way of understanding character. But occasionally I've made the homage more visible. My novel Downward to the Earth of 1969 is a kind of free transposition of his novella "Heart of Darkness" to science fiction, a borrowing that I signaled overtly by labeling my most tormented character with the name of Kurtz. "Heart of Darkness," when I first encountered it as a reader almost fifty years ago, had been packaged as half of a two-novella paperback collection, the other story being Conrad's "The Secret Sharer." And some time late in 1986, I felt the urge, I know not why—a love of symmetry? A compulsion toward completion?—to finish what I had begun in Downward to the Earth by writing a story adapted from the other great novella of that paperback of long ago.

This time I was less subtle than before, announcing my intentions not by using one of Conrad's character names but by appropriating his story's actual title. (This produced a pleasantly absurd result when my story was published in Isaac Asimov's Science Fiction Magazine and a reader wrote to the editor, somewhat indignantly, to ask whether I knew that the *title had already been used by Joseph Conrad!) I swiped not only the title but Conrad's basic story situation, that of the ship captain who finds a stowaway on board and eventually is drawn into a strange alliance with him. (Her, in my story.) But otherwise I translated the Conrad into purely science-fictional terms and produced something that I think represents completely original work, however much it may owe to the structure of a classic earlier story.*

"Translate" is perhaps not the appropriate term for what I did. A "translation," in the uncompromising critical vocabulary set forth by Damon Knight and James Blish in the 1950s upon which I based much of my own fiction-writing esthetic, is defined as an adaptation of a stock format of mundane fiction into s-f by the simple one-for-one substitution of science-fictiony noises for the artifacts of the mundane genre. That is, change "Colt .44" to "laser pistol" and "horse" to "greeznak" and "Comanche" to "Sloogl" and you can easily generate a sort of science fiction out of a standard western story, complete with cattle rustlers, scalpings, and cavalry rescues. But you don't get real science fiction; you don't get anything new and intellectually stimulating, just a western story that has greeznaks and Sloogls in it. Change "Los Angeles Police Department" to "Drylands Patrol" and "crack dealer" to "canal-dust dealer" and you've got a crime story set on Mars, but so what? Change "the canals of Venice" to "the marshy streets of Venusburg" and the sinister agents of S.M.E.R.S.H. to the sinister agents of A.A.A.A.R.G.H. and you've got a James Bond story set on the second planet, but it's still a James Bond story.

I don't think that that's what I've done here. The particular way in which Vox stows away aboard the Sword of Orion is nothing that Joseph Conrad could have understood, and arises, I think, purely out of the science-fictional inventions at the heart of the story. The way she leaves the ship is very different from anything depicted in Conrad's maritime fiction. The starwalk scene provides visionary possibilities quite unlike those afforded by a long stare into the vastness of the trackless Pacific. And so on. "The Secret Sharer" by Robert Silverberg is, or so I believe, a new and unique science-fiction story set, for reasons of the author's private amusement, within the framework of a well-known century-old masterpiece of the sea by Joseph Conrad.

"The Secret Sharer"—mine, not Conrad's—appeared in the September, 1988 issue of Asimov's and was a Nebula and Hugo nominee in 1988 as best novella of the year, but didn't get the trophies. It did win the third of the major s-f honors, the Locus award. Usually most of the Locus winners go

on to get Hugos as well, but that year it didn't happen. I regretted that. But Joseph Conrad's original version of the story didn't win a Hugo or a Nebula either, and people still read it admiringly to this day. You take your lumps in this business, and you go bravely onward: it's the only way. Conrad would have understood that philosophy.

1.

It was my first time to heaven and I was no one at all, no one at all, and this was the voyage that was supposed to make me someone.

But though I was no one at all I dared to look upon the million worlds and I felt a great sorrow for them. There they were all about me, humming along on their courses through the night, each of them believing it was actually going somewhere. And each one wrong, of course, for worlds go nowhere, except around and around and around, pathetic monkeys on a string, forever tethered in place. They seem to move, yes. But really they stand still. And I—I who stared at the worlds of heaven and was swept with compassion for them—I knew that though I seemed to be standing still, I was in fact moving. For I was aboard a ship of heaven, a ship of the Service, that was spanning the light-years at a speed so incomprehensibly great that it might as well have been no speed at all.

I was very young. My ship, then as now, was the *Sword of Orion*, on a journey out of Kansas Four bound for Cul-de-Sac and Strappado and Mangan's Bitch and several other worlds, via the usual spinarounds. It was my first voyage and I was in command. I thought for a long time that I would lose my soul on that voyage; but now I know that what was happening aboard that ship was not the losing of a soul but the gaining of one. And perhaps of more than one.

2.

Roacher thought I was sweet. I could have killed him for that; but of course he was dead already.

You have to give up your life when you go to heaven. What you get in return is for me to know and you, if you care, to find out; but the inescapable thing is that you leave behind anything that ever linked you to life on shore, and you become something else. We say that you give up the body and you get your soul. Certainly you can keep your body too, if you want it. Most do. But it isn't any good to you any more, not in the ways that you think a body is good to you. I mean to tell you how it was for me on my first voyage aboard the *Sword of Orion*, so many years ago.

I was the youngest officer on board, so naturally I was captain.

They put you in command right at the start, before you're anyone. That's the only test that means a damn: they throw you in the sea and if you can swim you don't drown, and if you can't you do. The drowned ones go back in the tank and they serve their own useful purposes, as push-cells or downloaders or mind-wipers or Johnny-scrub-and-scour or whatever. The ones that don't drown go on to other commands. No one is wasted. The Age of Waste has been over a long time.

On the third virtual day out from Kansas Four, Roacher told me that I was the sweetest captain he had ever served under. And he had served under plenty of them, for Roacher had gone up to heaven at least two hundred years before, maybe more.

"I can see it in your eyes, the sweetness. I can see it in the angle you hold your head."

He didn't mean it as a compliment.

"We can put you off ship at Ultima Thule," Roacher said. "Nobody will hold it against you. We'll put you in a bottle and send you down, and the Thuleys will catch you and decant you and you'll be able to find your way back to Kansas Four in twenty or fifty years. It might be the best thing."

Roacher is small and parched, with brown skin and eyes that shine with the purple luminescence of space. Some of the worlds he has seen were forgotten a thousand years ago.

"Go bottle yourself, Roacher," I told him.

"Ah, Captain, Captain! Don't take it the wrong way. Here, Captain, give us a touch of the sweetness." He reached out a claw, trying to stroke me along the side of my face. "Give us a touch, Captain, give us just a little touch!"

"I'll fry your soul and have it for breakfast, Roacher. There's sweetness for you. Go scuttle off, will you? Go jack yourself to the mast and drink hydrogen, Roacher. Go. Go."

"So sweet," he said. But he went. I had the power to hurt him. He knew I could do it, because I was captain. He also knew I wouldn't; but there was always the possibility he was wrong. The captain exists in that margin between certainty and possibility. A crewman tests the width of that margin at his own risk. Roacher knew that. He had been a captain once himself, after all.

There were seventeen of us to heaven that voyage, staffing a ten-kilo Megaspore-class ship with full annexes and extensions and all virtualities. We carried a bulging cargo of the things regarded in those days as vital in the distant colonies: pre-read vapor chips, artificial intelligences, climate nodes, matrix jacks, mediq machines, bone banks, soil converters, transit spheres, communication bubbles, skin-and-organ synthesizers, wildlife domestication plaques, gene replacement kits, a sealed consignment of obliteration sand and other proscribed weapons, and so on. We also had fifty billion dollars in the form of liquid currency pods, central-bank-to-central-bank transmission. In addition there was a passenger load of seven thousand colonists. Eight hundred of these were on the hoof and the others were stored in matrix form for body transplant on the worlds of destination. A standard load, in other words. The crew worked on commission, also as per standard, one percent of bill-of-lading value divided in customary lays. Mine was the 50th lay—that is, two percent of the net profits of the voyage—and that included a bonus for serving as captain; otherwise I would have had the 100th lay or something even longer. Roacher had the 10th lay and his jackmate Bulgar the 14th, although they weren't even officers. Which demonstrates the value of seniority in the Service. But seniority is the same thing as survival, after all, and why should survival not be rewarded? On my most recent voyage I drew the 19th lay. I will have better than that on my next.

3.

You have never seen a starship. We keep only to heaven; when we are to worldward, shoreships come out to us for the downloading. The closest we ever go to planetskin is a million shiplengths. Any closer and we'd be shaken apart by that terrible strength which emanates from worlds.

We don't miss landcrawling, though. It's a plague to us. If I had to step to shore now, after having spent most of my lifetime in heaven, I would die of the drop-death within an hour. That is a monstrous way to die; but why would I ever go ashore? The likelihood of that still existed for me at the time I first sailed the *Sword of Orion*, you understand, but I have long since given it up. That is what I mean when I say that you give up your life when you go to heaven. But of course what also goes from you is any feeling that to be ashore has anything to do with being alive. If you could ride a starship, or even see one as we see them, you would understand. I don't blame you for being what you are.

Let me show you the *Sword of Orion*. Though you will never see it as we see it.

What would you see, if you left the ship as we sometimes do to do the starwalk in the Great Open?

The first thing you would see was the light of the ship. A starship gives off a tremendous insistent glow of light that splits heaven like the blast of a trumpet. That great light both precedes and follows. Ahead of the ship rides a luminescent cone of brightness bellowing in the void. In its wake the ship leaves a photonic track so intense that it could be gathered up and weighed. It is the stardrive that issues this light: a ship eats space, and light is its offthrow.

Within the light you would see a needle ten kilometers long.

That is the ship. One end tapers to a sharp point and the other has the Eye, and it is several days' journey by foot from end to end through all the compartments that lie between. It is a world self-contained. The needle is a flattened one. You could walk about easily on the outer surface of the ship, the skin of the top deck, what we call Skin Deck. Or just as easily on Belly Deck, the one on the bottom side. We call one the top deck and the other the bottom, but when you are outside the ship these distinctions have no meaning. Between Skin and Belly lie Crew Deck, Passenger Deck, Cargo Deck, Drive Deck. Ordinarily no one goes from one deck to another. We stay where we belong. The engines are in the Eye. So are the captain's quarters.

That needle is the ship, but it is not the whole ship. What you will not be able to see are the annexes and extensions and virtualities. These accompany the ship, enfolding it in a webwork of intricate outstructures. But they are of a subordinate level of reality and therefore they defy vision. A ship tunnels into the void, spreading far and wide to find room for all that it must carry. In these outlying zones are kept our supplies and provisions, our stores of fuel, and all cargo traveling at second-class rates. If the ship transports prisoners, they will ride in an annex. If the ship expects to encounter severe probability turbulence during the course of the voyage, it will arm itself with stabilizers, and those will be carried in the virtualities, ready to be brought into being if needed. These are the mysteries of our profession. Take them on faith, or ignore them, as you will: they are not meant for you to know.

A ship takes forty years to build. There are two hundred seventy-one of them in service now. New ones are constantly under construction. They are the only link binding the Mother Worlds and the eight hundred ninety-eight Colonies and the colonies of the Colonies. Four ships have been lost since the beginning of the Service. No one knows why. The loss of a starship is the worst disaster I can imagine. The last such event occurred sixty virtual years ago.

A starship never returns to the world from which it was launched. The galaxy is too large for that. It makes its voyage and it continues onward through heaven in an endless open circuit. That is the service of the Service. There would be no point in returning, since thousands of worldward years sweep by behind us as we make our voyages. We live outside of time. We must, for there is no other way. That is our burden and our privilege. That is the service of the Service.

4.

On the fifth virtual day of the voyage I suddenly felt a tic, a nibble, a subtle indication that something had gone wrong. It was a very trifling thing, barely perceptible, like the scatter of eroded pebbles that tells you that the palaces and towers of a great ruined city lie buried beneath the mound on which you climb. Unless you are looking for such signals you will not see them. But I was primed for discovery that day. I was eager for it. A strange kind of joy came over me when I picked up that fleeting signal of wrongness.

I keyed the intelligence on duty and said, "What was that tremor on Passenger Deck?"

The intelligence arrived instantly in my mind, a sharp gray-green presence with a halo of tingling music.

"I am aware of no tremor, sir."

"There was a distinct tremor. There was a data-spurt just now."

"Indeed, sir? A data-spurt, sir?" The intelligence sounded aghast, but in a condescending way. It was humoring me. "What action shall I take, sir?"

I was being invited to retreat.

The intelligence on duty was a 49 Henry Henry. The Henry series affects a sort of slippery innocence that I find disingenuous. Still, they are very capable intelligences. I wondered if I had misread the signal. Perhaps I was too eager for an event, any event, that would confirm my relationship with the ship.

There is never a sense of motion or activity aboard a starship: we float in silence on a tide of darkness, cloaked in our own dazzling light. Nothing moves, nothing seems to live in all the universe. Since we had left Kansas Four I had felt that great silence judging me. Was I really captain of this vessel? Good: then let me feel the weight of duty upon my shoulders.

We were past Ultima Thule by this time, and there could be no turning back. Borne on our cloak of light, we would roar through heaven for week after virtual week until we came to worldward at the first of our destinations, which was Cul-de-Sac in the Vainglory Archipelago, out by the Spook Clusters. Here in free space I must begin to master the ship, or it would master me.

"Sir?" the intelligence said.

"Run a data uptake," I ordered. "All Passenger Deck input for the past half hour. There was movement. There was a spurt."

I knew I might be wrong. Still, to err on the side of caution may be naive, but it isn't a sin. And I knew that at this stage in the voyage nothing I could say or do would make me seem other than naive to the crew of the *Sword of Orion*. What did I have to lose by ordering a recheck, then? I was hungry for surprises. Any irregularity that 49 Henry Henry turned up would be to my advantage; the absence of one would make nothing worse for me.

"Begging your pardon, sir," 49 Henry Henry reported after a moment, "but there was no tremor, sir."

"Maybe I overstated it, then. Calling it a tremor. Maybe it was just an anomaly. What do you say, 49 Henry Henry?" I wondered if I was humiliating myself, negotiating like this with an intelligence. "There was something. I'm sure of that. An unmistakable irregular burst in the data-flow. An anomaly, yes. What do you say, 49 Henry Henry?"

"Yes, sir."

"Yes what?"

"The record does show an irregularity, sir. Your observation was quite acute, sir."

"Go on."

"No cause for alarm, sir. A minor metabolic movement, nothing more. Like turning over in your sleep." You bastard, what do you know about sleep? "Extremely unusual, sir, that you should be able to observe anything so small. I commend you, sir. The passengers are all well, sir."

"Very good," I said. "Enter this exchange in the log, 49 Henry Henry."

"Already entered, sir," the intelligence said. "Permission to decouple, sir?"

"Yes, you can decouple," I told it.

The shimmer of music that signaled its presence grew tinny and was gone. I could imagine it smirking as it went about its ghostly flitting rounds deep in the neural conduits of the ship. Scornful software, glowing with contempt for its putative master. The poor captain, it was thinking. The poor hopeless silly boy of a captain. A passenger sneezes and he's ready to seal all bulkheads.

Well, let it smirk, I thought. I have acted appropriately and the record will show it.

I knew that all this was part of my testing.

You may think that to be captain of such a ship as the *Sword of Orion* in your first voyage to heaven is an awesome responsibility and an inconceivable burden. So it is, but not for the reason you think.

In truth the captain's duties are the least significant of anyone's aboard the ship. The others have well-defined tasks that are essential to the smooth running of the voyage, although the ship could, if the need arose, generate virtual replacements for any and every crew member and function adequately on its own. The captain's task, though, is fundamentally abstract. His role is to witness the voyage, to embody it in his own consciousness, to give it coherence, continuity, by reducing it to a pattern of decisions and responses. In that sense the captain is simply so much software: he is the coding through which the voyage is expressed as a series of linear functions. If he fails to perform that duty adequately, others will quietly see to it that the voyage proceeds as it should. What is destroyed, in the course of a voyage that is inadequately captained, is the captain himself, not the voyage. My pre-flight training made that absolutely clear. The voyage can survive the most feeble of captains. As I have said, four starships have been lost since the

349

Service began, and no one knows why. But there is no reason to think that any of those catastrophes were caused by failings of the captain. How could they have been? The captain is only the vehicle through which others act. It is not the captain who makes the voyage, but the voyage which makes the captain.

5.

Restless, troubled, I wandered the eye of the ship. Despite 49 Henry Henry's suave mockery I was still convinced there was trouble on board, or about to be.

Just as I reached Outerscreen Level I felt something strange touch me a second time. It was different this time, and deeply disturbing.

The Eye, as it makes the complete descent from Skin Deck to Belly Deck, is lined with screens that provide displays, actual or virtual, of all aspects of the ship both internal and external. I came up to the great black bevel-edged screen that provided our simulated view of the external realspace environment and was staring at the dwindling wheel of the Ultima Thule relay point when the new anomaly occurred. The other had been the merest of subliminal signals, a nip, a tickle. This was more like an attempted intrusion. Invisible fingers seemed to brush lightly over my brain, probing, seeking entrance. The fingers withdrew; a moment later there was a sudden stabbing pain in my left temple.

I stiffened. "Who's there?"

"Help me," a silent voice said.

I had heard wild tales of passenger matrixes breaking free of their storage circuits and drifting through the ship like ghosts, looking for an unguarded body that they might infiltrate. The sources were unreliable, old scoundrels like Roacher or Bulgar. I dismissed such stories as fables, the way I dismissed what I had heard of the vast tentacular krakens that were said to swim the seas of space, or the beckoning mermaids with shining breasts who danced along the force-lines at spinaround points. But I had felt this. The probing fingers, the sudden sharp pain. And the sense of someone frightened, frightened but strong, stronger than I, hovering close at hand.

"Where are you?"

There was no reply. Whatever it was, if it had been anything at all, had slipped back into hiding after that one furtive thrust.

But was it really gone?

"You're still here somewhere," I said. "I know that you are."

Silence. Stillness.

"You asked for help. Why did you disappear so fast?"

No response. I felt anger rising.

"Whoever you are. Whatever. Speak up."

Nothing. Silence. Had I imagined it? The probing, the voiceless voice?

No. No. I was certain that there was something invisible and unreal hovering about me. And I found it infuriating, not to be able to regain contact with it. To be toyed with this way, to be mocked like this.

This is my ship, I thought. I want no ghosts aboard my ship.

"You can be detected," I said. "You can be contained. You can be eradicated."

As I stood there blustering in my frustration, it seemed to me that I felt that touch against my mind again, a lighter one this time, wistful, regretful. Perhaps I invented it. Perhaps I have supplied it retroactively.

But it lasted only a part of an instant, if it happened at all, and then I was unquestionably alone again. The solitude was real and total and unmistakable. I stood gripping the rail of the screen, leaning forward into the brilliant blackness and swaying dizzily as if I were being pulled forward through the wall of the ship into space.

"Captain?"

The voice of 49 Henry Henry, tumbling out of the air behind me.

"Did you feel something that time?" I asked.

The intelligence ignored my question. "Captain, there's trouble on Passenger Deck. Hands-on alarm: will you come?"

"Set up a transit track for me," I said. "I'm on my way."

Lights began to glow in mid-air, yellow, blue, green. The interior of the ship is a vast opaque maze and moving about within it is difficult without an intelligence to guide you. 49 Henry Henry constructed an efficient route for me down the curve of the Eye and into the main body of the ship, and thence around the rim of the leeward wall to the elevator down to Passenger Deck. I rode an air-cushion tracker keyed to the lights. The journey took no more than fifteen minutes. Unaided I might have needed a week.

Passenger Deck is an echoing nest of coffins, hundreds of them, sometimes even thousands, arranged in rows three abreast. Here our live cargo sleeps until we arrive and decant the stored sleepers into wakefulness. Machinery sighs and murmurs all around them, coddling them in their suspension. Beyond, far off in the dim distance, is the place for passengers of a different sort—a spiderwebbing of sensory cables that holds our thousands of disembodied matrixes. Those are the colonists who have left their bodies behind when going into space. It is a dark and forbidding place, dimly lit by swirling velvet comets that circle overhead emitting sparks of red and green.

The trouble was in the suspension area. Five crewmen were there already, the oldest hands on board: Katkat, Dismas, Rio de Rio, Gavotte, Roacher. Seeing them all together, I knew this must be some major event. We move on distant orbits within the immensity of the ship: to see as many as three members of the crew in the same virtual month is extraordinary. Now here were five. I felt an oppressive sense of community among them. Each of these five had sailed the seas of heaven more years than I had been alive. For at least a dozen voyages now they had been together as a team. I was the stranger in their midst, unknown, untried, lightly regarded, insignificant. Already Roacher had indicted me for my sweetness, by which he meant, I knew, a basic incapacity to act decisively. I thought he was wrong. But perhaps he knew me better than I knew myself.

They stepped back, opening a path between them. Gavotte, a great hulking thick-shouldered man with a surprisingly delicate and precise way of conducting himself, gestured with open hands: Here, Captain, see? See?

What I saw were coils of greenish smoke coming up from a passenger housing, and the glass door of the housing half open, cracked from top to bottom, frosted by temperature differentials. I could hear a sullen dripping sound. Blue fluid fell in thick steady gouts from a shattered support line. Within the housing itself was the pale naked figure of a man, eyes wide open, mouth agape as if in a silent scream. His left arm was raised, his fist was clenched. He looked like an anguished statue.

They had body-salvage equipment standing by. The hapless passenger would be disassembled and all usable parts stored as soon as I gave the word.

"Is he irretrievable?" I asked.

"Take a look," Katkat said, pointing to the housing readout. All the curves pointed down. "We have nineteen percent degradation already, and rising. Do we disassemble?"

"Go ahead," I said. "Approved."

The lasers glinted and flailed. Body parts came into view, shining, moist. The coiling metallic arms of the body-salvage equipment rose and fell, lifting organs that were not yet beyond repair and putting them into storage. As the machine labored the men worked around it, shutting down the broken housing, tying off the disrupted feeders and refrigerator cables.

I asked Dismas what had happened. He was the mind-wiper for this sector, responsible for maintenance on the suspended passengers. His face was open and easy, but the deceptive cheeriness about his mouth and cheeks was mysteriously negated by his bleak, shadowy eyes. He told me that he had been working much farther down the deck, performing routine service on the Strappado-bound people, when he felt a sudden small disturbance, a quick tickle of wrongness.

"So did I," I said. "How long ago was that?"

"Half an hour, maybe. I didn't make a special note of it. I thought it was something in my gut, Captain. You felt it too, you say?"

I nodded. "Just a tickle. It's in the record." I heard the distant music of 49 Henry Henry. Perhaps the intelligence was trying to apologize for doubting me. "What happened next?" I asked.

"Went back to work. Five, ten minutes, maybe. Felt another jolt, a stronger one." He touched his forehead, right at the temple, showing me where. "Detectors went off, broken glass. Came running, found this Cul-de-Sac passenger here undergoing convulsions. Rising from his bindings, thrashing around. Pulled himself loose from everything, went smack against the housing window. Broke it. It's a very fast death."

"Matrix intrusion," Roacher said.

The skin of my scalp tightened. I turned to him.

"Tell me about that."

He shrugged. "Once in a long while someone in the storage circuits gets to feeling footloose, and finds a way out and goes roaming the ship. Looking for a body to jack into, that's what they're doing. Jack into me, jack into Katkat, even jack into you, Captain. Anybody handy, just so they can feel flesh around them again. Jacked into this one here and something went wrong."

The probing fingers, yes. The silent voice. *Help me.*

"I never heard of anyone jacking into a passenger in suspension," Dismas said.

"No reason why not," said Roacher.

353

"What's the good? Still stuck in a housing, you are. Frozen down, that's no better than staying matrix."

"Five to two it was matrix intrusion," Roacher said, glaring.

"Done," Dismas said. Gavotte laughed and came in on the bet. So too did sinuous little Katkat, taking the other side. Rio de Rio, who had not spoken a word to anyone in his last six voyages, snorted and gestured obscenely at both factions.

I felt like an idle spectator. To regain some illusion of command I said, "If there's a matrix loose, it'll show up on ship inventory. Dismas, check with the intelligence on duty and report to me. Katkat, Gavotte, finish cleaning up this mess and seal everything off. Then I want your reports in the log and a copy to me. I'll be in my quarters. There'll be further instructions later. The missing matrix, if that's what we have on our hands, will be identified, located, and recaptured."

Roacher grinned at me. I thought he was going to lead a round of cheers.

I turned and mounted my tracker, and rode it following the lights, yellow, blue, green, back up through the maze of decks and out to the Eye.

As I entered my cabin something touched my mind and a silent voice said, "Please help me."

6.

Carefully I shut the door behind me, locked it, loaded the privacy screens. The captain's cabin aboard a Megaspore starship of the Service is a world in itself, serene, private, immense. In mine, spiral galaxies whirled and sparkled on the walls. I had a stream, a lake, a silver waterfall beyond it. The air was soft and glistening. At a touch of my hand I could have light, music, scent, color, from any one of a thousand hidden orifices. Or I could turn the walls translucent and let the luminous splendor of starspace come flooding through.

Only when I was fully settled in, protected and insulated and comfortable, did I say, "All right. What are you?"

"You promise you won't report me to the captain?"

"I don't promise anything."

"You will help me, though?" The voice seemed at once frightened and insistent, urgent and vulnerable.

"How can I say? You give me nothing to work with."

"I'll tell you everything. But first you have to promise not to call the captain."

I debated with myself for a moment and opted for directness.

"I am the captain," I said.

"No!"

"Can you see this room? What do you think it is? Crew quarters? The scullery?"

I felt turbulent waves of fear coming from my invisible companion. And then nothing. Was it gone? Then I had made a mistake in being so forthright. This phantom had to be confined, sealed away, perhaps destroyed, before it could do more damage. I should have been more devious. And also I knew that I would regret it in another way if it had slipped away: I was taking a certain pleasure in being able to speak with someone—something—that was neither a member of my crew nor an omnipotent, contemptuous artificial intelligence.

"Are you still here?" I asked after a while.

Silence.

Gone, I thought. Sweeping through the *Sword of Orion* like a gale of wind. Probably down at the far end of the ship by this time.

Then, as if there had been no break in the conversation: "I just can't believe it. Of all the places I could have gone, I had to walk right into the captain's cabin."

"So it seems."

"And you're actually the captain?"

"Yes. Actually."

Another pause.

"You seem so young," it said. "For a captain."

"Be careful," I told it.

"I didn't mean anything by that, Captain." With a touch of bravado, even defiance, mingling with uncertainty and anxiety. "Captain *sir*."

Looking toward the ceiling, where shining resonator nodes shimmered all up and down the spectrum as slave-light leaped from junction to junction along the illuminator strands, I searched for a glimpse of it, some minute electromagnetic clue. But there was nothing.

I imagined a web of impalpable force, a dancing will-o'-the-wisp, flitting erratically about the room, now perching on my shoulder, now clinging to some fixture, now extending itself to fill every open space: an airy thing, a sprite, playful and capricious. Curiously, not only was I unafraid but I found myself strongly drawn to it. There was something strangely appealing about this quick vibrating spirit, so bright with contradictions. And yet it had caused the death of one of my passengers.

"Well?" I said. "You're safe here. But when are you going to tell me what you are?"

"Isn't that obvious? I'm a matrix."

"Go on."

"A free matrix, a matrix on the loose. A matrix who's in big trouble. I think I've hurt someone. Maybe killed him."

"One of the passengers?" I said.

"So you know?"

"There's a dead passenger, yes. We're not sure what happened."

"It wasn't my fault. It was an accident."

"That may be," I said. "Tell me about it. Tell me everything."

"Can I trust you?"

"More than anyone else on this ship."

"But you're the captain."

"That's why," I said.

7.

Her name was Leeleaine, but she wanted me to call her Vox. That means "voice," she said, in one of the ancient languages of Earth. She was seventeen years old, from Jaana Head, which is an island off the coast of West Palabar on Kansas Four. Her father was a glass-farmer, her mother operated a gravity hole, and she had five brothers and three sisters, all of them much older than she was.

"Do you know what that's like, captain? Being the youngest of nine? And both your parents working all the time, and your cross-parents just as busy? Can you imagine? And growing up on Kansas Four, where it's a thousand kilometers between cities, and you aren't even in a city, you're on an *island*?"

"I know something of what that's like," I said.

"Are you from Kansas Four too?"

"No," I said. "Not from Kansas Four. But a place much like it, I think."

She spoke of a troubled, unruly childhood, full of loneliness and anger. Kansas Four, I have heard, is a beautiful world, if you are inclined to find beauty in worlds: a wild and splendid place, where the sky is scarlet and the bare basalt mountains rise in the east like a magnificent black wall. But to hear Vox speak of it, it was squalid, grim, bleak. For her it was a loveless place where she led a loveless life. And yet she told me of pale violet seas aglow with brilliant yellow fish, and trees that erupted with a shower of dazzling crimson fronds when they were in bloom, and warm rains that sang in the air like harps. I was not then so long in heaven that I had forgotten the beauty of seas or trees or rains, which by now are nothing but hollow words to me. Yet Vox had found her life on Kansas Four so hateful that she had been willing to abandon not only her native world but her body itself. That was a point of kinship between us: I too had given up my world and my former life, if not my actual flesh. But I had chosen heaven, and the Service. Vox had volunteered to exchange one landcrawling servitude for another.

"The day came," she said, "when I knew I couldn't stand it any more. I was so miserable, so empty: I thought about having to live this way for another two hundred years or even more, and I wanted to pick up the hills and throw them at each other. Or get into my mother's plummeter and take it straight to the bottom of the sea. I made a list of ways I could kill myself. But I knew I couldn't do it, not this way or that way or any way. I wanted to live. But I didn't want to live like *that*."

On that same day, she said, the soul-call from Cul-de-Sac reached Kansas Four. A thousand vacant bodies were available there and they wanted soul-matrixes to fill them. Without a moment's hesitation Vox put her name on the list.

There is a constant migration of souls between the worlds. On each of my voyages I have carried thousands of them, setting forth hopefully toward new bodies on strange planets.

Every world has a stock of bodies awaiting replacement souls. Most were the victims of sudden violence. Life is risky on shore, and death lurks everywhere. Salvaging and repairing a body is no troublesome matter, but once a soul has fled it can never be recovered. So the empty bodies of those who drown and those who are stung by lethal insects and those who are thrown from vehicles and those who are struck by falling branches as they work are collected and examined. If they are beyond repair they are disassembled and their usable parts set aside to be installed in others. But if their bodies can be made whole again, they are, and they are placed in holding chambers until new souls become available for them.

And then there are those who vacate their bodies voluntarily, per-haps because they are weary of them, or weary of their worlds, and wish to move along. They are the ones who sign up to fill the waiting bodies on far worlds, while others come behind them to fill the bodies they have abandoned. The least costly way to travel between the worlds is to surrender your body and go in matrix form, thus exchanging a discouraging life for an unfamiliar one. That was what Vox had done. In pain and despair she had agreed to allow the essence of herself, everything she had ever seen or felt or thought or dreamed, to be converted into a lattice of electrical impulses that the *Sword of Orion* would carry on its voyage from Kansas Four to Cul-de-Sac. A new body lay reserved for her there.

Her own discarded body would remain in suspension on Kansas Four. Some day it might become the home of some wandering soul from another world; or, if there were no bids for it, it might eventually be disassembled by the body-salvagers, and its parts put to some worthy use. Vox would never know; Vox would never care.

"I can understand trading an unhappy life for a chance at a happy one," I said. "But why break loose on ship? What purpose could that serve? Why not wait until you got to Cul-de-Sac?"

"Because it was torture," she said.

"Torture? What was?"

"Living as a matrix." She laughed bitterly. "Living? It's worse than death could ever be!"

"Tell me."

"You've never done matrix, have you?"

"No," I said. "I chose another way to escape."

"Then you don't know. You can't know. You've got a ship full of matrixes in storage circuits but you don't understand a thing about them. Imagine that the back of your neck itches, captain. But you have no arms to scratch with. Your thigh starts to itch. Your chest. You lie there itching everywhere. And you can't scratch. Do you understand me?"

"How can a matrix feel an itch? A matrix is simply a pattern of electrical—"

"Oh, you're impossible! You're *stupid*! I'm not talking about actual literal itching. I'm giving you a suppose, a for-instance. Because you'd never be able to understand the real situation. Look: you're in the storage circuit. All you are is electricity. That's all a mind really is, anyway: electricity. But you used to have a body. The body had sensation. The body had feelings. You remember them. You're a prisoner. A prisoner remembers all sorts of things that used to be taken for granted. You'd give anything to feel the wind in your hair again, or the taste of cool milk, or the scent of flowers. Or even the pain of a cut finger. The saltiness of your blood when you lick the cut. Anything. I hated my body, don't you see? I couldn't wait to be rid of it. But once it was gone I missed the feelings it had. I missed the sense of flesh pulling at me, holding me to the ground, flesh full of nerves, flesh that could feel pleasure. Or pain."

"I understand," I said, and I think that I truly did. "But the voyage to Cul-de-Sac is short. A few virtual weeks and you'd be there, and out of storage and into your new body, and—"

"Weeks? Think of that itch on the back of your neck, Captain. The itch that you can't scratch. How long do you think you could stand it, lying there feeling that itch? Five minutes? An hour? *Weeks?*"

It seemed to me that an itch left unscratched would die of its own, perhaps in minutes. But that was only how it seemed to me. I was not Vox; I had not been a matrix in a storage circuit.

I said, "So you let yourself out? How?"

"It wasn't that hard to figure. I had nothing else to do but think about it. You align yourself with the polarity of the circuit. That's a matrix too, an electrical pattern holding you in crosswise bands. You change the alignment. It's like being tied up, and slipping the ropes around until you can slide free. And then you can go anywhere you like. You key into any bioprocessor aboard the ship and you draw your energy from that instead of from the storage circuit, and it sustains you. I can move anywhere around this ship at the speed of light. Anywhere. In just the time you blinked your eye, I've been everywhere. I've been to the far tip and out on the mast, and I've been down through the lower decks, and I've been in the crew quarters and the cargo places and I've even been a little way off into something that's right outside the ship but isn't quite real, if you know what I mean. Something that just seems to be a cradle of probability waves surrounding us. It's like being a ghost. But it doesn't solve anything. Do you see? The torture still goes on. You want to feel, but you can't. You want to be connected again, your senses, your inputs. That's why I tried to get into the passenger, do you see? But he wouldn't let me."

I began to understand at last.

Not everyone who goes to the worlds of heaven as a colonist travels in matrix form. Ordinarily anyone who can afford to take his body with him will do so; but relatively few can afford it. Those who do travel in

ROBERT SILVERBERG

suspension, the deepest of sleeps. We carry no waking passengers in the Service, not at any price. They would be trouble for us, poking here, poking there, asking questions, demanding to be served and pampered. They would shatter the peace of the voyage. And so they go down into their coffins, their housings, and there they sleep the voyage away, all life-processes halted, a death-in-life that will not be reversed until we bring them to their destinations.

And poor Vox, freed of her prisoning circuit and hungry for sensory data, had tried to slip herself into a passenger's body.

I listened, appalled and somber, as she told of her terrible odyssey through the ship. Breaking free of the circuit: that had been the first strangeness I felt, that tic, that nibble at the threshold of my consciousness.

Her first wild moment of freedom had been exhilarating and joyous. But then had come the realization that nothing really had changed. She was at large, but still she was incorporeal, caught in that monstrous frustration of bodilessness, yearning for a touch. Perhaps such torment was common among matrixes; perhaps that was why, now and then, they broke free as Vox had done, to roam ships like sad troubled spirits. So Roacher had said. *Once in a long while someone in the storage circuits gets to feeling footloose, and finds a way out and goes roaming the ship. Looking for a body to jack into, that's what they're doing. Jack into me, jack into Katkat, even jack into you, Captain. Anybody handy, just so they can feel flesh around them again.* Yes.

That was the second jolt, the stronger one, that Dismas and I had felt, when Vox, selecting a passenger at random, suddenly, impulsively, had slipped herself inside his brain. She had realized her mistake at once. The passenger, lost in whatever dreams may come to the suspended, reacted to her intrusion with wild terror. Convulsions swept him; he rose, clawing at the equipment that sustained his life, trying desperately to evict the succubus that had penetrated him. In this frantic struggle he smashed the case of his housing and died. Vox, fleeing, frightened, careered about the ship in search of refuge, encountered me standing by the screen in the Eye, and made an abortive attempt to enter my mind. But just then the death of the passenger registered on 49 Henry Henry's sensors and when the intelligence made contact with me to tell me of the emergency Vox fled again, and hovered dolefully until I returned to my cabin. She had not meant to kill the passenger, she said. She was sorry that he had died. She felt some embarrassment, now, and fear. But no guilt. She rejected guilt for it almost defiantly. He had died? Well, so he had died. That was too bad. But how could she have known any such thing was going to happen? She was only looking for a body to take refuge in. Hearing that from her, I had a sense of her as someone utterly unlike me, someone volatile, unstable, perhaps violent. And yet I felt a strange kinship with her, even an identity. As though we were two parts of the same spirit; as though she and I were one and the same. I barely understood why.

"And what now?" I asked. "You say you want help. How?"

"Take me in."

"What?"

"Hide me. In you. If they find me, they'll eradicate me. You said so yourself, that it could be done, that I could be detected, contained, eradicated. But it won't happen if you protect me."

"I'm the *captain*," I said, astounded.

"Yes."

"How can I—"

"They'll all be looking for me. The intelligences, the crewmen. It scares them, knowing there's a matrix loose. They'll want to destroy me. But if they can't find me, they'll start to forget about me after a while. They'll think I've escaped into space, or something. And if I'm jacked into you, nobody's going to be able to find me."

"I have a responsibility to—"

"Please," she said. "I could go to one of the others, maybe. But I feel closest to you. Please. Please."

"Closest to me?"

"You aren't happy. You don't belong. Not here, not anywhere. You don't fit in, any more than I did on Kansas Four. I could feel it the moment I first touched your mind. You're a new captain, right? And the others on board are making it hard for you. Why should you care about *them*? Save me. We have more in common than you do with them. Please? You can't just let them eradicate me. I'm young. I didn't mean to hurt anyone. All I want is to get to Cul-de-Sac and be put in the body that's waiting for me there. A new start, my first start, really. Will you?"

"Why do you bother asking permission? You can simply enter me through my jack whenever you want, can't you?"

"The last one died," she said.

"He was in suspension. You didn't kill him by entering him. It was the surprise, the fright. He killed himself by thrashing around and wrecking his housing."

"Even so," said Vox. "I wouldn't try that again, an unwilling host. You have to say you'll let me, or I won't come in."

I was silent.

"Help me?" she said.

"Come," I told her.

8.

It was just like any other jacking: an electrochemical mind-to-mind bond, a linkage by way of the implant socket at the base of my spine. The sort of thing that any two people who wanted to make communion might do. There was just one difference, which was that we didn't use a jack. We skipped the whole intricate business of checking bandwiths and voltages and selecting the right transformer-adapter. She could do it all, simply by matching evoked potentials. I felt a momentary sharp sensation and then she was with me.

"Breathe," she said. "Breathe real deep. Fill your lungs. Rub your hands together. Touch your cheeks. Scratch behind your left ear. Please. Please. It's been so long for me since I've felt anything."

Her voice sounded the same as before, both real and unreal. There was no substance to it, no density of timbre, no sense that it was produced by the vibrations of vocal cords atop a column of air. Yet it was clear, firm, substantial in some essential way, a true voice in all respects except that there was no speaker to utter it. I suppose that while she was outside me she had needed to extend some strand of herself into my neural system in order to generate it. Now that was unnecessary. But I still perceived the voice as originating outside me, even though she had taken up residence within.

She overflowed with needs.

"Take a drink of water," she urged. "Eat something. Can you make your knuckles crack? Do it, oh, do it! Put your hand between your legs and squeeze. There's so much I want to feel. Do you have music here? Give me some music, will you? Something loud, something really hard."

I did the things she wanted. Gradually she grew more calm.

I was strangely calm myself. I had no special awareness then of her presence within me, no unfamiliar pressure in my skull, no slitherings along my spine. There was no mingling of her thoughtstream and mine. She seemed not to have any way of controlling the movements or responses of my body. In these respects our contact was less intimate than any ordinary human jacking communion would have been. But that, I would soon discover, was by her choice. We would not remain so carefully compartmentalized for long.

"Is it better for you now?" I asked.

"I thought I was going to go crazy. If I didn't start feeling something again soon."

"You can feel things now?"

"Through you, yes. Whatever you touch, I touch."

"You know I can't hide you for long. They'll take my command away if I'm caught harboring a fugitive. Or worse."

"You don't have to speak out loud to me any more," she said.

"I don't understand."

"Just *send* it. We have the same nervous system now."

"You can read my thoughts?" I said, still aloud.

"Not really. I'm not hooked into the higher cerebral centers. But I pick up motor, sensory stuff. And I get subvocalizations. You know what those are? I can hear your thoughts if you want me to. It's like being in communion. You've been in communion, haven't you?"

"Once in a while."

"Then you know. Just open the channel to me. You can't go around the ship talking out loud to somebody invisible, you know. *Send* me something. It isn't hard."

"Like this?" I said, visualizing a packet of verbal information sliding through the channels of my mind.

"You see? You can do it!"

"Even so," I told her. "You still can't stay like this with me for long. You have to realize that."

She laughed. It was unmistakable, a silent but definite laugh. "You sound so serious. I bet you're still surprised you took me in in the first place."

"I certainly am. Did you think I would?"

"Sure I did. From the first moment. You're basically a very kind person."

"Am I, Vox?"

"Of course. You just have to let yourself do it." Again the silent laughter. "I don't even know your name. Here I am right inside your head and I don't know your name."

"Adam."

"That's a nice name. Is that an Earth name?"

"An old Earth name, yes. Very old."

"And are you from Earth?" she asked.

"No. Except in the sense that we're all from Earth."

"Where, then?"

"I'd just as soon not talk about it," I said.

She thought about that. "You hated the place where you grew up that much?"

"Please, Vox—"

"Of course you hated it. Just like I hated Kansas Four. We're two of a kind, you and me. We're one and the same. You got all the caution and I got all the impulsiveness. But otherwise we're the same person. That's why we share so well. I'm glad I'm sharing with you, Adam. You won't make me leave, will you? We belong with each other. You'll let me stay until we reach Cul-de-Sac. I know you will."

"Maybe. Maybe not." I wasn't at all sure, either way.

"Oh, you will. You will, Adam. I know you better than you know yourself."

9.

So it began. I was in some new realm outside my established sense of myself, so far beyond my notions of appropriate behavior that I could not even feel astonishment at what I had done. I had taken her in, that was all. A stranger in my skull. She had turned to me in appeal and I had taken her in. It was as if her recklessness was contagious. And though I didn't mean to shelter her any longer than was absolutely necessary, I could already see that I wasn't going to make any move to eject her until her safety was assured.

But how was I going to hide her?

Invisible she might be, but not undetectable. And everyone on the ship would be searching for her.

There were sixteen crewmen on board who dreaded a loose matrix as they would a vampire. They would seek her as long as she remained at large. And not only the crew. The intelligences would be monitoring for her too, not out of any kind of fear but simply out of efficiency: they had nothing to fear from Vox but they would want the cargo manifests to come out in balance when we reached our destination.

The crew didn't trust me in the first place. I was too young, too new, too green, too *sweet*. I was just the sort who might be guilty of giving shelter to a secret fugitive. And it was altogether likely that her presence within me would be obvious to others in some way not apparent to me. As for the intelligences, they had access to all sorts of data as part of their routine maintenance operations. Perhaps they could measure tiny physiological changes, differences in my reaction times or circulatory efficiency or whatever, that would be a tipoff to the truth. How would I know? I would have to be on constant guard against discovery of the secret sharer of my consciousness.

The first test came less than an hour after Vox had entered me. The communicator light went on and I heard the far-off music of the intelligence on duty.

This one was 612 Jason, working the late shift. Its aura was golden, its music deep and throbbing. Jasons tend to be more brusque and less condescending than the Henry series, and in general I prefer them. But it was terrifying now to see that light, to hear that music, to know that the ship's intelligence wanted to speak with me. I shrank back at a tense awkward angle, the way one does when trying to avoid a face-to-face confrontation with someone.

But of course the intelligence had no face to confront. The intelligence was only a voice speaking to me out of a speaker grid, and a stew of magnetic impulses somewhere on the control levels of the ship. All the same, I perceived 612 Jason now as a great glowing eye, staring through me to the hidden Vox.

"What is it?" I asked.

"Report summary, Captain. The dead passenger and the missing matrix."

Deep within me I felt a quick plunging sensation, and then the skin of my arms and shoulders began to glow as the chemicals of fear went coursing through my veins in a fierce tide. It was Vox, I knew, reacting in sudden alarm, opening the petcocks of my hormonal system. It was the thing I had dreaded. How could 612 Jason fail to notice that flood of endocrine response?

"Go on," I said, as coolly as I could.

But noticing was one thing, interpreting the data something else. Fluctuations in a human being's endocrine output might have any number of causes. To my troubled conscience everything was a glaring signal of my guilt. 612 Jason gave no indication that it suspected a thing.

The intelligence said, "The dead passenger was Hans Eger Olafssen, 54 years of age, a native of—"

"Never mind his details. You can let me have a printout on that part."

"The missing matrix," 612 Jason went on imperturbably. "Leeleaine Eliani, 17 years of age, a native of Kansas Four, bound for Cul-de-Sac, Vainglory Archipelago, under Transmission Contract No. D-14871532, dated the 27th day of the third month of—"

"Printout on that too," I cut in. "What I want to know is where she is now."

"That information is not available."

"That isn't a responsive answer, 612 Jason."

"No better answer can be provided at this time, Captain. Tracer circuits have been activated and remain in constant search mode."

"And?"

"We have no data on the present location of the missing matrix."

Within me Vox reacted instantly to the intelligence's calm flat statement. The hormonal response changed from one of fear to one of relief. My blazing skin began at once to cool. Would 612 Jason notice that too, and from that small clue be able to assemble the subtext of my body's responses into a sequence that exposed my criminal violation of regulations?

"Don't relax too soon," I told her silently. "This may be some sort of trap."

To 612 Jason I said, "What data *do* you have, then?"

"Two things are known: the time at which the Eliani matrix achieved negation of its storage circuitry and the time of its presumed attempt at making neural entry into the suspended passenger Olafssen. Beyond that no data has been recovered."

"Its *presumed* attempt?" I said.

"There is no proof, Captain."

"Olafssen's convulsions? The smashing of the storage housing?"

"We know that Olafssen responded to an electrical stimulus, Captain. The source of the stimulus is impossible to trace, although the presumption is that it came from the missing matrix Eliani. These are matters for the subsequent inquiry. It is not within my responsibilities to assign definite causal relationships."

Spoken like a true Jason-series intelligence, I thought.

I said, "You don't have any effective way of tracing the movements of the Eliani matrix, is that what you're telling me?"

"We're dealing with extremely minute impedances, sir. In the ordinary functioning of the ship it is very difficult to distinguish a matrix manifestation from normal surges and pulses in the general electrical system."

"You mean, it might take something as big as the matrix trying to climb back into its own storage circuit to register on the monitoring system?"

"Very possibly, sir."

"Is there any reason to think the Eliani matrix is still on the ship at all?"

"There is no reason to think that it is not, Captain."

"In other words, you don't know anything about anything concerning the Eliani matrix."

"I have provided you with all known data at this point. Trace efforts are continuing, sir."

"You still think this is a trap?" Vox asked me.

"It's sounding better and better by the minute. But shut up and don't distract me, will you?"

To the intelligence I said, "All right, keep me posted on the situation. I'm preparing for sleep, 612 Jason. I want the end-of-day status report, and then I want you to clear off and leave me alone."

"Very good, sir. Fifth virtual day of voyage. Position of ship sixteen units beyond last port of call, Kansas Four. Scheduled rendezvous with relay forces at Ultima Thule spinaround point was successfully achieved at the hour of—"

The intelligence droned on and on: the usual report of the routine events of the day, broken only by the novelty of an entry for the loss of a passenger and one for the escape of a matrix, then returning to the standard data, fuel levels and velocity soundings and all the rest. On the first four nights of the voyage I had solemnly tried to absorb all this torrent of ritualized downloading of the log as though my captaincy depended on committing it all to memory, but this night I barely listened, and nearly missed my cue when it was time to give it my approval before clocking out for the night. Vox had to prod me and let me know that the intelligence was waiting for something. I gave 612 Jason the confirm-and-clock-out and heard the welcome sound of its diminishing music as it decoupled the contact.

"What do you think?" Vox asked. "It doesn't know, does it?"

"Not yet," I said.

"You really are a pessimist, aren't you?"

"I think we may be able to bring this off," I told her. "But the moment we become overconfident, it'll be the end. Everyone on this ship wants to know where you are. The slightest slip and we're both gone."

"Okay. Don't lecture me."

"I'll try not to. Let's get some sleep now."

"I don't need to sleep."

"Well, I do."

"Can we talk for a while first?"

"Tomorrow," I said.

But of course sleep was impossible. I was all too aware of the stranger within me, perhaps prowling the most hidden places of my psyche at this moment. Or waiting to invade my dreams once I drifted off. For the first time I thought I could feel her presence even when she was silent: a hot node of identity pressing against the wall of my brain. Perhaps I imagined it. I lay stiff and tense, as wide awake as I have ever been in my life. After a time I had to call 612 Jason and ask it to put me under the wire; and even then my sleep was uneasy when it came.

10.

Until that point in the voyage I had taken nearly all of my meals in my quarters. It seemed a way of exerting my authority, such as it was, aboard ship. By my absence from the dining hall I created a presence, that of the austere and aloof captain; and I avoided the embarrassment of having to sit in the seat of command over men who were much my senior in all things. It was no great sacrifice for me. My quarters were more than comfortable, the food was the same as that which was available in the dining hall, the servo-steward that brought it was silent and efficient. The question of isolation did not arise. There has always been something solitary about me, as there is about most who are of the Service.

But when I awoke the next morning after what had seemed like an endless night, I went down to the dining hall for breakfast.

It was nothing like a deliberate change of policy, a decision that had been rigorously arrived at through careful reasoning. It wasn't a decision at all. Nor did Vox suggest it, though I'm sure she inspired it. It was purely automatic. I arose, showered, and dressed. I confess that I had forgotten all about the events of the night before. Vox was quiet within me. Not until I was under the shower, feeling the warm comforting ultrasonic vibration, did I remember her: there came a disturbing sensation of being in two places at once, and, immediately afterward, an astonishingly odd feeling of shame at my own nakedness. Both those feelings passed quickly. But they did indeed bring to mind that extraordinary thing which I had managed to suppress for some minutes, that I was no longer alone in my body.

She said nothing. Neither did I. After last night's astounding alliance I seemed to want to pull back into wordlessness, unthinkingness, a kind of automaton consciousness. The need for breakfast occurred to me and I called up a tracker to take me down to the dining hall. When I stepped outside the room I was surprised to encounter my servo-steward, already on its way up with my tray. Perhaps it was just as surprised to see me going out, though of course its blank metal face betrayed no feelings.

"I'll be having breakfast in the dining hall today," I told it.

"Very good, sir."

My tracker arrived. I climbed into its seat and it set out at once on its cushion of air toward the dining hall.

The dining hall of the *Sword of Orion* is a magnificent room at the Eye end of Crew Deck, with one glass wall providing a view of all the lights of heaven. By some whim of the designers we sit with that wall below us, so that the stars and their tethered worlds drift beneath our feet. The other walls are of some silvery metal chased with thin swirls of gold, everything shining by the reflected light of the passing star-clusters. At the center is a table of black stone, with places allotted for each of the seventeen members of the crew. It is a splendid if somewhat ridiculous place, a resonant reminder of the wealth and power of the Service.

Three of my shipmates were at their places when I entered. Pedregal was there, the supercargo, a compact, sullen man whose broad dome of a head seemed to rise directly from his shoulders. And there was Fresco, too, slender and elusive, the navigator, a lithe dark-skinned person of ambiguous sex who alternated from voyage to voyage, so I had been told, converting from male to female and back again according to some private rhythm. The third person was Raebuck, whose sphere of responsibility was communications, an older man whose flat, chilly gaze conveyed either boredom or menace, I could never be sure which.

"Why, it's the captain," said Pedregal calmly. "Favoring us with one of his rare visits."

All three stared at me with that curious testing intensity which I was coming to see was an inescapable part of my life aboard ship: a constant hazing meted out to any newcomer to the Service, an interminable probing for the place that was most vulnerable. Mine was a parsec wide and I was certain they would discover it at once. But I was determined to match them stare for stare, ploy for ploy, test for test.

"Good morning, gentlemen," I said. Then, giving Fresco a level glance, I added, "Good morning, Fresco."

I took my seat at the table's head and rang for service.

I was beginning to realize why I had come out of my cabin that morning. In part it was a reflection of Vox's presence within me, an expression of that new component of rashness and impulsiveness that had entered me with her. But mainly it was, I saw now, some stratagem of my own, hatched on some inaccessible subterranean level of my double mind. In order to conceal Vox most effectively, I would have to take the offensive: rather than skulking in my quarters and perhaps awakening perilous suspicions in the minds of my shipmates, I must come forth, defiantly, challengingly, almost flaunting the thing that I had done, and go among them, pretending that nothing unusual was afoot and forcing them to believe it. Such aggressiveness was not natural to my temperament. But perhaps I could draw on some reserves provided by Vox. If not, we both were lost.

Raebuck said, to no one in particular, "I suppose yesterday's disturbing events must inspire a need for companionship in the captain."

I faced him squarely. "I have all the companionship I require, Raebuck. But I agree that what happened yesterday was disturbing."

"A nasty business," Pedregal said, ponderously shaking his neckless head. "And a strange one, a matrix trying to get into a passenger. That's new to me, a thing like that. And to lose the passenger besides— that's bad. That's very bad."

"It does happen, losing a passenger," said Raebuck.

"A long time since it happened on a ship of mine," Pedregal rejoined.

"We lost a whole batch of them on the *Emperor of Callisto*," Fresco said. "You know the story? It was thirty years ago. We were making the run from Van Buren to the San Pedro Cluster. We picked up a supernova pulse and the intelligence on duty went into flicker. Somehow dumped a load of aluminum salts in the feed-lines and killed off fifteen, sixteen passengers. I saw the bodies before they went into the converter. Beyond salvage, they were."

"Yes," said Raebuck. "I heard of that one. And then there was the *Queen Astarte*, a couple of years after that. Tchelitchev was her captain, little green-eyed Russian woman from one of the Troika worlds. They were taking a routine inventory and two digits got transposed, and a faulty delivery signal slipped through. I think it was six dead, premature decanting, killed by air poisoning. Tchelitchev took it very badly. *Very* badly. Somehow the captain always does."

"And then that time on the *Hecuba*," said Pedregal. "No ship of mine, thank God. That was the captain who ran amok, thought the ship was too quiet, wanted to see some passengers moving around and started awakening them—"

Raebuck showed a quiver of surprise. "You know about that? I thought that was supposed to be hushed up."

"Things get around," Pedregal said, with something like a smirk. "The captain's name was Catania-Szu, I believe, a man from Mediterraneo, very high-strung, the way all of them are there. I was working the *Valparaiso* then, out of Mendax Nine bound for Scylla and Charybdis and neighboring points, and when we stopped to download some cargo in the Seneca system I got the whole story from a ship's clerk named—"

"You were on the *Valparaiso*?" Fresco asked. "Wasn't that the ship that had a free matrix, too, ten or eleven years back? A real soul-eater, so the report went—"

"After my time," said Pedregal, blandly waving his hand. "But I did hear of it. You get to hear about everything, when you're downloading cargo. Soul-eater, you say, reminds me of the time—"

And he launched into some tale of horror at a spinaround station in a far quadrant of the galaxy. But he was no more than halfway through it when Raebuck cut in with a gorier reminiscence of his own, and then Fresco, seething with impatience, broke in on him to tell of a ship infested by three free matrixes at once. I had no doubt that all this was being staged for my enlightenment, by way of showing me how seriously such events were taken in the Service, and how the captains under whom they occurred went down in the folklore of the starships with ineradicable black marks. But their attempts to unsettle me, if that is what they were, left me undismayed. Vox, silent within me, infused me with a strange confidence that allowed me to ignore the darker implications of these anecdotes.

I simply listened, playing my role: the neophyte fascinated by the accumulated depth of spacegoing experience that their stories implied.

Then I said, finally, "When matrixes get loose, how long do they generally manage to stay at large?"

"An hour or two, generally," said Raebuck. "As they drift around the ship, of course, they leave an electrical trail. We track it and close off access routes behind them and eventually we pin them down in close quarters. Then it's not hard to put them back in their bottles."

"And if they've jacked into some member of the crew?"

"That makes it even easier to find them."

Boldly I said, "Was there ever a case where a free matrix jacked into a member of the crew and managed to keep itself hidden?"

"Never," said a new voice. It belonged to Roacher, who had just entered the dining hall. He stood at the far end of the long table, staring at me. His strange luminescent eyes, harsh and probing, came to rest on mine. "No matter how clever the matrix may be, sooner or later the host will find some way to call for help."

"And if the host doesn't choose to call for help?" I asked.

Roacher studied me with great care.

Had I been too bold? Had I given away too much?

"But that would be a violation of regulations!" he said, in a tone of mock astonishment. "That would be a criminal act!"

11.

She asked me to take her starwalking, to show her the full view of the Great Open.

It was the third day of her concealment within me. Life aboard the *Sword of Orion* had returned to routine, or, to be more accurate, it had settled into a new routine in which the presence on board of an undetected and apparently undetectable free matrix was a constant element.

As Vox had suggested, there were some who quickly came to believe that the missing matrix must have slipped off into space, since the watchful ship-intelligences could find no trace of it. But there were others who kept looking over their shoulders, figuratively or literally, as if expecting the fugitive to attempt to thrust herself without warning into the spinal jacks that gave access to their nervous systems. They behaved exactly as if the ship were haunted. To placate those uneasy ones, I ordered round-the-clock circuit sweeps that would report every vagrant pulse and random surge. Each such anomalous electrical event was duly investigated, and, of course, none of these investigations led to anything significant. Now that Vox resided in my brain instead of the ship's wiring, she was beyond any such mode of discovery.

Whether anyone suspected the truth was something I had no way of knowing. Perhaps Roacher did; but he made no move to denounce me, nor did he so much as raise the issue of the missing matrix with me at all after that time in the dining hall. He might know nothing whatever; he might know everything, and not care; he might simply be keeping his own counsel for the moment. I had no way of telling.

I was growing accustomed to my double life, and to my daily duplicity. Vox had quickly come to seem as much a part of me as my arm, or my leg. When she was silent—and often I heard nothing from her for hours at a time—I was no more aware of her than I would be, in any special way, of my arm or my leg; but nevertheless I knew somehow that she was there. The boundaries between her mind and mine were eroding steadily. She was learning how to infiltrate me. At times it seemed to me that what we were were joint tenants of the same dwelling, rather than I the permanent occupant and she a guest. I came to perceive my own mind as something not notably different from hers, a mere web of electrical force which for the moment was housed in the soft moist globe that was the brain of the captain of the *Sword of Orion*. Either of us, so it seemed, might come and go within that soft moist globe as we pleased, flitting casually in or out after the wraithlike fashion of matrixes.

At other times it was not at all like that: I gave no thought to her presence and went about my tasks as if nothing had changed for me. Then it would come as a surprise when Vox announced herself to me with some sudden comment, some quick question. I had to learn to guard myself against letting my reaction show, if it happened when I was with other members of the crew. Though no one around us could hear anything when she spoke to me, or I to her, I knew it would be the end for our masquerade if anyone caught me in some unguarded moment of conversation with an unseen companion.

How far she had penetrated my mind began to become apparent to me when she asked to go on a starwalk.

"You know about that?" I said, startled, for starwalking is the private pleasure of the spacegoing and I had not known of it myself before I was taken into the Service.

Vox seemed amazed by my amazement. She indicated casually that the details of starwalking were common knowledge everywhere.

But something rang false in her tone. Were the landcrawling folk really so familiar with our special pastime? Or had she picked what she knew of it out of the hitherto private reaches of my consciousness?

I chose not to ask. But I was uneasy about taking her with me into the Great Open, much as I was beginning to yearn for it myself. She was not one of us. She was planetary; she had not passed through the training of the Service.

I told her that.

"Take me anyway," she said. "It's the only chance I'll ever have."

"But the training—"

"I don't need it. Not if you've had it."

"What if that's not enough?"

"It will be," she said. "I know it will, Adam. There's nothing to be afraid of. You've had the training, haven't you? And I am you."

12.

Together we rode the transit track out of the Eye and down to Drive Deck, where the soul of the ship lies lost in throbbing dreams of the far galaxies as it pulls us ever onward across the unending night.

We passed through zones of utter darkness and zones of cascading light, through places where wheeling helixes of silvery radiance burst like auroras from the air, through passages so crazed in their geometry that they reawakened the terrors of the womb in anyone who traversed them. A starship is the mother of mysteries. Vox crouched, frozen with awe, within that portion of our brain that was hers. I felt the surges of her awe, one after another, as we went downward.

"Are you really sure you want to do this?" I asked.

"Yes!" she cried fiercely. "Keep going!"

"There's the possibility that you'll be detected," I told her.

"There's the possibility that I won't be," she said.

We continued to descend. Now we were in the realm of the three cyborg push-cells, Gabriel, Banquo, and Fleece. Those were three members of the crew whom we would never see at the table in the dining hall, for they dwelled here in the walls of Drive Deck, permanently jacked in, perpetually pumping their energies into the ship's great maw. I have already told you of our saying in the Service, that when you enter you give up the body and you get your soul. For most of us that is only a

figure of speech: what we give up, when we say farewell forever to planetskin and take up our new lives in starships, is not the body itself but
the body's trivial needs, the sweaty things so dear to shore people. But
some of us are more literal in their renunciations. The flesh is a meaningless hindrance to them; they shed it entirely, knowing that they can
experience starship life just as fully without it. They allow themselves
to be transformed into extensions of the stardrive. From them comes
the raw energy out of which is made the power that carries us hurtling through heaven. Their work is unending; their reward is a sort of
immortality. It is not a choice I could make, nor, I think, you: but for
them it is bliss. There can be no doubt about that.

"Another starwalk so soon, Captain?" Banquo asked. For I had been
here on the second day of the voyage, losing no time in availing myself
of the great privilege of the Service.

"Is there any harm in it?"

"No, no harm," said Banquo. "Just isn't usual, is all."

"That's all right," I said. "That's not important to me."

Banquo is a gleaming metallic ovoid, twice the size of a human
head, jacked into a slot in the wall. Within the ovoid is the matrix of
what had once been Banquo, long ago on a world called Sunrise where
night is unknown. Sunrise's golden dawns and shining days had not
been good enough for Banquo, apparently. What Banquo had wanted
was to be a gleaming metallic ovoid, hanging on the wall of Drive Deck
aboard the *Sword of Orion*.

Any of the three cyborgs could set up a starwalk. But Banquo was
the one who had done it for me that other time and it seemed best
to return to him. He was the most congenial of the three. He struck
me as amiable and easy. Gabriel, on my first visit, had seemed austere, remote, incomprehensible. He is an early model who had lived the
equivalent of three human lifetimes as a cyborg aboard starships and
there was not much about him that was human any more. Fleece, much
younger, quick-minded and quirky, I mistrusted: in her weird edgy way
she might just somehow be able to detect the hidden other who would
be going along with me for the ride.

You must realize that when we starwalk we do not literally leave
the ship, though that is how it seems to us. If we left the ship even
for a moment we would be swept away and lost forever in the abyss
of heaven. Going outside a starship of heaven is not like stepping outside an ordinary planet-launched shoreship that moves through normal

space. But even if it were possible, there would be no point in leaving the ship. There is nothing to see out there. A starship moves through utter empty darkness.

But though there may be nothing to see, that does not mean that there is nothing out there. The entire universe is out there. If we could see it while we are traveling across the special space that is heaven we would find it flattened and curved, so that we had the illusion of viewing everything at once, all the far-flung galaxies back to the beginning of time. This is the Great Open, the totality of the continuum. Our external screens show it to us in simulated form, because we need occasional assurance that it is there.

A starship rides along the mighty lines of force which cross that immense void like the lines of the compass rose on an ancient mariner's map. When we starwalk, we ride those same lines, and we are held by them, sealed fast to the ship that is carrying us onward through heaven. We seem to step forth into space; we seem to look down on the ship, on the stars, on all the worlds of heaven. For the moment we become little starships flying along beside the great one that is our mother. It is magic; it is illusion; but it is magic that so closely approaches what we perceive as reality that there is no way to measure the difference, which means that in effect there is no difference.

"Ready?" I asked Vox.

"Absolutely."

Still I hesitated.

"Are you *sure*?"

"Go on," she said impatiently. "Do it!"

I put the jack to my spine myself. Banquo did the matching of impedances. If he were going to discover the passenger I carried, this would be the moment. But he showed no sign that anything was amiss. He queried me; I gave him the signal to proceed; there was a moment of sharp warmth at the back of my neck as my neural matrix, and Vox's traveling with it, rushed out through Banquo and hurtled downward toward its merger with the soul of the ship.

We were seized and drawn in and engulfed by the vast force that is the ship. As the coils of the engine caught us we were spun around and around, hurled from vector to vector, mercilessly stretched, distended by an unimaginable flux. And then there was a brightness all about us, a brightness that cried out in heaven with a mighty clamor. We were outside the ship. We were starwalking.

"Oh," she said. A little soft cry, a muted gasp of wonder.

The blazing mantle of the ship lay upon the darkness of heaven like a white shadow. That great cone of cold fiery light reached far out in front of us, arching awesomely toward heaven's vault, and behind us it extended beyond the limits of our sight. The slender tapering outline of the ship was clearly visible within it, the needle and its Eye, all ten kilometers of it easily apparent to us in a single glance.

And there were the stars. And there were the worlds of heaven.

The effect of the stardrive is to collapse the dimensions, each one in upon the other. Thus inordinate spaces are diminished and the galaxy may be spanned by human voyagers. There is no logic, no linearity of sequence, to heaven as it appears to our eyes. Wherever we look we see the universe bent back upon itself, revealing its entirety in an infinite series of infinite segments of itself. Any sector of stars contains all stars. Any demarcation of time encompasses all of time past and time to come. What we behold is altogether beyond our understanding, which is exactly as it should be; for what we are given, when we look through the Eye of the ship at the naked heavens, is a god's-eye view of the universe. And we are not gods.

"What are we seeing?" Vox murmured within me.

I tried to tell her. I showed her how to define her relative position so there would be an up and a down for her, a backward, a forward, a flow of time and event from beginning to end. I pointed out the arbitrary coordinate axes by which we locate ourselves in this fundamentally incomprehensible arena. I found known stars for her, and known worlds, and showed them to her.

She understood nothing. She was entirely lost.

I told her that there was no shame in that.

I told her that I had been just as bewildered, when I was undergoing my training in the simulator. That everyone was; and that no one, not even if he spent a thousand years aboard the starships that plied the routes of heaven, could ever come to anything more than a set of crude equivalents and approximations of understanding what starwalking shows us. Attaining actual understanding itself is beyond the best of us.

I could feel her struggling to encompass the impact of all that rose and wheeled and soared before us. Her mind was agile, though still only half-formed, and I sensed her working out her own system of explanations and assumptions, her analogies, her equivalencies. I gave her no more help. It was best for her to do these things by herself; and in any case I had no more help to give.

I had my own astonishment and bewilderment to deal with, on this my second starwalk in heaven.

Once more I looked down upon the myriad worlds turning in their orbits. I could see them easily, the little bright globes rotating in the huge night of the Great Open: red worlds, blue worlds, green ones, some turning their full faces to me, some showing mere slivers of a crescent. How they cleaved to their appointed tracks! How they clung to their parent stars!

I remembered that other time, only a few virtual days before, when I had felt such compassion for them, such sorrow. Knowing that they were condemned forever to follow the same path about the same star, a hopeless bondage, a meaningless retracing of a perpetual route. In their own eyes they might be footloose wanderers, but to me they had seemed the most pitiful of slaves. And so I had grieved for the worlds of heaven; but now, to my surprise, I felt no pity, only a kind of love. There was no reason to be sad for them. They were what they were, and there was a supreme rightness in those fixed orbits and their obedient movements along them. They were content with being what they were. If they were loosed even a moment from that bondage, such chaos would arise in the universe as could never be contained. Those circling worlds are the foundations upon which all else is built; they know that and they take pride in it; they are loyal to their tasks and we must honor them for their devotion to their duty. And with honor comes love.

This must be Vox speaking within me, I told myself.

I had never thought such thoughts. Love the planets in their orbits? What kind of notion was that? Perhaps no stranger than my earlier notion of pitying them because they weren't starships; but that thought had arisen from the spontaneous depths of my own spirit and it had seemed to make a kind of sense to me. Now it had given way to a wholly other view.

I loved the worlds that moved before me and yet did not move, in the great night of heaven.

I loved the strange fugitive girl within me who beheld those worlds and loved them for their immobility.

I felt her seize me now, taking me impatiently onward, outward, into the depths of heaven. She understood now; she knew how it was done. And she was far more daring than ever I would have allowed me to be. Together we walked the stars. Not only walked but plunged and swooped and soared, traveling among them like gods. Their hot breath singed us. Their throbbing brightness thundered at us. Their serene movements boomed a mighty music at us. On and on we went, hand in hand, Vox leading, I letting her draw me, deeper and deeper into the shining abyss that was the universe. Until at last we halted, floating in mid-cosmos, the ship nowhere to be seen, only the two of us surrounded by a shield of suns.

In that moment a sweeping ecstasy filled my soul. I felt all eternity within my grasp. No, that puts it the wrong way around and makes it seem that I was seized by delusions of imperial grandeur, which was not at all the case. What I felt was myself within the grasp of all eternity, enfolded in the loving embrace of a complete and perfect cosmos in which nothing was out of place, or ever could be.

It is this that we go starwalking to attain. This sense of belonging, this sense of being contained in the divine perfection of the universe.

When it comes, there is no telling what effect it will have; but inner change is what it usually brings. I had come away from my first starwalk unaware of any transformation; but within three days I had impulsively opened myself to a wandering phantom, violating not only regulations but the nature of my own character as I understood it. I have always, as I think I have said, been an intensely private man. Even though I had given Vox refuge, I had been relieved and grateful that her mind and mine had remained separate entities within our shared brain.

Now I did what I could to break down whatever boundary remained between us.

I hadn't let her know anything, so far, of my life before going to heaven. I had met her occasional questions with coy evasions, with half-truths, with blunt refusals. It was the way I had always been with everyone, a habit of secrecy, an unwillingness to reveal myself. I had been even more secretive, perhaps, with Vox than with all the others, because of the very closeness of her mind to mine. As though I feared that by giving her any interior knowledge of me I was opening the way for her to take me over entirely, to absorb me into her own vigorous, undisciplined soul.

But now I offered my past to her in a joyous rush. We began to make our way slowly backward from that apocalyptic place at the center of everything; and as we hovered on the breast of the Great Open, drifting between the darkness and the brilliance of the light that the ship created, I told her everything about myself that I had been holding back.

I suppose they were mere trivial things, though to me they were all so highly charged with meaning. I told her the name of my home planet. I let her see it, the sea the color of lead, the sky the color of smoke. I showed her the sparse and scrubby gray headlands behind our house, where I would go running for hours by myself, a tall slender boy pounding tirelessly across the crackling sands as though demons were pursuing him.

I showed her everything: the somber child, the troubled youth, the wary, overcautious young man. The playmates who remained forever strangers, the friends whose voices were drowned in hollow babbling echoes, the lovers whose love seemed without substance or meaning. I told her of my feeling that I was the only one alive in the world, that everyone about me was some sort of artificial being full of gears and wires. Or that the world was only a flat colorless dream in which I somehow had become trapped, but from which I would eventually awaken into the true world of light and color and richness of texture. Or that I might not be human at all, but had been abandoned in the human galaxy by creatures of another form entirely, who would return for me some day far in the future.

I was lighthearted as I told her these things, and she received them lightly. She knew them for what they were—not symptoms of madness, but only the bleak fantasies of a lonely child, seeking to make sense out of an incomprehensible universe in which he felt himself to be a stranger and afraid.

"But you escaped," she said. "You found a place where you belonged!"

"Yes," I said. "I escaped."

And I told her of the day when I had seen a sudden light in the sky. My first thought then had been that my true parents had come back for me; my second, that it was some comet passing by. That light was a starship of heaven that had come to worldward in our system. And as I looked upward through the darkness on that day long ago, straining to catch a glimpse of the shoreships that were going up to it bearing cargo and passengers to be taken from our world to some unknowable place at the other end of the galaxy, I realized that that starship was my true home. I realized that the Service was my destiny.

And so it came to pass, I said, that I left my world behind, and my name, and my life, such as it had been, to enter the company of those who sail between the stars. I let her know that this was my first voyage, explaining that it is the peculiar custom of the Service to test all new officers by placing them in command at once. She asked me if I had found happiness here; and I said, quickly, Yes, I had, and then I said a moment later, Not yet, not yet, but I see at least the possibility of it.

She was quiet for a time. We watched the worlds turning and the stars like blazing spikes of color racing toward their far-off destinations, and the fiery white light of the ship itself streaming in the firmament as if it were the blood of some alien god. The thought came to me of all that I was risking by hiding her like this within me. I brushed it aside. This was neither the place nor the moment for doubt or fear or misgiving.

Then she said, "I'm glad you told me all that, Adam."

"Yes. I am too."

"I could feel it from the start, what sort of person you were. But I needed to hear it in your own words, your own thoughts. It's just like I've been saying. You and I, we're two of a kind. Square pegs in a world of round holes. You ran away to the Service and I ran away to a new life in somebody else's body."

I realized that Vox wasn't speaking of my body, but of the new one that waited for her on Cul-de-Sac.

And I realized too that there was one thing about herself that she had never shared with me, which was the nature of the flaw in her old body that had caused her to discard it. If I knew her more fully, I thought, I could love her more deeply: imperfections and all, which is the way of love. But she had shied away from telling me that, and I had never pressed her on it. Now, out here under the cool gleam of heaven, surely we had moved into a place of total trust, of complete union of soul.

I said, "Let me see you, Vox."

"See me? How could you—"

"Give me an image of yourself. You're too abstract for me this way. *Vox.* A voice. Only a voice. You talk to me, you live within me, and I still don't have the slightest idea what you look like."

"That's how I want it to be."

"Won't you show me how you look?"

"I won't look like anything. I'm a matrix. I'm nothing but electricity."

"I understand that. I mean how you looked *before*. Your old self, the one you left behind on Kansas Four."

She made no reply.

381

I thought she was hesitating, deciding; but some time went by, and still I heard nothing from her. What came from her was silence, only silence, a silence that had crashed down between us like a steel curtain.

"Vox?"

Nothing.

Where was she hiding? What had I done?

"What's the matter? Is it the thing I asked you?"

No answer.

"It's all right, Vox. Forget about it. It isn't important at all. You don't have to show me anything you don't want to show me."

Nothing. Silence.

"Vox? Vox?"

The worlds and stars wheeled in chaos before me. The light of the ship roared up and down the spectrum from end to end. In growing panic I sought for her and found no trace of her presence within me. Nothing. Nothing.

"Are you all right?" came another voice. Banquo, from inside the ship. "I'm getting some pretty wild signals. You'd better come in. You've been out there long enough as it is."

Vox was gone. I had crossed some uncrossable boundary and I had frightened her away.

Numbly I gave Banquo the signal, and he brought me back inside.

13.

Alone, I made my way upward level by level through the darkness and mystery of the ship, toward the Eye. The crash of silence went on and on, like the falling of some colossal wave on an endless shore. I missed Vox terribly. I had never known such complete solitude as I felt now. I had not realized how accustomed I had become to her being there, nor what impact her leaving would have on me. In just those few days of giving her sanctuary, it had somehow come to seem to me that to house two souls within one brain was the normal condition of mankind, and that to be alone in one's skull as I was now was a shameful thing.

As I neared the place where Crew Deck narrows into the curve of the Eye a slender figure stepped without warning from the shadows.

"Captain."

My mind was full of the loss of Vox and he caught me unawares. I jumped back, badly startled.

"For the love of God, man!"

"It's just me. Bulgar. Don't be so scared, Captain. It's only Bulgar."

"Let me be," I said, and brusquely beckoned him away.

"No. Wait, Captain. Please, wait."

He clutched at my arm, holding me as I tried to go. I halted and turned toward him, trembling with anger and surprise.

Bulgar, Roacher's jackmate, was a gentle, soft-voiced little man, wide-mouthed, olive-skinned, with huge sad eyes. He and Roacher had sailed the skies of Heaven together since before I was born. They complemented each other. Where Roacher was small and hard, like fruit that has been left to dry in the sun for a hundred years, his jackmate Bulgar was small and tender, with a plump, succulent look about him. Together they seemed complete, an unassailable whole: I could readily imagine them lying together in their bunk, each jacked to the other, one person in two bodies, linked more intimately even than Vox and I had been.

With an effort I recovered my poise. Tightly I said, "What is it, Bulgar?"

"Can we talk a minute, Captain?"

"We are talking. What do you want with me?"

"That loose matrix, sir."

My reaction must have been stronger than he was expecting. His eyes went wide and he took a step or two back from me.

Moistening his lips, he said, "We were wondering, Captain—wondering how the search is going—whether you had any idea where the matrix might be—"

I said stiffly, "Who's *we*, Bulgar?"

"The men. Roacher. Me. Some of the others. Mainly Roacher, sir."

"Ah. So Roacher wants to know where the matrix is."

The little man moved closer. I saw him staring deep into me as though searching for Vox behind the mask of my carefully expressionless face. Did he know? Did they all? I wanted to cry out, *She's not there any more, she's gone, she left me, she ran off into space.* But apparently what was troubling Roacher and his shipmates was something other than the possibility that Vox had taken refuge with me.

Bulgar's tone was soft, insinuating, concerned. "Roacher's very worried, Captain. He's been on ships with loose matrixes before. He knows how much trouble they can be. He's really worried, Captain. I have to tell you that. I've never seen him so worried."

"What does he think the matrix will do to him?"

"He's afraid of being taken over," Bulgar said.

"Taken over?"

"The matrix coming into his head through his jack. Mixing itself up with his brain. It's been known to happen, Captain."

"And why should it happen to Roacher, out of all the men on this ship? Why not you? Why not Pedregal? Or Rio de Rio? Or one of the passengers again?" I took a deep breath. "Why not me, for that matter?"

"He just wants to know, sir, what's the situation with the matrix now. Whether you've discovered anything about where it is. Whether you've been able to trap it."

There was something strange in Bulgar's eyes. I began to think I was being tested again. This assertion of Roacher's alleged terror of being infiltrated and possessed by the wandering matrix might simply be a roundabout way of finding out whether that had already happened to me.

"Tell him it's gone," I said.

"Gone, sir?"

"Gone. Vanished. It isn't anywhere on the ship any more. Tell him that, Bulgar. He can forget about her slithering down his precious jackhole."

"*Her?*"

"Female matrix, yes. But that doesn't matter now. She's gone. You can tell him that. Escaped. Flew off into heaven. The emergency's over." I glowered at him. I yearned to be rid of him, to go off by myself to nurse my new grief. "Shouldn't you be getting back to your post, Bulgar?"

Did he believe me? Or did he think that I had slapped together some transparent lie to cover my complicity in the continued absence of the matrix? I had no way of knowing. Bulgar gave me a little obsequious bow and started to back away.

"Sir," he said. "Thank you, sir. I'll tell him, sir."

He retreated into the shadows. I continued uplevel.

I passed Katkat on my way, and, a little while afterward, Raebuck. They looked at me without speaking. There was something reproachful but almost loving about Katkat's expression, but Raebuck's icy, baleful stare brought me close to flinching. In their different ways they were saying, *Guilty, guilty, guilty.* But of what?

Before, I had imagined that everyone whom I encountered aboard ship was able to tell at a single glance that I was harboring the fugitive, and was simply waiting for me to reveal myself with some foolish slip.

Now everything was reversed. They looked at me and I told myself that they were thinking, *He's all alone by himself in there, he doesn't have anyone else at all*, and I shrank away, shamed by my solitude. I knew that this was the edge of madness. I was overwrought, overtired; perhaps it had been a mistake to go starwalking a second time so soon after my first. I needed to rest. I needed to hide.

I began to wish that there were someone aboard the *Sword of Orion* with whom I could discuss these things. But who, though? Roacher? 612 Jason? I was altogether isolated here. The only one I could speak to on this ship was Vox. And she was gone.

In the safety of my cabin I jacked myself into the mediq rack and gave myself a ten-minute purge. That helped. The phantom fears and intricate uncertainties that had taken possession of me began to ebb.

I keyed up the log and ran through the list of my captainly duties, such as they were, for the rest of the day. We were approaching a spinaround point, one of those nodes of force positioned equidistantly across heaven which a starship in transit must seize and use in order to propel itself onward through the next sector of the universe. Spinaround acquisition is performed automatically but at least in theory the responsibility for carrying it out successfully falls to the captain: I would give the commands, I would oversee the process from initiation through completion.

But there was still time for that.

I accessed 49 Henry Henry, who was the intelligence on duty, and asked for an update on the matrix situation.

"No change, sir," the intelligence reported at once.

"What does that mean?"

"Trace efforts continue as requested, sir. But we have not detected the location of the missing matrix."

"No clues? Not even a hint?"

"No data at all, sir. There's essentially no way to isolate the minute electromagnetic pulse of a free matrix from the background noise of the ship's entire electrical system."

I believed it. 612 Jason Jason had told me that in nearly the same words.

I said, "I have reason to think that the matrix is no longer on the ship, 49 Henry Henry."

"Do you, sir?" said 49 Henry Henry in its usual aloof, half-mocking way.

"I do, yes. After a careful study of the situation, it's my opinion that the matrix exited the ship earlier this day and will not be heard from again."

"Shall I record that as an official position, sir?"

"Record it," I said.

"Done, sir."

"And therefore, 49 Henry Henry, you can cancel search mode immediately and close the file. We'll enter a debit for one matrix and the Service bookkeepers can work it out later."

"Very good, sir."

"Decouple," I ordered the intelligence.

49 Henry Henry went away. I sat quietly amid the splendors of my cabin, thinking back over my starwalk and reliving that sense of harmony, of love, of oneness with the worlds of heaven, that had come over me while Vox and I drifted on the bosom of the Great Open. And feeling once again the keen slicing sense of loss that I had felt since Vox's departure from me. In a little while I would have to rise and go to the command center and put myself through the motions of overseeing spinaround acquisition; but for the moment I remained where I was, motionless, silent, peering deep into the heart of my solitude.

"I'm not gone," said an unexpected quiet voice.

It came like a punch beneath the heart. It was a moment before I could speak.

"Vox?" I said at last. "Where are you, Vox?"

"Right here."

"Where?" I asked.

"Inside. I never went away."

"You never—"

"You upset me. I just had to hide for a while."

"You knew I was trying to find you?"

"Yes."

Color came to my cheeks. Anger roared like a stream in spate through my veins. I felt myself blazing.

"You knew how I felt, when you—when it seemed that you weren't there any more."

"Yes," she said, even more quietly, after a time.

I forced myself to grow calm. I told myself that she owed me nothing, except perhaps gratitude for sheltering her, and that whatever pain she had caused me by going silent was none of her affair. I reminded myself also that she was a child, unruly and turbulent and undisciplined.

After a bit I said, "I missed you. I missed you more than I want to say."

"I'm sorry," she said, sounding repentant, but not very. "I had to go away for a time. You upset me, Adam."

"By asking you to show me how you used to look?"

"Yes."

"I don't understand why that upset you so much."

"You don't have to," Vox said. "I don't mind now. You can see me, if you like. Do you still want to? Here. This is me. This is what I used to be. If it disgusts you don't blame me. Okay? Okay, Adam? Here. Have a look. Here I am."

14.

There was a wrenching within me, a twisting, a painful yanking sensation, as of some heavy barrier forcibly being pulled aside. And then the glorious radiant scarlet sky of Kansas Four blossomed on the screen of my mind.

She didn't simply show it to me. She took me there. I felt the soft moist wind on my face, I breathed the sweet, faintly pungent air, I heard the sly rustling of glossy leathery fronds that dangled from bright yellow trees. Beneath my bare feet the black soil was warm and spongy.

I was Leeleaine, who liked to call herself Vox. I was seventeen years old and swept by forces and compulsions as powerful as hurricanes.

I was her from within and also I saw her from outside.

My hair was long and thick and dark, tumbling down past my shoulders in an avalanche of untended curls and loops and snags. My hips were broad, my breasts were full and heavy: I could feel the pull of them, the pain of them. It was almost as if they were stiff with milk, though they were not. My face was tense, alert, sullen, aglow with angry intelligence. It was not an unappealing face. Vox was not an unappealing girl.

From her earlier reluctance to show herself to me I had expected her to be ugly, or perhaps deformed in some way, dragging herself about in a coarse, heavy, burdensome husk of flesh that was a constant reproach to her. She had spoken of her life on Kansas Four as being so dreary, so sad, so miserable, that she saw no hope in staying there. And had given up her body to be turned into mere electricity, on the promise that she could have a new body—any body—when she reached Cul-de-Sac. I *hated my body*, she had told me. *I couldn't wait to be rid of it.* She had refused even to give me a glimpse of it, retreating instead for hours into a desperate silence so total that I thought she had fled.

All that was a mystery to me now. The Leeleaine that I saw, that I was, was a fine sturdy-looking girl. Not beautiful, no, too strong and strapping for that, I suppose, but far from ugly: her eyes were warm and intelligent, her lips full, her nose finely modeled. And it was a healthy body, too, robust, vital. Of course she had no deformities; and why had I thought she had, when it would have been a simple matter of retrogenetic surgery to amend any bothersome defect? No, there was nothing wrong with the body that Vox had abandoned and for which she professed such loathing, for which she felt such shame.

Then I realized that I was seeing her from outside. I was seeing her as if by relay, filtering and interpreting the information she was offering me by passing it through the mind of an objective observer: myself. Who understood nothing, really, of what it was like to be anyone but himself.

Somehow—it was one of those automatic, unconscious adjustments—I altered the focus of my perceptions. All old frames of reference fell away and I let myself lose any sense of the separateness of our identities.

I was her. Fully, unconditionally, inextricably.

And I understood.

Figures flitted about her, shadowy, baffling, maddening. Brothers, sisters, parents, friends: they were all strangers to her. Everyone on Kansas Four was a stranger to her. And always would be.

She hated her body not because it was weak or unsightly but because it was her prison. She was enclosed within it as though within narrow stone walls. It hung about her, a cage of flesh, holding her down, pinning her to this lovely world called Kansas Four where she knew only pain and isolation and estrangement. Her body—her perfectly acceptable, healthy body—had become hateful to her because it was the emblem and symbol of her soul's imprisonment. Wild and incurably restless by temperament, she had failed to find a way to live within the smothering predictability of Kansas Four, a planet where she would never be anything but an internal outlaw. The only way she could leave Kansas Four was to surrender the body that tied her to it; and so she had turned against it with fury and loathing, rejecting it, abandoning it, despising it, detesting it. No one could ever understand that who beheld her from the outside.

388

But I understood.

I understood much more than that, in that one flashing moment of communion that she and I had. I came to see what she meant when she said that I was her twin, her double, her other self. Of course we were wholly different, I the sober, staid, plodding, diligent man, and she the reckless, volatile, impulsive, tempestuous girl. But beneath all that we were the same: misfits, outsiders, troubled wanderers through worlds we had never made. We had found vastly differing ways to cope with our pain. Yet we were one and the same, two halves of a single entity.

We will remain together always now, I told myself.

And in that moment our communion broke. She broke it—it must have been she, fearful of letting this new intimacy grow too deep—and I found myself apart from her once again, still playing host to her in my brain but separated from her by the boundaries of my own individuality, my own selfhood. I felt her nearby, within me, a warm but discrete presence. Still within me, yes. But separate again.

15.

There was shipwork to do. For days, now, Vox's invasion of me had been a startling distraction. But I dared not let myself forget that we were in the midst of a traversal of heaven. The lives of us all, and of our passengers, depended on the proper execution of our duties: even mine. And worlds awaited the bounty that we bore. My task of the moment was to oversee spinaround acquisition.

I told Vox to leave me temporarily while I went through the routines of acquisition. I would be jacked to other crewmen for a time; they might very well be able to detect her within me; there was no telling what might happen. But she refused. "No," she said. "I won't leave you. I don't want to go out there. But I'll hide, deep down, the way I did when I was upset with you."

"Vox—"I began.

"No. Please. I don't want to talk about it."

There was no time to argue the point. I could feel the depth and intensity of her stubborn determination.

"Hide, then," I said. "If that's what you want to do."

I made my way down out of the Eye to Engine Deck.

The rest of the acquisition team was already assembled in the Great Navigation Hall: Fresco, Raebuck, Roacher. Raebuck's role was to see to it that communications channels were kept open, Fresco's to set up the navigation coordinates, and Roacher, as power engineer, would monitor fluctuations in drain and input-output cycling. My function was to give the cues at each stage of acquisition. In truth I was pretty much redundant, since Raebuck and Fresco and Roacher had been doing this sort of thing a dozen times a voyage for scores of voyages and they had little need of my guidance. The deeper truth was that they were redundant too, for 49 Henry Henry would oversee us all, and the intelligence was quite capable of setting up the entire process without any human help. Nevertheless there were formalities to observe, and not inane ones. Intelligences are far superior to humans in mental capacity, interfacing capability, and reaction time, but even so they are nothing but servants, and artificial servants at that, lacking in any real awareness of human fragility or human ethical complexity. They must only be used as tools, not decision-makers. A society which delegates responsibilities of life and death to its servants will eventually find the servants' hands at its throat. As for me, novice that I was, my role was valid as well: the focal point of the enterprise, the prime initiator, the conductor and observer of the process. Perhaps anyone could perform those functions, but the fact remained that *someone* had to, and by tradition that someone was the captain. Call it a ritual, call it a highly stylized dance, if you will. But there is no getting away from the human need for ritual and stylization. Such aspects of a process may not seem essential, but they are valuable and significant, and ultimately they can be seen to be essential as well.

"Shall we begin?" Fresco asked.

We jacked up, Roacher directly into the ship, Raebuck into Roacher, Fresco to me, me into the ship.

"Simulation," I said.

Raebuck keyed in the first code and the vast echoing space that was the Great Navigation Hall came alive with pulsing light: a representation of heaven all about us, the lines of force, the spinaround nodes, the stars, the planets. We moved unhinderedly in free fall, drifting as casually as angels. We could easily have believed we were starwalking.

The simulacrum of the ship was a bright arrow of fierce light just below us and to the left. Ahead, throbbing like a nest of twining angry serpents, was the globe that represented the Lasciate Ogni Speranza spinaround point, tightly-wound dull gray cables shot through with strands of fierce scarlet.

"Enter approach mode," I said. "Activate receptors. Begin threshold equalization. Begin momentum comparison. Prepare for acceleration uptick. Check angular velocity. Begin spin consolidation. Enter displacement select. Extend mast. Prepare for acquisition receptivity."

At each command the proper man touched a control key or pressed a directive panel or simply sent an impulse shooting through the jack hookup by which he was connected, directly or indirectly, to the mind of the ship. Out of courtesy to me, they waited until the commands were given, but the speed with which they obeyed told me that their minds were already in motion even as I spoke.

"It's really exciting, isn't it?" Vox said suddenly.

"For God's sake, Vox! What are you trying to do?"

For all I knew, the others had heard her outburst as clearly as though it had come across a loudspeaker.

"I mean," she went on, "I never imagined it was anything like this. I can feel the whole—"

I shot her a sharp, anguished order to keep quiet. Her surfacing like this, after my warning to her, was a lunatic act. In the silence that followed I felt a kind of inner reverberation, a sulky twanging of displeasure coming from her. But I had no time to worry about Vox's moods now.

Arcing patterns of displacement power went ricocheting through the Great Navigation Hall as our mast came forth—not the underpinning for a set of sails, as it would be on a vessel that plied planetary seas, but rather a giant antenna to link us to the spinaround point ahead— and the ship and the spinaround point reached toward one another like grappling many-armed wrestlers. Hot streaks of crimson and emerald and gold and amethyst speared the air, vaulting and rebounding. The spinaround point, activated now and trembling between energy states, was enfolding us in its million tentacles, capturing us, making ready to whirl on its axis and hurl us swiftly onward toward the next way-station in our journey across heaven.

"Acquisition," Raebuck announced.

"Proceed to capture acceptance," I said.

"Acceptance," said Raebuck.

"Directional mode," I said. "Dimensional grid eleven."

"Dimensional grid eleven," Fresco repeated.

The whole hall seemed on fire now.

"Wonderful," Vox murmured. "So beautiful—"

"*Vox!*"

"Request spin authorization," said Fresco.

"Spin authorization granted," I said. "Grid eleven."

"Grid eleven," Fresco said again. "Spin achieved."

A tremor went rippling through me—and through Fresco, through Raebuck, through Roacher. It was the ship, in the persona of 49 Henry Henry, completing the acquisition process. We had been captured by Lasciate Ogni Speranza, we had undergone velocity absorption and redirection, we had had new spin imparted to us, and we had been sent soaring off through heaven toward our upcoming port of call. I heard Vox sobbing within me, not a sob of despair but one of ecstasy, of fulfillment.

We all unjacked. Raebuck, that dour man, managed a little smile as he turned to me.

"Nicely done, Captain," he said.

"Yes," said Fresco. "Very nice. You're a quick learner."

I saw Roacher studying me with those little shining eyes of his. Go on, you bastard, I thought. You give me a compliment too now, if you know how.

But all he did was stare. I shrugged and turned away. What Roacher thought or said made little difference to me, I told myself.

As we left the Great Navigation Hall in our separate directions Fresco fell in alongside me. Without a word we trudged together toward the transit trackers that were waiting for us. Just as I was about to board mine he—or was it she?—said softly, "Captain?"

"What is it, Fresco?"

Fresco leaned close. Soft sly eyes, tricksy little smile; and yet I felt some warmth coming from the navigator.

"It's a very dangerous game, Captain."

"I don't know what you mean."

"Yes, you do," Fresco said. "No use pretending. We were jacked together in there. I felt things. I know."

There was nothing I could say, so I said nothing.

After a moment Fresco said, "I like you. I won't harm you. But Roacher knows too. I don't know if he knew before, but he certainly knows now. If I were you, I'd find that very troublesome, Captain. Just a word to the wise. All right?"

16.

Only a fool would have remained on such a course as I had been following. Vox saw the risks as well as I. There was no hiding anything from anyone any longer; if Roacher knew, then Bulgar knew, and soon it would be all over the ship. No question, either, but that 49 Henry Henry knew. In the intimacies of our navigation-hall contact, Vox must have been as apparent to them as a red scarf around my forehead.

There was no point in taking her to task for revealing her presence within me like that during acquisition. What was done was done. At first it had seemed impossible to understand why she had done such a thing; but then it became all too easy to comprehend. It was the same sort of unpredictable, unexamined, impulsive behavior that had led her to go barging into a suspended passenger's mind and cause his death. She was simply not one who paused to think before acting. That kind of behavior has always been bewildering to me. She was my opposite as well as my double. And yet had I not done a Vox-like thing myself, taking her into me, when she appealed to me for sanctuary, without stopping at all to consider the consequences?

"Where can I go?" she asked, desperate. "If I move around the ship freely again they'll track me and close me off. And then they'll eradicate me. They'll—"

"Easy," I said. "Don't panic. I'll hide you where they won't find you."

"Inside some passenger?"

"We can't try that again. There's no way to prepare the passenger for what's happening to him, and he'll panic. No. I'll put you in one of the annexes. Or maybe one of the virtualities."

"The what?"

"The additional cargo area. The subspace extensions that surround the ship."

She gasped. "Those aren't even real! I was in them, when I was traveling around the ship. Those are just clusters of probability waves!"

"You'll be safe there," I said.

"I'm afraid. It's bad enough that *I'm* not real any more. But to be stored in a place that isn't real either—"

"You're as real as I am. And the outstructures are just as real as the rest of the ship. It's a different quality of reality, that's all. Nothing bad will happen to you out there. You've told me yourself that you've already been in them, right? And got out again without any problems.

393

They won't be able to detect you there, Vox. But I tell you this, that if you stay in me, or anywhere else in the main part of the ship, they'll track you down and find you and eradicate you. And probably eradicate me right along with you."

"Do you mean that?" she said, sounding chastened.

"Come on. There isn't much time."

On the pretext of a routine inventory check—well within my table of responsibilities—I obtained access to one of the virtualities. It was the storehouse where the probability stabilizers were kept. No one was likely to search for her there. The chances of our encountering a zone of probability turbulence between here and Cul-de-Sac were minimal; and in the ordinary course of a voyage nobody cared to enter any of the virtualities.

I had lied to Vox, or at least committed a half-truth, by leading her to believe that all our outstructures are of an equal level of reality. Certainly the annexes are tangible, solid; they differ from the ship proper only in the spin of their dimensional polarity. They are invisible except when activated, and they involve us in no additional expenditure of fuel, but there is no uncertainty about their existence, which is why we entrust valuable cargo to them, and on some occasions even passengers.

The extensions are a level further removed from basic reality. They are skewed not only in dimensional polarity but in temporal contiguity: that is, we carry them with us under time displacement, generally ten to twenty virtual years in the past or future. The risks of this are extremely minor and the payoff in reduction of generating cost is great. Still, we are measurably more cautious about what sort of cargo we keep in them.

As for the virtualities—

Their name itself implies their uncertainty. They are purely probabilistic entities, existing most of the time in the stochastic void that surrounds the ship. In simpler words, whether they are actually there or not at any given time is a matter worth wagering on. We know how to access them at the time of greatest probability, and our techniques are quite reliable, which is why we can use them for overflow ladings when our cargo uptake is unusually heavy. But in general we prefer not to entrust anything very important to them, since a virtuality's range of access times can fluctuate in an extreme way, from a matter of microseconds to a matter of megayears, and that can make quick recall a chancy affair.

Knowing all this, I put Vox in a virtuality anyway.

I had to hide her. And I had to hide her in a place where no one would look. The risk that I'd be unable to call her up again because of virtuality fluctuation was a small one. The risk was much greater that she would be detected, and she and I both punished, if I let her remain in any area of the ship that had a higher order of probability.

"I want you to stay here until the coast is clear," I told her sternly. "No impulsive journeys around the ship, no excursions into adjoining outstructures, no little trips of any kind, regardless of how restless you get. Is that clear? I'll call you up from here as soon as I think it's safe."

"I'll miss you, Adam."

"The same here. But this is how it has to be."

"I know."

"If you're discovered, I'll deny I know anything about you. I mean that, Vox."

"I understand."

"You won't be stuck in here long. I promise you that."

"Will you visit me?"

"That wouldn't be wise," I said.

"But maybe you will anyway."

"Maybe. I don't know." I opened the access channel. The virtuality gaped before us. "Go on," I said. "In with you. In. Now. Go, Vox. Go."

I could feel her leaving me. It was almost like an amputation. The silence, the emptiness, that descended on me suddenly was ten times as deep as what I had felt when she had merely been hiding within me. She was gone, now. For the first time in days, I was truly alone.

I closed off the virtuality.

When I returned to the Eye, Roacher was waiting for me near the command bridge.

"You have a moment, Captain?"

"What is it, Roacher."

"The missing matrix. We have proof it's still on board ship."

"Proof?"

"You know what I mean. You felt it just like I did while we were doing acquisition. It said something. It spoke. It was right in there in the navigation hall with us, Captain."

I met his luminescent gaze levelly and said in an even voice, "I was giving my complete attention to what we were doing, Roacher.

Spinaround acquisition isn't second nature to me the way it is to you. I had no time to notice any matrixes floating around in there."

"You didn't?"

"No. Does that disappoint you?"

"That might mean that you're the one carrying the matrix," he said.

"How so?"

"If it's in you, down on a subneural level, you might not even be aware of it. But we would be. Raebuck, Fresco, me. We all detected something, Captain. If it wasn't in us it would have to be in you. We can't have a matrix riding around inside our captain, you know. No telling how that could distort his judgment. What dangers that might lead us into."

"I'm not carrying any matrixes, Roacher."

"Can we be sure of that?"

"Would you like to have a look?"

"A jackup, you mean? You and me?"

The notion disgusted me. But I had to make the offer.

"A—jackup, yes," I said. "Communion. You and me, Roacher. Right now. Come on, we'll measure the bandwidths and do the matching. Let's get this over with."

He contemplated me a long while, as if calculating the likelihood that I was bluffing. In the end he must have decided that I was too naive to be able to play the game out to so hazardous a turn. He knew that I wouldn't bluff, that I was confident he would find me untenanted or I never would have made the offer.

"No," he said finally. "We don't need to bother with that."

"Are you sure?"

"If you say you're clean—"

"But I might be carrying her and not even know it," I said. "You told me that yourself."

"Forget it. You'd know, if you had her in you."

"You'll never be certain of that unless you look. Let's jack up, Roacher."

He scowled. "Forget it," he said again, and turned away. "You must be clean, if you're this eager for jacking. But I'll tell you this, Captain. We're going to find her, wherever she's hiding. And when we do—"

He left the threat unfinished. I stood staring at his retreating form until he was lost to view.

17.

For a few days everything seemed back to normal. We sped onward toward Cul-de-Sac. I went through the round of my regular tasks, however meaningless they seemed to me. Most of them did. I had not yet achieved any sense that the *Sword of Orion* was under my command in anything but the most hypothetical way. Still, I did what I had to do.

No one spoke of the missing matrix within my hearing. On those rare occasions when I encountered some other member of the crew while I moved about the ship, I could tell by the hooded look of his eyes that I was still under suspicion. But they had no proof. The matrix was no longer in any way evident on board. The ship's intelligences were unable to find the slightest trace of its presence.

I was alone, and oh! it was a painful business for me.

I suppose that once you have tasted that kind of round-the-clock communion, that sort of perpetual jacking, you are never the same again. I don't know: there is no real information available on cases of possession by free matrix, only shipboard folklore, scarcely to be taken seriously. All I can judge by is my own misery now that Vox was actually gone. She was only a half-grown girl, a wild coltish thing, unstable, unformed; and yet, and yet, she had lived within me and we had come toward one another to construct the deepest sort of sharing, what was almost a kind of marriage. You could call it that.

After five or six days I knew I had to see her again. Whatever the risks.

I accessed the virtuality and sent a signal into it that I was coming in. There was no reply; and for one terrible moment I feared the worst, that in the mysterious workings of the virtuality she had somehow been engulfed and destroyed. But that was not the case. I stepped through the glowing pink-edged field of light that was the gateway to the virtuality, and instantly I felt her near me, clinging tight, trembling with joy.

She held back, though, from entering me. She wanted me to tell her it was safe. I beckoned her in; and then came that sharp warm moment I remembered so well, as she slipped down into my neural network and we became one.

"I can only stay a little while," I said. "It's still very chancy for me to be with you."

"Oh, Adam, Adam, it's been so awful for me in here—"

"I know. I can imagine."

"Are they still looking for me?"

"I think they're starting to put you out of their minds," I said. And we both laughed at the play on words that that phrase implied.

I didn't dare remain more than a few minutes. I had only wanted to touch souls with her briefly, to reassure myself that she was all right and to ease the pain of separation. But it was irregular for a captain to enter a virtuality at all. To stay in one for any length of time exposed me to real risk of detection.

But my next visit was longer, and the one after that longer still. We were like furtive lovers meeting in a dark forest for hasty delicious trysts. Hidden there in that not-quite-real outstructure of the ship we would join our two selves and whisper together with urgent intensity until I felt it was time for me to leave. She would always try to keep me longer; but her resistance to my departure was never great, nor did she ever suggest accompanying me back into the stable sector of the ship. She had come to understand that the only place we could meet was in the virtuality.

We were nearing the vicinity of Cul-de-Sac now. Soon we would go to worldward and the shoreships would travel out to meet us, so that we could download the cargo that was meant for them. It was time to begin considering the problem of what would happen to Vox when we reached our destination.

That was something I was unwilling to face. However I tried, I could not force myself to confront the difficulties that I knew lay just ahead.

But she could.

"We must be getting close to Cul-de-Sac now," she said.

"We'll be there soon, yes."

"I've been thinking about that. How I'm going to deal with that."

"What do you mean?"

"I'm a lost soul," she said. "Literally. There's no way I can come to life again."

"I don't under—"

"Adam, don't you see?" she cried fiercely. "I can't just float down to Cul-de-Sac and grab myself a body and put myself on the roster of colonists. And you can't possibly smuggle me down there while nobody's looking. The first time anyone ran an inventory check, or did passport control, I'd be dead. No, the only way I can get there is to be neatly packed up again in my original storage circuit. And even if I could figure out how to get back into that, I'd be simply handing myself over for punishment or even eradication. I'm listed as missing on the manifest, right? And I'm wanted for causing the death of that passenger. Now I turn up again, in my storage circuit. You think they'll just download me nicely to Cul-de-Sac and give me the body that's waiting for me there? Not very likely. Not likely that I'll ever get out of that circuit alive, is it, once I go back in? Assuming I *could* go back in in the first place. I don't know how a storage circuit is operated, do you? And there's nobody you can ask."

"What are you trying to say, Vox?"

"I'm not trying to say anything. I'm saying it. I have to leave the ship on my own and disappear."

"No. You can't do that!"

"Sure I can. It'll be just like starwalking. I can go anywhere I please. Right through the skin of the ship, out into heaven. And keep on going."

"To Cul-de-Sac?"

"You're being stupid," she said. "Not to Cul-de-Sac, no. Not to anywhere. That's all over for me, the idea of getting a new body. I have no legal existence any more. I've messed myself up. All right: I admit it. I'll take what's coming to me. It won't be so bad, Adam. I'll go starwalking. Outward and outward and outward, forever and ever."

"You mustn't," I said. "Stay here with me."

"Where? In this empty storage unit out here?"

"No," I told her. "Within me. The way we are right now. The way we were before."

"How long do you think we could carry that off?" she asked.

I didn't answer.

"Every time you have to jack into the machinery I'll have to hide myself down deep," she said. "And I can't guarantee that I'll go deep enough, or that I'll stay down there long enough. Sooner or later they'll notice me. They'll find me. They'll eradicate me and they'll throw you out of the Service, or maybe they'll eradicate you too. No, Adam. It couldn't possibly work. And I'm not going to destroy you with me. I've done enough harm to you already."

"Vox—"

"No. This is how it has to be."

18.

And this is how it was. We were deep in the Spook Cluster now, and the Vainglory Archipelago burned bright on my realspace screen.

Somewhere down there was the planet called Cul-de-Sac. Before we came to worldward of it, Vox would have to slip away into the great night of heaven.

Making a worldward approach is perhaps the most difficult maneuver a starship must achieve; and the captain must go to the edge of his abilities along with everyone else. Novice at my trade though I was, I would be called on to perform complex and challenging processes. If I failed at them, other crewmen might cut in and intervene, or, if necessary, the ship's intelligences might override; but if that came to pass my career would be destroyed, and there was the small but finite possibility, I suppose, that the ship itself could be gravely damaged or even lost.

I was determined, all the same, to give Vox the best send-off I could.

On the morning of our approach I stood for a time on Outerscreen Level, staring down at the world that called itself Cul-de-Sac. It glowed like a red eye in the night. I knew that it was the world Vox had chosen for herself, but all the same it seemed repellent to me, almost evil. I felt that way about all the worlds of the shore people now. The Service had changed me; and I knew that the change was irreversible. Never again would I go down to one of those worlds. The starship was my world now.

I went to the virtuality where Vox was waiting.

"Come," I said, and she entered me.

Together we crossed the ship to the Great Navigation Hall.

The approach team had already gathered: Raebuck, Fresco, Roacher, again, along with Pedregal, who would supervise the downloading of cargo. The intelligence on duty was 612 Jason. I greeted them with quick nods and we jacked ourselves together in approach series.

Almost at once I felt Roacher probing within me, searching for the fugitive intelligence that he still thought I might be harboring. Vox shrank back, deep out of sight. I didn't care. Let him probe, I thought. This will all be over soon.

"Request approach instructions," Fresco said.

"Simulation," I ordered.

The fiery red eye of Cul-de-Sac sprang into vivid representation before us in the hall. On the other side of us was the simulacrum of the ship, surrounded by sheets of white flame that rippled like the blaze of the aurora.

I gave the command and we entered approach mode.

We could not, of course, come closer to planetskin than a million shiplengths, or Cul-de-Sac's inexorable forces would rip us apart. But we had to line the ship up with its extended mast aimed at the planet's equator, and hold ourselves firm in that position while the shoreships of Cul-de-Sac came swarming up from their red world to receive their cargo from us.

612 Jason fed me the coordinates and I gave them to Fresco, while Raebuck kept the channels clear and Roacher saw to it that we had enough power for what we had to do. But as I passed the data along to Fresco, it was with every sign reversed. My purpose was to aim the mast not downward to Cul-de-Sac but outward toward the stars of heaven.

At first none of them noticed. Everything seemed to be going serenely. Because my reversals were exact, only the closest examination of the ship's position would indicate our 180-degree displacement.

Floating in the free fall of the Great Navigation Hall, I felt almost as though I could detect the movements of the ship. An illusion, I knew. But a powerful one. The vast ten-kilometer-long needle that was the *Sword of Orion* seemed to hang suspended, motionless, and then to begin slowly, slowly to turn, tipping itself on its axis, reaching for the stars with its mighty mast. Easily, easily, slowly, silently—

What joy that was, feeling the ship in my hand!

The ship was mine. I had mastered it.

"Captain," Fresco said softly.

"Easy on, Fresco. Keep feeding power."

"Captain, the signs don't look right—"

"Easy on. Easy."

"Give me a coordinates check, Captain."

"Another minute," I told him.

"But—"

"Easy on, Fresco."

Now I felt restlessness too from Pedregal, and a slow chilly stirring of interrogation from Raebuck; and then Roacher probed me again, perhaps seeking Vox, perhaps simply trying to discover what was going on. They knew something was wrong, but they weren't sure what it was.

We were nearly at full extension, now. Within me there was an electrical trembling: Vox rising through the levels of my mind, nearing the surface, preparing for departure.

"Captain, we're turned the wrong way!" Fresco cried.

"I know," I said. "Easy on. We'll swing around in a moment."

"He's gone crazy!" Pedregal blurted.

I felt Vox slipping free of my mind. But somehow I found myself still aware of her movements, I suppose because I was jacked into 612 Jason and 612 Jason was monitoring everything. Easily, serenely, Vox melted into the skin of the ship.

"*Captain!*" Fresco yelled, and began to struggle with me for control.

I held the navigator at arm's length and watched in a strange and wonderful calmness as Vox passed through the ship's circuitry all in an instant and emerged at the tip of the mast, facing the stars. And cast herself adrift.

Because I had turned the ship around, she could not be captured and acquired by Cul-de-Sac's powerful navigational grid, but would be free to move outward into heaven. For her it would be a kind of floating out to sea, now. After a time she would be so far out that she could no longer key into the shipboard bioprocessors that sustained the patterns of her consciousness, and, though the web of electrical impulses that was the Vox matrix would travel outward and onward forever, the set of identity responses that was Vox herself would lose focus soon, would begin to waver and blur. In a little while, or perhaps not so little, but inevitably, her sense of herself as an independent entity would be lost. Which is to say, she would die.

I followed her as long as I could. I saw a spark traveling across the great night. And then nothing.

"All right," I said to Fresco. "Now let's turn the ship the right way around and give them their cargo."

19.

That was many years ago. Perhaps no one else remembers those events, which seem so dreamlike now even to me. The *Sword of Orion* has carried me nearly everwhere in the galaxy since then. On some voyages I have been captain; on others, a downloader, a supercargo, a mind-wiper, even sometimes a push-cell. It makes no difference how we serve, in the Service.

I often think of her. There was a time when thinking of her meant coming to terms with feelings of grief and pain and irrecoverable loss, but no longer, not for many years. She must be long dead now, however durable and resilient the spark of her might have been. And yet she still lives. Of that much I am certain. There is a place within me where I can reach her warmth, her strength, her quirky vitality, her impulsive sud-denness. I can feel those aspects of her, those gifts of her brief time of sanctuary within me, as a living presence still, and I think I always will, as I make my way from world to tethered world, as I journey onward everlastingly spanning the dark light-years in this great ship of heaven.

HOUSE OF BONES

Terry Carr was a first-rate editor, responsible for such masterpieces of science fiction as The Left Hand of Darkness, And Chaos Died, *and* Neuromancer. *He was a much underrated writer, too, who published one classic story ("The Dance of the Changer and the Three") and a number of fine ones that received less attention than they deserved. He was also a warmhearted, funny, decent human being who was one of my closest friends for almost thirty years.*

The one thing he wasn't was physically durable. Though he was tall and athletic-looking, his body began to give out by the time he was about forty-five, and in the spring of 1987 he died, two months after his fiftieth birthday, after a melancholy period of accelerating decline that for the most part had remained unknown outside his immediate circle.

Beth Meacham, then the editor-in-chief at Tor Books, was one of many in the science-fiction field who had learned her craft by working with Terry and by emulating his precepts. In the weeks after his death she sought to find some way of showing her gratitude to him, and in May, 1987, she hit upon the idea of assembling an anthology of original stories by writers who had had some professional association with Terry and who felt that his impact on their careers had been substantial. I was one of those that Beth invited to contribute, along with Fritz Leiber, Kate Wilhelm, Ursula K. Le Guin, Gene Wolfe, Roger Zelazny, and a dozen or so others.

I had just finished writing "House of Bones." Terry was keenly interested in prehistory, and had a fundamental belief that human beings were basically good, however unlikely that might seem if one judged by outward appearance alone. "House of Bones" seemed to me to be the perfect story for the memorial anthology, and I sent it to Beth. Terry's Universe was published in May of 1988, thirteen months after his death. "House of Bones" was the first story in the book.

After the evening meal Paul starts tapping on his drum and chanting quietly to himself, and Marty picks up the rhythm, chanting too. And then the two of them launch into that night's installment of the tribal epic, which is what happens, sooner or later, every evening.

It all sounds very intense but I don't have a clue to the meaning. They sing the epic in the religious language, which I've never been allowed to learn. It has the same relation to the everyday language, I guess, as Latin does to French or Spanish. But it's private, sacred, for insiders only. Not for the likes of me.

"Tell it, man!" B.J. yells. "Let it roll!" Danny shouts.

Paul and Marty are really getting into it. Then a gust of fierce stinging cold whistles through the house as the reindeerhide flap over the doorway is lifted, and Zeus comes stomping in.

Zeus is the chieftain. Big burly man, starting to run to fat a little. Mean-looking, just as you'd expect. Heavy black beard streaked with gray and hard, glittering eyes that glow like rubies in a face wrinkled and carved by windburn and time. Despite the Paleolithic cold, all he's wearing is a cloak of black fur, loosely draped. The thick hair on his heavy chest is turning gray too. Festoons of jewelry announce his power and status: necklaces of seashells, bone beads, and amber, a pendant of yellow wolf teeth, an ivory headband, bracelets carved from bone, five or six rings.

Sudden silence. Ordinarily when Zeus drops in at B.J.'s house it's for a little roistering and tale-telling and butt-pinching, but tonight he has come without either of his wives, and he looks troubled, grim. Jabs a finger toward Jeanne.

"You saw the stranger today? What's he like?"

There's been a stranger lurking near the village all week, leaving traces everywhere—footprints in the permafrost, hastily covered-over campsites, broken flints, scraps of charred meat. The whole tribe's keyed. Strangers aren't common. I was the last one, a year and a half ago. God only knows why they took me in: because I seemed so pitiful to them, maybe. But the way they've been talking, they'll kill this one on sight if they can. Paul and Marty composed a Song of the Stranger last week and Marty sang it by the campfire two different nights. It was in the religious language so I couldn't understand a word of it. But it sounded terrifying.

Jeanne is Marty's wife. She got a good look at the stranger this afternoon, down by the river while netting fish for dinner. "He's short," she tells Zeus. "Shorter than any of you, but with big muscles, like Gebravar." Gebravar is Jeanne's name for me. The people of the tribe are strong, but they didn't pump iron when they were kids. My muscles fascinate them. "His hair is yellow and his eyes are gray. And he's ugly. Nasty. Big head, big flat nose. Walks with his shoulders hunched and his head down." Jeanne shudders. "He's like a pig. A real beast. A goblin. Trying to steal fish from the net, he was. But he ran away when he saw me."

Zeus listens, glowering, asking a question now and then—did he say anything, how was he dressed, was his skin painted in any way. Then he turns to Paul.

"What do you think he is?"

"A ghost," Paul says. These people see ghosts everywhere. And Paul, who is the bard of the tribe, thinks about them all the time. His poems are full of ghosts. He feels the world of ghosts pressing in, pressing in. "Ghosts have gray eyes," he says. "This man has gray eyes."

"A ghost, maybe, yes. But what kind of ghost?"

"What *kind*?"

Zeus glares. "You should listen to your own poems," he snaps. "Can't you see it? This is a Scavenger Folk man prowling around. Or the ghost of one."

General uproar and hubbub at that.

I turn to Sally. Sally's my woman. I still have trouble saying that she's my wife, but that's what she really is. I call her Sally because there once was a girl back home who I thought I might marry, and that was her name, far from here in another geological epoch.

I ask Sally who the Scavenger Folk are.

"From the old times," she says. "Lived here when we first came. But they're all dead now. They—"

That's all she gets a chance to tell me. Zeus is suddenly looming over me. He's always regarded me with a mixture of amusement and tolerant contempt, but now there's something new in his eye. "Here is something you will do for us," he says to me. "It takes a stranger to find a stranger. This will be your task. Whether he is a ghost or a man, we must know the truth. So you, tomorrow: you will go out and you will find him and you will take him. Do you understand? At first light you will go to search for him, and you will not come back until you have him."

I try to say something, but my lips don't want to move. My silence seems good enough for Zeus, though. He smiles and nods fiercely and swings around, and goes stalking off into the night.

They all gather around me, excited in that kind of animated edgy way that comes over you when someone you know is picked for some big distinction. I can't tell whether they envy me or feel sorry for me. B.J. hugs me, Danny punches me in the arm, Paul runs up a jubilant-sounding number on his drum. Marty pulls a wickedly sharp stone blade about nine inches long out of his kit-bag and presses it into my hand.

"Here. You take this. You may need it."

I stare at it as if he had handed me a live grenade.

"Look," I say. "I don't know anything about stalking and capturing people."

"Come *on*," B.J. says. "What's the problem?"

B.J. is an architect. Paul's a poet. Marty sings, better than Pavarotti. Danny paints and sculpts. I think of them as my special buddies. They're all what you could loosely call Cro-Magnon men. I'm not. They treat me just like one of the gang, though. We five, we're some bunch. Without them I'd have gone crazy here. Lost as I am, cut off as I am from everything I used to be and know.

"You're strong and quick," Marty says. "You can do it."

"And you're pretty smart, in your crazy way," says Paul. "Smarter than *he* is. We aren't worried at all."

If they're a little condescending sometimes, I suppose I deserve it. They're highly skilled individuals, after all, proud of the things they can do. To them I'm a kind of retard. That's a novelty for me. I used to be considered highly skilled too, back where I came from.

"You go with me," I say to Marty. "You and Paul both. I'll do whatever has to be done but I want you to back me up."

"No," Marty says. "You do this alone."

"B.J.? Danny?"

"No," they say. And their smiles harden, their eyes grow chilly. Suddenly it doesn't look so chummy around here. We may be buddies but I have to go out there by myself. Or I may have misread the whole situation and we aren't such big buddies at all. Either way this is some kind of test, some rite of passage maybe, an initiation. I don't know. Just when I think these people are exactly like us except for a few piddling differences of customs and languages, I realize how alien they really are. Not savages, far from it. But they aren't even remotely like modern people.

They're something entirely else. Their bodies and their minds are pure *Homo sapiens* but their souls are different from ours by 20,000 years.

To Sally I say, "Tell me more about the Scavenger Folk."

"Like animals, they were," she says. "They could speak but only in grunts and belches. They were bad hunters and they ate dead things that they found on the ground, or stole the kills of others."

"They smelled like garbage," says Danny. "Like an old dump where everything was rotten. And they didn't know how to paint or sculpt."

"This was how they screwed," says Marty, grabbing the nearest woman, pushing her down, pretending to hump her from behind. Everyone laughs, cheers, stamps his feet.

"And they walked like this," says B.J., doing an ape-shuffle, banging his chest with his fists.

There's a lot more, a lot of locker-room stuff about the ugly shaggy stupid smelly disgusting Scavenger Folk. How dirty they were, how barbaric. How the pregnant women kept the babies in their bellies twelve or thirteen months and they came out already hairy, with a full mouth of teeth. All ancient history, handed down through the generations by bards like Paul in the epics. None of them has ever actually seen a Scavenger. But they sure seem to detest them.

"They're all dead," Paul says. "They were killed in the migration wars long ago. That has to be a ghost out there."

Of course I've guessed what's up. I'm no archaeologist at all—West Point, fourth generation. My skills are in electronics, computers, time-shift physics. There was such horrible political infighting among the archaeology boys about who was going to get to go to the past that in the end none of them went and the gig wound up going to the military. Still, they sent me here with enough crash-course archaeology to be able to see that the Scavengers must have been what we call the

Neanderthals, that shambling race of also-rans that got left behind in the evolutionary sweepstakes.

So there really had been a war of extermination between the slow-witted Scavengers and clever *Homo sapiens* here in Ice Age Europe. But there must have been a few survivors left on the losing side, and one of them, God knows why, is wandering around near this village.

Now I'm supposed to find the ugly stranger and capture him. Or kill him, I guess. Is that what Zeus wants from me? To take the stranger's blood on my head? A very civilized tribe, they are, even if they do hunt huge woolly elephants and build houses out of their whitened bones. Too civilized to do their own murdering, and they figure they can send me out to do it for them.

"I don't think he's a Scavenger," Danny says. "I think he's from Naz Glesim. The Naz Glesim people have gray eyes. Besides, what would a ghost want with fish?"

Naz Glesim is a land far to the northeast, perhaps near what will someday be Moscow. Even here in the Paleolithic the world is divided into a thousand little nations. Danny once went on a great solo journey through all the neighboring lands: he's a kind of tribal Marco Polo.

"You better not let the chief hear that," B.J. tells him.

"He'll break your balls. Anyway, the Naz Glesim people aren't ugly. They look just like us except for their eyes."

"Well, there's that," Danny concedes. "But I still think—"

Paul shakes his head. That gesture goes way back, too. "A Scavenger ghost," he insists.

B.J. looks at me. "What do you think, Pumangiup?" That's his name for me.

"Me?" I say. "What do I know about these things?"

"You come from far away. You ever see a man like that?"

"I've seen plenty of ugly men, yes." The people of the tribe are tall and lean, brown hair and dark shining eyes, wide faces, bold cheekbones. If they had better teeth they'd be gorgeous. "But I don't know about this one. I'd have to see him."

Sally brings a new platter of grilled fish over. I run my hand fondly over her bare haunch. Inside this house made of mammoth bones nobody wears very much clothing, because the structure is well insulated and the heat builds up even in the dead of winter. To me Sally is far and away the best looking woman in the tribe, high firm breasts, long supple legs, alert, inquisitive face. She was the mate of a man who had to be killed last summer because he became infested with ghosts. Danny and B.J. and a couple of the others bashed his head in, by way of a mercy killing, and then there was a wild six-day wake, dancing and wailing around the clock. Because she needed a change of luck they gave Sally to me, or me to her, figuring a holy fool like me must carry the charm of the gods. We have a fine time, Sally and I. We were two lost souls when we came together, and together we've kept each other from tumbling even deeper into the darkness.

"You'll be all right," B.J. says. "You can handle it. The gods love you."

"I hope that's true," I tell him.

Much later in the night Sally and I hold each other as though we both know that this could be our last time. She's all over me, hot, eager. There's no privacy in the bone-house and the others can hear us, four couples and I don't know how many kids, but that doesn't matter. It's dark. Our little bed of fox-pelts is our own little world.

There's nothing esoteric, by the way, about these people's style of love-making. There are only so many ways that a male human body and a female human body can be joined together, and all of them, it seems, had already been invented by the time the glaciers came.

At dawn, by first light, I am on my way, alone, to hunt the Scavenger man. I rub the rough strange wall of the house of bones for luck, and off I go.

The village stretches for a couple of hundred yards along the bank of a cold, swiftly-flowing river. The three round bone-houses where most of us live are arranged in a row, and the fourth one, the long house that is the residence of Zeus and his family and also serves as the temple and house of parliament, is just beyond them. On the far side of it is the new fifth house that we've been building this past week. Further down, there's a workshop where tools are made and hides are scraped, and then a butchering area, and just past that there's an immense garbage dump and a towering heap of mammoth bones for future construction projects.

A sparse pine forest lies east of the village, and beyond it are the rolling hills and open plains where the mammoths and rhinos graze. No one ever goes into the river, because it's too cold and the current is too strong, and so it hems us in like a wall on our western border. I want to teach the tribesfolk how to build kayaks one of these days. I should also try to teach them how to swim, I guess. And maybe a few years farther along I'd like to see if we can chop down some trees and build a bridge. Will it shock the pants off them when I come out with all this useful stuff? They think I'm an idiot, because I don't know about the different grades of mud and frozen ground, the colors of charcoal, the uses and qualities of antler, bone, fat, hide, and stone. They feel sorry for me because I'm so limited. But they like me all the same. And the gods *love* me. At least B.J. thinks so.

I start my search down by the riverfront, since that's where Jeanne saw the Scavenger yesterday. The sun, at dawn on this Ice Age autumn morning, is small and pale, a sad little lemon far away. But the wind is quiet now. The ground is still soft from the summer thaw, and I look for tracks. There's permafrost five feet down, but the topsoil, at least, turns spongy in May and gets downright muddy by July. Then it hardens again and by October it's like steel, but by October we live mostly indoors.

There are footprints all over the place. We wear leather sandals, but a lot of us go barefoot much of the time, even now, in 40-degree weather. The people of the tribe have long, narrow feet with high arches. But down by the water near the fish-nets I pick up a different spoor, the mark of a short, thick, low-arched foot with curled-under toes. It must be my Neanderthal. I smile. I feel like Sherlock Holmes. "Hey, look, Marty," I say to the sleeping village. "I've got the ugly bugger's track. B.J.? Paul? Danny? You just watch me. I'm going to find him faster than you could believe."

Those aren't their actual names. I just call them that, Marty, Paul, B.J., Danny. Around here everyone gives everyone else his own private set of names. Marty's name for B.J. is Ungklava. He calls Danny Tisbalalak and Paul is Shibgamon. Paul calls Marty Dolibog. His name for B.J. is Kalamok. And so on all around the tribe, a ton of names, hundreds and hundreds of names for just forty or fifty people. It's a confusing system. They have reasons for it that satisfy them. You learn to live with it.

A man never reveals his true name, the one his mother whispered when he was born. Not even his father knows that, or his wife. You could put hot stones between his legs and he still wouldn't tell you that true name of his, because that'd bring every ghost from Cornwall to Vladivostok down on his ass to haunt him. The world is full of angry ghosts, resentful of the living, ready to jump on anyone who'll give them an opening and plague him like leeches, like bedbugs, like every malign and perverse bloodsucking pest rolled into one

We are somewhere in western Russia, or maybe Poland. The landscape suggests that: flat, bleak, a cold grassy steppe with a few oaks and birches and pines here and there. Of course a lot of Europe must look like that in this glacial epoch. But the clincher is the fact that these people build mammoth-bone houses. The only place that was ever done was Eastern Europe, so far as anybody down the line knows. Possibly they're the oldest true houses in the world.

What gets me is the immensity of this prehistoric age, the spans of time. It goes back and back and back and all of it is alive for these people. We think it's a big deal to go to England and see a cathedral a thousand years old. They've been hunting on this steppe thirty times as long. Can you visualize 30,000 years? To you, George Washington lived an incredibly long time ago. George is going to have his 300th birthday very soon. Make a stack of books a foot high and tell yourself that that stands for all the time that has gone by since George was born in 1732. Now go on stacking up the books. When you've got a pile as high as a ten-story building, that's 30,000 years.

A stack of years almost as high as that separates me from you, right this minute. In my bad moments, when the loneliness and the fear and the pain and the remembrance of all that I have lost start to operate on me, I feel that stack of years pressing on me with the weight of a mountain. I try not to let it get me down. But that's a hell of a weight to carry. Now and then it grinds me right into the frozen ground.

The flatfooted track leads me up to the north, around the garbage dump, and toward the forest. Then I lose it. The prints go round and round, double back to the garbage dump, then to the butchering area, then toward the forest again, then all the way over to the river. I can't make sense of the pattern. The poor dumb bastard just seems to have been milling around, foraging in the garbage for anything edible, then taking off again but not going far, checking back to see if anything's been caught in the fish net, and so on. Where's he sleeping? Out in the open, I guess. Well, if what I heard last night is true, he's as hairy as a gorilla; maybe the cold doesn't bother him much.

Now that I've lost the trail, I have some time to think about the nature of the mission, and I start getting uncomfortable.

I'm carrying a long stone knife. I'm out here to kill. I picked the military for my profession a long time ago, but it wasn't with the idea of killing anyone, and certainly not in hand-to-hand combat. I guess I see myself as a representative of civilization, somebody trying to hold back the night, not as anyone who would go creeping around planning to stick a sharp flint blade into some miserable solitary tramp.

But I might well be the one that gets killed. He's wild, he's hungry, he's scared, he's primitive. He may not be very smart, but at least he's shrewd enough to have made it to adulthood, and he's out here earning his living by his wits and his strength. This is his world, not mine. He may be stalking me even while I'm stalking him, and when we catch up with each other he won't be fighting by any rules I ever learned. A good argument for turning back right now.

On the other hand if I come home in one piece with the Scavenger still at large, Zeus will hang my hide on the bone-house wall for disobeying him. We may all be great buddies here but when the chief gives the word, you hop to it or else. That's the way it's been since history began and I have no reason to think it's any different back here.

I simply have to kill the Scavenger. That's all there is to it.

I don't want to get killed by a wild man in this forest, and I don't want to be nailed up by a tribal court-martial either. I want to live to get back to my own time. I still hang on to the faint chance that the rainbow will come back for me and take me down the line to tell my tale in what I have already started to think of as the future. I want to make my report.

The news I'd like to bring you people up there in the world of the future is that these Ice Age folk don't see themselves as primitive. They know, they absolutely *know*, that they're the crown of creation. They have a language—two of them, in fact—they have history, they have music, they have poetry, they have technology, they have art, they have architecture. They have religion. They have laws. They have a way of life that has worked for thousands of years, that will go on working for thousands more. You may think it's all grunts and war-clubs back here, but you're wrong. I can make this world real to you, if I could only get back there to you.

But even if I can't ever get back, there's a lot I want to do here. I want to learn that epic of theirs and write it down for you to read. I want to teach them about kayaks and bridges, and maybe more. I want to finish building the bone-house we started last week. I want to go on horsing around with my buddies B.J. and Danny and Marty and Paul. I want Sally. Christ, I might even have kids by her, and inject my own futuristic genes into the Ice Age gene pool.

I don't want to die today trying to fulfill a dumb murderous mission in this cold bleak prehistoric forest.

The morning grows warmer, though not warm. I pick up the trail again, or think I do, and start off toward the east and north, into the forest. Behind me I hear the sounds of laughter and shouting and song as work gets going on the new house, but soon I'm out of earshot. Now I hold the knife in my hand, ready for anything. There are wolves in here, as well as a frightened half-man who may try to kill me before I can kill him.

I wonder how likely it is that I'll find him. I wonder how long I'm supposed to stay out here, too—a couple of hours, a day, a week?—and what I'm supposed to use for food, and how I keep my ass from freezing after dark, and what Zeus will say or do if I come back empty-handed.

I'm wandering around randomly now. I don't feel like Sherlock Holmes any longer.

Working on the bone-house, that's what I'd rather be doing now. Winter is coming on and the tribe has grown too big for the existing four houses. B.J. directs the job and Marty and Paul sing and chant and play the drum and flute, and about seven of us do the heavy labor.

"Pile those jawbones chin down," B.J. will yell, as I try to slip one into the foundation the wrong way around. "*Chin down*, bozo! That's better." Paul bangs out a terrific riff on the drum to applaud me for getting it right the second time. Marty starts making up a ballad about how dumb I am, and everyone laughs. But it's loving laughter. "Now that backbone over there," B.J. yells to me. I pull a long string of mammoth vertebrae from the huge pile. The bones are white, old bones that have been lying around a long time. They're dense and heavy. "Wedge it down in there good! Tighter! Tighter!" I huff and puff under the immense weight of the thing, and stagger a little, and somehow get it where it belongs, and jump out of the way just in time as Danny and two other men come tottering toward me carrying a gigantic skull.

The winter-houses are intricate and elaborate structures that require real ingenuity of design and construction. At this point in time B.J. may well be the best architect the world has ever known. He carries around a piece of ivory on which he has carved a blueprint for the house, and makes sure everybody weaves the bones and skulls and tusks into the structure just the right way. There's no shortage of construction materials. After 30,000 years of hunting mammoths in this territory, these people have enough bones lying around to build a city the size of Los Angeles.

The houses are warm and snug. They're round and domed, like big igloos made out of bones. The foundation is a circle of mammoth skulls with maybe a hundred mammoth jawbones stacked up over them in fancy herringbone patterns to form the wall. The roof is made of hides stretched over enormous tusks mounted overhead as arches. The whole thing is supported by a wooden frame and smaller bones are chinked in to seal the openings in the walls, plus a plastering of red clay. There's an entranceway made up of gigantic thighbones set up on end. It may all sound bizarre but there's a weird kind of beauty to it and you have no idea, once you're inside, that the bitter winds of the Pleistocene are howling all around you.

The tribe is semi-nomadic and lives by hunting and gathering. In the summer, which is about two months long, they roam the steppe, killing mammoths and rhinos and musk oxen, and bagging up berries and nuts to get them through the winter. Toward what I would guess is August the weather turns cold and they start to head for their village of bone houses, hunting reindeer along the way. By the time the really bad weather arrives—think Minnesota-and-a-half—they're settled in for the winter with six months' worth of meat stored in deep-freeze pits in the permafrost. It's an orderly, rhythmic life. There's a real community here. I'd be willing to call it a civilization. But—as I stalk my human prey out here in the cold—I remind myself that life here is harsh and strange. Alien. Maybe I'm doing all this buddy-buddy nickname stuff simply to save my own sanity, you think? I don't know.

If I get killed out here today the thing I'll regret most is never learning their secret religious language and not being able to understand the big historical epic that they sing every night. They just don't want to teach it to me. Evidently it's something outsiders aren't meant to understand.

The epic, Sally tells me, is an immense account of everything that's ever happened: the *Iliad* and the *Odyssey* and the *Encyclopedia Britannica* all rolled into one, a vast tale of gods and kings and men and warfare and migrations and vanished empires and great calamities. The text is so big and Sally's recounting of it is so sketchy that I have only the foggiest idea of what it's about, but when I hear it I want desperately to understand it. It's the actual history of a forgotten world, the tribal annals of thirty millennia, told in a forgotten language, all of it as lost to us as last year's dreams.

If I could learn it and translate it I would set it all down in writing so that maybe it would be found by archaeologists thousands of years from now. I've been taking notes on these people already, an account of what they're like and how I happen to be living among them. I've made twenty tablets so far, using the same clay that the tribe uses to make its pots and sculptures, and firing it in the same beehive-shaped kiln. It's a godawful slow job writing on slabs of clay with my little bone knife. I bake my tablets and bury them in the cobblestone floor of the house. Somewhere in the 21st or 22nd century a Russian archaeologist will dig them up and they'll give him one hell of a jolt. But of their history, their myths, their poetry, I don't have a thing, because of the language problem. Not a damned thing.

Noon has come and gone. I find some white berries on a glossy-leaved bush and, after only a moment's hesitation, gobble them down. There's a faint sweetness there. I'm still hungry even after I pick the bush clean.

If I were back in the village now, we'd have knocked off work at noon for a lunch of dried fruit and strips of preserved reindeer meat, washed down with mugs of mildly fermented fruit juice. The fermentation is accidental, I think, an artifact of their storage methods. But obviously there are yeasts here and I'd like to try to invent wine and beer. Maybe they'll make me a god for that. This year I invented writing, but I did it for my sake and not for theirs and they aren't much interested in it. I think they'll be more impressed with beer.

A hard, nasty wind has started up out of the east. It's September now and the long winter is clamping down. In half an hour the temperature has dropped fifteen degrees, and I'm freezing. I'm wearing a fur parka and trousers, but that thin icy wind cuts right through. And it scours up the fine dry loose topsoil and flings it in our faces. Some day that light yellow dust will lie thirty feet deep over this village, and over B.J. and Marty and Danny and Paul, and probably over me as well.

Soon they'll be quitting for the day. The house will take eight or ten more days to finish, if early-season snowstorms don't interrupt. I can imagine Paul hitting the drum six good raps to wind things up and everybody making a run for indoors, whooping and hollering. These are high-spirited guys. They jump and shout and sing, punch each other playfully on the arms, brag about the goddesses they've screwed and the holy rhinos they've killed. Not that they're kids. My guess is that they're 25, 30 years old, senior men of the tribe. The life expectancy here seems to be about 45. I'm 34. I have a grandmother alive back in Illinois. Nobody here could possibly believe that. The one I call Zeus, the oldest and richest man in town, looks to be about 53, probably is younger than that, and is generally regarded as favored by the gods because he's lived so long. He's a wild old bastard, still full of bounce and vigor. He lets you know that he keeps those two wives of his busy all night long, even at his age. These are robust people. They lead a tough life, but they don't know that, and so their souls are buoyant. I definitely will try to turn them on to beer next summer, if I last that long and if I can figure out the technology. This could be one hell of a party town.

Sometimes I can't help feeling abandoned by my own time. I know it's irrational. It has to be just an accident that I'm marooned here. But there are times when I think the people up there in 2013 simply shrugged and forgot about me when things went wrong, and it pisses me off tremendously until I get it under control.

I'm a professionally trained hard-ass. But I'm 20,000 years from home and there are times when it hurts more than I can stand.

Maybe beer isn't the answer. Maybe what I need is a still. Brew up some stronger stuff than beer, a little moonshine to get me through those very black moments when the anger and the really heavy resentment start breaking through.

In the beginning the tribe looked on me, I guess, as a moron. Of course I was in shock. The time trip was a lot more traumatic than the experiments with rabbits and turtles had led us to think.

There I was, naked, dizzy, stunned, blinking and gaping, retching and puking. The air had a bitter acid smell to it—who expected that, that the air would smell different in the past?—and it was so cold it burned my nostrils. I knew at once that I hadn't landed in the pleasant France of the Cro-Magnons but in some harsher, bleaker land far to the east. I could still see the rainbow glow of the Zeller Ring, but it was vanishing fast, and then it was gone.

The tribe found me ten minutes later. That was an absolute fluke. I could have wandered for months, encountering nothing but reindeer and bison. I could have frozen; I could have starved. But no, the men I would come to call B.J. and Danny and Marty and Paul were hunting near the place where I dropped out of the sky and they stumbled on me right away. Thank God they didn't see me arrive. They'd have decided that I was a supernatural being and would have expected miracles from me, and I can't do miracles. Instead they simply took me for some poor dope who had wandered so far from home that he didn't know where he was, which after all was essentially the truth.

I must have seemed like one sad case. I couldn't speak their language or any other language they knew. I carried no weapons. I didn't know how to make tools out of flints or sew a fur parka or set up a snare for a wolf or stampede a herd of mammoths into a trap. I didn't know anything, in fact, not a single useful thing. But instead of spearing me on the spot they took me to their village, fed me, clothed me, taught me their language. Threw their arms around me and told me what a great guy I was. They made me one of them. That was a year and a half ago. I'm a kind of holy fool for them, a sacred idiot.

I was supposed to be here just four days and then the Zeller Effect rainbow would come for me and carry me home. Of course within a few weeks I realized that something had gone wonky at the uptime end, that the experiment had malfunctioned and that I probably wasn't ever

419

going to get home. There was that risk all along. Well, here I am, here I stay. First came stinging pain and anger and I suppose grief when the truth finally caught up with me. Now there's just a dull ache that won't go away.

In early afternoon I stumble across the Scavenger Man. It's pure dumb luck. The trail has long since given out—the forest floor is covered with soft pine duff here, and I'm not enough of a hunter to distinguish one spoor from another in that—and I'm simply moving aimlessly when I see some broken branches, and then I get a whiff of burning wood, and I follow that scent twenty or thirty yards over a low rise and there he is, hunkered down by a hastily thrown-together little hearth roasting a couple of ptarmigans on a green spit. A scavenger he may be, but he's a better man than I am when it comes to skulling ptarmigans.

He's really ugly. Jeanne wasn't exaggerating at all.

His head is huge and juts back a long way. His mouth is like a muzzle and his chin is hardly there at all and his forehead slopes down to huge brow-ridges like an ape's. His hair is like straw, and it's all over him, though he isn't really shaggy, no hairier than a lot of men I've known. His eyes are gray, yes, and small, deep-set. He's built low and thick, like an Olympic weightlifter. He's wearing a strip of fur around his middle and nothing else. He's an honest-to-God Neanderthal, straight out of the textbooks, and when I see him a chill runs down my spine as though up till this minute I had never really believed that I had traveled 20,000 years in time and now, holy shit, the whole concept has finally become real to me.

He sniffs and gets my wind, and his big brows knit and his whole body goes tense. He stares at me, checking me out, sizing me up. It's very quiet here and we are primordial enemies, face to face with no one else around. I've never felt anything like that before.

We are maybe twenty feet from each other. I can smell him and he can smell me, and it's the smell of fear on both sides. I can't begin to anticipate his move. He rocks back and forth a little, as if getting ready to spring up and come charging, or maybe bolt off into the forest.

But he doesn't do that. The first moment of tension passes and he eases back. He doesn't try to attack, and he doesn't get up to run. He just sits there in a kind of patient, tired way, staring at me, waiting to see what I'm going to do. I wonder if I'm being suckered, set up for a sudden onslaught.

I'm so cold and hungry and tired that I wonder if I'll be able to kill him when he comes at me. For a moment I almost don't care.

Then I laugh at myself for expecting shrewdness and trickery from a Neanderthal man. Between one moment and the next all the menace goes out of him for me. He isn't pretty but he doesn't seem like a goblin, or a demon, just an ugly thick-bodied man sitting alone in a chilly forest.

And I know that sure as anything I'm not going to try to kill him, not because he's so terrifying but because he isn't.

"They sent me out here to kill you," I say, showing him the flint knife.

He goes on staring. I might just as well be speaking English, or Sanskrit.

"I'm not going to do it," I tell him. "That's the first thing you ought to know. I've never killed anyone before and I'm not going to begin with a complete stranger. Okay? Is that understood?"

He says something now. His voice is soft and indistinct, but I can tell that he's speaking some entirely other language.

"I can't understand what you're telling me," I say, "and you don't understand me. So we're even."

I take a couple of steps toward him. The blade is still in my hand. He doesn't move. I see now that he's got no weapons and even though he's powerfully built and could probably rip my arms off in two seconds, I'd be able to put the blade into him first. I point to the north, away from the village, and make a broad sweeping gesture. "You'd be wise to head off that way," I say, speaking very slowly and loudly, as if that would matter. "Get yourself out of the neighborhood. They'll kill you otherwise. You understand? *Capisce? Verstehen Sie?* Go. Scat. Scram. I won't kill you, but they will."

I gesture some more, vociferously pantomiming his route to the north. He looks at me. He looks at the knife. His enormous cavernous nostrils widen and flicker. For a moment I think I've misread him in the most idiotically naive way, that he's been simply biding his time getting ready to jump me as soon as I stop making speeches.

Then he pulls a chunk of meat from the bird he's been roasting, and offers it to me.

"I come here to kill you, and you give me lunch?"

He holds it out. A bribe? Begging for his life?

"I can't," I say. "I came here to kill you. Look, I'm just going to turn around and go back, all right? If anybody asks, I never saw you." He waves the meat at me and I begin to salivate as though it's pheasant under glass. But no, no, I can't take his lunch. I point to him, and again to the north, and once more indicate that he ought not to let the sun set on him in this town. Then I turn and start to walk away, wondering if this is the moment when he'll leap up and spring on me from behind and choke the life out of me.

I take five steps, ten, and then I hear him moving behind me.

So this is it. We really are going to fight.

I turn, my knife at the ready. He looks down at it sadly. He's standing there with the piece of meat still in his hand, coming after me to give it to me anyway.

"Jesus," I say. "You're just lonely."

He says something in that soft blurred language of his and holds out the meat. I take it and bolt it down fast, even though it's only half cooked—dumb Neanderthal!—and I almost gag. He smiles. I don't care what he looks like, if he smiles and shares his food then he's human by me. I smile too. Zeus is going to murder me. We sit down together and watch the other ptarmigan cook, and when it's ready we share it, neither of us saying a word. He has trouble getting a wing off, and I hand him my knife, which he uses in a clumsy way and hands back to me.

After lunch I get up and say, "I'm going back now. I wish to hell you'd head off to the hills before they catch you."

And I turn, and go.

And he follows me like a lost dog who has just adopted a new owner.

So I bring him back to the village with me. There's simply no way to get rid of him short of physically attacking him, and I'm not going to do that. As we emerge from the forest a sickening wave of fear sweeps over me. I think at first it's the roast ptarmigan trying to come back up, but no, it's downright terror, because the Scavenger is obviously planning to stick with me right to the end, and the end is not going to be good. I can see Zeus' blazing eyes, his furious scowl. The thwarted Ice Age chieftain in a storm of wrath. Since I didn't do the job, they will. They'll kill him and maybe they'll kill me too, since I've revealed myself to be a dangerous moron who will bring home the very enemy he was sent out to eliminate.

"This is dumb," I tell the Neanderthal. "You shouldn't be doing this."

He smiles again. You don't understand shit, do you, fellow?

We are past the garbage dump now, past the butchering area. B.J. and his crew are at work on the new house. B.J. looks up when he sees me and his eyes are bright with surprise.

He nudges Marty and Marty nudges Paul, and Paul taps Danny on the shoulder. They point to me and to the Neanderthal. They look at each other. They open their mouths but they don't say anything. They whisper, they shake their heads. They back off a little, and circle around us, gaping, staring.

Christ. Here it comes.

I can imagine what they're thinking. They're thinking that I have really screwed up. That I've brought a ghost home for dinner. Or else an enemy that I was supposed to kill. They're thinking that I'm an absolute lunatic, that I'm an idiot, and now they've got to do the dirty work that I was too dumb to do. And I wonder if I'll try to defend the Neanderthal against them, and what it'll be like if I do. What am I going to do, take them all on at once? And go down swinging as my four sweet buddies close in on me and flatten me into the permafrost? I will. If they force me to it, by God I will. I'll go for their guts with Marty's long stone blade if they try anything on the Neanderthal, or on me.

I don't want to think about it. I don't want to think about any of this.

Then Marty points and claps his hands and jumps about three feet in the air.

"Hey!" he yells. "Look at that! He brought the ghost back with him!"

And then they move in on me, just like that, the four of them, swarming all around me, pressing close, pummelling hard. There's no room to use the knife. They come on too fast. I do what I can with elbows, knees, even teeth. But they pound me from every side, open fists against my ribs, sides of hands crashing against the meat of my back. The breath goes from me and I come close to toppling as pain breaks out all over me at once. I need all of my strength, and then some, to keep from going down under their onslaught, and I think, this is a dumb way to die, beaten to death by a bunch of berserk cave men in 20,000 B.C.

But after the first few wild moments things become a bit quieter and I get myself together and manage to push them back from me a little way, and I land a good one that sends Paul reeling backward with blood spouting from his lip, and I whirl toward B.J. and start to take him out, figuring I'll deal with Marty on the rebound. And then I realize that they aren't really fighting with me any more, and in fact that they never were.

It dawns on me that they were smiling and laughing as they worked me over, that their eyes were full of laughter and love, that if they had truly wanted to work me over it would have taken the four of them about seven and a half seconds to do it.

They're just having fun. They're playing with me in a jolly rough-house way.

They step back from me. We all stand there quietly for a moment, breathing hard, rubbing our cuts and bruises. The thought of throwing up crosses my mind and I push it away.

"You brought the ghost back," Marty says again.

"Not a ghost," I say. "He's real."

"Not a ghost?"

"Not a ghost, no. He's live. He followed me back here."

"Can you believe it?" B.J. cries. "Live! Followed him back here! Just came marching right in here with him!" He turns to Paul. His eyes are gleaming and for a second I think they're going to jump me all over again. If they do I don't think I'm going to be able to deal with it. But he says simply, "This has to be a song by tonight. This is something special."

"I'm going to get the chief," says Danny, and runs off.

"Look, I'm sorry," I say. "I know what the chief wanted. I just couldn't do it."

"Do what?" B.J. asks. "What are you talking about?" says Paul.

"Kill him," I say. "He was just sitting there by his fire, roasting a couple of birds, and he offered me a chunk, and—"

"*Kill* him?" B.J. says. "You were going to kill him?"

"Wasn't that what I was supposed—"

He goggles at me and starts to answer, but just then Zeus comes running up, and pretty much everyone else in the tribe, the women and the kids too, and they sweep up around us like the tide. Cheering, yelling, dancing, pummelling me in that cheerful bones-mashing way of theirs, laughing, shouting. Forming a ring around the Scavenger Man and throwing their hands in the air. It's a jubilee. Even Zeus is grinning. Marty begins to sing and Paul gets going on the drum. And Zeus comes over to me and embraces me like the big old bear that he is.

"I had it all wrong, didn't I?" I say later to B.J. "You were all just testing me, sure. But not to see how good a hunter I am."

He looks at me without any comprehension at all and doesn't answer. B.J., with that crafty architect's mind of his that takes in everything.

"You wanted to see if I was really human, right? If I had compassion, if I could treat a lost stranger the way I was treated myself."

Blank stares. Deadpan faces.

"Marty? Paul?"

They shrug. Tap their foreheads: the timeless gesture, ages old.

Are they putting me on? I don't know. But I'm certain that I'm right. If I had killed the Neanderthal they almost certainly would have killed me. That must have been it. I need to believe that that was it. All the time that I was congratulating them for not being the savages I had expected them to be, they were wondering how much of a savage *I* was. They had tested the depth of my humanity; and I had passed. And they finally see that I'm civilized too.

At any rate the Scavenger Man lives with us now. Not as a member of the tribe, of course, but as a sacred pet of some sort, a tame chimpanzee, perhaps. He may very well be the last of his kind, or close to it; and though the tribe looks upon him as something dopey and filthy and pathetic, they're not going to do him any harm. To them he's a pitiful bedraggled savage who'll bring good luck if he's treated well. He'll keep the ghosts away. Hell, maybe that's why they took me in, too.

As for me, I've given up what little hope I had of going home. The Zeller rainbow will never return for me, of that I'm altogether sure. But that's all right. I've been through some changes. I've come to terms with it.

We finished the new house yesterday and B.J. let me put the last tusk in place, the one they call the ghost-bone, that keeps dark spirits outside. It's apparently a big honor to be the one who sets up the ghost-bone. Afterward the four of them sang the Song of the House, which is a sort of dedication. Like all their other songs, it's in the old language, the secret one, the sacred one. I couldn't sing it with them, not having the words, but I came in with oom-pahs on the choruses and that seemed to go down pretty well.

I told them that by the next time we need to build a house, I will have invented beer, so that we can all go out when it's finished and get drunk to celebrate properly.

Of course they didn't know what the hell I was talking about, but they looked pleased anyway.

And tomorrow, Paul says, he's going to begin teaching me the other language. The secret one. The one that only the members of the tribe may know.

CPSIA information can be obtained at www.ICGtesting.com
Printed in the USA
LVOW12s1656221014

410014LV00004B/930/P